PROMISED IN FIRE

JASMINE WALT

DYNAMO PRESS

PROLOGUE

"**I**s this really the only way?"

The dragon princess clung to Einar's arm as the three figures stood within the heart of Mount Furian, a slender bridge of stone the only thing separating them from the lake of molten lava below. Violent winds generated by the open portal waiting behind her whipped around the inside of the volcano, yanking her long red hair out behind her like an angry banner. But the golden crown on her head did not budge, and neither did her resolve to find some way, *any* way, to bring the most beloved of her kin with her to the realm beyond.

"You already know that it is, Ylena." Einar gently pried the princess's hands from his tattooed forearm. Stylized flames swirled up his arm and wrapped around his bicep, nearly identical to the ones on her own arm. Pain shimmered in amber eyes that had witnessed far too much death and anguish, but he masked it behind an encouraging smile. "My blood is a small price to pay for the safety of our people."

"But why does he have to stay behind?" Ylena whipped her body toward the third figure, anger blazing in her golden eyes.

"Why can't he give you some of his blood to seal the portal and then come with us? Haven't we already lost enough?"

The third figure spread its arms, white robes fanning out behind it like wings. A soft white glow emanated from its body, shielding the true nature of its face, and even whether it was male or female. Such was the nature of Radiants. Though they watched over Ediria, they were not of this world, and existed in a place beyond the understanding of those who lived here.

"You wish me to give you a loophole that does not exist," the Radiant said in a voice like a clear bell. "All magic requires sacrifice, Princess Ylena, and the portal is no exception. Einar must stay behind, or the shadow creatures will be able to follow you into your new realm."

Ylena's eyes hardened as she looked to the mouth of the cave. Beyond lay Hearthfyre, the kingdom her people had fought for millennia to keep. For thousands of years the dragons had successfully fought off the fae, and they'd been so close to achieving peace between the races. Her brother had been sent to marry the fae princess—*had* married the fae princess, and should have been blissfully enjoying his honeymoon with his bride now.

Instead, he'd been murdered during the wedding feast. In retaliation, the dragon queen—*her mother*—had beheaded the fae king, and any hope for peace had crumbled beneath a tide of violence and a thirst for revenge. The fae king's successor had not wasted any time, drawing on a new, evil power that allowed him to wipe nearly all the dragons from the face of Ediria.

There were less than a hundred left, and if they did not seal the portal soon, there wouldn't be any survivors at all. Not with the monstrous shadow creatures that now infested their land, poisoning everything that had once been good and bright and wonderful.

"I miss him too, Ylena." Einar took the princess by the shoulders and turned her to face him. His eyes were hard, his jaw like granite. "Daryan and I were brothers in all but name, you know that. Neither of us will ever get to see his smile or hear his jokes or feel the warmth of his fire again. But I know that if he had still been alive, it would have been him staying behind to ensure our people's future. It is my job to do that for him now, just as it is your job to lead our people into this new world, and take advantage of this chance the Radiants have given us."

Ylena gave a shaky sigh. "I know," she said softly. Looking down, she unclasped a golden cuff from around her bicep, then took Einar's left hand in hers.

"Ylena, no." Einar tried to pull away, but the dragon princess held fast. "You need—"

"Hush." She fastened the cuff around his wrist, and the large, ruby-colored stone flashed as the piece of jewelry clasped shut. "You need this far more than I do. As a link to our people, as a reminder for what you're doing and why you are doing it. And Daryan would have wanted you to have it."

She gave him a watery smile, and Einar had to clear his throat against the lump that had suddenly formed there.

"May your flame never go out," he said gruffly.

"May your fire shine brightest in the dark," she returned.

The warrior and the Radiant watched as the dragon princess took one step, then two, toward the portal. The winds kicked up even higher as she approached the enormous swirling circle, the pit beyond an inky purple so dark, it was nearly black. The Radiant could feel the dragon warrior's longing, his burning wish that if he could not join his people beyond the portal, that he could at least *see* where they were going, so he might dream about their new lives in the future.

"The realm beyond is a land of plenty," the Radiant assured him. "Fields of green, vast, open oceans, fresh, clear skies. Plenty of room for dragons to hunt and fish and fly."

"And predators?" Einar asked softly. "What enemies will they have to face?"

The Radiant wondered if he should tell the dragon warrior about the humans. Creatures shorter lived than the fae, and without magic, but with such ferocious intelligence and creativity that they had reshaped their world nearly beyond recognition.

Instead, he merely said, "There is nothing in this new realm that can outwit the cunning of a dragon. As long as Princess Ylena is there to lead them, your kin will be safe."

Einar nodded, the lingering doubt vanishing from his face. Shoulders set with resolve, he unsheathed the dagger strapped to his hip, then rolled back the sleeve of his tunic to expose his forearm. Without a shred of emotion, he dragged the sharp edge of the blade along his skin. Blood poured from the wound, and the portal hummed in response, sensing the offering. A fresh wind kicked up around the warrior's legs, sweeping the blood away before it could hit the ground and sucking it straight into the void.

A flare of violet light burst from the portal, and the warrior dropped to his knees, briefly stunned by the kinetic burst of energy. The Radiant raised its arms again, chanting in the language of the ancients. Each word reverberated through the inside of the volcano like a lightning strike, and the warrior gritted his teeth, trembling from the sheer force of it.

Finally, on the last word, the portal collapsed on itself. It disappeared with a sucking sound, leaving behind a deafening silence. Not even the magma below stirred. It was as if the world was collectively holding its breath, waiting to see if the portal would open again.

But it did not. The spell held. The dragons were safe.

Einar let out a long sigh. "Is this where you leave me?" he asked, turning his head up to look at the Radiant. The resolve and determination from before had fled, as had the raw anguish from earlier. There was only a bone-deep exhaustion left behind, the kind one saw in those who were on the verge of giving up on life.

The Radiant nodded. "I must. But I can give you one more boon before I go. Something to make you more comfortable."

The warrior nodded. "Put me to sleep then. A long, dreamless slumber from which I cannot wake."

The Radiant hesitated. "Are you sure? You do not wish even for dreams, then?"

"So I can be trapped with the nightmares of my past?" A shadow stirred behind Einar's eyes, some dark memory threatening to surface. "No, it's better this way. Unless you'd rather kill me." His lips twisted into a mirthless smirk.

The Radiant shook his head. "You are now the keeper of this gate, and will remain so as long as you are alive. If you die, the portal will open again, and your kin will be at risk of a shadow creature invasion."

Einar nodded grimly. "Eternal sleep it is, then."

The dragon warrior closed his eyes, and the swirling flames on his arm came to life, the fiery ropes spiraling around his body as he shifted. Two legs turned into four, smooth skin became rippling scales, long hair transformed into spikes and a thrashing tail. Wings sprouting, snout elongating, body lengthening, until a twenty-foot-long dragon towered above the Radiant.

But instead of taking flight, the great beast curled up at the Radiant's feet, and closed his golden eyes. He was ready.

The Radiant surveyed the dragon for a long moment before it laid hands on his snout. It would do as the dragon wished and put him in a deep slumber, devoid of dreams and pain.

But it would not be eternal, and it would not be here. For the dragon's story was not over. It was only just beginning.

1

Adara

"I still think this is a stupid idea, Adara."

I swore as a root tendril exploded from the ground, nearly tripping me as I raced through the forest. Leaping over it, I glared in the direction of the voice, which was a mistake. The distraction caused me to run straight into a waiting vine, which wrapped itself around my waist and tried to haul me up a tree.

"Do you think you could not talk to me while you're trying to kill me?" I yelled as I yanked my short sword from its scabbard. I hacked furiously at the vine, which was at least four inches thick, and broke free before it could hoist me too high. I landed on my feet, then kept running. The sound of rushing water reached my ears, and I soon caught sight of the stream waiting just ahead. A series of slippery rocks provided the easiest path across, but I ignored them, knowing that the moss growing on them could be weaponized against me. Instead, I pumped my legs faster, building up speed, then cleared the ten-foot-wide stream in one bound.

There it is, I thought, staring at the red flag waving in the wind just twenty yards ahead. All I needed to do was grab it, and I'd win.

"Smart choice," Mavlyn said, dropping from a bloodberry tree ten yards away. Her auburn hair was tied up in a high ponytail, and the forest green tunic and bark-colored leggings she wore provided the perfect camouflage when she was hiding up in trees and didn't want to be spotted. "But did you really think I'd let you make it to the finish line without a fight?"

She pulled a few seeds from a pouch at her belt, and they exploded in her palms, growing into long, purplish-blue vines. The vines wrapped around her arms, becoming an extension of them, then shot toward me, their pointed tips as deadly as any sword.

"Not really." I drew the short sword again and swung it in an arc, blocking the first vine before it could hit me, and slicing through the second. The piece of the second vine I'd hacked off dropped to the ground, but the remaining half was already growing back, preparing to strike again. I would have to be fast if I wanted to get to Mavlyn.

"Careful," Mavlyn warned. I ducked and weaved between the vines, trying to reach her, but she controlled them expertly, keeping me at bay. "You're not paying attention to your surroundings."

I felt something wrap around my ankle, and I cursed as my feet were yanked out from underneath me. "Oh come on!" I yelled as I sliced at the root wrapped around my ankle. I managed to get free, but not before Mavlyn's vines snaked up my body. They wrapped around my arms, forcing them to my sides, and kept growing until they bound my entire torso.

"This is unfair and you know it," I seethed as Mavlyn came to stand over me. One of the vines squeezed my wrist, causing my hand to spasm, and the sword fell from my fingers. "The tryouts won't be nearly this difficult. You're just punishing me because you don't want me to join the military."

Mavlyn snorted. She picked up the fallen sword—a loan from her father, who was thankfully out of town—and used the tip to draw circles in the earth. I winced; he didn't know we'd borrowed it, and I wasn't sure he'd appreciate her dragging it in the dirt like that.

"The fact that I'm pushing you this hard means that you'll ace the tryouts with no sweat," she pointed out. "You should be thanking me for that. But—" she swung the sword in an arc and jabbed it in my general direction—"You're right. I am punishing you, because this is a dumb idea. You should be attending university with me next month, not joining the military so you can run off and get yourself killed by shadow creatures."

She waved a hand, and I sighed in relief as the vines unraveled. Mavlyn was an expert at turning just about any plant into a weapon, but wielding actual weapons wasn't her specialty, and I didn't need her accidentally decapitating me with her father's sword. I rushed to my feet before she could change her mind and retreated several paces to get clear of the vines.

"There's no point in me going to the university with you," I argued. "I can barely summon a bead of moisture with my magic. They'll never let me in."

To prove my point, I lifted my hand and tried to summon a few snowflakes from the air. My fingers tingled, and the air shimmered around me as condensation began to form. Frowning, I tugged harder on that inner core of magic, trying to summon more power.

But it was no use. The magic churned inside me, jagged and wild, but stuck fast, like lightning trapped in a bottle. A headache clamped down on my temples, and I gritted my teeth in frustration.

"Adara, stop." Mavlyn said. The blend of pity and regret in

her voice scraped at my already raw nerves, and I recoiled from my magic in response. "We both know that you have issues with using your water magic. That's why I want you to come with me to Talamh, so you can find a water fae to help you unblock your powers. *That's* what you should be doing, not running off to get yourself killed."

I shook my head, wiping my hand on my leggings. A few droplets of condensation had stuck to my fingers—the most I could manage. Every once in a while I could do more, like freeze a mugful of tea, or shape a handful of water into an icicle, but those moments were rare and happened less and less the older I got.

Talamh University only took the best and the brightest, and as a magically incompetent water fae, I definitely did *not* qualify.

"I don't want to talk about this again," I said, marching past Mavlyn. I plucked the red flag from the dirt and brandished it at her as though it could keep her opinions at bay. "I know you want me to come to university with you, but I've never been the schoolbook type. I need to get out and see the rest of the kingdom, find the place I really belong. And joining the military is the best way for me to do that."

Mavlyn scowled, but she fell into step with me, heading up the path back to the village. We'd grown up together here in Fenwood, a tiny village deep within Domhain, the Earth Realm. It was one of the four realms of Ediria, each one belonging to a different type of elemental fae.

As a water fae, I had been an outsider from the day I was born. In the bigger cities, like Talamh, there were fae who wielded other elements, but in a small village like Fenwood, they didn't exist. Everyone I'd grown up with was an earth fae, including my mother. I was the only water fae in the entire village, and I'd inherited that talent from a father who'd died before I was even born.

"I just don't like you going off to join the military at a time like this," Mavlyn said as we picked our way along the path. "King Aolis has been recruiting like crazy, which can only mean that the threat of the shadow creatures is growing. How are you going to defend yourself against those things if they put you on the front lines?"

"I don't know, but that's what the training is for," I pointed out. "Dune tells me that the army's been working on special weapons to kill them more effectively."

But Mavlyn was right. The shadow creatures, which had been creeping out of the Deadlands to the west and slowly invading the rest of Ediria, were a real problem. No one knew exactly where they had come from, but they were born of shadow magic, which was a deadly type of magic that infected and corrupted everything it came into contact with. Normal plants and animals morphed into cruel, murderous creatures that stalked our lands and terrorized our people, and if they bit you, you would be infected with shadow magic too.

I'd seen the effects of that firsthand, once, from a traveler who was attacked on the road, and there was no cure. Even my mother, one of the most talented healers in all of Domhain, had been able to do nothing for him. She'd been forced to put him out of his misery before he'd turned into a monster himself. We'd burned the body as far away from the village as possible, and had buried the ashes to ensure that he didn't infect anyone else.

"Dune is an idiot," Mavlyn declared as the trees thinned and her backyard came into view. "And speaking of Dune, don't think I don't realize that part of the reason you're doing this is so you can chase after him like a lovesick puppy."

My face flamed. "That is *not* true—"

"Did someone mention my name?"

Mavlyn and I stopped dead as Dune Terran walked around

the side of her house and into the backyard. My breath caught at the sight of him—tall and broad-shouldered and brimming with confidence, he swaggered toward us as if he owned the very land beneath his feet. The dying light set off his golden-brown skin to perfection, and brought out the highlights in his gilded chestnut hair.

I knew from experience just how soft his hair was. I'd let those strands slip through my fingers many times when we'd stolen kisses in dark corners and alleyways. Felt his hard body against mine as he'd trailed those kisses down my neck and whispered filthy things in my ear.

As the headman's second son, he was one of the most eligible bachelors in the village. He could have any female he wanted, and there were many.

And yet, he had chosen *me*.

"I don't remember inviting you onto my property." Mavlyn curled her lip at Dune as he approached. The arrogant smile on his face faded a little as a wall of grass exploded three feet into the air, blocking his approach. "What are you doing here?"

"I was looking for Adara." His hazel eyes found mine, and they glinted knowingly, as if he'd been aware of what I was thinking. A dimple formed in his left cheek as his lips curved up. "We have a date tonight."

"Oh." I blushed, my hands flying to my hair. The lavender-blue strands probably looked like a rat's nest after this afternoon's training session, and I was sure I smelled like sweat and dirt and other more unpleasant things. "I was going to wash up first."

"What have you two been doing?" Dune raised an eyebrow, likely noting the grass stains on my clothing. "Gardening? Never mind, I don't want to know." He snatched up my hand and pressed a kiss to it before Mavlyn or I could say anything. "Just come with me. My father needs me for the rest of the evening, and I've got to be up early for the tryouts tomorrow, but I want to spend some time with you first. That is, if you're not too busy."

Mavlyn raised her eyebrows from behind Dune, but I ignored her. He didn't know that I was going to take part in the tryouts, or that Mavlyn had been helping me train for them—I wanted it to be a surprise.

"I'm not too busy," I said, my heart beating faster. The fact that Dune wanted to spend time with me when he had so many other things he could be doing made my heart soar. Sure, the stolen moments we had together were always in dark, secluded places, but I knew that was because his father wouldn't approve of his son courting a water fae.

But once we passed the military tryouts together, we wouldn't have to worry about his father, or what any of the other villagers thought. We could be together openly. Of course, that was providing that we got assigned to the same division, but—

"Good, then come on. I've got something special to show you."

He tugged at my hand, and I hesitated, looking back at Mavlyn. The annoyance on her face said it all—she didn't approve. Mavlyn and Dune had never gotten along, bickering and fighting since they were children, but I'd always had a huge crush on him.

He was handsome, popular, charismatic, and every female in the village wanted him...but he wasn't with any of those females right now.

He was with *me.*

"I'd love to," I said, turning away from Mavlyn. Maybe she couldn't be happy for me, but that didn't mean I had to put up with her judgment. I grasped Dune's hand tighter and let him lead me away from Mavlyn. For once in my life, happiness was in my grasp, and I was going to chase it no matter what anyone thought.

Even my best friend.

2

Adara

"Are you ready?"

I grinned at the sound of Dune's teasing voice in my ear. He'd taken me into a different part of the forest than where Mavlyn and I had trained, closer to his house, then put a blindfold on me. It had taken everything in me not to giggle like a little girl as he'd steered me down the path with his hands on my shoulders, but I couldn't help it. I felt as giddy as a water nymph walking on land for the first time.

Dune and I had always had a rocky relationship. When we were young teenagers, we would fight constantly, him bullying and teasing me, while I volleyed back the insults just as hard. The spark of chemistry between us had always pulled us together, and we both reveled in the conflict, but because of his status in the village and mine, we were enemies.

Or so I'd thought, until one night a few months ago. We'd run into each other during the harvest festival, and engaged in one of our usual spats. I couldn't even remember what the fight was about, but it had ended with me pressed against the wall and his tongue in my mouth.

It was the first time a male had kissed me, and the rush had gone straight to my head. One night of kissing had turned into two, then three, then more.

If it had been only kissing, I probably could have stopped it. It would have been easy to convince myself that Dune and I didn't have a future together, and walked away.

But...it wasn't just kissing. It was long nights under the stars, snuggling as Dune talked about his hopes and dreams, his fears. His desire to make his father proud, his need to prove himself in the shadow of his older brother. His thirst for adventure and burning need to get out and see the world.

I'd never known that we were so similar on the inside, but the more time I spent with Dune, the more certain I was that we were made for each other. That this magnetic pull between us was a sign we were meant to be together, regardless of what society or his father thought.

And now, here Dune was, taking me on a real "date", for the first time. The butterflies in my stomach were out of control, my skin practically vibrating beneath Dune's touch. I couldn't wait to see what he had in store for me.

I took a deep breath, trying to contain my excitement. "I'm ready."

Dune took the blindfold off, revealing the scene before us. A picnic blanket, a basket, and two pillows awaited us in the middle of a clearing. My heart fluttered as I noticed the touches he'd put in—fairy lights dancing between the leaves, the bottle of honey wine and the bouquet of flowers sitting on a nearby tree stump, the way he'd positioned us right beneath a patch of dappled sunlight, which streamed through the trees in rays of golden orange as the sun dipped beneath the horizon.

I was going to have to head home soon, before my mother worried.

But I'd be damned if I wasn't going to enjoy this first.

"This is amazing." I spun toward Dune and threw my arms around him. His muscular arms came around my waist, pulling me into him, and I breathed in his earthy scent as another wave of giddiness rushed through me. "I didn't know you could be so romantic," I teased, pulling back so I could look up into his face.

"You make me want to be." He gave me one of those devilish grins, causing heat to blossom in my lower belly. I tried to fight the blush that rose to my cheeks, but I couldn't help it, and his grin only widened in response.

"Come on." He took my hand and pulled me down to the blanket. I reached for the picnic basket, excited to see what he'd packed, but before I could reach it he pushed me back, covering my body with his own. The weight of him pressed me down into the earth as his lips touched mine, and before I knew it I was lost in another one of his kisses, my hands in his hair, his fingers digging into my hips, that heady, masculine scent making my head spin.

"Adara," he groaned, trailing kisses down my jaw, my neck. "I need you."

That sexy growl made the heat in my lower belly burn even hotter, but when he cupped his hand around the mound between my thighs, my entire body tensed. A kernel of doubt sprouted in the back of my mind, and I pushed his hand away and tried to rise.

"I don't know if I'm ready for that, Dune."

Dune lifted his head just enough to scowl down at me. "What do you mean, you're not ready?" He pressed a hand between my legs again, and I gasped as a surge of pleasure rippled through me. "Even with the fabric of your leggings in the way, I can feel you're wet. You want me, Adara. You've *always* wanted me."

I bit my lip as he ground the heel of his hand into me, fighting back a moan. Dune was right—I'd always wanted him. I'd fantasized more than once about taking our kissing sessions further, of having him deep inside me, and now, here was my chance.

You're just a plaything to him, Adara. Mavlyn's voice echoed in my ear. She'd said that to me more than once, and I'd always tuned her out. *The moment he gets what he wants from you, he'll leave you in the dust.*

I so badly wanted to tune those words out again. But...what if she was right? What if Dune really *was* just using me?

"I do want you," I told him. "I'm just not ready to sleep with you, that's all. This...thing that we have is new, and I'm still getting to know this side of you."

Dune rolled his eyes, removing his hand from between my legs. He rolled onto his side and propped his head on his hand, digging his elbow into the ground. "We've been 'getting to know each other' for weeks, Adara, and our time is almost up. The tryouts are tomorrow, and when I'm accepted I'll be shipping out right away. Don't you want to give me a good send off before I go?"

A good send off? I stared at him, shocked at this abrupt shift in attitude. "Is that what this is about? Getting your rocks off before you leave?"

Dune's expression softened. "It's not like that," he crooned, reaching for my hip so he could pull me into him. "This isn't only about me. I want you to feel good too." His lips found my neck, sending a hot shiver down my spine. "I want to make this one last memory with you before I go."

I sighed, pushing at his chest again. I might have given in, but that last sentence...I had to tell him the truth.

"If you're trying to rush the sex between us because you're worried about never seeing me again, you don't have to." I smiled up at him as his brow furrowed in confusion. "I'm joining the military, too."

Dune looked at me for a long moment, then threw back his head and laughed. "Giant's teeth," he gasped as he rolled onto his back, his broad chest vibrating. "That was a good one, Adara!"

I sat up, my heart growing cold in my chest as I watched him laugh at me. "I'm not joking, Dune."

He stopped laughing abruptly and looked me dead in the eye. "You've got to be joking," he said. "There's no way a girl like you could make it through the military tryouts. Not when you can't even use your magic."

"Excuse me?" Hot tears burned the corners of my eyes at his outright dismissal of me. "You have no idea what I'm capable of, Dune." As a child, I'd often snuck out to watch the village warriors train, and mimicked their moves with crudely fashioned sticks. The local militia leader had allowed it, and when I'd started changing from a child into an adult, he'd taken it upon himself to show me the basics of both hand to hand and sword combat.

A shadow creature had killed him while he was out on patrol, robbing me of the closest thing I'd had to a father figure. But I'd forced Mavlyn to be my training partner, refusing to let the things he'd taught me go to waste, and had continued to sharpen my skills over the years.

If I was certain about anything in life, it was that I was meant to fight. Joining the military was the best way to put my skills to use—not studying to be a healer like my mother wanted, and not going to university where I would be shunned because of my stunted magic.

Dune snorted. "You're a water fae who can't even summon a

rainstorm," he said, "and somehow don't have a drop of earth magic in you even though your mother is a talented healer. What use is the military going to have for you?"

"You don't have to have strong magic to join the military," I argued. "Only the willingness and ability to fight."

Dune shrugged. "Maybe, but you do have to be a warrior, and I don't think you have it in you."

A lump formed in my throat at Dune's callous attitude. "Why are you being like this?" I choked out. "I thought you'd be happy that I was joining too. I wanted to follow you, so that we could be together."

"Be together?" Dune gave me a look of disbelief. "Adara...you and I can't be together. You know that."

The earth seemed to tilt from beneath me, and I thanked the Radiants that I was laying down. "But we are," I insisted, though the words sounded hollow even to my ears. I clutched at the pendant nestled against my chest—a strange blue-white stone set into a golden circlet. It was an heirloom from my late father, a reminder of my heritage, and a protection amulet that I often reached for when I was upset or stressed. "We've been fighting this attraction to each other for so long because we're not "supposed" to be together, but here we are. Don't you think that's a sign that we're meant to be?"

Dune laughed. "The only thing it's a sign of is that we want to fuck," he said. "That doesn't mean we're written in the stars, or that I want to marry you, Adara."

Hot shame flooded me, and I leapt to my feet, scattering the contents of the picnic basket everywhere. Dune cursed as the bread, meats and cheeses spilled across the forest floor, but for once I didn't care what he thought. I spun on my heel and tried to run as my heart shattered in my chest, not wanting him to see the tears flowing freely down my cheeks.

He didn't deserve my tears, not after this.

"Oh, come on, Adara!" Dune grabbed my wrist, trying to pull me back to him. "I'm just trying to give you a dose of reality—"

I spun into Dune, twisting my hand palm up and pulling my arm in. His grip on my wrist broke instantly, and I kept spinning, snapping my leg into a side kick. My booted foot slammed into his middle, and he bent double, wheezing.

How's that for a dose of reality, part of me wanted to shoot back at him, but my desire to get away was stronger. I left him in the clearing, trying to catch his breath, humiliation eating away at the hole in my chest as I ran.

Mavlyn had been right. Dune had just been playing with me, treating my heart and my body like a prize to be won, then discarded. But she was wrong about one thing—I was leaving him in the dust, not the other way around. And I would never, ever make this mistake again.

3

Adara

"Oh good, you're home," Mother said as I walked into the apothecary. She was sitting at the counter, shredding gillyroot into a bowl, her head bent forward in concentration. "Will you help me finish shredding these? Mr. Fern is picking up a batch of diver's potion tomorrow, and it needs to brew overnight."

"Of course." I approached the counter, hoping that my eyes weren't too red from crying. I'd taken the long way home, trying to give myself enough time to calm down so I didn't enter the house looking like a total mess. I grabbed one of the purplish-blue roots, then took a knife from the counter and scraped it vertically along the root, creating thin slices I would chop up into tinier pieces later. I couldn't count the number of times I'd stood at this counter, helping mother chop and measure ingredients for potions.

"How was your day?" Mother glanced up at me. Even dressed simply in a long, yellow gown and apron, with her moss-green hair plaited into a crown to keep it out of the way, she was a vision. Wide, emerald eyes with thick lashes, high cheekbones, and a full mouth that smiled often and loved to make others laugh. There was an energy about her that was beyond her looks, a sort of magnetism that drew others to her. Many of the single males in the village had tried to court her, but she'd refused all of their offers. She was dedicated to her craft, she told them, and she had no need for a male when her heart was already filled with the most important thing in her life.

Me.

"It was fine," I said, hoping that my voice didn't sound too rough. But Mother's eyes narrowed, and she took a closer look at my face.

"Your cheeks are blotchy, and you sound like you have a cold," she said. "Have you been crying?"

"I—" Tears welled in my eyes. "It's Dune. We...we're not together anymore."

"Oh, sweetling." Mother put her knife and root down, and came around the counter to hug me. I sucked in a shuddering breath as she pulled me in close, enveloping me in the scent of honeysuckles and earth-warmed soil. "I'm so sorry. What happened?"

She led me out of the apothecary, and into the main part of the house. Our home wasn't very big—a simple, open space with two beds, a sitting area by the wood stove, and a tub in the corner with a privacy screen that we used for bathing. But it was all we needed, and I had many happy memories here.

We sat down in the two chairs by the stove, and I told Mother what happened in between sips of Tranquil Tea. The calming brew took the edge off my pain, allowing me to take my first full breath since leaving Dune in the woods.

"That oaf," Mother fumed when I'd finished. Her emerald eyes glittered with righteous anger. "I suspected he wasn't interested in pursuing anything serious with you, but he didn't have to be such an ass about it. I ought to slip some wyrmroot in his porridge tomorrow."

A wet laugh burst from my lips. "That would definitely ruin the tryouts for him," I said. Wyrmroot was a cure for constipation, but if you didn't have a blockage, it gave you terrible diarrhea.

"Oh, well we can't have that." Mother leaned over to kiss the top of my head, then smoothed a hand over my lavender-blue hair. "As much as you and I would enjoy that kind of petty revenge, I'd much rather see that boy make the tryouts and leave. It's for the best that you two part ways, Adara. You need to focus on your herbalism studies, not moon after males who aren't even worthy of you."

I bit my lip against the familiar retort rising in my throat. Although I was reasonably skilled at chopping ingredients and identifying plants and herbs, I had no talent or love for herbalism. Mother had always pushed me to follow in her footsteps as a healer, because herbalism didn't require innate magic to master, but to me it was a chore, not a labor of love.

She didn't know that I planned to sneak out and participate in the tryouts tomorrow. And I had no intention of telling her, because if I did, she would do everything in her power to stop me.

"Let's finish chopping up the gillyroot so I can get to bed," I told her, rising from my chair. "I'm tired and I want to go to sleep early."

We went back into the apothecary shop, and continued the task while Mother quizzed me, asking me to identify the various herbs and ingredients that hung from the ceiling and lined the shelves in glass jars. As I did, she took the shredded roots into her hands and held them briefly to infuse them with magic. The pieces of root began to glow lavender after just a few seconds, perfuming the air with their potent scent, and then she put the activated roots into a second bowl before repeating the process.

No matter how many plants I memorized and how many recipes I brewed, I would *never* be able to make potions as potent and effective as Mother's. I hadn't inherited her special talent for enhancing the natural properties of plants, or any other earth magic that would help me.

We were nearly finished preparing the roots when the door opened, and a male walked in. I stared at him with open curiosity—he was obviously a traveler, judging by the heavy pack he carried and the sturdy, dust covered boots he wore.

"Good evening," he greeted us, tipping his hat respectfully. "Do you have any everbright potion for sale? I was told you brew it here."

"I do." Mother wiped her hands on her apron, then moved to one of the shelves. She reached for a row of bottles filled with a golden potion that shimmered like liquid metal. "How many do you need?"

"Five."

Mother paused. "That's going to cost you."

"I know." He sighed heavily. "But there aren't too many healers around that sell the stuff, and I don't know when I'm going to find it next. You can't travel without it these days, not with all these shadow creatures roaming about."

"How bad is it out there?" I asked, a little apprehensive of the answer. If this man was traveling the roads alone, surely that meant it couldn't be too dangerous. But the lines of worry around his eyes and mouth told a different story.

The traveler turned to face me, his eyes sharpening with interest. They were a stunning green, with a gold ring around the pupils I'd never seen on any earth fae before. "A water fae," he said, looking me up and down. "Don't see too many of you in small villages like this."

No, there weren't. In the nineteen years I'd lived in Fenwood, I'd only seen a water fae once—a female who'd come to the village when I was only four years old, at the behest of my mother. I didn't remember her name or where she'd come from, but she'd worn fine clothing and had a powerful aura around her, marking her as a Greater Fae.

Most fae in Ediria were lesser fae—males and females who could only control one aspect of an element. For example, Mavlyn could command plants to do her bidding, while Dune had the ability to manipulate the earth itself. But a Greater Earth Fae was able to do both, as well as anything else once could think of using earth magic for.

I didn't know how Mother had gotten a Greater Fae to come and assess my magic, but the fae had spent an hour with me, and then told her that there was something inside me that was blocking my magic, twisting the pathways so that very little of it could come out. And that until that blockage was resolved, I would never be able to use it.

Unfortunately, I'd never been able to figure out what the blockage was or how to remove it, no matter how many hours I spent meditating or practicing control. And at this rate, I didn't think I ever would.

"This is my daughter, Adara," Mother said. "Her father was a water fae. And my name is Chaya. What did you say your name was, again?"

"Kiryan." His eyes never left mine. "To answer your question, it depends on where you are. Here in Domhain, shadow creature attacks are still rare, because the air fae are doing a pretty good job of killing them before they can make it past the Gaoth Aire mountains and into the rest of the kingdom. But their numbers must be increasing, because more are slipping through. I was attacked by a shadow nymph a few days ago, and

I was out of everbright. If she'd managed to bite me, I would have died."

I winced. Shadow creatures were actually normal creatures and animals who'd been corrupted by shadow magic. The nymph who'd attacked this man had probably once been a peaceful wood nymph before the taint had warped her into something malicious and unrecognizable.

No one knew exactly why the shadow magic had infected our world, but we all knew the infection had started in the Deadlands, where the dragons had once lived before King Aolis had wiped them out. Some suspected that maybe the dragons had been dabbling in shadow magic, and the taint they'd left behind simply multiplied, running rampant through the Deadlands. The leaders of the three elemental houses—Air, Water, and Earth—combined forces with the king to create a wall around the Deadlands to contain the shadow creatures. But the Air Mountains ran directly into the Deadlands, making it a weak spot that required constant defenders. And sometimes, creatures made it through.

"Well, let's load you up with a few bottles, then." Mother grabbed six off the shelf, then brought them to the counter.

"I asked for five," the man pointed out.

"Yes." She smiled. "The sixth one is on the house."

"Are you sure?" the man hesitated. "I know how costly these are—"

"The cost of these is nothing compared to the value of your life," she interrupted. "I'm sure you have your reasons for braving these roads alone, and I would hate for you to find yourself at the mercy of a shadow creature again with no potion to help you."

The traveler inclined his head. "Blessings upon you, then."

He gave my mother four silver coins from his money pouch, then took his pack off so he could put the potions inside it. Everbright potion was a funny thing—originally used by deep divers who wanted to illuminate their surroundings, it lit you up from the inside out with a temporary glow that lasted up to three hours. But someone discovered that the light effect was also a cure for shadow magic infections, provided that you took the potion right away. If you waited too long, or were bitten too many times, the shadow magic would become too potent for the potion to work. But if you were fast enough, it saved lives.

Unfortunately, the herb that was used to make the potion was hard to find, because the stuff only grew near seawater. Mother had to have it imported from either Talamh, which aside from being the capital, was the closest port city to Fenwood, or from Lochanlee, the Water Realm. So as much as she wished she could make it affordable for everyone, she had to charge top price for it.

The traveler wished us well, and Mother locked the door behind him as he left. "He is either very brave or very foolish to be traveling the roads in this day and age by himself," she told me. "Honestly, Adara, it's a good thing that you and Dune weren't serious. He's going to go off and get himself killed, all in service to a spineless king who's done nothing to protect our kingdom."

"What?" I gaped at Mother, shocked at the treasonous words she'd spoken. I'd never heard anyone speak about King Aolis that way—he was widely considered a hero, the only monarch to kill off the dragons and put an end to the Dragon-Fae War that had plagued our kingdom for millennia. He'd brought peace to our lands after thousands of years of fighting. "How can you say he's doing nothing? He's been recruiting like mad, sending more soldiers to fight the shadow creatures—"

"You mean more lesser fae to die while the King and his pretentious advisors sit in their castles and manors and do nothing," Mother shot back. She looked like she wanted to keep rant-ing, but she must have seen the look on my face, so she simply shook her head. "Never you mind, Adara. I've already said too much about this. Go on off to bed—I'll finish up here."

"All right. Good night, Mother." I gave her a kiss on the cheek, then headed to bed. Questions chased each other in my head like fairy lights during mating season, but I knew better than to ask. Once Mother ended a discussion, there was no prying anything more out of her.

As I laid down on my bed and stared up at the ceiling, I fingered the protection amulet, tracing the rounded edges of the stone. I wondered if it would provide any protection against the shadow creatures, should they send me out to fight them, or if the military provided us with everbright potion to carry on our patrols.

I wasn't sure if joining the military was the right choice or not. But I was still going to go to the tryouts, because I would be damned if I let Dune or Mother or anyone else scare me off. I might be magically incompetent, but I knew I had what it took to be a warrior. And tomorrow, I was going to show Dune just how wrong he'd been about me.

4

———

Adara

"This was a mistake, wasn't it?"

I swallowed hard as I stared out at the massive crowd that had gathered for the tryouts. There had to be at least a hundred earth fae here with all sorts of talent. Many of them were showing off their skills to one another as they waited in otherwise orderly lines, bending metal or flowers or the earth itself into fantastic shapes. Even the weakest of them had more magic at their beck and call than I ever would, and I felt woefully out of my depth.

"Yes, but that's irrelevant right now." Mavlyn jabbed her elbow into my ribcage. We were standing at the top of a knoll overlooking the field, along with the mare we'd borrowed from Mavlyn's parents. "I didn't train with you for months, then get up in the middle of the night and ride with you for three hours just for you to chicken out. Get down there and show those soldiers what you're made of."

"Yeah. Okay. You're right." I squared my shoulders and started down the hillside. A line for the registration desk had formed at the bottom of the hill, and I joined it, hoping that I was prepared enough. I'd borrowed Mavlyn's father's short sword for the occasion in case I needed it, but the bow and arrows I carried, and the hunting leathers I wore, were mine. Beyond the desk, and past the orderly lines of waiting candidates, was a massive field where the tryouts were to take place. They'd segmented the field into various sections, and I did my best to guess the purpose of each one. The obstacle course was easy enough to spot—there were two, one set up for the horses that waited nearby, and another that was obviously meant to be done on foot. There was also a tent with rows of desks lined up beneath it, like the ones in the village schoolhouse, an archery range, and a combat ring. Plenty of space for spectators to gather around each arena and watch, too, so Mavlyn would be there to cheer me on.

I scanned the area for Dune as I waited in line, my stomach tightening with dread and determination. Part of me hoped I wouldn't see him at all, but my ego demanded that I seek him out because I wanted *him* to see *me*. What was the point in acing these tryouts if I couldn't rub his face in it?

Better to do this to spite Dune rather than to be with him, I told myself. I knew Mavlyn would approve of that sentiment, even though she disagreed with the whole situation to begin with. Part of me started to wonder if she was right, but I'd been training for this for months. It was too late to back out now. I had to go through with this for my own sake, if no one else's.

And there he is. My eyes snagged on his tall, broad form, and my stupid heart did a swoop in my chest, betraying me. Why did he have to be so handsome? Gritting my teeth, I envisioned the butterflies in my stomach dying a quick, fiery death, and fanned the imaginary sparks and ashes into a blaze of righteous anger. I didn't care how handsome he was, how special he'd tried to make me feel, or how sweet and sexy his kisses had been.

He was still ugly on the inside, and he didn't deserve me.

"Name?"

A gruff voice startled me out of my thoughts, and I jumped. Somehow, I'd made it to the front of the line without realizing! My cheeks heated with embarrassment as the officer behind the desk raised his eyebrow. His mahogany-colored skin and moss green hair marked him as an earth fae, just like all the other soldiers here. I stuck out like a sore thumb with my lavender-blue hair and pale skin, and we both knew it.

"Adara Greenwood," I said.

He wrote that down on his clipboard. "Greenwood?" he repeated, raising an eyebrow. "That's an earth fae name. Were you born here in the earth realm?"

"Yes," I answered, though truthfully I didn't know where exactly I was born. I only knew my mother had brought me to Fenwood shortly after my birth, and I'd lived there all my life. "My mother is an earth fae, and she raised me in Fenwood, not Lochanlee, so I took her name."

He grunted. "Do you have any earth element abilities, or just water?"

"Umm." I scratched the back of my neck, not sure how to answer the question. "Just water, but I can't really use that very well either. You should just mark me down as a dud."

The soldier frowned, as though he disapproved of the use of that term. "Fair enough. I'll automatically mark you down as a level one then. You won't need to do any of the magical trials. But I'll warn you, your combat skills had better be top-notch. General Slaugh wants useful candidates, not cannon fodder, so if you're trying to commit suicide by military, I'd suggest you throw yourself on your sword and save yourself the trouble."

My cheeks flamed, and I lifted my chin. "I'm here to prove my worth, sir," I said stiffly. "I want to serve Ediria with my *life*. There's no honor in a pointless death."

The soldier gave me another once over, and something that looked a little like respect crossed his features. "If you really mean that, you'll do just fine," he said.

I blinked at the unexpected encouragement, and the knot of dread in my stomach loosened a little. *Maybe this won't be so bad,* I thought as I joined the other candidates. I deliberately picked the line next to Dune's—he was at the front of his line while I was at the back, so he didn't see me, but I wanted to make sure we ended up in the same sections together so I could beat him in every challenge.

"Candidates!" A gravely voice boomed from the front. We all jerked to attention, our collective gazes swinging to the front of the field. The officers stood in a row, and in front of them was a fae who looked like he'd walked straight out of a nightmare. Over six feet tall, clad in black armor that seemed to absorb the sun rather than reflect it, he was a hulking figure who had obviously once been handsome. But terrible burns marred the left side of his skull, forming a landscape of trauma that was hard to look at directly. His hair and the cartilage of his ear were completely burned away on that side, leaving nothing but warped, angry, melted skin, and a black eyepatch covered the area where his left eye should have been. Even the left side of his mouth was mutilated, the once-soft flesh twisted into an eternal grimace.

In contrast, the other half of his face was almost perfect. Wavy red hair covered the right side of his scalp, framing that side of his face nicely. The burns had been kind enough to leave him a side part that started from the left side of his head instead of straight down the middle so that he could grow it long enough to cover most of his scalp, and if not for the scarred flesh I would have assumed he'd chosen the hairstyle on purpose, as unconventional as it was. His remaining eye was a gorgeous, emerald green, his umber skin was smooth, his cheekbones were high and wide, and his triangular jaw looked like it could cut through even the thickest panes of glass.

I knew him in an instant, though I'd never seen him in person. This was General Slaugh, King Aolis's right-hand man. Leader of the Shadow Guard, and second in command of the Edirian military. He'd fought in the Dragon-Fae War, and it was dragon fire that had disfigured his face, and supposedly the left side of his body, though his armor covered that up well enough.

Giant's teeth, I thought as I stared at him. I hadn't realized the general was overseeing these tryouts personally. The pressure to perform settled heavily on my shoulders, and I stood up straighter, determined not to be intimidated.

General Slaugh waited a beat, then continued on. "It is good to see so many faces here this morning," he said. "As you know, King Aolis has put out a call for young, able-bodied fae to join our ranks so that we can fight against the growing threat of the shadow creatures that plague our land. These tryouts are meant to assess both your fitness and your abilities to ensure that you have what it takes to be a warrior, so if you are crippled or deficient in any way, step out of line and turn back. We have no room for weakness here."

A few of the fae shifted uneasily on their feet, but no one tried to leave, and I didn't blame them. Doing so would be far too humiliating. Feeling the weight of someone's stare, I glanced to my left to see Dune watching me from the front of his line. His eyebrows were raised, and the taunting expression on his face was easy enough to read. *Take the hint. Go home.*

I merely smirked back at him, confident that I'd be wiping that derisive look off his face soon enough.

"That's what I like to see," General Slaugh boomed. He punched his fist into the sky, and the ground beneath our feet rumbled in response. "Let the tryouts begin!"

The vibrations of the earth surged into my feet, and we all

moved forward as one. The General's sergeants leaped into action, ushering each line toward a different section of the field. As I anticipated, Dune's line merged with mine into one group, and we ended up beneath the tents together. I made sure to sit at the desk right in front of his—close enough to taunt him, far enough away that he wouldn't be able to look at my paper and cheat. Academics had never been his strong suit, and I had no intention of letting him profit off my superior intelligence.

As one of the sergeants—the same one who'd signed me in at the front desk—handed out quills, ink, paper, and a thick tome bound in treated bark, Dune leaned across his desk so he could talk into my ear. "You know that if you sit this close to me I'm going to do my best to make your life miserable, right?" he said in a low voice.

The tips of my ears quivered in response to the challenge in his voice. "Do your worst," I responded in a honey-sweet voice, keeping my gaze forward. "It's never been enough to stop me before."

Dune huffed, but sat back as the sergeant returned to the proctor's desk at the front of the tent so he could address the group. A timer sat on the desk in front of him, set to sixty minutes. "This first test is meant to assess your literacy level," he told us. "You will have until the bell goes off to complete it. Please begin."

The sergeant smacked the button on the timer, and it chimed, signifying the beginning of the countdown. A flurry of activity followed as everyone in the tent scrambled to open their books, and I smiled as Dune swore under his breath behind me. Unlike him, I had this in the bag and I knew it. Most of the villagers in Fenwood didn't take literacy very seriously—they really didn't need it since their magic was fairly intuitive—but Mother had taken it upon herself to ensure I was well-read so that I could study her herbalism and medical texts.

Looks like being magically incompetent is working out in my favor so far, I thought smugly.

The test was simple enough—the sergeant had listed which passages to read on the blackboard up front, and had also written down a series of questions that we were to answer for each passage that were meant to show critical thinking skills. The text wasn't difficult to read at all—a collection of fables, much more enjoyable to read than *1001 Herbal Remedies* or *Fae Anatomy Explained.*

I managed to make it halfway through the literacy test before Dune started tormenting me. I was in the middle of writing the answers to the fifth set of questions when my desk began to tremble. Sighing, I did my best to ignore it—it wasn't as if I could turn around and punch him in the face—but the vibrations caused the tip of my quill to skitter across the page, ruining the sentence I'd been writing.

"This is low, even for you," I grumbled, and Dune chuckled in response. Glancing down, I saw that two inches of earth had somehow crept up each one of the desk's legs, making them look as if someone had dipped them in mud. I could hear his quill scratching even as he used the mud to make my desk vibrate, and I gritted my teeth. Clearly, I'd underestimated his ability to multi-task.

"Candidate." The sergeant, who was pacing the aisles between the desks to make sure no one was cheating, stopped by my seat. "Is there a reason you're talking during the test?"

The tips of my ears burned as every gaze in the room turned to me, and Dune coughed behind me to hide his laughter. "My desk seems to be vibrating for some reason," I told him, as calmly as I could manage. "It's affecting my ability to write my answers, so I got a little frustrated."

The sergeant glanced at the legs of my chair, then at Dune sitting behind me. The dry look on his face told me that this wasn't the first time he'd witnessed shenanigans of this sort, and he picked up my test and scanned what I'd written. His eyebrows rose, and he slapped the test back down on the table, picked up my quill, then scribbled a giant A at the top of the page and circled it.

"You're obviously literate, Greenwood, so I see no reason to prolong your suffering. Report to the next tryout. You'll have to wait for the rest of the group before you can begin, but you can watch what they're doing to get a sense of the next challenge."

"Yes sir." Grinning, I got to my feet and nodded at the sergeant, then left the tent. I glanced over my shoulder on the way out to see Dune fuming in his seat, and I stifled a laugh. His attempt to bully me into giving up had obviously backfired, and I couldn't have been more delighted about it.

I ducked out of the tent and headed to the next field, which was the obstacle course. They'd laid the course out on a quarter-mile long track, with twenty separate obstacles spaced out in intervals— I spotted a rope ladder, rock wall, fords, beams, trip wires, and at least two pits, amongst other things. A sergeant stood in the center of the track, a clipboard in one hand and a stopwatch in the other as he timed each candidate, and I watched along with the remaining candidates as the current one made his way through the course.

"I don't know how he does it so easily," a candidate to my left panted as the fae running the course crawled beneath the net of trip wires at top speed, then raced up the waiting ramp at the end and jumped straight down, landing in a crouch. The candidate who'd spoken was standing with three others that had obviously completed the course—they were all drenched in a sheen of sweat, some of them sporting scrapes and cuts for their trouble. "At the rate he's going he'll finish in half the time it took me."

"I think his father is an officer," another candidate, this one from the group that hadn't gone yet, commented. "That's why he's better prepared than we are. The obstacle course our militia runs yearly has maybe half the number of obstacles this one does."

"I'm just glad none of these obstacles are magical," I chimed in. Though even if they had been, I would have been fine thanks to Mavlyn's training. The obstacle courses she'd set for me hadn't been as rigid as this, but she'd run interference constantly using her plants, forcing me to stay aware of my surroundings while remaining focused on each task at the same time.

The candidates gave me an odd look, and I became uncomfortably aware that I was the odd fae out in more ways than one. "I should hope not," a female candidate said in a snooty voice. "They're not allowing us to use our magic to complete the course, so it seems only fair that the obstacles aren't magic, either."

"What are you doing with our group anyway?" one of the fae who'd finished the course asked. "Weren't you sent to the tent with Group A?"

"I was, but I finished my test early, so the proctor let me come over here to watch while I wait for the others."

"Lucky," the fae grumbled. "You're getting a head start over your group."

I thought about pointing out that having a head start over the rest of my group didn't matter—after all, this wasn't a competition—but then I remembered Dune's face as I walked out of the tent, and swallowed the words. I'd promised myself that I would show Dune I had what it took to pass the tryouts, but I wanted more than that now. I wanted to outdo him in every arena, and if having a head start helped me do that, then I wasn't going to spit on the opportunity.

The fae on the track finished the course, and the snooty

female went next. It took her five more minutes than the last candidate to complete it on account of repeatedly falling off the balance beams, and the sergeant shook his head as she cleared the last obstacle, marking something on his clipboard. He tore the sheet of paper off and handed it to her as she finished, and the candidate left the field, looking dejected.

"I'm guessing there's a minimum time?" I asked the candidate on my left, the one who'd spoken first. Considering that he and his friends were still on the field, I imagined that they'd all completed the course within the time limit.

He nodded, running a hand through his sweat drenched hair. It stuck up from his scalp in dark green spikes, making him look like an oddly colored hedgehog. "We each get ten minutes."

Ten minutes for twenty obstacles? Giant's teeth, the general hadn't been kidding when he'd said they only wanted the best.

I watched the rest of the candidates finish the course in relative silence, studying how they approached each obstacle and making notes on which techniques seemed to work the best. As the last candidate finished, my group approached the course, with Dune in the lead. I grinned as I noticed the ink spatters on his left hand and cheek—he'd obviously tried to write as fast as possible to finish the test within the allotted hour, and judging by his grumpy expression, it hadn't been a breeze for him.

The sergeant running the obstacle course sent the other group away, then lined us up and explained the rules for the course. Ten-minute time limit, no magic allowed, and each individual obstacle had to be completed before you moved onto the next one.

"Miss Greenwood, since you got here before everyone else, you can have the privilege of going first."

Oh. I swallowed hard, glancing at the rest of my group. Even though I'd just had the chance to watch the last group and study them, I wasn't a fan of being the first in our group to go. But just beyond them, past Dune's smirking face, I spied Mavlyn standing on the sidelines, waving. The sight of her there bolstered my confidence, and I lifted my chin and turned to the sergeant. It didn't matter what the others thought. My best friend was here to cheer me on, and I was going to make her proud.

"Yes sir." I stepped out of the line and faced the sergeant. "Ready when you are."

The sergeant retreated to the center of the track, then blew on a silver whistle. I sprang into action, climbing up the ladder rope, dropping to the other side, and heading straight for the ford. Tiny stumps, maybe five inches in diameter each, jutted out of the shallow water, but I jumped from one to the other with ease, then slid right into a crawl beneath the net of trip wires awaiting me next.

Three obstacles down, seventeen to go.

I felt the eyes of the other candidates on me as I raced up a steep incline, then dropped straight down into the waiting pit below. The pit was circular, its walls smooth and made of stone —the only way up was a series of holes carved into the opposite side, meant to be scaled with a set of wooden stakes. I snatched the stakes from the ground and plunged them into the highest set of holes I could reach, then hastily pulled myself up. My arms ached a little from the effort, but my years of archery had strengthened my upper body, so I made it to the top with ease.

Next were the first set of balance beams. Each one was progressively higher off the ground than the last, but unlike the fae who'd failed this challenge earlier, I didn't bother using my arms—which were tired from the pit anyway—to pull myself up. Instead, I took a running leap toward the first one and launched myself in the air, timing it perfectly so that I landed directly in the center of the first one. Not wanting to lose any momentum, I leaped to the second one, then the third, then from there straight onto the waiting monkey bars. The metal bars were almost too smooth for my sweaty hands, and I nearly slipped and fell, but by some stroke of luck I managed to hold fast.

Dragon's breath, I swore as my body began to tremble. Anxiety rushed into my limbs, shortening my breath. The ground was a long way down from here—if I fell, I would have to run all the way back to the balance beams to make it up, which would cost me precious time.

"Come on, Adara!" Mavlyn shrieked from the sidelines. "You can do this!"

My best friend's encouraging words snuffed out the anxiety, giving me space to suck in a deep breath and push on. Swinging my body forward, I caught the next set of bars and made quick work of them, then leaped onto the waiting rope at the end and shimmied to the bottom.

A series of trip wires awaited next, which I crossed with ease thanks to Mavlyn's constant assaults on my ankles with her vines. Following that was a set of vertical bars I had to scale, then a trio of balance beams I had to go over, then under. Another pit after that, this one filled with sand, but with corners that allowed me to shimmy up and out.

Twelve down, I told myself as I crawled out of the pit. Eight to go.

The remaining obstacles were easy enough—a series of tunnels and beams to crawl through and jump over, more ladders and pits, and two more walls to scale.

"Seven minutes and thirteen seconds!" the sergeant called as I completed the last obstacle—a rock wall that I had to climb without the assistance of a rope or safety net. He gave me a very impressed once over as I walked off the track and headed toward him for his assessment. "I don't think I've ever seen a lesser fae complete this course that quickly."

I shrugged, a little uncomfortable with the praise. "My magic is weak, so I've had to overcompensate in other ways," I joked. In truth, I'd always been faster and stronger than the other fae my age, even from when I was a small child. I'd always figured that was the trade-off for being magically incompetent.

The sergeant snorted, then marked something on his clipboard before waving me off. Instead of standing next to the other candidates, I crossed the field and joined Mavlyn, who was practically bouncing on the balls of her feet with excitement.

"That was amazing, Adara!" she squealed, throwing her arms around me. The grass beneath my feet hummed in tune with her emotions, and I couldn't hold back a grin even as she squeezed the breath out of me. "You should have seen the look on Dune's face as he watched you clear the course. He looks like he swallowed your mother's most bitter healing draught."

I laughed. "It's about time Dune got a taste of his own medicine," I said, turning to glance at him across the field. True to Mavlyn's description, he was sour-faced and sullen—an expression I'd never seen on him before. I was used to seeing the swaggering, confident Dune, the one who taunted and teased and didn't care what anyone else thought of him. To see him so obviously bothered by my success sent a heady rush through me, bolstering my confidence even further.

"I honestly don't know what I was worried about," I said, shaking my head. "You did such a good job preparing me for this. I owe you one."

"I don't know why you were worried either," Mavlyn teased. "You're strong and fast and crazy talented, and you've been training for this for ages. As long as you trounce Dune like the sorry sack of dragon dung he is, I'll consider your debt paid. I don't even care if you decide to leave me for the military as long as you accomplish that."

I rolled my eyes. "Only you would take this as an opportunity to guilt trip me," I said.

Mavlyn grinned and jabbed her elbow into my side. "Hey, what are friends for?"

I stayed with Mavlyn as the rest of our group finished the course. Half of them failed and were sent off the field, but Dune passed with flying colors. He made it through each of the obstacles on the first try, but he failed to beat my time by thirty seconds, so I could hardly be annoyed about that.

"He's a worthy adversary, much as I hate to admit it," Mavlyn said as he walked off the track. "You're going to have to give it your all if you want to beat him across the boards."

"That was always the plan."

I moved onto the next tryout—archery—feeling much more confident. Dune and I tied for performance with that one, but I outdid him in the horsemanship obstacle course, and also in melee combat. With each tryout that we completed, he grew more and more visibly frustrated, and by the time we got to the single combat arena, he was practically fuming.

As the sergeant explained the rules of the challenge, my scalp began to prickle with awareness, as though someone was watching me. Instinctively, I scanned the crowd on the sidelines, and I nearly jumped out of my skin to find General Slaugh staring at me intently. His emerald green eye narrowed as he studied me, and a chill raced across my skin. My instincts warned me that drawing this fae's attention to me was *not* a good thing, though I couldn't fathom why. After all, I'd excelled at every tryout so far, so it wasn't as if General Slaugh could possibly disapprove of me. If my plan was to join the military and ascend its ranks, wouldn't catching the general's attention be a good thing?

Luckily, the general turned his attention away from me before I could give into the urge to melt into the crowd and hide. But my relief was short-lived as he stepped into the combat ring

—really just a circular patch of earth stripped of grass—and faced our group.

"Thank you, sergeant," he said as the sergeant finished explaining the rules. "Normally, I would have Sergeant Onyx test you all today, but in light of the growing threat of the shadow creatures, I've taken on the responsibility myself. Each of you will join me in the ring for one three-minute round so I can assess your abilities. If I fail to land a fatal blow on you within that round, you pass the tryouts." He paused here, for dramatic effect, then added, "and if any candidate lands a blow on me, fatal or not, I'll commission them as an officer on the spot."

A murmur raced through the candidates, and I stood up a little straighter. Lesser fae were never commissioned as officers —unless you were a Greater Fae, you had to work your way up the ranks. My misgivings about drawing General Slaugh's attention evaporated—this was my chance to prove myself, and I wouldn't back down simply because I was a little intimidated.

General Slaugh turned to Sergeant Onyx, who hastily saluted. He seemed taken aback by the general's sudden decision, but he quickly recovered his wits and turned his attention to his clipboard. "Sandra Lockwood," he called. "You're up first."

The fae standing next to me stiffened, but she stepped forward and joined General Slaugh in the ring. The sergeant handed them wooden practice swords, and I watched carefully as they squared off with each other. The match up was absurd in many ways—General Slaugh was a Greater Fae with superior strength and speed, not to mention battle-hardened, and he easily outweighed his opponent by a good hundred pounds— but Sandra used her diminutive size to her advantage, evading most of his blows expertly and weaving around his guard so she could strike at his most vulnerable spots. The rest of us watched with bated breath as the candidate darted in and out of range—

she nearly landed a hit to his inner thigh, but General Slaugh was faster than her, and he blocked it at the last second with the hilt of his hand and a half sword before the sergeant blew on his whistle, signifying the end of the match.

"Well done," General Slaugh told her, and she strode out of the ring with a triumphant smile on her face.

"Dune Terran," the sergeant announced, and Dune stepped into the ring next. He chose a long sword from the rack of wooden weapons, and as he squared off with the General, I had to admit they appeared to be a much more even match. Dune was nearly the same height and build, and the weapon he'd chosen was similar to the General's in length, giving them approximately the same amount of reach.

But as the two engaged, it became obvious that General Slaugh was holding back. As a Greater Fae, he had superior size and strength to everyone here, but instead of using it to crush the candidates, he matched their physical prowess and focused on testing the weaknesses of their techniques. Dune had a tendency to over commit with his swings, but he was also quick to recover, dancing out of Slaugh's reach before he could take advantage and land a blow. Their wooden swords clashed over and over as they darted in and out of range, and just as the sergeant lifted the whistle to his lips, Dune pivoted and slashed his wooden blade across the side of Slaugh's ribs.

The audience let out a collective gasp, and the entire world seemed to freeze for a split second.

"Well, well." Slaugh's single green eye glinted as the whistle went off. "Not a fatal blow, but a blow nonetheless. Congratulations, candidate."

"Thank you, sir." Dune saluted, his entire being brimming with pride. The look of joy on his face almost made me forget I hated him, and I wished for a moment that I could congratulate him. I knew how much he wanted to impress his father and older brother, how much it would mean to him to come home and tell them the news.

But when he turned to rejoin the candidates, the smug expression on his face killed that budding desire. "Let's see if you can beat that," he said as he passed, bumping his broad shoulder into mine.

I resisted the urge to snap back, instead settling for rolling my eyes. "Adara Greenwood," the sergeant called, and I jumped a little. Giant's Teeth. Was it my turn already?

Swallowing hard, I stepped into the ring and selected a short sword from the rack of wooden weapons. It was around the same size and weight of the one I borrowed from Mavlyn's father, though the hilt was smoother and a little more slippery than I was used to. I'd have to be careful not to let it accidentally fly out of my hand. Taking a deep breath, I gave it a few experimental swings.

"You seem nervous, candidate," General Slaugh commented, watching me closely.

I immediately stopped swinging the sword and turned to face him. "No more nervous than any other candidate facing a battle-hardened soldier for the first time in their life, Sir," I countered, aware that Dune was watching. Slaugh hadn't addressed any of the other candidates like this, or seemed particularly interested in them.

The General barked out a harsh laugh. The bright sunlight beating down overhead cast the burns on his face into sharp relief, making him look even more intimidating. Swallowing hard, my gaze flickered away from his face, snagging on his shadow. My eyes widened a little as I stared at it—tendrils of darkness flickered at the shadow's edges, like little tentacles. Jerking my gaze back to the general, I scanned his form, expecting to see matching tendrils, but there weren't any.

What was going on here?

If the general noticed my reaction, he didn't let on. "You've got some sass in you," he commented. "Let's see if you have the skills to back up that attitude."

He struck without warning, closing the distance between us in an instant. One moment he was on the other side of the ring, the next he was only three feet away, swinging his long sword straight at my head. I barely managed to get my short sword up in time to block the blow, and the force of it reverberated straight up my arms, making me grit my teeth.

Why was the General singling me out like this? He'd let the other candidates strike first. Was it really because I'd been sassy? Or was it because I was an oddity, the only water fae in a field full of earth fae? I couldn't imagine it was because I'd scored so highly on the other tryouts, but maybe that was a factor, too.

It doesn't matter, I told myself. If the General wanted to be harder on me, there was nothing I could do to change that. The only thing that mattered was how I responded.

Tightening my grip on my short sword, I sprang back out of his reach, which was considerable. I was at a disadvantage, pitting my short sword against his much longer blade, so I would just have to play the game better.

So I did something that I knew he wouldn't expect.

Absolutely nothing.

The General scowled as I lowered my sword and let it hang loosely at my side. "You dare drop your guard in front of me?" he snarled, raising his own weapon. He closed the distance and struck again, and I danced out of his reach once more. Smiling, I let him chase me around the ring for a bit, taunting him by darting in just close enough for him to strike, then blocking the blow and pulling back. We were moving at lightning speed, far faster than the other candidates, and I could see the suspicion glinting behind the general's eyes. Clearly, he hadn't expected to run into anyone with my physical prowess.

"Stop running away, candidate," the general barked as I jumped out of his reach once again. "You can't win battles if your only strategy is to retreat."

"I'm not retreating," I said, smiling sweetly. "I'm simply waiting for the opportune moment."

The General blinked at me, pausing for a fraction of a second and giving me the opening I was looking for. Raising my sword, I dashed in for a wild strike, and as expected, he reacted, swinging his sword wide to block. But because he'd grown accustomed to my feints, he reacted too slowly, allowing me to close the distance, then swing my own blade into the hilt of his sword. It flew from his armored fist, and the blow sent him spinning to his knees, back facing me, completely exposed.

The audience gasped as I touched the blade to the back of the general's exposed neck, then retreated and bowed respectfully. Fear and triumph fought for dominance inside me, but I schooled my expression as the general slowly rose to his feet and turned to face me. Not a single person moved or spoke as he stared at me, his own expression as unreadable as mine.

"A fatal blow," he finally said. "A candidate hasn't landed a fatal blow on me in at least fifty years."

"There's a reason for that, General," a voice rang out, and I whipped my head around as Dune stepped into the ring. His eyes narrowed, and spots of angry color rose high on his cheekbones as he jabbed a finger in my direction. "You're far too experienced to be bested by a candidate, but Adara hasn't been fighting fair. She's been cheating this entire time, and I can prove it!"

Adara

"Cheating?" I whirled to face Dune properly, my hands balling into fists in response to the unwarranted accusation. "What are you talking about?"

Dune bared his teeth as he stalked up to me. "I can't believe I didn't think of it before," he said, his hand darting out. His fingers closed around the chain I'd tucked beneath my tunic shirt and leather breastplate, and he pulled out the protection amulet my late father had left me. My skin turned ice cold—I'd never taken it off in my life, and it hadn't occurred to me to remove it before the tryouts. Had wearing it given me some kind of advantage?

"She's been wearing this primal stone the entire time," he told the General, shaking the blue-white in his direction. "It's the only thing that explains why she's so much stronger and faster than the rest of us."

"Primal stone?" I repeated, confused. I'd never even heard of a primal stone—what was he talking about? "This is a protection amulet—there's no way it could have given me extra strength or speed. Let go of it!"

I tried to pry the chain from Dune's grip, but he yanked hard, and it broke from around my neck. Smirking, he took a step in the general's direction, the amulet dangling from his fist.

"Let's see if you can use your super speed and strength now," he taunted.

"Give it back, you lowlife!" I lunged forward with my hand outstretched, unleashing every bit of fury I had within me. Something hot bloomed in my chest as I moved, surging out of me, and before I even knew what was happening, a gout of fire burst from my hand and barreled straight toward Dune.

Dune yelped, diving out of the way. The stream of fire shot past him, narrowly missing the General, who'd gone ramrod stiff. His eyes were glassy, disfigured face frozen with fear. The audience who'd been standing by to watch the tryouts screamed as the flames slammed into the earth right in front of them, setting the grass ablaze. Within seconds a fire was raging through the field, and fae were running in all directions, trying to get away.

I stood stock still as I took in all the commotion, shock rooting me to the spot. The scent of burning grass and flesh singed my nostrils, the screams of fae all around me assaulting my eardrums. How was this happening? Had that fire really come from me?

This is impossible, I thought numbly even as the fire raged around me.

"Put that fire out!" the general roared, snapping out of his fugue first. Dune sprang into action at the command, racing toward the flames. He raised his arms to the sky, and a wave of earth surged from the ground at his command. He used the soil to quash the flames, preventing them from spreading further. A few feet away, several fae had caught fire and were rolling in the grass and beating at their clothing, trying to put it out. The urge to help them seized me, and I took a few steps in their direction.

But before I could go any further, the general appeared in front of me.

"Not so fast," he growled, but before he could grab me, roots burst from the ground and wrapped around his ankles. Instinctively, I leaped out of his reach and spun around to see Mavlyn behind me, partially hidden in the crowd. Her arms were outstretched, and sweat beaded on her brow as she used her magic to hold the significantly more powerful general.

"Get out of here, Adara!" she shrieked. "I'll cover you!"

I glanced back to see General Slaugh sprawled on the ground. More roots burst from the dirt, snagging at the general's arms and legs, trying to hold him. He roared in anger, ripping at them, and the terrifying noise snapped me out of my shock and spurred me into action. Turning away, I sprinted for the equestrian arena. Mavlyn's horse, Butterfly, was still there, tied to a post, though she was stomping her hooves nervously at all the commotion. Refusing to think too hard about it, I untied her, leaped onto her back, and dug my heels into her flanks.

Butterfly sprang into motion, and I clung to her back as we cantered through the field, leaping over fleeing fae and dodging burning patches of grass. A few soldiers tried to stop us, snatching futilely at Butterfly's reins, but she was too fast, and in no time we'd cleared the field.

The mare surged into a full gallop as we hit the main road, and I gave her free rein to run, wanting to put as much distance between us and the general as possible. The wind ripped and tugged at my hair as we sped up and down the hills, like an extension of the general's grasping hands, and for the first ten minutes I kept glancing back, certain I'd see pursuers catching up at any moment. But no one was following—the soldiers must have been too busy trying to contain the chaos, and possibly dealing with wounded as well. Guilt twisted in my chest as I recalled the fire racing across the field. That had been *my* doing.

But how? I didn't understand how that fire could have possibly come from me. I was a water fae, and an impotent one at that. It should be completely impossible for me to wield fire—water and fire were incompatible elements, and no fae in the history of our race had been born with the ability to wield both. Not to mention that I didn't have any fire fae in my family tree—they'd been driven to extinction nearly three thousand years ago, when the dragons had invaded our realm.

Could the fire have been trapped in the primal stone—if that's what the amulet had truly been? But no, the fire had surged from my hands, not from the stone, which Dune had been holding. I'd felt it, *seen* it—the fire had been an extension of my fury, and Dune had been my target.

As we crested yet another hill, Fenwood Village finally came into view. The sight of the stone houses nestled at the edge of the forest sent a surge of relief through me, and I tugged on the reins, signaling for Butterfly to slow her pace. We entered the village at a trot, and Butterfly started toward Mavlyn's home, but I tugged on the reins again, guiding her toward my house instead. The villagers I passed sent me alarmed looks—my hair was probably a wild mess, and I knew Butterfly's flanks were lathered in sweat. But I ignored the questions on their faces. I needed to get to Mother, to tell her what happened. Surely she would have an explanation for all of this.

Not wanting to leave Mavlyn's horse neglected, I rubbed Butterfly down as best as I could, then tied her up in our yard and rushed into the house.

"Adara!" Mother cried as I slammed the door behind me, my heart still pounding hard in my chest. She'd been tending to a bubbling pot of porridge on the wood stove, but she abandoned it now, anger blazing in her green eyes as she advanced on me.

"Where have you been?" she demanded, jabbing her wooden stirring spoon in my direction. Flecks of hot porridge spattered my sweat-stained skin, but I barely felt it. "Sneaking out of the house before sunrise, without even leaving a note behind—how could you? You've had me worried sick!"

"Mother, please, I'm sorry." I put my hands on her shoulders and looked her square in the eye. "I know you're angry right now, but I need you to let me speak before the general and his men get here. They're coming for me."

Mother's skin went ashen beneath her copper complexion. "General Slaugh?" she asked, dawning horror in her eyes. "Please, Adara, tell me you didn't go to the tryouts. Tell me that isn't where you've been all day."

I swallowed hard trepidation rising in my throat. "I didn't just go to the tryouts, Mother. I took part in them."

"Took part?" Mother stared at me, aghast. "Why would you do such a thing? I've been training you to be a healer, Adara, not a warrior—"

"—because I can't use my water magic, right?" I spat, cutting her off. "Or at least that's what you've been telling me my whole life, and I foolishly believed it. But there's something else, isn't there, Mother? Some secret you've been keeping that explains the *real* reason you won't let me leave the village, and why you insist on training me in an art you know I have no love for."

What little color was left in Mother's face drained away, and she grasped the back of the nearest chair for support. Her gaze went to my neck, where the amulet chain had once been. "The necklace," she whispered. "You took it off. That's how you know."

"Know what?" I cried, slamming my fist against the top of the small wooden table we shared our meals at. The fire in the wood stove surged in response, and Mother screamed, jumping out of the way before her skirts caught fire. "Know that I have fire magic? Is that what this is? Is that why the stove nearly exploded just now?"

"Adara, you need to calm down." Mother spoke in an even tone, but there was a desperate look in her eyes as she grasped my hands. "Please, tell me what happened today. Why did you take the necklace off, and what did General Slaugh see, exactly?"

I didn't want to calm down. I wanted to rant and rage and vent my fury at this entire situation, at the lies and secrets I sensed bubbling to the surface. But the sight of the stove flickering behind Mother gave me pause—it had clearly responded to my emotions, and the fire I'd used earlier, that I'd nearly incinerated Dune with, had also been a product of my anger.

So I took a deep breath, sat down, and told Mother exactly what happened.

"You foolish, foolish child." Mother said when I'd finished. She had long since ceased sitting in the chair—she'd begun pacing when I got to the part about General Slaugh calling me into the ring. "Going to the tryouts, drawing the attention of the general, taking off your protection amulet—everything that could have possibly gone wrong—"

"Stop calling it a protection amulet!" I snapped, cutting Mother off. She stopped pacing and turned to stare at me, astonishment on her beautiful face. "Dune said that it was a primal stone. What does that mean? Was this even really a gift from my father? What other secrets have you been keeping?" My voice rose with each question, and sparks began to shoot from my fingertips. "You keep blaming me for everything that happened today, but you're the one who's been keeping me in the dark this entire time! What kind of mother does that?"

The words whipped out of me before I could stop myself, and my stomach dropped as tears filled my mother's eyes. "I'm sorry," I blurted out. "I didn't mean—"

"No, you're right." Mother's expression crumpled, and her

shoulders sagged. "I've been trying so hard to shield you, to protect you from the truth, but I should have known I couldn't keep it from you forever. This is my fault. I—"

A loud knock sounded at the door, and Mother immediately stopped speaking. "Go out through the apothecary entrance," she hissed, moving toward the front door. "I'll take care of General Slaugh."

"Absolutely not!" I jumped to my feet, my dagger already in hand. "I'm not leaving you to face the general alone, not when it's me he wants!"

"Adara, please." Mother grabbed my arm and began shoving me toward the shop door. "I don't have time to explain now, but you cannot, under *any* circumstances, allow the general to capture you."

"But—"

The front door flew open with a loud bang, and Mother and I froze. General Slaugh marched inside, his single eye narrowed, his mutilated lips pressed together. It struck me then that his eye was the exact same shade as Mother's, but I didn't have time to think that through further as my attention caught on the male following behind the general.

"There she is." Dune pointed at me, a smirk on his face. There was a sick light shining in his eyes that made my stomach twist. How had I ever thought he was handsome, when he was so horrid on the inside? "Told you we'd find her, General."

But the general wasn't paying any attention to Dune's words. In fact, he wasn't paying any attention to me either. He'd stopped in his tracks, his gaze fixed on one person and one person only.

My mother.

"Gelsyne?" His face went slack with shock, as if he couldn't believe what he was seeing. "I thought you were dead."

Gelsyne? I glanced at my mother, expecting to see the same confusion I felt mirrored in her eyes. But she only squared her shoulders, a determined look on her face as she confronted the general.

"Gelsyne is dead," she said firmly, placing her body in front of mine as if to shield me from General Slaugh's gaze. "I'm Chaya, the village healer, and you're trespassing in my home. Please take your leave. It's late, and my daughter and I require rest."

General Slaugh scoffed, his gaze landing on me. "Your daughter? I find that hard to believe." He took another step toward me, his single emerald eye scanning me from top to bottom with intense interest. "A water fae with the ability to wield fire," he murmured. "So the prophecy is real, after all."

"Prophecy?" I tried to step around my mother, but she flung out her arm, blocking me. "What are you talking about?"

The general laughed again. "Oh this is too good," he said, shaking his head. "You've kept her in the dark, haven't you Gelsyne? That's how you've managed to keep her hidden so long, even though the king has been searching for her. He's been scouring the newborns in both Lochanlee and the Beanntan Deigh for the past twenty years, testing each one of them for fire magic. It never occurred to him to search Domhain for her."

"That's because King Aolis has scrambled harpy eggs for a brain," Gelsyne snapped. "Go back and tell your king you've failed, cousin. I'll never let you take Adara, not so long as there's breath in my body."

"Then we'll just have to fix that, won't we?"

Slaugh's form rippled, and the air surrounding him grew hazy. His armor melted into his skin as his muscles swelled and his shape changed, legs shortening, arms lengthening, black and silver hair sprouting as he changed into a hulking silverback gorilla. Roaring, he crossed the room in one bounding leap, then grabbed my mother by the torso and slammed her into the wall.

Her head cracked against the stone, and she cried out in pain as those huge fingers tightened around her ribcage.

"Mother!" I rushed to her aid, but Dune stepped into my path, his own sword raised.

"Not so fast," he tsked. "You're coming with us."

"Get out of my way," I snarled. Fire sprang to my fingertips, and this time I embraced it. Satisfaction surged in me as Dune took a fearful step back, and I let the flames build into twin fire balls, urging them to grow brighter, hotter—

"NO!"

My mother flung out a free hand in my direction, power rippling from her in waves of sparkling green light. The earth rumbled beneath our feet, then opened directly under me like a sprung trap. Our eyes met for a split second as I fell into the darkness below, and in her gaze I saw myriad emotions—guilt, regret, anger, determination.

But most importantly, love.

Then the ground swallowed me whole, and I saw no more.

6

Adara

"No!" I screamed as the earth closed over my head. I clawed at the dirt, trying to dig my way back, but before I could get more than a handful, a hidden force propelled me forward with the strength of a tidal wave.

"Stop, stop, stop, stop, STOP!" I wailed, but the earth kept moving. It was carrying me away from the house at impossible speeds, rattling my brain, shoving my heart into my throat and turning my bones liquid. Panic screeched through my nerves, and it took everything I had in me not to pass out as the earth rumbled around me.

Just when I thought I was going to be stuck underground forever, the earth spat me out. I landed hard on the ground, choking and sputtering, wiping dirt from my eyes and coughing it from my lungs. My entire body trembled with shock, and I closed my eyes against my surroundings, which were spinning so fast I wanted to throw up. Sucking in a deep breath, I stayed where I was, and forced myself to think calming thoughts.

Eventually my heart stopped pounding, and the roaring in

my ears died down, replaced by the sound of wildlife rustling in the bushes nearby. I cracked my eyes open, and sighed in relief when instead of a spinning world, I was met by a canopy of mercifully still tree branches. They were almost completely bare, stripped of their leaves by the north winds heralding the coming winter.

Groaning, I pushed myself to my feet. I felt battered, as if I'd been kicked and punched repeatedly all over my body. Which, in a way, I had. Scowling, I turned around, inspecting my surroundings, trying to figure out where I was. The earth surrounding my feet looked completely undisturbed, as though a hole hadn't opened up and ejected me into the middle of a forest. And it did look like I was smack dab in the middle—I couldn't see anything beyond the trees except, well, more trees. Oh, and fog. Swirls of it, clinging to the trunks, turning the air murky.

"Great," I muttered. How was I supposed to get back to my mother? I shuddered to think of what General Slaugh might be doing to her. I had no doubt it had been her who'd sent me away —but how? My whole life I thought she'd been a healer, her talent lying in her ability to draw out the concentrated essence of any plant and use it to make potent remedies. The fact that Mother been able to manipulate the earth, with enough power to send me miles away from home, meant that she was a Greater Fae.

More secrets she's been keeping from me.

Bitterness tried to take root in my heart, but I pushed it out. There was no time for that. Right now, my mother was in grave danger, and I needed to find my way back before something horrible happened to her. I had no idea where to go, so I just started walking forward, following the narrow deer trail before me. If I kept moving, I would eventually reach the end of the forest, or at least *some* kind of landmark that would tell me where to go next.

The surrounding forest quieted at the sound of my footfalls, and nerves prickled at the back of my neck, aware of the creatures watching my progress silently. Lifting my hand, I tugged on the hidden power that had awoken in me, and concentrated. A flame sparked to life in my palm, hovering just above my skin. There was still plenty of daylight, but fire was useful for keeping predators away, so I kept the flame burning in my hand as I walked. I would just have to be careful not to lose control of it, the way I had during the tryouts.

I wish I had more travel experience, I thought glumly as I walked through the dense forest. I'd only traveled beyond Fenwood a handful of times, usually on trips with my mother to neighboring villages, and once to Talamh, to find rare herbs or texts she needed. I'd always thought it odd that such an educated fae chose to live in a small town like Fenwood, away from the halls of learning she'd obviously grown up around. But after tonight, I wondered if she'd chosen Fenwood for a specific reason. To keep me safe, away from prying eyes.

But why had I needed to be hidden? My powers were definitely unusual—I still couldn't fathom how I had the ability to wield fire—but I didn't understand why the king was so desperate to capture me. General Slaugh had mentioned a prophecy—what was that about? And why had my mother stopped me from using my fire magic on him and Dune? The two obviously had no love lost between each other. If Mother really was a Greater Fae, she and Slaugh would be from the same house. So how had they become enemies?

These thoughts continued to chase themselves around in my head, digging up more and more questions as I walked. Hour after hour I moved through the trees, until my temples pounded and my feet ached and I wanted nothing more than to lie down. Between the tryouts and the traumatic experience of being swallowed and crushed by the earth, every inch of my body was crying out in pain.

But I couldn't stop. Not when my mother was in danger.

"Lost, are you, little one?"

I whipped my head around at the baritone voice. An earth fae perched on a rock, smoking a pipe. His long, pointed ears stuck out from beneath a wild mane of curling white hair. His dark skin was wrinkled with age, and his faded, threadbare tunic had clearly seen better days, but his eyes, a startling green with gold-rimmed pupils, were bright and sharp.

Those eyes. I'd seen them before, on someone else. But where? I wracked my brain as I tried to remember, but I was so tired I could barely think straight.

"Who are you?" I finally asked, looking around to see if there were any other signs of civilization. Perhaps a house nearby, where this man lived? "And where am I?"

"Ahhh, so you are lost." He puffed out three concentric circles of blue-grey smoke. I knew that color well—it was the exact shade of my hair. "We're in the Barrowood Forest, girl."

I swallowed, hard. If memory served, Barrowood Forest was a good twenty miles east of Fenwood, halfway to Talamh. It would take me hours to get home, provided I was even going in the right direction! Plus, the forest was said to be haunted, home to spirits both fell and friendly. No wonder I was getting chills all over my body.

"Can you help me get out of here?" I asked him. "I need to get home to my mother. She's in grave danger."

The elderly fae smiled, and nodded his head to the left. "Those who need help should follow the lights. They'll take you where you need to go."

I turned in the direction he was pointing, and stared. A fork split off from the path I'd been walking. Tiny, glowing blue orbs of light hovered along the new path at intervals, and I blinked several times, trying to decide if what I was seeing was real. I was pretty sure neither the path nor the lights had been there before —surely I would have noticed.

"How—" I turned back to address him, but the fae had vanished. The plume of smoke hovering in the air was the only indication he'd been there at all.

"Giant's teeth," I grumbled, turning back to the path. I wasn't sure if it was a good idea to follow this stranger's advice, but really, what choice did I have? It wasn't like my current path was getting me anywhere, and if I was being honest, I really, *really* needed to find a safe place to shelter for a few hours. The light filtering through the trees had turned the reddish-gold color of sunset, and I was so tired I had begun to sway on my feet.

Gathering my strength, I set off along the path. The glowing orbs were oddly soothing, easing some of my fear and exhaustion, beckoning me forward with a silent call. Encouraged, I lengthened my stride instinctively. I didn't know where I was going, but I had the feeling that this path led somewhere important, to something that I needed to see.

After about an hour of walking, the path widened into a sort of overgrown drive, littered with roots and vines that would have tripped me up if not for the floating lights illuminating the path. Eventually, I came across an old, rusted gate. It was at least ten feet tall, covered in ivy, and lay open, half twisted off its hinges by some unseen force. Beyond it lay the ruins of an old castle, a remnant from a forgotten age long abandoned. Parts of the roof and walls were exposed, and the stones were covered in moss, but it looked sturdy enough to take shelter in, at least for the night.

Drawing my cloak tighter around me, I approached the ruin cautiously. The front door was locked, and the nearest hole in the wall was ten feet up, too high to climb. I considered the problem for a moment, wondering if I could use my fire magic, but I decided it was too risky. Instead, I grabbed a large brick lying nearby and brought it down on top of the doorknob with all my strength. The force of the blow smashed the knob, and the mechanism fell apart, clattering to the ground in pieces.

Here we go, I thought as the door swung inward. I stepped over the threshold and conjured my fireball again, using the flickering light to illuminate the interior. The inside of the tower was spacious, and looked like it had once been used as a kind of library or study. There was a large desk and chair in one area, what looked like laboratory equipment in another area, and a small group of couches and chairs where one could sit and read. Bookshelves packed with dusty tomes lined every inch of the walls, rising upward in a spiral pattern all the way to the very top of the tower. Rolling ladders were spaced at intervals on each level, and part of me itched to climb up there and explore the tomes on the shelves. Unfortunately, a sizeable chunk of the winding staircase had fallen away, rendering the upper levels inaccessible.

But the most arresting thing in the room was neither the books nor the staircase nor the laboratory. It was the massive stone dragon that lay curled up in front of the staircase, blocking access to it entirely.

My breath caught in my throat as I stared at the sculpture. Dragons hadn't been seen in decades—the last ones were killed off before I was born, during the final days of the Dragon-Fae war that had plagued Ediria for millennia. The dragons had been trying to steal our land for centuries, and King Aolis—who had been general and the right hand of the king at that time—had eradicated them and taken back the lands they had stolen. According to the stories, the Radiants had blessed him with a special weapon after the dragons assassinated the former king, which he'd used to avenge his king and safeguard Ediria from all threats.

The last thing any fae would want to do was memorialize any dragon in stone, and especially not a lifelike sculpture such as this. Even curled up in sleep, the dragon towered over me by a good twenty feet. Its head alone was twice the length of my entire body, and the spikes jutting from its back and tail were the length of my forearm. The artist had put meticulous detail into the piece, right down to the individual scales that made up its hide.

Unable to help myself, I reached out and ran a hand across the stone scales. A shiver raced up my arm and down my spine —the stone was warm to the touch despite the cold weather. Was this really what dragons had looked like? What would it have been like to face one in battle?

I was about to pull my hand back when suddenly, the statue rippled. I gasped as the hard, grey stone transformed, turning into ruby-colored scales that shimmered in the light cast by my fireball. A growl rumbled from the sculpture, and I scrambled backward, a scream building in my throat.

Limbs shifted. Wings unfurled. Spiked tail swished. Fear turned my knees into molten liquid, and it took everything in me not to collapse to the ground as one large, golden eye opened, the reptilian pupil fixing straight on me.

The sculpture wasn't a sculpture. It was a real dragon.

And I was about to be dinner.

7

Einar

Warmth.

I stirred at the foreign sensation, of fingers splayed against my hide, questioning, feeling. Who dared to touch me with such a delicate appendage, to pull me from the darkness that had become my home, my prison that I had so willingly embraced to see my family to safety?

I tried to sink back into the darkness, to shrug off this prick at my consciousness, but the warmth began to penetrate my hide and seep into my blood. My bones. My muscles stirred against my will, the sleeping spell sloughing off my hide like a layer of dust.

A growl rumbled up from the rusty bowels of my chest, and I cracked an eye open, determined to find the trespasser who dared disturb my slumber.

A female stared back at me, her cornflower blue eyes wide with terror. The growl in my throat cut off abruptly, and I stared back, momentarily transfixed by her beauty. Milky white skin, button nose, rosebud lips. Curves that beckoned and taunted all at once. Her lavender-blue hair was a wild mane around her heart-shaped face, and it begged me to run my fingers through it, to see if it was as soft and silky as it looked.

At least, until I saw the pointed ears peeking out from underneath it. Barely visible in the firelight coming from her palm, but there.

Fae. She's a fucking fae.

Rage ripped through me, obliterating any desire I had for the female. I bellowed loud enough to shake the walls, and the fae stumbled backwards, shielding her face. My muscles bunched as I prepared to launch myself at her, to tear her limb from limb for what her people had done to mine.

"No! Please, don't hurt me!"

The dulcet tone of her voice awakened something with me, and I froze, an invisible tether bringing me up short before I could attack. I snarled as I realized what was happening, as the bindings tightened around my soul, rooting me to the spot, forcing me to obey her command.

The mating bond.

A beam from the ceiling fell, dislodged by my roar. The female screamed, and I reacted instinctively, whipping out one of my wings to shield her. The length of wood bounced harmlessly off my wing, but I misjudged my own momentum, and accidentally knocked her over with the appendage even as I sought to protect her. She fell back and smacked her head into the ground with a loud *thunk*.

Shit.

An unwelcome sense of guilt pierced my chest, and I tossed the beam aside, then shifted into my bi-pedal form. My wings furled into my back, torso shrinking, limbs lengthening, scales melting away into smooth skin. I rushed over to the fae—*my mate*, an inner voice in my head reminded me—and dropped to my knees beside her, then hauled her head into my lap.

"Hey. Hey!" I shook her shoulders, fear and anger biting into my words. "Wake up!"

The fae stirred in my lap. Her eyes fluttered open, hazy at first, and for a moment, we simply gazed at each other. Looking into those eyes felt like coming home, and that made me furious.

My home had been destroyed, long ago, by this female's kind. There *was* no home for me anymore, not in this forsaken realm.

The fae's cheeks turned pink as she seemed to realize how inappropriate our position was. "Who are you?" she asked as she struggled into an upright position.

"Hold on," I said gruffly, pinning her back down. I grabbed a piece of wood lying nearby and blew a flame onto it so I could see her better. Then I checked her pupils and felt the back of her head for any lumps.

"Stop it." She pushed my hands away and sat up, scooting herself off my lap. I resisted the urge to pull her back onto me—*she's a fae, she's the enemy*, I reminded myself. "I'm fine." She rubbed the back of her head a bit, sending a fresh pang of guilt through me. "You didn't answer my question. Who are you?"

"My name is Einar," I said, fisting my hands to keep myself from touching her. Even through my anger, the need to claim her, to put my mark over every square inch of her flesh, writhed within me like a living creature desperate to get free. "I'm the dragon you woke up."

Her eyes went wide, and she looked past me to where I'd been lying in my dragon form, and then back to me. "You... you're..." she seemed to fumble for the right words. "Well that explains how you lit that fire," she finished lamely.

"I'm not the only one who lit a fire in this room." I frowned as I recalled the fireball she'd been holding when she woke me. "How are you able to wield fire magic? I thought none of the fae had that power anymore."

"Well you would know, wouldn't you?" she said, a little snarkily. "Since the dragons killed all the fire fae when they came to Ediria."

I growled low in my throat at the familiar lie that had spawned generations of hatred between our two races. "The dragons never touched the fire fae," I spat. "They were gone before we arrived in Ediria."

"Oh, so they just *happened* to disappear right around the time your kind arrived?" the fae mocked sweetly. "How convenient for you."

My nails bit into my palms as I once again resisted the urge to touch her—except this time I wanted to wrap my hands around her throat and strangle her. "Where are we?" I asked, trying to change the subject. The last thing I remembered was inside the heart of Mount Furian. I'd been put to sleep there, not inside a tower ruin. How had I gotten here? And more importantly, why here specifically?

"We're in Barrowood Forest," the fae answered. "Where exactly in the forest, I don't know. I followed the spirit lights here."

"Spirit lights? What nonsense are you talking about?"

The fae shrugged, looking a little uncomfortable. "I was lost, and an elder I met in the woods told me if I followed the lights they would take me to where I needed to go. The legends say that Barrowood Forest is haunted by spirits, so I figured the lights must be ghosts or something."

I frowned as I considered her words. "Those sound like aural lights." Aural lights were the work of the Radiants, beings of light who watched over our world. Since Radiants were from the spirit world, they rarely manifested in this realm, but they sometimes sent signs when they wanted to influence certain people or events.

Evidently, the Radiants had decided it was time for me to

awaken. So they sent the one person with the power to break the sleeping spell—my mate.

But why? I seethed internally, furious at this betrayal. It was imperative that I remain asleep, tucked away from fae eyes and ears. That was the only way to ensure that the portal remained closed and my people remained safe. Why would the Radiants put us at risk now, after all they'd done to help us?

"Are you okay?" the fae asked, her eyebrows arched. "You look like you're about to explode."

I sighed, scrubbing a hand across my face. "What's your name?" I asked, resigned to the fact that I was going to need to know more about the fae before I could figure out how to extricate myself from this mess. "And why were you lost in the forest?"

The fae crossed her arms over her chest, which had the very unfortunate effect of pushing her breasts together. A vision unfurled in my head of her sprawled out beneath me, hair tousled, face flushed, her upper body completely bare to my hungry gaze. My hands cupping her breasts, drawing one rosy nipple into my mouth so I could lick and suckle. Her breathy cries echoing off the walls, long legs wrapping around my waist—

"*Hello?*" the fae's voice cut through my vision, and I blinked to find her staring crossly at me. "Did you hear *anything* I said?"

"Sorry." I shook my head vigorously, my ears burning with embarrassment. I was behaving like a whelp! "I've been asleep for a long time. I'm still trying to adjust."

The fae huffed. "I said my name is Adara, and that I'm tired of answering all these questions. I want to know what *you're* doing here, and why you were a stone statue before I woke you up."

Adara. The name suited her, though I'd never tell her so. "I have no idea what I'm doing here," I told her. "If memory serves,

Barrowood Forest is in the earth realm, and when the Radiants put me to sleep, I was in Hearthfyre, deep within the heart of Mount Furian."

"Hearthfyre?" Adara frowned. "You mean the Deadlands? And you said the *Radiants* are the ones who put you to sleep?"

"The Deadlands?" I repeated, incensed. "Is that what your people are calling my homeland?"

"Well, it hasn't been your homeland for some time now," Adara said primly. "The Dragon-Fae War ended nearly twenty years ago." She tilted her head to the side as she considered me. "Is that how long you've been asleep for?"

"Must be," I groused. "Not nearly long enough. I intended to sleep for eternity."

"Why?" Adara screwed her face up in distaste. "That sounds miserable."

"No more miserable than living out your life as the last of your race in a realm that hates your kind. And I don't need your pity," I snapped as her expression began to soften. "I made a sacrifice so that my people could live, and I don't regret it."

She scowled. "What do you mean, so that your people could live? I thought King Aolis killed all the dragons."

"Right," I drawled. "*All* of them."

Adara rolled her eyes. "Well obviously not *all*, since you're here." Without warning, she jumped to her feet and began pacing the room. "Giant's teeth, I don't have time for this."

"Time for what?" I asked.

"To argue with a crotchety old dragon!" Adara threw up her hands. "I don't understand why those lights brought me to you. The elder said they'd take me where I need to go, but what I need is to get back to my village and find out what happened to my mother. And you aren't helping at all!"

"Adara, wait—" I started, but she was already storming out into the night. I sat on the worn rug for a moment, waiting to see if I could let her go. It would be so much easier if we could just part ways here—she seemed young, still wet behind the ears, and I wasn't in the mood to play nanny.

But after a minute, the mate bond began to tug at me. Gritting my teeth, I tried to resist, but it quickly turned into a burning sensation. With every minute that passed, the pain spread farther and farther, until my entire body was screaming.

Snarling, I pushed myself to my feet and stalked out the door. There was nothing for it. I was going to have to follow her, even if she ended up leading me to my own demise.

8

King Aolis

"Y our Highness, General Slaugh has returned."

King Aolis frowned, turning away from the Gaoth Aire general he was meeting with. It was customary for him to spend his mornings in the throne room, hearing out the requests of his people, and he did not appreciate being interrupted.

"What of it?" he addressed his sergeant-at-arms, a tall water fae clad in the black matte armor all members of his Shadow Guard wore. "I do not need to be informed every time the general comes and goes from the castle, Kian. If Slaugh needs to see me, he can do so once I'm finished here."

The sergeant cleared his throat. "The general understands you are busy, but he insists this is of the utmost importance. He has a prisoner in tow—a female crucial to helping him accomplish the...mission."

King Aolis straightened in his throne, the air fae before him immediately forgotten. "Send him in," he commanded. He waved a hand at the fae, who had traveled all the way from the air realm to meet with him. "You're dismissed, general."

"But Your Highness!" the general protested, outrage flashing in his mercurial eyes. His pale blue leather armor, reinforced with silver plates, creaked as he straightened his own tall form, standing his ground. "We haven't finished discussing the plan for reinforcements—"

"As I explained to you, I am actively recruiting more soldiers to help in the fight against the shadow creatures," King Aolis said, his tone clipped. "We will send reinforcements when we can. In the meantime, you and your Lightning Riders must continue to guard the border. That is your duty now, just as it was during the Dragon-Fae War."

The general opened his mouth to argue, but King Aolis lazily curled a hand around the black spear that sat to his left in an ornate stand. The spear hummed in his palm, coming to life, and Aolis steeled himself against the hunger that rippled through him in response. Everyone in Ediria respected the Spear of Destiny, the legendary weapon Aolis had used to exterminate the dragons and bring peace to the kingdom.

It was a good thing the general did not know that this was not the true Spear of Destiny, or that wielding it came with a terrible price Aolis could rarely afford to pay. Not if he wanted to maintain the little control he had left over his own mind.

The general's face went pale, and he snapped his mouth shut. "My apologies, Sire," he said, bowing stiffly. "I have forgotten myself. I will return to the Gaoth Aire now."

"Good. Send Lord Oren my regards."

The air fae general left, and King Aolis suppressed a sigh. He knew that this was not the last he would hear from the Gaoth Aire—they had grown tired of fighting off the shadow creatures at the border, largely on their own with very little support from the other kingdoms. So far, the hostages Aolis had taken from each of the Houses ensured that the other realms remained under his thumb, but he knew the subservience of their rulers would only go so far. If the shadow creatures grew too far out of control, they would come for him regardless of the safety of their children.

That was why he'd thrown the general out, and allowed Slaugh to interrupt him. He desperately needed this mission to succeed, and he was not yet ready for the air fae nobility to get wind of the fact that he'd made any progress with it.

"Send General Slaugh in," Aolis ordered the sergeant-at-arms, his tone rife with impatience. The sergeant stuck his head through the double doors, and a second later, they opened wide to admit Slaugh. Aolis gripped his spear a little tighter as the general strode in, his body humming with anticipation. A female trailed behind him, her head bowed so that her long, dark hair hid her face. She wore a dark green dress that was torn at the hem and the left sleeve, and he spotted a healing gash on her forearm. Her hands were bound in front of her, her shoulders slumped forward in defeat. Clearly there had been a scuffle, but Slaugh had managed to bring her in.

Could this be the one he was searching for? The girl of ice and fire, who would drive back the shadow creatures and unite the kingdom?

"Your Highness." Slaugh sank down onto one knee in front of the dais and bowed his head. The female, however, remained standing, and shock hit Aolis like a slap to the face as she finally lifted her head. Familiar emerald eyes stared out at him from behind a comely face he'd once seen almost daily, but instead of smiling at him as they once had, they glittered with unsuppressed rage.

"Aolis." She bit the word out, her teeth bared. "It's been a long time."

"Gelsyne." Aolis managed to keep most of the surprise out of his voice. He knew he should command her to kneel, but he was so stunned by her appearance that he didn't bother. "I haven't seen you since you and Princess Olette ran from the wedding feast. When the Oracle informed me of Olette's death, I assumed you had perished as well. Why did you never come back to court?"

"Because I have no desire to serve a traitor king," Gelsyne spat.

King Aolis stiffened. "All who live in this realm serve me, regardless of whether or not they are members of my court," he growled. The shadows in the room flickered as he spoke, reacting to his mood, and Gelsyne's eyes narrowed as the shadows began to lengthen.

"Not just a traitor king, then," she sneered. "A corrupted one, too."

King Aolis sucked in a sharp breath. He clamped down on the rising hunger inside him, and reluctantly, the shadows retreated. For a heartbeat, he had almost lost control. That was unacceptable.

"General." He addressed Slaugh this time, motioning for him to rise. "Where did you find this wench, and why have you brought her to me instead of executing her for treason?" Kidnapping the princess was considered a capital crime, and he'd put out an execution order for Gelsyne decades ago. Slaugh did not need Aolis's permission to carry it out.

Slaugh smirked as he rose to his feet. "I found Gelsyne hiding out in a backwoods village in Domhain. She's been living there the last eighteen years pretending to be a lesser fae, working as the village's healer and going by the name Chaya, according to the Headman's younger son. But it wasn't Gelsyne who caught my interest. It was her *daughter*, Adara. She came to the tryouts today, and during the combat trial she nearly killed a candidate using fire magic."

"Fire magic?" King Aolis repeated. His pulse raced, and he had to fight the urge to leap up from his throne in excitement. "Are you certain?"

"She shot a fireball from her hand and nearly set an entire field aflame," Slaugh said dryly. "Which should have been an impossibility, given that she's a water fae."

"A water fae?" Aolis's gaze cut back to Gelsyne, whose complexion had gone pale beneath her dark skin. "How did you come to have a water fae for a daughter, Gelsyne?" He was curious to know more about the girl's parentage. As Greater Fae with both the powers of air and water at his command, he was likely related to the girl, even if only distantly.

Gelsyne lifted her chin. "I will go to my grave before I give you any information that will help you capture Adara."

"It's too bad you no longer harbor any loyalty toward this court, Gelsyne," Aolis said in a tragic voice. "This would be much less painful for both of us if you would cooperate. You see, I am not merely interested in your daughter because of her fire magic, though that is a rare talent indeed. I'm interested because she is key to defeating the shadow creatures, which is why I cannot allow you to stop me from finding her."

Gelsyne snorted. "Say what you wish, Aolis, but we all know that you care more about holding onto the throne than you do about saving the kingdom. If that weren't true, you wouldn't have had Daryan assassinated at the wedding feast. Your own hatred and jealousy over the dragon who won Olette's heart was more important to you than ending—"

Slaugh's gauntleted hand cracked across Gelsyne's face, cutting her off. The former courtier cried out as she stumbled back, a fresh gash opening across her cheek. Blood spilled from the wound, dripping down her jaw and splattering the bodice of her dress, and the dark force curled in Aolis's chest stirred again.

Go ahead, the darkness inside him whispered. *Take her. Just a taste. For us.*

"That's enough," Aolis said through gritted teeth. He wasn't sure if he was speaking to the darkness, or to Slaugh, or to Gelsyne, but he couldn't allow this situation to spiral out of control. "Your treasonous words are not welcome at this court, Gelsyne. Take her to the dungeons," he commanded. "I will interrogate her later." Aolis wanted to do it now, but he knew his control was tenuous at best right now. He needed to make sure he had the darkness inside him fully in hand before he questioned Gelsyne.

"But Your Majesty," Slaugh protested. "Surely you have more important things to do. I am more than capable of handling the interrogation myself. She undoubtedly has information that will help us capture the girl."

Aolis shook his head. "No. I will handle this myself." Both fae ignored Gelsyne's struggles as she was removed from the throne room, her curses echoing off the stone walls. "Take two of your most trusted soldiers, and bring Adara to me. I will send word if I extract any relevant information from Gelsyne, but finding the girl cannot wait."

Aolis needed to see Adara for himself to be sure, but there was little doubt in his mind that she was the child from the Oracle's prophecy, the one he'd been searching for these last two decades. Finding her was the key to saving his kingdom and keeping his seat on the stolen throne beneath him.

Because Gelsyne was right. He was a traitor. But he'd done what he had to secure the future of his kingdom, and he couldn't allow his sins to be in vain.

9

Adara

"Madness," I muttered to myself as I stormed out of the ruin. This entire situation was absolute chaos. When I'd woken up this morning, I'd been a magically impotent fae. My only goal had been to get into the Edirian army, so I could prove to Dune and my mother that they were wrong about me, that there *was* a place and a purpose for me outside the stifling safety of Fenwood Village. That even in a world where magical ability was prized above all else, I still had value.

But in the span of just a few hours, my entire life had been irrevocably altered. Now, I was a wanted fae with powerful fire magic humming in my veins—magic that everyone thought extinct in fae bloodlines. And if that weren't bad enough, I'd somehow managed to find—and piss off—the only living dragon in Ediria.

Honestly, it was a miracle I was still breathing.

I didn't know what the aural lights had had in mind when they'd brought me to him, but Einar was anything but helpful. All he wanted to do was fight with me, and I didn't have time for that. Slaugh could have badly wounded my mother, or worse, killed her in retaliation for helping me escape. And given that Einar seemed to hate fae with a passion, I could hardly expect him to assist me anyway.

"Unbelievable," I grumbled under my breath. I was so busy fuming over the situation that I almost didn't hear the soft growl. My body reacted before my brain registered the sound, and I came to an abrupt halt in the middle of a clearing.

"What..." I stared, and the words died in my throat as a dire wolf stepped into the clearing—a massive beast with coal-black fur and fangs the size of my hand. Even from several yards away, I could already tell that the top of its head reached my shoulder, and that its jaws were capable of chomping my torso in half.

But the worst thing about the wolf was not its fangs or its jaws or its hulking size. It was the tendrils of darkness rippling from the ends of its fur, and the inky blackness that bled from its pupils and into the whites of its eyes, swallowing them whole.

This wasn't just a dire wolf. It had become something twisted, something cursed.

A shadow creature.

Terror iced my veins as three more wolves stepped into the clearing, and I grasped for my short sword. My palms went clammy when they met my leather-clad thigh instead, and I realized I'd left the sword at the tryouts during the combat trial, when I'd had to switch it out for the wooden sword to fight Slaugh. My dagger was still in my boot, but I knew it would be of little use against such massive beasts. My fire magic would be a better bet.

"Easy there," I warned, taking a slow step back. I raised my palms and tried to call upon my fire magic, but the flames that sprang to my fingertips were weak, dimmed by the fear churning in my gut. The wolves bared their teeth in response, their snarls ripping through the stillness of the night. The fire died in my hand completely, and I swallowed hard, bracing myself for the inevitable rush.

The first wolf leapt at me, shadows bleeding from its open maw as its big, black body sailed through the air. A cry of terror burst from my lips, but my body sprang into action and I dodged just in time. The beast slammed into the tree behind me with a yelp, but the other three were already rushing me. I avoided the snapping jaws of one, but the second one's muzzle closed around my forearm, wicked sharp teeth sinking into my tender flesh.

No! My brain screamed the denial even as the veins surrounding the wound turned black. This was how shadow magic spread—the infected creatures passed it on by biting or scratching their victims. I hadn't had a chance to take any ever-bright before my mother had forcibly propelled me from the house, so there was no chance I would recover from this.

Abruptly, the fight went out of me, and my shoulders sagged. There was no point in resisting, not anymore. Better to let the wolves tear me apart than to become a shadow creature. The infected were driven by a mindless hunger that forced them to seek out others, to continue to spread the infection, and I wouldn't do that to my people. I wouldn't bring this terrible sickness to them.

A second wolf bit into me, fangs sinking into my calf, and this time, I screamed. But a deafening roar drowned out the sound, and the wolves froze as a shadow fell over us, large and ominous enough to block out the light from the dying sun.

My breath caught in my throat, and I glanced up. Ruby red scales flashed from above, wings spread taut, an even larger maw opening wide as something white hot-flashed from the back of a reptilian throat.

That was all the warning I got before a torrent of flames rained down from the sky, dousing the entire clearing. The wolves howled in agony, teeth ripping from my flesh as they sought to escape the inferno, but it was too late for them.

Just as it was too late for me.

I threw my arms up over my head as the wolves burnt to cinders around me, as if my measly appendages could protect me from the firestorm. But though the flames licked at my skin, they felt warm and soft, like a lover's caress. The wolves' cries faded into smoke and ash, and the icy fear inside me evaporated, melted away by a rush of relief.

A loud rumble abruptly cut that relief off as the dragon landed heavily in the clearing. He beat his wings forcefully, generating a torrent of wind that snatched at the flames, drawing them away. I cried out in protest as they left me, trying to snatch them back, but the wind whisked them straight into Einar's open mouth, and I watched in astonishment as he swallowed them.

A deafening silence fell as the dragon and I stared at each other. Not a single living thing stirred—the only movement came from the black smoke that curled up from the charred remains of the dire wolves.

The dragon's form rippled, and I gasped as he shifted right in front of me. Ruby red scales gave way to smooth, tanned skin, dark, shoulder-length hair, and a ruggedly handsome face that, when I'd first met him, was twisted in anger and disgust.

But while there were still lines of anger evident in his expression, there was something else. A reluctant curiosity simmered in his golden eyes as he studied me, like I was a frustrating puzzle he couldn't quite turn away from.

I took advantage of the moment to get a good look at him—it had been difficult to see him properly in the castle. The sun had properly set by now, and moonlight rippled across his body, casting him in sharp relief. He was all broad shoulders and carved muscle, his chest bare, his legs covered in tight trousers that outlined his powerful thighs and calves. Stylized flames swirled across his right pectoral muscle and all the way down his adjacent arm, but the rest of his tanned skin was bare of adornment save for a golden cuff adorned with a single red stone on his left wrist.

Despite his terrifying display of strength—or perhaps because of it—I found myself wanting to reach out and trace the lines of his tattoo. Maybe even lower, across that muscled abdomen, and down to the v that disappeared down his trousers...

"You need to stop looking at me like that," Einar said roughly, breaking the silence.

I jolted from my reverie. "Like what?" I asked, my cheeks heating. Giant's teeth, had I been staring at him that long?

"Like you want to lick me from head to toe." I thought he was teasing me, but his expression was deadly serious. His eyes were gold once more, but they gleamed with hunger, and I became excruciatingly aware that I was toe to toe with an alpha predator the likes of which hadn't been seen for decades.

And yet, unlike the dire wolves, I didn't want to run away. I wanted to come closer, to challenge him, to see just how deep that hunger went, and how far he would go to satisfy it.

What is wrong *with me?* I shouldn't be thinking like this, not when I was on the brink of death.

Clearing my throat, I did my best to change the subject. "You rescued me," I said. "Why? You made it clear that you hate all fae."

"Sheer curiosity." His mouth tightened as he scanned the clearing, his gaze lingering on the wolves. "I watched from the sky as they attacked you, and saw your idiotic reaction. Why did you give in to them like that? Why didn't you use your fire magic?"

Tears scalded the corners of my eyes at his accusatory tone, embarrassment burning away any feelings of attraction I might have had. Einar thought I was a failure, just like Dune. "I didn't want to give up, but one of them bit me," I said hotly, lifting my arm to show him. "I appreciate you coming to my rescue, but you might as well kill me before the shadow magic they infected me with takes over. I'd rather die than become a shadow creature."

Einar raised an eyebrow, crossing his beefy arms over his muscular chest. "Doesn't look like you're infected with shadow magic to me," he said pointedly.

"I—what?" I glanced at my arm, then gasped. I expected to see black veins pulsing through my skin, spreading up my arm and heading for my heart. But aside from the torn flesh, which was healing inexplicably fast, my arm looked completely normal.

"This doesn't make any sense," I said faintly, my head spinning with confusion. "Those dire wolves were infected with shadow magic. I *saw* the taint spread into my skin when it bit me."

"That's impossible," Einar said flatly. "You must have been seeing things." He toed one of the beasts with his bare foot, his upper lip curling. "No one escapes the effects of shadow magic. Not even dragons."

I glanced sideways at him. "You sound like you're speaking from firsthand experience."

"Of course I am," Einar sneered. "Your wonderful King Aolis's expert use of it is the reason he won the war."

My mouth dropped open. "You think King Aolis used shadow magic to kill the dragons?"

"I know he did. I witnessed it myself."

The raw pain in Einar's voice stole my breath, and for a moment, I was speechless. The idea that King Aolis had used shadow magic, a power that no elemental fae could wield, was preposterous. Everyone knew he'd used the legendary Spear of Destiny, gifted to him by the Radiants, to drive the dragons back to their borders and kill them off. As beings of light, there was no way the Radiants would have given him a relic crafted from shadow magic.

And yet, the anguish burning in Einar's eyes couldn't be faked. He definitely believed King Aolis had used shadow magic to kill his people. And if I was being honest, it wasn't as if I actually knew the truth about anything, especially since I hadn't been alive during the war. In fact, it was becoming more and more obvious with each passing second that I knew nothing at all.

"This conversation isn't going anywhere," I said with a huff. "Thanks for saving me, but I have to go now. I need to find my mother and get some answers."

I turned away, but before I could take a step, Einar was suddenly in front of me. "You're not going anywhere." His massive hands curled around my shoulders as he loomed over me, and I swallowed hard, steeling myself for a fight. "Not until I get some answers of my own."

Einar

T he moment I curled my fingers around Adara's shoulders, my desire for answers evaporated, leaving me with the burning need to pull her closer, to bury my nose in her hair and inhale her scent. I gritted my teeth, fighting against the temptation, against the instinct to claim what every inch of my body screamed was mine.

You don't want her, I reminded myself—a mantra I would be repeating for the days to come. *This is just the mating bond talking. She's still a filthy, murderous fae.*

Adara's eyes narrowed, as if she were sensing weakness. Moving so fast I could barely track the motion, she gripped my left arm with both hands, then spun around and dropped her weight. Before I knew what was happening, she'd hauled me up her back, then flipped me over, sending me flying across the clearing.

I crashed into the ground several feet away with a surprised 'oof'.

"Go find someone else to give you answers," she called in a

scathing voice over her shoulder, her footsteps scuffing against the dirt as she strode away. "I don't have time to play with you."

I snorted. Did she really think she could walk away from me so easily? I volleyed to my feet, then somersaulted through the air, landing right in front of her. A punch flew straight toward my head, but this time I was expecting it, and I caught it with my fist.

She gritted her teeth, and I arched an eyebrow. "Where was this fighting spirit before, when you were getting eaten alive by dire wolves?"

"Get out of my way." Adara wrenched her fist out of my grip, and swung for me again. I blocked the blow, then countered with one of my own, enjoying the combative interaction despite myself. It had been a long time since I'd sparred with anyone, and though I would never admit it aloud to this female, she clearly had some talent.

"Not until you give me some answers." I dropped to the ground and swung my leg toward her ankles, trying to sweep her. She jumped up at the last second, then snapped her foot out, the sole of her dusty boot flying straight for my nose. But I'd already anticipated that, and I rolled onto my shoulders, avoiding the blow. Upside down, I glommed onto her leg with all four of my limbs, pushed on her hip with my foot, and pulled her ankle at the same time.

"Giant's teeth!" she swore as we fell to the ground in a tangle of limbs. I popped up and spun around, then covered her body with mine and pinned her beneath me. Spitting mad, she flung every curse I'd ever heard—and a few that were new to my ears—at me as she tried to buck me off, but I kept my knees and elbows tight against her, refusing to give her any space.

Which turned out to be a mistake, I realized as her scent enveloped me. The salt of an ocean breeze, the perfume of water lilies, and lying just beneath, the hint of burning embers. My body responded instantly, lust surging hot in my veins, and I became painfully aware of every dip and curve of Adara's body as it molded against mine. I could feel myself growing hard, and I instinctively flinched back, not wanting her to feel any evidence of my arousal.

Unfortunately, that gave her the space to buck me off. Planting her hands on my rib cage, she threw me forward, then shoved herself between my legs and scrambled out. I flipped my body around just in time to catch the silver glint of a knife in her hand, and I braced myself, expecting her to lunge for me.

But she didn't. Instead, she remained where she was. One knee on the ground, the other foot planted, dagger clutched in her fist with the sharp edge of the blade facing me. Her long hair had come free of its braid to frame her face in wild, lavender-blue waves, and her pale skin glowed in the moonlight as she regarded me warily out of those cornflower blue eyes.

I'd never seen anything so beautiful, or so deadly, in my life.

"Where did you learn to fight like that?" she asked in a breathless voice. A flush stained her alabaster cheeks, her chest rising and falling rapidly from our recent exertions. "I've trained with soldiers before and I've never experienced anything like that."

Fresh pain bit into my chest as an old memory surfaced, cutting through the arousal. Daryan and I used to grapple all the time, both as whelps and young males, pitting my superior strength and size against his speed and wiliness. Those scraps had taught me that natural strength was not enough to win battles, that skill, timing, and the willingness to wait for the right moment could make all the difference in the world.

And yet, none of that had mattered in the end. Daryan was dead and gone, and leaving me with a void in my heart and nothing, not even the ashes of my homeland, to comfort me.

"A friend," I bit out. I allowed my hatred of the fae to creep back into my heart and fill that void, pushing out any lingering feelings of desire. "I won't speak his name aloud—your pointed fae ears are unworthy of hearing it."

Adara rolled her eyes. "Ahh, back to hating me again. Perfect." She sighed and leaned back a little so that her bottom touched the ground, taking the weight off her knee. "I would take this opportunity to leave, but I've used a lot of energy fighting you, so I'll just take a nap instead." She leaned her head back against the tree behind her and closed her eyes, lavender-blue lashes fanning against her milk-white skin.

"If only I could go back to sleep," I muttered. "That's all I want."

Adara cracked one eye open. "*All* you want?" she asked. "I thought you wanted answers."

I shrugged a shoulder. "Answers are necessary if I have to live in this forsaken kingdom alone, but I wouldn't need them if I could return to my enchanted sleep. I have no desire to live out the rest of my days in a land plagued by shadows and populated by fae who would kill me on sight if they knew I existed."

"Hmm." Adara's other eye opened, and she tapped her chin thoughtfully. "What if I could put you back to sleep?"

I'd been propped up on my elbow before, but now I sat up fully. "How?" I asked, skeptical. The fae only wielded elemental magic, not spells—they didn't have the same power that the Radiant used to put me into that eternal sleep.

Not that it turned out to be eternal, I groused. I was going to have a word with the Radiant, if I ever saw him again.

"My mother," Adara said. "She's a powerful healer, and she makes some of the most potent potions and remedies in the kingdom. She'll be able to fix you a sleeping draught that can keep you asleep for a very long time. And probably give you a few extras, in case you wake up sooner than you'd like," she added with an arched brow.

I grumbled under my breath. That wasn't quite the same as eternal sleep...but it was something. The longer I remained awake and mobile, the greater the chances I could be killed, and that was a risk I couldn't take. Not when my life was the only thing keeping the portal sealed.

"What do I need to do to get my hands on this potion?" I asked.

Adara smiled. "Just take me back to my village."

I crossed my arms over my chest. "I have a feeling it's not that simple," I said dryly. "You said before that you needed to get back to the village to find out what *happened* to your mother. What exactly did you mean by that?"

Adara's eyes clouded with worry. "That's a bit of a long story, and I'm not sure I want to tell it to you." She tilted her head up to look at the sky, allowing silvery moonlight to spill across her face once more. "The important part is that my mother and I were attacked by one of King Aolis's soldiers, and that she used earth magic to send me away from him. That means she faced him all on her own, and I need to know what the outcome of that was. Whether she defeated him, or, or..." her lower lip trembled.

My heart wrenched with pity for Adara, but my brain was too caught up with the implications of what she'd said. "You told me your mother was a healer. How could she have used earth magic to send you away? That's not within the purview of herb lore, unless there's a teleportation potion I'm not aware of."

"That's one of the things I need answers about, because I don't understand it either," Adara said crossly. "I don't understand anything right now—why I have fire magic, why the general came for me and my mother, why she lied about being a Greater Fae, any of it! When I woke up this morning I didn't even *know* I had fire magic."

I stared at her. "You just found out *today*?"

"Yes!"

"Well that explains your lack of control over it," I said, and her cheeks turned pink. "All right, all right." I held up a hand before she could respond. "I agree that sitting here arguing and talking when neither of us have any idea what is going on is not a productive use of our time. But I also fail to see why I should take you back to the village when you can't guarantee that I'll get the sleeping draught."

"Because you have nothing better to do," Adara said flatly.

I opened my mouth, then closed it. "You have a point," I grumbled, flicking my gaze skyward. The moon sat high and full in the sky, which was good for visibility, but there was also heavy cloud cover, which meant any fae still awake would be unlikely to see me. "Very well, I'll take you. Just make sure to hold on tight," I warned as I began to shift. "If you fall off, I can't promise to catch you."

That was a lie, of course. Until I figured out how to get rid of the mating bond, I couldn't harm Adara. But she didn't need to know that, and it would be better for both of us if she had a healthy dose of respect and fear where I was concerned. As a female, she wasn't compelled by the mating bond the same way that I was—she could easily ignore any emotions from the bond, and they would diminish the more I acted like a cad around her.

The last thing I needed was for her to feel safe around me, because that was the next step toward developing feelings. And if Adara began to care for me in any way, my chances of severing the mating bond between us were doomed.

11

Adara

"I'm not sure I can do this."

Einar growled low in his throat, thrashing his spiked tail impatiently. The motion kicked up dust into the air, and I coughed, shielding my face against the sudden onslaught. A chilly gust of wind whipped through the air, and I wrapped my arms around myself, unusually cold. As a water fae with an affinity for ice, I rarely noticed the cold. It was my nerves getting to me.

"Don't look at me like that," I said as he glared balefully at me out of one eye. "You're a giant, twenty-foot-long lizard with spikes jutting out of your spine. If I make one wrong move while we're in the sky, I'll accidentally impale myself."

That large, gold-rimmed eye rolled skyward. *"Stop being such a coward,"* he'd chided me when I'd said almost the exact same thing to him when he'd still been in bi-pedal form. He'd taken great pains to explain to me exactly how to climb on and where to hold so that I wouldn't hurt myself. *"We have a deal, and unlike your kind, dragons never break their word. I will see you safely home to your mother. You just need to get onto my back."*

Sucking in a deep breath, I approached the dragon. I placed a hand against his golden scales, and I paused, taking a moment to savor the novelty of the situation. I was touching a living, breathing dragon, and he wasn't trying to tear my head off. Had any fae before me enjoyed such a privilege? Had any fae ever ridden a dragon before? The idea that I might be the first was exciting enough to push my fear away, and I wedged my foot into the spot behind Einar's foreleg, then grabbed a spike and used it to pull myself onto his back.

Einar rumbled his approval as I got myself situated. There was a large spike the size of my torso at the base of his neck, perfect for grabbing onto, and about a yard of spike-free space just above and between his wings. I laid my body flat along that space and wrapped my arms around the spike.

"Are you sure I'll be able to stay on?" I asked, anxiety creeping into my voice. "If I accidentally let go of the spike while you're doing some kind of fancy flying—"

Einar flapped his wings, cutting me off, and I screamed as the sudden motion nearly sent me flying off his back. Burying my face into his scaly hide, I held onto the spike for dear life as he took a running start, wings flapping once, twice, then three times before he launched himself into the air. My stomach bounced in time to his wings as he beat them furiously, and I swallowed hard against the gorge threatening to rise in my throat.

But soon enough, we stopped climbing, and Einar's wings slowed from a staccato beat to the occasional flap. I lay still for a long moment before I gathered the courage to lift my head and risk a look around.

The sight took my breath away.

From the ground, the sky had been one giant, steel-colored

blanket of clouds. I'd thought the view from up here would be dreary, but Einar had flown us above the cloud layer and caught an updraft. We coasted above a sea of puffy clouds, the moon shining high above us, endless midnight stretching for miles in every direction. Little gaps in the clouds allowed me to glimpse the ground below us, and every time I caught sight of the forests or glens, a rush of giddiness swept through me.

This entire experience was surreal, and I was loving every minute of it.

Wonderingly, I ran a hand along Einar's scales. A sheen of iridescence rippled across the ruby surfaces, and despite the frigid temperatures up here, they were warm to the touch. From what I understood, dragons had iron in their hides, which acted as a natural repellent against all fae magic. That, coupled with their ability to fly and breathe fire, was why they had made such a formidable enemy.

I'd expected to experience some kind of weakness or fatigue, since I was pressing my entire body against a massive amount of iron. But all I felt was the steady heat emanating from Einar's body, and the moon-touched wind kissing my cheeks. It reminded me of long winter nights sitting by the wood stove with Mother, listening to her spin tales of the outside world while blizzards raged beyond our walls.

Mother. My chest ached at the thought of her, and my hand flew to the spot on my chest where the amulet had always rested. But the pads of my fingers met only flesh and fabric, and my stomach dropped as I remembered how Dune had so gleefully ripped the necklace from me.

I couldn't decide how to feel about that. On the one hand, Dune's betrayal and vitriol dug into my chest like a knife wound—it had only been a day or so since I'd thought myself in love with him, ready to travel to the ends of the kingdom so I could stay by his side. But on the other hand, if he'd never taken that chain from me, I would have never discovered my fire magic.

It's little wonder Slaugh wants to take me back to the king, I mused as I reached out a hand, letting it drift through a tuft of cloud. Ice crystals clung to my fingers as they passed through, but they melted as soon as I placed my hand back against Einar's scales. Fire and water magic were incompatible, and as far as I knew, no fae had ever been born with the ability to wield both. Greater Fae were sometimes born with the ability to wield two elements, but they were always complementary. Water and air, earth and air, earth and water, and once upon a time, when the fire fae had still lived, fire and air, and earth and fire.

I wasn't sure when the last fire-wielding fae had died out, but it had been a very, very long time ago. Only a handful had survived the genocide when the dragons came to our world, and their bloodline had been diluted to extinction over the millennia since.

There must be a fire fae somewhere in my family tree. That was the only thing that explained my magic. Mother had obviously known about it—she hadn't seemed surprised when I'd told her, and the 'protection' amulet she'd made me wear all my life had clearly kept my magic suppressed. That explained why I'd never been able to wield more than a thimbleful of my water magic—that gemstone had kept me from using all but the tiniest bit of my power.

I was just wondering if I might be able to use my water magic now, when Einar suddenly angled his body downward, preparing to descend. We dove through a thick layer of cloud cover that left me sputtering, and I blinked as Fenwood came into view. Smoke drifted lazily from the chimneys of the village huts and cabins, and a pang hit my chest as my gaze snagged on Mavlyn's house. Had she made it back home? Did she know I was missing? She'd used her magic to help me flee, and if any of the soldiers noticed, they would have detained her. Guilt swamped me at the thought of her sitting in a dark cell somewhere, in chains, because of me. I needed to find her, too, and make sure she was okay.

I thought Einar would land right outside the village, but instead he went around it and headed for Fenwood Lake. The lake sat in the middle of Fenwood Forest, three miles from the village, but it offered enough privacy for us to land without being spotted. Feeling jittery, I leaped off Einar's back, then took a minute to straighten my rumpled clothing while he shifted back into bipedal form.

"Seems like you survived," he observed with an arched eyebrow, taking in my windswept hair and flushed skin. His golden eyes glittered in the darkness, his full lips curling up with just a hint of smugness. "You even look like you might have enjoyed yourself."

"Let's not get ahead of ourselves." I raked my fingers through my hair and plaited it back into its braid, not quite looking him in the eye. I had enjoyed the experience very much, but that didn't mean I needed to admit it to him. "Come on. The village is this way."

We trekked through the forest, taking the well-worn path I'd used countless times. As a water fae, I'd always found comfort in the clear, still waters of the lake, and had often used it as both refuge and escape, diving deep beneath the surface and staying there for as long as I could. The kelp forests and the colorful fish that darted between them made me feel like I was in another world, and while I still needed to come up for air, I could stay down there for a solid thirty minutes, far longer than any earth fae could manage. It was the perfect way to avoid chores, or get away from the burning taunts of the other children when I'd had enough.

Anxiety pushed me to pick up the pace, and I lengthened my

stride until we were practically running. If Einar wanted to complain, he showed no sign of it, matching my pace smoothly. The trees thinned, and my heart plummeted as my house came into view. A huge chunk of the roof had been torn off, and large, thorny vines as thick as my torso snaked out of the opening, draping over the sides of the house. A sense of *wrongness* emanated from them, and my steps faltered as my brain tried to catch up with what my body already knew.

"Adara, stop." Einar snatched my arm, pulling me to a halt. "Those vines are infected with shadow magic. I can sense it, even from here."

Horror curdled in my gut as I remembered the tendrils of darkness that clung to Slaugh's shadow. Had he been shadow touched? Did the king know? Questions tumbled through my mind as I stood there, staring, but I knew I wouldn't get any answers here.

I had to go inside.

Einar cursed as I wrenched my arm from his grasp, and darted through the back door, which was wide open. There was no sign of my mother, but every sign that there had been a struggle. Furniture was upended, dishes smashed, the floorboards ripped up where Mother had torn the ground open and shoved me inside to get me away. The thorny vines I'd seen from outside had burst from the ground in the space between our beds, and they pulsed darkly as they clung to the wall and ceiling. I was careful to avoid them as I moved through the room, checking for any bodies or other clues as to what had happened.

Tears sprang to my eyes as I made my way into the workroom to find every single vial and jar smashed, their precious contents bled out all over the dirt. The fresh herbs that hung from the ceiling had been torn down and trampled, the cauldron lying on its side and sporting a nasty dent.

"Why would they do this?" I cried as Einar stood silent

behind me. "Why destroy not just our home, but my mother's life's work?"

"To send a message," Einar said somberly. His gilded eyes were heavy with memories as he looked around the room—probably scenes of brutality against his own people. "To let you know what they're capable of, and what happens if you defy them."

"It's senseless, this violence." I shook my head, unable to wrap my mind around any of it.

"Who exactly was it that came here last night?" Einar asked. "And what did they say they wanted?"

I sighed. I'd given Einar only the barest details, and he hadn't seemed inclined to ask more. "His name is General Slaugh," I told him. "He saw me use fire magic at the tryouts, and came here looking for me."

I gave Einar a summary of what had happened, telling him about my struggles with magic, my amulet, the fight with Slaugh, and Dune's subsequent betrayal. "He mentioned something about a prophecy, too, and he seemed to know my mother by another name, Gelsyne," I finished. "I wish I could remember more, but everything happened so fast."

Einar's jaw flexed. "I've clashed with General Slaugh on the battlefield before," he said. "He's a monster, absolutely ruthless—I've seen him step on the dying bodies of his own comrades to get to an enemy. I'm the one who gave him those burns, after he and ten of his soldiers brought down one of my cousins."

"Wonderful," I muttered. It was a good thing Slaugh wasn't here right now—I had a feeling he would lose his mind if he came face to face with the dragon who'd disfigured him. I looked around the room once more and shook my head. "I don't know why the villagers haven't burned this place to the ground, now that it's infected. I need to find Mavlyn, see if she made it home. Hopefully she'll be able to tell me more."

"Are you sure that's wise?" Einar asked as he followed me out the front door. "It might be better to keep a low profile right now, especially if this Dune person is trying to get rid of you."

"I don't care about that right now." Anger built inside me with each stride, until my fingertips crackled, and I felt as though the very air around me were about to catch fire. "Finding my mother is more important."

I stalked into the village, my rage growing. The night air seemed to sizzle around me, and I gritted my teeth, doing my best to control myself. Setting the village on fire was the last thing I wanted to do.

But it was hard not to be angry, not when it was so obvious that no one had lifted a finger to help my mother. I saw no other evidence of fighting in the streets, no other buildings or houses damaged. Slaugh had come for me, and when he hadn't gotten what he wanted, he'd destroyed my home, and...and...

Don't think about it, I warned myself as tears seared my eyes. I didn't know what Mother's fate was. Not yet.

The moon was halfway through its descent by the time I reached Mavlyn's house, the barest hints of twilight lightening the horizon. As quietly as I could manage, I knocked on the door, hoping I was loud enough to wake them up, but quiet enough not to alert the neighbors. I heard shuffling inside the house, and then the door opened, revealing Seema, Mavlyn's mother. She was almost identical in looks to Mavlyn, except that her face was harder, less youthful, and her auburn hair, which she'd braided for bedtime, was threaded with a few wisps of silver.

"Adara!" Seema exclaimed, her jade green eyes going wide. "Oh, thank the Radiants you're safe!"

A light flickered to life from the house across the street, and I winced. "Did Mavlyn make it home safe?" I asked, pitching my voice low. "I left her behind at the tryouts, and I didn't have time—"

I stopped at the pitter patter of bare feet on floorboards, hope rising in my chest. Mavlyn's face popped up behind her mother's shoulder, and the next thing I knew she was out on the porch, her arms banded tight around me as she hugged me with all her strength.

"Mav," I choked out, hugging her back. "Mav, I'm so glad you're safe. How did you get back without the soldiers capturing you? Do you know what happened to my mother?"

"The soldiers didn't even notice what I'd done," Mavlyn said impatiently, pulling back to look at me. Tears welled in her eyes as she inspected me, and she shook her head. "When I came back, you and your mother were gone. I thought General Slaugh had taken you both!"

"Taken?" So she hadn't been killed. Dread twisted inside my gut even as relief made my knees wobble, and I couldn't decide which emotion to give in to. "Did you see them take her away?" I asked Mavlyn's mother.

Seema's lips pursed, and she glanced from me to Einar, who had stood by silently this entire time. His glittering eyes scanned the street for danger, and I noticed more gazes peeking out from between curtains, candlelight spilling through moonlit-frosted windows. We were drawing too much attention. Seema seemed to weigh a decision in her mind before she finally stepped back and opened the door wider.

"We should discuss this inside," she said. "It's not safe for you out here."

"The only place Adara is going," a familiar voice said, ringing with authority, "is to a holding cell until General Slaugh returns."

I spun around at the sound of Dune's voice to see him walking up the street toward us. Backing him up were ten other males—members of our militia, all carrying weapons. My stomach dropped at the sight of the people I'd grown up with all turned against me, fear and anger in their eyes, swords bristling.

"You bastard," I spat. Flames sprang to life in my palms, and Mavlyn's mother gasped from behind me. "It wasn't enough for you to try and discredit me during the tryouts—you had to bring General Slaugh directly to my door. Are you satisfied, now that he's taken my mother away and destroyed our home?"

Dune flinched, but he didn't lower his sword. "I didn't mean for that to happen, but it's not my fault," he insisted. "If you'd surrendered, the general wouldn't have taken Chaya."

"Surrendered?" I seethed. The flames in my hands grew brighter, casting shadows on the males' faces and highlighting the fear in their eyes. They were clearly uncomfortable with my display of power, not that I blamed them. "For what? I did nothing wrong, and the general had no right to attack my mother. He tried to kill her!"

"The general had every right to attack your mother, and you are not the only reason she was taken away," a deep voice interrupted. I went completely still as Headman Terran stepped out of the shadows. He was taller and lankier than his son, with streaks of white running through his chestnut hair, but his strong jaw, hazel eyes, and the effortless magnetism he wielded were identical to Dune's. "Gelsyne committed treason when she fled from the court all those years ago and refused to swear allegiance to our new king. The only reason I allowed her to stay in our village was because of her skill as a healer, but I told her that if the crown ever discovered her existence, I would not protect her. She knew the risks."

Dune's eyes widened, and my head spun at this revelation. "You knew Adara's mother was in hiding?" he asked, sounding as stunned as I felt.

"I did," the headman admitted. "But I couldn't turn her away, not when she had a newborn babe to take care of and nowhere else to go."

"What about Adara's fire magic?" Mavlyn asked. "Did you know about that?"

"I didn't." The headman's gaze hardened as he looked at me. "Adara, a fae hasn't been born with fire magic in hundreds of years. You should know how important someone with your abilities would be in the fight against the shadow creatures. Why would you deny the king the use of your power? Isn't that why you tried to join the military, so you could serve him and protect our kingdom?"

My gaze cut to Dune again, who was staring at me with a calculating look in his eyes. He had been one of the reasons I'd wanted to join, but yes, I had wanted to aid in the fight against the shadow creatures as well as find my place out in the big, wide world I'd never been allowed to explore.

Did the headman have a point? Should I surrender, and allow myself to be taken to the king?

"You cannot, under any *circumstances, allow the general to capture you."* My mother's words, the last she'd spoken to me before she'd sent me away, echoed in my head.

Part of me wondered if I should trust them, when she'd been keeping so many things from me. But everything she'd done, including the lies she'd told, had been to protect me. And even if I wanted to discount her words, I couldn't ignore what I'd seen.

"I don't know what I want," I finally said. "But I do know that I can't trust a shadow-touched fae, even if he does work for the king."

Gasps rippled through the crowd, and I realized the entire village had turned out to watch the commotion. Mothers and fathers, sons and daughters, all barefoot and clad in nightgowns and robes as they watched the exchange with rapt expressions.

"Shadow-touched?" Mavlyn's mother asked, her tone pitched high with worry. "What do you mean?"

"The girl is speaking nonsense," the headman said brusquely. "The general isn't shadow-touched. He would have been frothing at the mouth and raving mad."

"No, she isn't." Einar spoke up for the first time. He stepped in front of me, almost as if he were using his big body to shield me, and for some reason, the knot of tension in my chest loosened. "But shadow-touched isn't the right word. The general was *wielding* shadow magic, not being controlled by it."

"Wielding?" the headman sputtered. "That's preposterous. No fae can wield shadow magic. We can only use the magic we're born with—"

"If that's the case, then how was King Aolis able to kill the dragons?" Einar challenged.

"He used the Spear of Destiny, of course, but that's different," the headman argued. "The spear is imbued with Radiant magic; everyone knows the king can't wield Radiant power on his own."

Einar snorted. "Radiant magic. Right."

The headman scowled. "Just who *are* you, anyway? You're not a member of our village."

Einar opened his mouth, but I cut him off. "He's a friend of mine from Glendar," I said quickly, referencing a neighboring village a few miles away. I didn't think it was a good idea to tell them that Einar was a dragon. They'd try to kill him on the spot, and given how much Einar seemed to hate the fae, I had a feeling he'd end up razing the village in retaliation. Even if the headman and his son had turned against me, and the villagers had always treated me like an outsider, they didn't deserve to die.

"I've been to Glendar dozens of times, and I've never seen him," Dune said. He looked Einar up and down, taking in his powerful body and the swirling flame tattoo on his chest. I thanked the Radiants that Einar's shoulder-length hair was long enough to hide his ears—the lack of pointed tips would have been a dead giveaway.

"I don't know why you care so much," I snapped at Dune. "It's me you wanted so badly to get rid of, wasn't it?"

"That's enough," the headman barked before Dune could respond. He clapped his hands, and the militia raised their swords again, taking a step toward me. "This discussion is over. Adara, please come quietly. There's no need to make a scene here."

"She's not going anywhere."

The crowd murmured as Seema planted herself between me and Dune's men. She raised her hands, and the earth beneath our feet began to rumble. Stones shot up from deep beneath the ground and hovered in the air, awaiting her command. "If you want them, you'll have to go through me."

"And me." Mavlyn raised her hands as well, calling to the nearby flora. Thorny rose vines snaked around her arms, extending past her hands like barbed tentacles.

"Seema!" the headman protested. "Be reasonable! You're a member of the village council!"

"Yes, I am," Seema said firmly, "and as a member, I have to say I'm very disturbed by your attitude, Headman. Regardless of your reasons for accepting Adara and Chaya into our village, the fact remains that they *are* members, and are under our protection. This General Slaugh didn't have an order or decree from the king when he arrived, did he?" she asked Dune.

Dune's cheeks colored. "Well, no, but—"

"But nothing," Seema said firmly. "We might be part of the Kingdom of Ediria, but we're citizens of Domhain first. We don't allow outsiders to come in and snatch our people away without cause."

While Seema argued with the headman, Mavlyn sidled up to

me. "Take this and go to Talamh," she whispered in my ear. She unclasped the antler bracelet she always wore around her wrist and fastened it to mine, then tapped the tree sigil in the center of the moonstone. "Show this bracelet to Lady Mossi's guards and tell them you need sanctuary. She'll help you."

"Lady Mossi?" Einar said sharply. "As in the head of House Ithir, and the ruler of Domhain?"

"That's right." Mavlyn smirked. "She's my great, great aunt, twice removed, or something like that. She'll be honor-bound to take you in if you show her that bracelet."

Einar snorted, but I squeezed Mavlyn's hand tight, overcome with gratitude. "You don't have to do this," I told her. "This isn't your fight."

"You would do the same for me, wouldn't you?" Mavlyn challenged.

"Well, yes, but—"

"But nothing. Now go!"

She shoved me toward the road and stepped forward at the same time, drawing Dune's attention. The earth vibrated as she shot vines in his direction, and she knocked Dune's sword from his hand even as the ground turned liquid beneath her feet. Alarmed, I sprang toward Mavlyn as she began to sink, but before I could close my hand around hers, a larger hand grabbed me by the elbow and hauled me back.

"Get out of here, Adara!" Seema shouted. She flung one of her stones straight at Dune's head, forcing him to duck, and breaking his concentration. The ground beneath Mavlyn's feet solidified, but one of the villagers yanked her free before she was attacked. Surprised, I watched as they threw themselves into the fray, some siding with the militia members, others with Mavlyn and Seema.

"Come on," Einar said, tugging at my arm. "As long as you're here, the fighting will continue. We have to get away."

His words pulled me back to my senses, and I turned my attention away from the fighting. "This way," I said, darting through Mavlyn's open front door. We raced through the house and out the back, but one of the militia must have spotted us, because he was waiting for us around the back with three others.

Einar snarled and lunged toward the man. Panic rose inside me at the killing intent in his eyes, and I reacted instinctively, flinging out a hand. But it wasn't my fire magic that responded this time. Instead, the moisture clinging to the grass reacted, droplets coalescing into crystals as they rose into the air. They swirled up the enemy fae's legs, encasing them in layers of ice that rooted them to the ground.

"Stop!" I grabbed Einar and wrenched him back. "We're not killing them," I said hotly when he spun to face me, mouth open in a snarl. "These people are just following orders! They're not my enemy."

"Soldiers are also just following orders," Einar growled. "But that didn't stop your king from slaughtering ours in battle, now did it?"

"Oh shut up," I snapped, darting around the frozen fae even as they struggled to free themselves of the ice. I knew it wouldn't hold them for long, so I put on a burst of speed, disappearing beneath the cover of the forest. Einar followed, and we ran as fast as we could, until we'd reached the edge of the lake once more.

"We can't stop here for long," I said, panting as I leaned my hand against a tree trunk. "They'll track us here." I held up my left wrist, flashing the bracelet Mavlyn had clasped there. "We need to get to Talamh and find Lady Mossi. It's our only hope."

"You mean *your* only hope," Einar retorted, eyes flashing. "You're asking me, a dragon, to fly you into one of the three fae seats of power. They'll slaughter me on the spot."

I eyed him up and down, taking in his long hair, his tattoos, and his golden eyes. "Yes, they will. But I think I have a solution."

He eyed me warily, no doubt seeing the wheels turning behind my eyes. "And what solution would that be?"

I grinned. "We're going to turn you into a fae."

Einar

"This is never going to work."

Adara frowned. "What are you talking about? Of course it's going to work, as long as you behave yourself and stop touching your ears."

She smacked my hand down as I was reaching up to touch the pointed tips—again—and I scowled. "I can't help it," I snapped, my hand stinging. "It's strange, having putty stuck to my ears." I glanced down at my arm, which she'd covered with some kind of powder. It blended into my skin perfectly, hiding my flame tattoos. "And do you have any idea how disrespectful it is to cover these flames? It's the equivalent of spitting on my ancestors' graves."

Adara rolled her eyes. "I'm pretty sure your ancestors are okay with a little grave spitting if it means you get to stay alive," she said. "Now be quiet for a minute. I need to check on this potion."

I snapped my mouth shut as Adara knelt down by the fire. She picked up the wooden spoon I'd fashioned and stirred the contents of the clay pot—also made by me—then dipped a finger into the piping hot liquid and licked it. The sight of her pink tongue darting out as she drew her finger into her mouth, lush lips puckering closed, sent a shot of heat straight to my groin, and I gritted my teeth against the unwelcome lust.

I would not give in to the mating bond. No matter how tempting this female was.

I had to admit she was intriguing, though. Aside from the fact that she could wield fire *and* ice—an impossibility, according to the laws of elemental magic—she was clearly a skilled fighter, and on top of that, she seemed to have herbalism skills. She was a pretty package wrapped in a shroud of mystery, and despite myself, I wanted to penetrate those layers, to solve the puzzle she so clearly represented.

The two of us had fled Fenwood, making it most of the way to Talamh before the sunrise forced me to land. As the last dragon alive, flying was risky enough at night, but during the day it would be suicide. We'd landed outside a grove of trees growing just a few yards from a riverbend, and had taken shelter there. Adara had fallen asleep beneath the trees, and I'd kept watch, my eyes and ears on alert for any threat. There were no predators, but I had managed to catch a few rabbits, and the smell of roasting meat had woken her.

I'd expected her to go back to sleep after we'd eaten, but instead she told me to make her a pot using the clay from the riverbed, then disappeared into the woods. She came back several hours later with an armful of herbs and berries, then set to work grinding them up and adding them to the pot, which I'd hardened with dragon fire while she'd been gone.

The ears, she'd shaped with riverbed clay, using some kind of viscous additive from one of the leaves to make them pliable, almost rubbery. The powder was dirt, mixed with some ground up petals that mimicked the shade of my skin. This potion she'd been working on for the past three hours would supposedly change the color of my eyes.

"How do you know how to do all this?" I asked her. "None of this is healing magic."

Adara glanced over at me. Her cornflower blue eyes deepened with sadness even as a smile tugged at the corner of her lips. "When I was a child, I used to love to dress up and pretend I was one of the forest creatures. My mother thought she could tempt me into loving herbalism and potion making by introducing me to what she called 'pretend magic'—using plant extracts to change my appearance. At first, I loved it," she admitted, pushing away from the fire so she could sit on a nearby rock. Her gaze grew distant as she relived those childhood memories. "I could make my hair and skin any color I wanted, and I did. I wore different colors of the rainbow every day, and all the other children were jealous. They used to beg me to dye them too, and for a little while, I was the most popular kid in the village."

"But then?" I prompted, noting the shimmer of pain in her eyes, at the clear sign that this story did not have the happy ending it should have.

"But then one day, a girl whose hair I refused to dye snapped at me, and told me I was a pretender, that everyone knew I was just trying to fit in. And even though I knew she was just trying to get back at me, her words still hit me hard... because she was right. I'd been coloring my hair green, and making my skin dark, so that I could look like an earth fae and blend in with the others. But no matter how much I mimicked them on the outside, on the inside, I still didn't have a drop of earth magic. I wasn't one of them, and I never would be."

Her shoulders dropped, and then lifted again in a shrug. "So, I stopped dyeing my hair and my skin. I went back to looking like a water fae again. And I lost my love for potions and herbs completely, much to the disappointment of my mother."

Her lips twisted in a mirthless smirk, and she turned back to the fire. I stared at her as she worked, watching the way her lavender-blue hair shone in the dappled sunlight. Her pale skin shimmered with a sort of moonstone iridescence when it caught the light just the right way, and my fingers ached with remembrance at how smooth it had felt during the few times I'd touched her.

I wanted to tell her she was breathtaking, that she should never feel the need to hide or change herself for the sake of pleasing others. That she was perfect just the way she was.

That's just the mate bond talking, I told myself. I'd come across many beautiful fae females before—usually on the battlefield—and never once had I felt the urge to tell any of them they were breathtaking.

And yet, a nagging sensation persisted, forcing my mouth open, for words to spill from my lips unbidden.

"I think you're beau--mmphhh."

Adara's head snapped up, and she blinked at me. "What?"

I removed the hand I'd clapped over my mouth and cleared my throat. "I said you should hurry up," I grumbled, turning my head to the side so she couldn't look into my eyes and see the truth there. "We've still got to walk all the way to Talamh and gain entrance to Lady Mossi's stronghold."

Adara raised her eyebrows. "Are you sure that's what you said?" She got to her feet and walked toward me, hips swaying gently with the movement. I swallowed a curse as she crouched down directly in front of me and placed two fingers on my pulse. A lightning bolt of desire shot straight from my neck and into my loins, and I clenched my jaw.

"You don't seem to have any swelling there, or a fever," she said, moving her hand from my neck to my forehead. Every touch sent little shivers of pleasure through my body, and I fisted my hands at my sides, trying to keep myself perfectly still.

"Stop. Touching. Me." I forced out between gritted teeth.

She sat back a little, her expression pinched with annoyance. "I'm just trying to make sure you're well before I give you the potion. It's usually harmless, but if a person is sick it can make their symptoms worse." Her eyes narrowed. "And while you don't seem to have a fever, your face *is* a little flushed."

"I'm not sick," I snapped, snatching her wrist before she could touch me again.

But that turned out to be a mistake, giving my body the chance to betray me. Because instead of pushing her away, I pulled her *onto* me.

Straight into my lap.

Adara gasped, and I toppled backward in surprise. She landed on top of me, her curves molding to my body, and I hissed as my skin heated in response. I froze as her long legs settled around my waist, as her small hands curved around my biceps, as the heat between her legs sank into me. My cock stiffened to full attention, and there was no hiding it this time, not when we were pressed so closely together.

Her cornflower blue eyes widened, and this time it was her cheeks that stained with color. A blush that spread from the roots of her hair and disappeared beneath the neckline of her tunic. Her nipples stiffened beneath the fabric, scraping against my chest, and the air thickened with the scent of her arousal.

I wanted to push her off, to shove her away as far as possible.

But my body wouldn't allow me, because every part of me screamed to touch her. To strip her bare and lick every inch of her shimmering skin until I reached the source of that delicious scent. The primal part of me knew she'd taste even better than she smelled, and I swallowed hard as my mouth watered.

But I didn't give in, because I knew I wouldn't be able to stop if I did. The urge to claim her was too intense. All I could do was remain still, and pray to the Radiants that Adara had more self-control than I did.

The sound of water hissing filled the air, and Adara's head snapped up, her gaze tearing from mine. "Giant's teeth!" she swore, leaping from my body. She rushed over to the bubbling clay pot and snatched it from the flames, then set it on a cool rock nearby. Relief swept through me as she stirred the contents, and I sucked in a gulping breath, willing my heart to slow, my blood to cool, my muscles to relax.

"Phew, that was a close one." She put the wooden spoon aside and brought the pot to me, crouching down next to me. "It's ready; drink up so we can get going."

Her eyes settled on a spot near my nose as she offered me the contents, refusing to meet my gaze. It seemed that she, too, was not willing to acknowledge what nearly passed between us, and I was grateful for that.

"All right." I took the bowl from her, trying not to think too hard about this. If she was planning on poisoning me, now would be the perfect time to do it. Sweat broke out across my skin, and for a brief moment, I considered tossing the potion into the grass.

Instead, I tipped my head back, and swallowed the contents in one go.

13

Adara

For a heart-stopping moment, I worried that I'd gotten the potion wrong. Einar sat there, blinking at me, his eyes still that same, damning gold color that would give us away. Biting my lip, I wondered if there were any other options. Could I tear a strip of cloth off my tunic and wrap it around his eyes like a blind fold?

"Oww!" Einar slapped a hand over his eyes. "What in the blazes is happening?"

"It's working!" I crowed, relief lightening the tension in my chest. "Perfect. Now we won't have to pretend that you're blind."

"What?" His eyelids flew open, brows drawing into a scowl, and I grinned. They were a boring moss green now, no hint of gold to be seen. "Were you going to blind me if this didn't work?"

I snorted. "You're so dramatic," I said, getting to my feet. I kicked some dirt over the fire we'd made, then stomped on it for good measure to put it out. "Come on, let's get going. We need to make it to Talamh before dark."

Einar muttered something *very* uncomplimentary under his

breath, but he didn't argue as he followed me out of the trees. We set out for the capital, walking alongside the river. I knew from studying maps of the kingdom that it led straight to the city, though Mother had never taken me there. A constant anxiety for her simmered in the back of my mind, but I had to admit the thought of finally visiting a big city for the first time in my life was exciting.

I glanced sidelong at Einar as we walked, who was staring straight ahead, a stoic expression on his handsome face. My skin tingled as I remembered the way my body responded to him when he'd yanked me on top of him. A savage hunger had roared to life inside me, and the intensity of it had stunned me as much as the lust that had burned behind his golden eyes.

I'd never felt such desire for anyone, not even Dune. And while Dune and I had never made love, we'd done a lot more than just touch each other.

And where did that get you? A voice in my head scolded. The taboo nature of our relationship coupled with the yearning I'd felt for Dune had blinded me to reality, had spurred me to spin fantasies in my head of a future that was never going to come to pass.

Besides, it was clear that despite the mutual attraction between us, Einar loathed me. He was only helping me because it suited him. The fact that I felt anything other than annoyance toward him was proof that lust was a treacherous thing, not to be trusted, and certainly never something to base decisions on.

If Dune had taught me anything, it was that hearts were selfish things, capable of fooling even the sharpest of minds with sweet lies and false promises. My mind was the only thing I could trust. And it was only as reliable as my ability to keep my gaze clear and focused and on the road ahead.

"Your ice magic," Einar said, breaking the silence between us. He was still looking straight ahead, but I could tell his attention was on me. "Is that the only kind of water magic you can use?"

"As far as I know." I turned my gaze in the direction he was looking just as we rounded the edge of the forest. A winding road snaked ahead of us, and in the distance, the city of Talamh waited ahead, the tops of tall buildings peeking out behind towering walls. The spires of Castle Ithir rose above it all, where Lady Mossi ruled the earth realm. The antler bracelet Mavlyn had given me sat heavy on my wrist, and I hoped it would be enough to gain an audience with the head of House Ithir. Mavlyn's relation was very distant, after all, and I looked too much like a water fae to endear myself to Lady Mossi. Rumor had it she was fiercely loyal to her own kin, but distrustful of outsiders, and with no obvious earth fae traits, that put me at a disadvantage.

"I've never been able to effectively wield my ice magic, though, not before today," I went on, more to fill the silence than anything else. "I think the amulet—or whatever that stone was —suppressed both sides of my magic, the fire and the ice."

"Interesting." Einar's eyes flickered briefly in my direction. "You clearly have better control over the ice, but that's not surprising considering that you obviously favor your water fae heritage." His lips pursed. "Your kind always were a pain in the ass to fight. Nearly as bad as the air fae."

I arched an eyebrow. "The air fae were worse?" Since dragons were fire creatures, I would have imagined water fae would have been the hardest to fight.

Einar nodded. "The lightning riders would chase us through the skies and use their spears to attack our wings until we had no choice but to land. It is too awkward to fight in dragon form on the ground, so we were forced to shift, and without our iron hide to protect us we are vulnerable to magical attacks." He shuddered. "I can't count the number of dragon soldiers I've seen frozen in ice or crushed by earth or stone."

"I'm sure my people can say the same about the number of fae who've been burnt to a crisp or ripped apart by dragon claws," I said dryly, though I felt a twinge of guilt. I didn't like hearing about such terrible deaths, regardless of which side the victims had been on.

Einar's jaw worked, but he said nothing, and that was probably for the best since we were approaching Talamh's gates. The portcullis was raised, but one of the guards standing on either side of the entrance stopped us before we could go through.

"State your names and your business," he demanded. He wore the House Ithir sigil—a circle with a tree in the middle, its branches and roots mirroring each other as they spread through sky and soil—proudly on his breastplate, marking him as one of Lady Mossi's soldiers as opposed to the Edirian army.

"Adara and Einar of Fenwood," I said. "We've come to beg an audience with Lady Mossi."

I held up my wrist to show him the antler bracelet. The guard's eyes narrowed, and he grabbed my wrist, holding it still so he could examine the sigil carved there, identical to the one stamped on his armor.

"These bracelets are only given to those related to House Ithir by blood," he said, still not dropping my arm. His gaze moved over my face suspiciously. "How would a water fae come by one of these?"

My stomach dropped, and my mind blanked as my anxiety bubbled to the surface. How much could I tell him without putting myself in danger?

"Those details are for Lady Mossi's ears only," Einar said, drawing the guard's attention away. He stood his ground, and though his stance was relaxed, his stare even, I felt a subtle shift in the air as tension rose between them. "You are honor-bound to take us to her, so please, lead the way."

The guard pressed his lips into a flat line, clearly annoyed. He fell back and exchanged a few muttered words with the other guard, who disappeared through the gate. Long minutes passed as we waited, and I resisted the urge to shift my weight from foot to foot. Looking nervous would imply there was something for me to *be* nervous about, which would only raise suspicion.

Finally, the second guard reappeared, with a third in tow. The golden leaves adorning the shoulders of his armor marked him as a higher rank than the others, probably a captain. He looked us both up and down, gaze landing on my bracelet, then gave me a terse nod.

"Come on, then. I'll take you to Lady Mossi."

We followed the soldier through the gates and into the hustle and bustle of the city. I expected it to be crowded and dirty, but to my surprise, the streets were clean, the air fragrant with blossoms. Flowering plants crawled up the sides of the buildings, covering them almost completely and making them look more like massive, geometrically shaped garden sculptures than dwellings. Countless gardens, both wild and manicured, teemed with life, and I grew almost dizzy as I tried to sort through all the garden scents.

A few fae glanced at us as we walked the wide street, heading toward the castle at the city center, but most paid us no mind. While most were earth fae, I spotted a few air fae as well. They were easily identifiable, not just by their white and gold hair, but by the way they flitted through the streets, blasting past other city-dwellers as they rode frigid air currents and leaving more than a few of them a little disgruntled.

"Tartlet, dear?"

I startled at the sound of the voice, and my eyes went wide at the sight of a water fae standing right outside of a bakery. Short, arctic blue hair framed her pale face, and her eyes, a matching shade, twinkled cheerfully as she held out a tray filled with tiny bits of pastry. My stomach grumbled a little as the scents of butter, sugar, and yeast wafted toward me, but I barely paid any mind as I stared at this fae who looked more like me than anyone I'd seen in a long, long time.

Her brow creased, bottom lip worrying. "Is there something on my nose?" she asked, swiping at the pointed tip.

"Oh!" My ears burned with embarrassment as I realized how rude I was being. "No...I just..." I glanced over to see Einar gesturing to me impatiently—he and the captain were already several buildings ahead. "Never mind. I'm sorry."

Feeling ten kinds of foolish, I hurried to rejoin the others, too embarrassed to take a pastry even though I was hungry.

"These city sections," Einar said as we passed from what was clearly a shopping district into a more residential area, "They're organized into circles, not blocks like an ordinary city. Is that for defense?"

"Yes," the captain confirmed. "There was a period during the Wars where Talamh was targeted frequently, so Lady Danah, Lady Mossi's mother, had the districts organized into rings, to make them more easily defensible. During attacks, we raise earth domes around each section to protect the citizens, and because we have so many gardens growing within the city walls, there is enough food and water to last each district for several days."

"Interesting," Einar murmured, and I glanced sideways at him. His gaze filled with memories, and I wondered if he'd ever taken part in an attack on Talamh. Just how old was he, anyway? I knew that like Greater Fae, dragons could live for hundreds of years. Lady Mossi was reported to be close to three hundred years old herself, which meant that these city-spheres would have been constructed even longer ago than that, if her mother had been the one to build them.

As we got closer to the castle, the buildings grew taller, and more tightly packed together. We passed Talamh University, a sprawling campus that took up an entire district on its own, and I fingered the bracelet on my wrist as I thought of Mavlyn. She was right—there were water fae in this city, and if I could find one on the street giving out pastry samples, there was probably one at the university, too.

But then again, it wasn't as if any water fae would have been able to help me solve my magic problem. If I'd taken Mavlyn's suggestion and gone to the university with her, I would have just run into more frustration. In a way, I'd actually made the right decision, even if I was beginning to think it had brought me more trouble than it was worth.

After about thirty minutes of walking, we finally reached the castle gates. Like the rest of the buildings in the city, ivy crawled along the stone exteriors of the walls, but this ivy was a reddish-black that leant the castle a deadly wash of color.

"Necro-ivy," Einar said darkly as the gates opened.

"You know it?" I asked, a little surprised.

"I do." He didn't say more—couldn't, not with the captain in earshot—but I had a feeling that he'd watched a few of his fellow dragons succumb to its terrible effects. The ivy that covered the other buildings in this city was merely decorative— although a fae like Mavlyn could weaponize it—but necro-ivy was deadly. The leaves secreted a terrible poison that necrotized living tissue on contact. One touch would turn your skin black, a second would penetrate your flesh, working its way into your bone marrow. It spread quickly, and the only way to save yourself was to cut off the infected skin immediately.

I'd never seen the effects firsthand, but I remembered reading about it in one of mother's herbalism books. I shuddered at the gruesome images my mind conjured, and my skin prickled as we walked through the gates, the gleaming vines a little too close for comfort. They seemed to crouch on the walls like waiting spiders, ready to spring, and I was grateful that, on their own, at least, they couldn't move.

But as we moved into the inner courtyard of the castle, I caught sight of something that distracted me completely.

"Griffins!" I gasped, nearly tripping over my own feet in shock. A thrill that was both terror and excitement shuddered through me as I got a good look at them. There were twelve scattered around the courtyard, massive creatures that were both bird and beast. The front halves of their bodies were all eagle, with diamond-white feathers, golden beaks and claws, but their back halves were the powerful hindquarters of a lion, gilded brown fur rippling over powerful muscles. Their wings, which were golden-brown near the spine but faded into white at the tips, were tucked into their sides as they lazed in the sunshine, but though their posture was relaxed, their ice-blue eyes were shrewd as they watched us enter their domain.

"Why aren't they chained up?" I asked as we walked past, keeping one wary eye on them.

The captain laughed, and the other soldiers smirked. "You can't chain up a griffin," he said. "They'd rip the chains right out of the ground with those powerful beaks, then tear your intestines out for good measure. Besides, there's no need to. They are loyal to Lady Mossi, and to their riders, and they get fed plenty here. They go off to hunt every once in a while, or to stretch their wings, but they've no need to wander off for any length of time."

"Riders?"

The captain raised an eyebrow, incredulous. "You've never heard of Lady Mossi's famed griffin riders?"

My cheeks colored, and I ducked my head a little. "There are a lot of things I've never heard of," I admitted.

The captain shook his head. "They're renowned throughout Ediria," he said. "We're the only ones who've managed to successfully tame and ride them, so it's kind of a big deal. And their claws and beaks are one of the few things that can tear through dragon hide, so they were used often throughout the wars."

"I bet." I glanced sidelong at Einar, looking for a reaction, but his expression was stoic as we entered the main building of the castle. A sense of awareness came over me as I realized how this experience must affect him—surrounded by fae, and being hit with constant reminders of the ways we'd hurt and killed his people.

True, the dragons weren't blameless, and had killed many more of us than we had of them. Even so, this was the equivalent of walking into a dragon lair, and he was handling it with a sense of calm I wasn't sure I could have managed under similar circumstances.

The captain led us down a corridor and into a large, domed building made entirely of windows. A greenhouse, I realized, staring around the place in wonder. The glass walls stretched high overhead, at least several dozen feet, allowing golden light to fill the entire space. Butterflies of all sizes and colors fluttered from flower to tree branch to bush, and I marveled at the sheer variety of plant life thriving within these walls.

"Shoes and weapons," the guard standing just inside ordered.

I blinked at him. "Shoes?" I echoed, bewildered by the request.

He nodded. "Lady Mossi doesn't like for the grass to be trampled."

I glanced at the plush carpet of grass, which I realized

covered every square inch of the place, then back at the guard's boots. "You haven't taken yours off," I noted.

He raised an eyebrow. "I'm a guard," he said, as if that were self-explanatory.

I supposed it was. After all, if there was an attack, it wasn't as if the guards had time to put on their boots before rushing to defend the castle. And by the same token, if a visitor tried to attack or flee, their lack of shoes would be one more handicap to slow them down.

Einar had already taken off his boots, so I followed suit, then stepped onto the grass. My feet sunk into the thick, soft blades, and a sense of peace swept through me as my toes curled. By the way Einar's shoulders relaxed, I could tell the grass was having a similar effect on him.

A prickle of awareness trickled through my spine, and I kept my eyes and ears open as I walked. Lady Mossi's powerful magic was clearly embedded into every inch of this space. It was important for me to remember that.

And yet, I couldn't help but be enchanted by the atrium garden as I walked through it. Plants both magical and mundane flourished in every section, and bees, butterflies, and tiny fireflies floated lazily through the floral-scented air. Mother would have had a field day if she were here, exclaiming over the various herbs and flowers and all their properties.

The thought of her sobered me, reminding me why I was here. I couldn't allow myself to be carried away by the beauty of this place. I had a job to do.

At the center of the atrium, two more guards marked the end of the path. They stepped aside to let us pass, and we entered a clearing ringed by black-trunked trees with ruby-red leaves. Golden apples hung heavy from their branches, and I had to swallow hard to contain a squeal of excitement. These were the famed Ithir Apples, supposedly able to cure any illness or disease, even shadow magic infections. I'd read about them long ago, but had forgotten—they only grew here in the atrium, and were jealously guarded for their mythical properties.

I expected the center of the atrium to be an ostentatious throne room, but it was decorated more like a sitting area, with white lounging furniture, luxurious pink pillows, and a koi pond filled with shimmering rainbow fish. I could easily imagine Lady Mossi sitting there with her ladies-in-waiting, enjoying tea and pastries or feeding the fish as she plotted and planned.

But today, she sat on her throne, which I imagined was more befitting when receiving subjects and visitors. It was a simple, yet quietly powerful piece of furniture, made from antler bone, the House Ithir sigil carved at the very top. Three chartreuse-colored stones were set along the edges of the seatback, their yellowish-green depths sparkling as they caught the filtered sunlight streaming from above.

"My Lady." The captain stopped in front of the throne and bowed, sweeping his hand back to indicate us standing behind him. "Adara and Einar of Fenwood. These are the two fae who came to the city gates, claiming a blood tie to House Ithir."

Lady Mossi's amber eyes flashed as they flicked from the soldier to me and Einar. She was a vision, dressed in a shimmering, low-cut gown woven into a tapestry of autumn colors. Threads of gold, russet, and emerald twined with burnt orange, saffron, and aubergine, somehow creating a harmonious medley that shifted and shimmered over her curves. Her long, sage-colored hair flowed in loose waves over her shoulders, framing a heart-shaped face with a long nose and full, cupid's bow lips. Her skin, the color of red clay, seemed to glow from within, and a golden filigree necklace with a large, blue-white stone sat heavy between her collarbones.

I froze, my eyes locked on that stone. It was the same color as the amulet I used to wear, the stone that had kept my powers suppressed for decades.

But why would Lady Mossi be wearing one? Surely the head of House Ithir would have full access and control of her magic, wouldn't she?

"A blood tie?" she repeated, lips thinning as she took us in. I knew what she saw—an earth fae who looked like a low-born savage, bare chested and long-haired, and me, with my obvious water fae features. "It must be a very distant one."

Hastily, I bowed, remembering my manners, my place. Einar followed suit, though judging by the set of his jaw and the stiffness of his movements, I could tell he did so begrudgingly. It must chafe, having to bow to someone who was undoubtedly responsible for many of the deaths of his people, but I couldn't feel sympathy for him. He had to play this part if he wanted to survive.

"My apologies, Lady Mossi," I said, straightening. My skin prickled with nerves, and I knew I only had one shot to convince her. "I didn't mean to imply that my companion and I are related to House Ithir. That honor belongs to my best friend, Mavlyn Edendown. She gave her bracelet to me and told me that if I showed it to you, you would help me."

"Edendown." Lady Mossi straightened in her seat, some of the suspicion clearing from her face. She extended a fine-boned hand. "Let me see this bracelet."

I handed it to the captain, who approached the throne and set it in Lady Mossi's hand. She turned it over, fingertips brushing over the sigil, long-lashed eyes drifting shut. A soft, golden light hummed briefly from the carved piece of antler, then faded away.

"Yes," she finally said, opening her eyes. "Edendown is a distant branch, founded from my cousin's illegitimate child. Despite his status, he did our house a great favor once, and so we gifted him with this token." She handed the bracelet back to the captain, who returned it to me. It felt warm against my skin as I re-clasped it around my wrist, as if it had been sitting on a rock, absorbing the rays of the late afternoon sun. "I can sense that it was given to you freely, so I will hear your request. What can I do to help you?"

I cleared my throat. "My mother, Chaya Greenwood, was taken by General Slaugh and his men. I need your help to get her back."

A silence fell over the room, like a blanket of freshly fallen snow, smothering the peaceful greenery of this place and leaving a chill in its wake. "General Slaugh?" she repeated. "He is the King's right hand, the head of his military. If he has taken your mother, there is nothing I can do."

"Please, Lady Mossi." I dropped to my knees, desperation clawing at me like a griffin's talons. "My mother did nothing wrong. The general took her because he was searching for me. She didn't deserve to be ripped from her home."

Lady Mossi's eyes narrowed. "Searching for you? Why?"

Einar shot me a warning look, but I ignored him. "Because of my magic," I explained, holding out my right hand.

I drew on the incandescent core of power within me, so different from the cool flow of ice magic that had been stoppered up inside me all my life. A flame flickered to life above my palm, and Einar cursed, but Lady Mossi's gasp drowned his voice out.

"Fire magic?" Her lips parted, wide amber eyes flickering as they reflected the firelight emanating from my palm. "But...you are a water fae. How is this possible?"

"I don't know," I admitted. "My mother never explained it to me. She made me wear a stone similar to yours—" I pointed to the blue-white stone around her neck— "and told me it was a protection amulet, but the moment it was taken off me, my fire magic came out of nowhere. I think I probably had it all my life, but the stone suppressed it, so I could never use any of my powers. Fire or water."

The fire in my hand started to dance, flames branching and twining up my fingers in response to my agitated emotions. Quickly, I snapped my fingers closed into a fist, snuffing out the flames. The last thing I needed to do was lose control in front of such a powerful earth fae. We stood in the heart of her power, where she was at her strongest—she would crush us both without blinking if she perceived either of us as a threat.

"That's very interesting," Lady Mossi murmured. "She must have given you a primal stone to wear."

"A primal stone?" Dune had mentioned the term before, but I hadn't had a chance to ask anyone about it.

"Yes." Her fingers drifted to the necklace, and the stone seemed to glow brighter as she touched it. "Primal stones are used to store magic—fae use it to keep reserves of elemental magic, so we can draw on it when needed. But there are some that contain old spells, placed there by witchlings long ago. Your friend there seems to be in possession of one."

She pointed at Einar, who automatically touched the cuff at his wrist. Now that I looked at it, I saw a faint, starry light shimmering from within the ruby stone set into the piece of gold jewelry.

"Witchling magic?" I repeated, turning my attention back to Lady Mossi. "I thought witchlings were just a myth." I'd read about them in stories—an ancient race that could call upon both shadow and light magic without the aid of the spirits, casting spells that could bend reality to their whim.

"A legend, more like, and one lost to time. I don't believe anyone has seen a witchling, not in at least a thousand years." Lady Mossi's eyes glittered as she assessed me again, and I wished I could get a read on the emotions swirling in their depths. "You say your mother never explained your powers to you? You were never aware of your fire magic?"

I shook my head, putting all thoughts of witchlings aside for the moment. "No. That's one of the reasons I need to find her. I need her to tell me what this all means, why the king wants me, what this proph—"

"*Adara*," Einar growled, cutting me off before I could finish the sentence. A muscle ticced in his jaw, his golden eyes blazing with ire.

Lady Mossi raised a sage-colored eyebrow at him. "Is there a problem, Einar?" she asked. Her tone was light, like sunlight rippling across a lake, and yet there was a thread of steel underneath, a warning.

My cheeks flushed as I looked back and forth between the two of them, dragon and fae, locked in a staring contest. I knew why Einar had snapped at me—he thought I was getting carried away, revealing too much.

And perhaps I was. I didn't actually *know* Lady Mossi, after all. And just because she was an authority figure, in a position of power, didn't mean I could trust her. After all, my encounter with General Slaugh was proof enough of that.

But then again, Mavlyn had trusted her enough to send me to her. And this bracelet around my wrist meant she was honor-bound to help me. That had to be enough. Right?

Einar shrugged. "I apologize, but Adara talks too much sometimes. You're a very busy person, and I'm sure you have better things to do than listen to us prattle on."

"Oh, I assure you, this has been anything but boring," Lady Mossi said as I gnashed my teeth, resisting the urge to kick Einar in the shin. She tapped her bottom lip with the pad of her index finger, deliberating. "Helping you two would be a direct action against the king, so it's not a decision I can make lightly."

I bit my own bottom lip, feeling as if this opportunity was

slipping through my fingers. Grasping for something, anything, I blurted out the only thing that came to mind.

"Does the name Gelsyne mean anything to you?"

The entire atrium went still, as if divine fingers had reached in and plucked this moment, this scene, straight out of time. I held my breath as Lady Mossi stared at me, wondering if I'd said the wrong thing.

"Gelsyne is my granddaughter," Lady Mossi finally said, her voice sharp as crushed glass. "She died in the Dragon-Fae Wars. What would her name mean to a youngling like you?"

I swallowed hard, feeling Einar's eyes boring into me, but I pressed on. "General Slaugh called my mother by that name earlier, before she sent me away. She used powerful earth magic, magic that only a Greater Fae could have wielded." Even Dune wouldn't have been able to send me that far away, that fast. And if my mother really was a Greater Fae, that made her a member of House Ithir and a relative of Lady Mossi. "I... I think that might be her real name."

Lady Mossi's eyes filled with tears. She was out of her throne in an instant, closing the distance between us, taking my pale hands into her dark ones. The scents of sage and honey enveloped me in an instant as her amber eyes searched my face, clearly looking for traces of earth fae heritage.

Traces I'd never managed to find, no matter how hard I'd looked.

Finally, she cleared her throat and stepped back. "I find it hard to believe that Gelsyne would have birthed a child with no earth magic of her own," she said, "but if she raised you, then you are her daughter regardless of where your bloodline comes from." Her eyes hardened with determination. "If General Slaugh has my granddaughter in his clutches, I will do whatever it takes to get her back."

Hope surged within me, a brilliant ray of warmth that

pierced shadowy fear and uncertainty that had clung to my insides since this started. "So you'll help us rescue her?"

"Yes." She gripped my shoulder, and though her fingers dug in hard enough to bruise, the touch was a comfort nonetheless. "You have my word."

14

Lady Mossi

The bolt of Lady Mossi's bedroom door tumbled with a loud *click* as she turned the key in the lock. The sound seemed to echo in the loud chamber, and she jumped a little, like a youngling caught with her hand in the honeycomb jar.

It was a ridiculous reaction, considering that she was the queen of Domhain, safe and secure in her own chambers, in her own castle.

Of course, she wasn't allowed to use the title of *queen*. Her family was forced to drop all royal titles, eons ago, when the dragons first invaded Hearthfyre. The other fae realms—earth, water, air—had come together into one realm in order to solidify their forces and band together against the monsters who had slaughtered their fire fae brethren.

It had been Lady Mossi's own grandfather, King Edrin, who had convinced the others. We would be stronger together, he'd argued, stronger than we would trying to fight the dragons from three fronts.

And for a long time, that was true.

But things are different now, Lady Mossi mused as she crossed the vast space, passing the sitting area, the bathing chamber, the enormous bed piled high with pillows, fragrant, blossoming vines hanging from the top of the gilt four-poster frame. The dragons were gone, and King Aolis had only a tentative hold on Ediria, too tied up in fighting off the shadow magic infection to pay attention to the everyday minutiae of actually running a kingdom. Meanwhile, the earth kingdom continued to supply food to the rest of Ediria, even though the water and air fae were no longer holding up their end of the agreement, or at least not with the frequency that was once promised.

Lady Mossi pinched the bridge of her nose, trying to stave off the headache brewing there. The headache that crept up on her every time she thought about the injustice that was the power balance in our kingdom.

Like everywhere else in the castle, an abundance of plants thrived in her bedchambers. The atrium boasted a wide variety —trees, shrubs, herbs, flowers, vines, magical, decorative, poisonous, and practical—and was meant to show off the verdant wealth and power of the earth realm.

But the plants that grew here were her personal favorites, and she kept them for her pleasure alone.

Sitting down in front of her vanity, Lady Mossi reached out to touch one of the flowers blooming along the vine that clung to the bleached wooden frame of her mirror. The petals, a shade of violet so dark that they were nearly black, opened in response to her skimming fingers, revealing the starry brightness within. A thick perfume wafted out, and she breathed it in deeply, allowing the narcotic fragrance to work its way through her system, calming her frayed nerves.

Gelsyne is alive.

Anger and joy blazed inside Lady Mossi. Unlike the other fae races, earth fae were incredibly fertile, and she'd produced many children. But out of all the grandchildren they'd given her, Gelsyne had been her favorite. Her fascination with flora had bonded them, and the two had spent long hours in the atrium, tending to the plants, discussing all the different properties of the flowers and herbs and ways they could be used, both to heal and to hurt.

She'd grieved when King Cyrian, Aolis's predecessor, had summoned her to court to serve as Princess Olette's companion. But Gelsyne had wanted it, and Lady Mossi had never had the heart to refuse her anything.

When Lady Mossi heard that Gelsyne had been killed, every single plant in the atrium had wilted beneath the devastating weight of her anguish.

It had taken her years to build it back up to its former glory. And now, to hear that Gelsyne been alive all this time, and had never once reached out to her?

It was like a poisonous thorn, shoved straight into the center of her barely-healed heart.

Lady Mossi took in another breath, settling herself a little more, then pulled open one of the vanity drawers. Inside a small box of sandalwood lay a primal stone, but unlike the one at her throat, this one was corrupted, dark shadow magic swirling within its circular depths.

He'd told her it was witchling magic, that the stone kept it contained so that it couldn't hurt her, but Lady Mossi had never believed him. So she slipped on the silk glove she kept for this purpose, then picked up the stone. A shiver ratcheted through her limbs as she clutched it—the stone was frigid, and she could feel the foul magic within grasping for her life force, eager to suck every bit of warmth and light out of her.

"General Slaugh," Lady Mossi said to the mirror in front of her. "I need to speak to you."

One moment passed, then two, then three. She was nearly

ready to throw the stone back in the box when the surface of the mirror clouded over. A shadow swirled within the silver depths, before coalescing into the tall, disfigured form she knew so well.

"Auntie," Slaugh said in his rough voice. It always made her think of stones scraping against each other, forever trying to create a spark that refused to catch. Lady Mossi remembered when that voice used to be deep and smooth, before dragon fire had torched his throat. His wavy red hair flopped over to cover the burned side of his scalp, and he wore a loose tunic and leggings with the collar open and the sleeves rolled up, exposing the distorted skin on his chest and arms. Lady Mossi blinked, unused to seeing him dressed so informally—he must be in his private chambers, getting ready for bed.

But then again, she rarely ever saw her nephew outside of official business. Not since he'd become General Aolis—now *King Aolis*'s right hand, wielder of all of Ediria's military might.

"Nephew," Lady Mossi returned, hiding her thoughts behind a practiced smile. "I heard you were recently in Domhain, recruiting more of my people to be slaughtered, and yet you didn't come to say hello."

Slaugh snorted. "I've been busy, and I wasn't anywhere near Talamh, in any case." He ran a hand through his hair, exposing some of the warped skin of his scalp. "Besides, as much as I'd like to see you, I've had more important business to take care of."

Lady Mossi arched a brow. "This business wouldn't have anything to do with a blue-haired female with fire magic, would it?"

Slaugh immediately jumped to his feet, bracing his hands on whatever surface his mirror was sitting on. "What do you know about her?" he demanded, eagerness transforming his face. "Do you have her?"

"First, you need to answer me this." Lady Mossi held up a

hand, staving off his questions. "Is it true that you have Gelsyne?"

Slaugh sighed. "Yes. She used her magic to get the girl away from me, so I took her instead. She's languishing in our dungeons right now, and King Aolis is having her interrogated. From what we've managed to get so far, she's been raising Adara in that village since she was a baby, and she used a primal stone to keep her powers hidden. But we know nothing beyond that, not even who the father was."

"Yes, I figured out that much as well," Lady Mossi said. She buried her hands in her skirts so that Slaugh couldn't see they'd clenched into fists. "I suppose it doesn't matter to you that Gelsyne is your cousin, does it?"

Slaugh's expression hardened. "She's a traitor," he said in a voice like granite. "And besides, my loyalty to the king supersedes my ties to House Ithir. You know that."

Something in Lady Mossi's chest twisted in response to the ugly truth of his words. "I know it better than anyone else," she countered.

"Is there a reason you've summoned me?" Slaugh asked, lips thinning. "That stone I gave you was for emergency use only."

"Yes." Lady Mossi sat up a little straighter, lifting her chin. "I'm prepared to make a trade. The girl for Gelsyne...and Avani."

"Avani?" Slaugh raised an incredulous brow. "The king will never agree to give her back to you. You know the rules—one hostage for each realm in the kingdom."

"I do know the rules." Lady Mossi's lip curled involuntarily at the reminder of both Aolis's strength and weakness. Strength, that he was able to intimidate each of the house leaders by forcing them to hand over a loved one, and weakness, because a true ruler would never need to resort to such tactics. "But I have a feeling that Aolis will pay any price for Adara, and this is mine.

My granddaughters for Adara, and you must bring them here. I won't allow you to take Adara in good faith."

"Careful, Lady Mossi," Slaugh warned. "The king may not take kindly to such harsh demands."

Lady Mossi's fingers twitched in her skirts, her jaw clenching with fury. "Aolis may be king," she said in a low voice, "but it is *I* who controls the food supply for most of the kingdom. If he wishes to take offense to my terms, he does so at the rest of Ediria's peril."

A tense silence filled the air, and Slaugh pressed his lips together as he considered her words. "It will take me a few days," he said after a long moment. "Make sure that Adara remains in your care in the meantime. If she escapes before I arrive, there will be dire consequences for you."

He disappeared before Lady Mossi could express her outrage at being threatened by her own kin. She dropped the stone back into the box, then ripped the glove off and tossed it into the fireplace. But even as she watched the scrap of fabric burn, even as the shiver of revulsion crawled through her, she felt a blossom of hope unfurl in her chest.

Soon, Lady Mossi would get her granddaughters back. And once she had them, no one, not even Aolis, would be able to stop her from taking what was hers.

15

Einar

"I don't like this."

Adara rolled her eyes at me. "You've been saying that ever since we arrived," she said, twirling a loop of fire around her fingers. We were sitting cross-legged out on the balcony of Adara's bedroom, all furniture and flammables removed from the area so she could practice her fire magic without risking a conflagration.

"And it's no less true than it was yesterday." I twirled my own loop of fire, then snagged it around both of my forefingers and gently tugged. The string of flame grew longer, expanding until it was long enough to loop over my head like a necklace. "We've been cooped up in this castle for three days now, watched like hawks by the guards every time we leave our rooms, and Lady Mossi hasn't reported back on any progress finding your mother."

Adara sighed. "These things take time," she said, trying to copy my move. She tugged on the loop of fire she'd created, trying to lengthen the flame, but instead it grew wider, sprouting extra tendrils and twisting up her wrists. "And of course Lady Mossi isn't just going to let us come and go from the castle. Not when I'm being hunted."

The flames began to dance up her left arm, and this time it was *my* turn to roll my eyes. "You're not concentrating enough," I chastised, grabbing her arm to intercept the flames before they could climb too high. An electric sizzle jolted up my hand at the contact, but I did my best to ignore it as I coaxed the flames from Adara's body. Dutifully, they collected themselves into my hand, and I abruptly closed my palm, snuffing them out.

"And who's fault is that?" Adara crossed her arms over her chest, pushing her breasts together and giving me a far too tantalizing view of her cleavage. Lady Mossi had sent fresh clothes for both of us—supple brown leather pants, a cream-colored cotton shirt, and a forest green jerkin for me, while Adara was given a sleeveless blue overdress with a golden bustier and dark leggings underneath. Golden epaulets clutched her otherwise bare shoulders, and a matching pair of bracers covered her forearms. Lady Mossi had claimed the outfit was from a late water fae cousin of hers, and I had to admit it suited her very well.

A little too well, I admitted to myself, dragging my gaze back up to her face. It was frustrating, how easily distracted I was by her body. The mating bond was a relentless force, constantly pushing me to claim what it insisted was mine by divine right.

"You need to be able to control your magic regardless of the circumstances," I told her, forcing my mind back to the issue at hand. "Do you think the enemy is going to politely wait while you gather your focus? That they won't attack you, goad you, distract you, do whatever they possibly can to get through your defenses?"

"Of course not," Adara snapped, her eyes flashing, "but I'm

not at that level yet, Einar. I only discovered I had fire magic four days ago. You can't expect me to wield it as easily as you can."

"Maybe not," I agreed, "but that doesn't mean I'm not going to push you. You signed up for this when you asked me to teach you," I reminded her when she opened her mouth to protest. "If you don't like it, you can find someone else."

She glared at me. "You know there isn't anyone else who can teach me. The fire fae are all gone, thanks to your people."

I shot to my feet, fury obliterating my desire to help. "We're done here," I growled, stalking away from her.

A haze of red came over my vision, and I resisted the urge to lash out at something. I was so tired of hearing that same old line, of being punished for a crime that, even if my ancestors *had* committed, happened nearly three thousand years ago. A crime that the fae had used as an excuse to drive us nearly to extinction.

I made it three steps before a delicate hand closed around my wrist. That familiar jolt sizzled up my arm, and I halted abruptly, my feet rooted to the spot by her touch.

"Wait." Adara's voice was softer now, tinged with what sounded like regret. "I'm sorry, Einar. I shouldn't have said that."

My shoulders relaxed, a deep exhale sawing from my lungs, and I inwardly kicked myself at the reaction. I should wrench my arm from her grip and keep walking, head back to my rooms and leave her here. Let her set fire to the place for all I cared.

Instead, I slowly turned, bringing her face to face with me, letting her see the raw emotions in my eyes.

Adara sucked in a breath as our gazes collided. Her fingers still curled around my wrist, my pulse thrumming against the pale digits. Part of me wanted to take that hand and pull her in closer, to feel her body flush against mine the way she had been back in the forest when she'd accidentally fallen on top of me. Heat coiled low in my belly at the thought of it, and I found my other hand lifting up, skimming my thumb along her cheek-bone, running it over her lower lip.

Her eyes widened, and she jerked back as if I'd slapped her.

The pain of that rejection lanced through me, a white hot spear of denial that seared the inside of my chest. Unable to face it, I spun on my heel and stalked back inside, out of her rooms and into my own.

This time, she didn't stop me.

Breaths coming in fast, I paced the small sitting area near my bed, hands shoved into my hair, insides churning with emotion. *This is a good thing,* I tried to tell myself. *You want her to reject you. You want her to push you away, so that the mating bond doesn't take root. You've been trying to make her hate you since you first met.*

Then why, when I was succeeding, did I feel like such a damned failure?

Letting out a gusty exhale, I strode toward the window in the room and flung it open. The sun had set, and only a hint of twilight remained, tinging the verdant horizon with a hint of pale yellow as night settled in.

I knew there was a chance I would be seen, but instinct drove me hard, pushing me toward the open sky. I couldn't stand to be in this place, caged by walls that stank of fae magic, for even a second longer.

So, before I could think it through, I took a few steps back, then dashed toward the window and dove through it.

Immediately, I began to plummet, the ground rushing up to meet me from ten stories above. I allowed myself to fall for a brief moment, the wind screaming a shrill warning in my ears, and then my wings burst from my back, the satiny membranes unfurling to catch the current. Scales sprouted along the ends of my extremities—hands, feet, forearms, shins—,claws curved from the tips of my toes and fingers, and I grinned fiercely, exposing razor sharp fangs.

It had been a long time since I'd assumed my halfling form. It was a skill that only the strongest of dragons could manage, holding oneself between forms, and it felt damn good to know that even after all these years, I still had it.

I pumped my wings once, twice, three times, until I caught an updraft that carried me far from the castle. Closing my eyes, I coasted for a while, simply enjoying the freedom of flying. There was no agenda, no place I needed to be, no rider on my back to carry to safety.

If I wanted to, I could just keep flying.

But where to? I wondered as I drifted through a cloud. Icy particles clung to my skin, reminding me of the blue-haired faery girl with moonlit skin and bewitching eyes I'd left behind. The mating bond tugged at my heart, trying to pull me back to her, and a deep ache settled in my chest.

For a long time, I'd prayed every night to the spirits of my ancestors to help me find my mate. Completing that soul bond was one of the greatest joys in a dragon's life, and I'd been envious as I watched my friends, hatchlings I'd grown up with and fought alongside, find their life partners and experience the bliss of joining with their missing halves.

But as I'd fought more battles, watched more and more of my friends lose their lives, I became thankful I didn't have a mate. Thankful that she would never experience the soul-rending pain of watching me die in battle, and that she would never subject me to the same agony. In a life lived on the edge of death, it seemed to me that there was no room for love, no room for anything but desperate survival.

To be gifted the thing I'd once wanted most in the world, under such tragic circumstances, was almost more than I could bear.

Daryan's face swam into my mind's eye as I flew, his ember-colored eyes glowing with joy as he held his fae betrothed's hands. The two of them had adored each other so much, their love so strong it had nearly brought the two races together, had nearly put an end to the bloodshed.

But the two of them were dead now, their ashes lost to time and grief, and shadows had risen in their wake, devouring the land and everything they had fought for.

If that wasn't a cautionary tale against love and soul-bonds, I didn't know what was.

Still, I thought, circling around a particularly dense cloud and heading back to the castle, I'd made a deal with Adara. And while I refused to claim her as my mate, I couldn't deny the deep-seated need inside me to see this thing through, to unearth the truths hidden between the cracks and crevices of Adara's past, and the chance to confront the fae responsible for Daryan's death.

I was convinced that Aolis had orchestrated Daryan's murder. He had been madly in love with Olette, and the two had been engaged before she'd given herself to the dragon prince instead. If anyone had been motivated to kill my best friend at his own wedding feast, it was the general-turned-king.

I just needed to be careful not to get myself killed, or the sacrifice I'd made all those years ago would be for nothing.

The castle came back into view, and I coasted over to the roof of the south tower, not quite ready to head back into my room yet. Tucking my wings behind me, I sank into a crouch as I carefully surveyed my surroundings. The pulsing, reddish-black vines that covered the walls of the castle clung to the roof tiles as well, and I eyed it warily. The scales covering my feet and hands ensured I wouldn't get poisoned if I accidentally stepped on one, but the plants could still touch my exposed skin, and I didn't like being so close to them.

Still, a fresh breeze was blowing up here, so I tilted my head back and sucked in a deep breath, then slowly let the icy air out.

My body relaxed as I allowed the current to carry my worries and negative emotions away. The sting in my heart eased, my mind finally clearing.

It was a good thing that Adara pushed me away, I decided. In fact, I was thankful for it. Of the two of us, she clearly had better control over her emotions, and I shuddered to think what might have happened if I'd given in to the mating bond. Aside from the fact that I didn't want it, Adara wasn't even aware of it. She would be furious if she ended up being mated to me with no foreknowledge on the matter.

Putting Adara out of my mind, I let my gaze wander over the castle grounds, noting where the guards were stationed and any potential escape routes. As I did, voices drifted to me on the wind, and I caught snippets of what sounded like urgent conversation.

Curious, I spread my wings and then leapt from the roof, catching another current. I glided down to a balcony several stories below, just above what looked to be the armory. The voices were coming from inside, and my ears quivered as I strained to hear what they were saying.

"...coming tomorrow," a male complained. "Apparently there's a prisoner he's supposed to be taking back to the king."

"A prisoner?" another voice asked, sounding puzzled. "The only one in the dungeons is Jiffry, and I don't see what the king would want with him seeing as how he's only been charged with public nudity."

"No, not Jiffry." I could practically hear the other fae rolling his eyes. "That little bastard is in and out every other month for some stupid infraction or other. I'm amazed the captain hasn't ordered him to be executed out of sheer annoyance. But anyway, it's that blue-haired girl, the one staying in the north tower. Apparently the king's taken such an interest in her, he's willing to trade Lady Avani back for her."

"Really?" The second fae's voice rose in surprise. "I didn't realize she was so important."

The two fae continued talking, but I could no longer hear them above of the roaring in my ears. Blue-haired girl. Prisoner. A trade.

Lady Mossi wasn't holding Adara here to keep her safe. She was planning on using her as a bargaining chip, and if she had her way, Adara would be back in enemy hands *tomorrow*.

16

Adara

The door slammed as Einar stormed out of the room, leaving a cloud of anger and hurt in his wake. Shocked, I stared at the white door, my hand lifting to touch my lips in the spot where his finger had just been. My lower lip was still tingling at the contact, my mind whirling as I tried to process what had just happened.

I hadn't been able to help my reaction. I wasn't prepared for Einar to touch me the way he had, wasn't ready for the surge of emotions that had overwhelmed me. Something wicked and wanton had risen inside me, and I'd nearly darted my tongue out to lick his skin. I'd wanted to taste him, to feel him, to pull him closer so I could press his powerful body pressed against mine.

The intense carnal need had shocked me so badly that I'd recoiled instinctively, not sure how to handle it. And judging by the way Einar had stormed out, I'd obviously hurt his feelings.

That's a little ridiculous, a voice in my head said. *You're not*

obligated to accept his advances, and there's no need for him to have a
tantrum just because you rejected him.

Right. I shook my head a little, jostling myself out of my
stupor, and began to pace. Truthfully, I didn't know what Einar
had been thinking, touching me like that. Half the time he acted
like he hated me, so what was he playing at with such intimacy?

I'd already tried to give my heart to someone who clearly
didn't love me back, and I had no intention of being manipulated
like that again. I didn't know what kind of game Einar was playing, but I had no intention of getting caught up in it. My only
goal was to find my mother, and I couldn't let him distract me.

Still, I thought as I paused by the window, looking out at the
last rays of sunlight as they kissed the horizon. *Einar has a point.* I
hadn't seen Lady Mossi since the initial welcome feast she'd
given us on our first day in the palace, and that had been nearly
three days ago. I'd thought the two of us would come up with a
plan to rescue Mother together, but instead she'd told me to
leave it to her and focus on honing my magic instead.

That's what I'd been doing these past couple of days, cooped
up in the north tower with no one but Einar and the guards for
company. We were escorted by guards everywhere we went, and
so far, my requests to speak to Lady Mossi had been rebuffed.

With every day that passed with no news of my mother, my
anxiety rose a little higher. I'd done my best so far to give Lady
Mossi the benefit of the doubt, but I couldn't afford to do so any
longer.

I needed to confront her, and find out what was really
going on.

I considered my options for a moment, then strode to the
door of my chambers and opened it. A winding staircase awaited
at the end of a short landing, and I followed it down to the
bottom of the tower, passing Einar's room along the way.

Part of me wondered if I should knock on his door and at least tell him I was meeting with Lady Mossi.

But a small, petty part of me insisted that if he wanted to sulk in his room, then far be it from me to interfere.

And it was that voice I chose to listen to tonight.

As I exited the tower and made my way through the courtyard, two guards peeled off from their posts outside the north tower and fell into step a few feet behind me. Lady Mossi had insisted they were there for my protection, but I knew her intentions couldn't be so magnanimous. We were strangers staying in her home, and she wanted to monitor us.

I would have done the same in her position, but it still chafed.

I followed the path to the atrium, heading straight for the double door entrance. Moonlight spilled across the windowpanes, making them glitter like sheets of ice. Two guards stood in front of the doors, and they closed ranks as I approached, blocking me from entering.

"Lady Mossi isn't receiving visitors tonight."

"Oh." I came to a halt and tapped a finger against my lips. "That's too bad. I'd hate to leave without saying goodbye."

"Leave?" one of the soldiers guarding the atrium frowned, and I felt the other two guards that had followed me close ranks behind me, blocking my path from the other side. "I'm sorry, but Lady Mossi gave specific instructions that you remain here until further notice."

I arched an eyebrow. "Am I a prisoner, then?" I asked them. A spark ignited at the tip of my forefinger, bursting into a tiny flame, and I drew lazy circles in the air, leaving streaks of fiery light in my wake as I spelled out the word. P-R-I-S-O-N-E-R.

The guards stiffened, and they glanced furtively at each other. "No, of course not," the other one said. He cleared his throat, then stepped aside and opened one of the double doors. "Please, go on in."

I hid a smile as I passed by him, leaving all four guards in the atrium. I had a feeling none of them wanted to face Lady Mossi's ire, but neither were they prepared to fight a fae with fire magic.

The moment I stepped into the atrium, I felt a shift in the air. The atmosphere in here was hotter, more humid, and droplets of water clung to my skin as I made my way down the path that led to the throne. Hundreds of floral scents hung heavy in the air, sticky and cloying in a way they hadn't been the first time I'd set foot in here.

It was as if there was a hunger lurking somewhere in these bushes, something dark and sinister just waiting to devour me.

A shiver crawled up my spine, but I set my shoulders and pressed on until I reached the clearing. I expected to find Lady Mossi sitting in her throne, or on one of the chaises, but instead she lay on her side in the grass, right at the edge of the pond. Her fingers skimmed the water, and a puckering koi swam up to kiss and nibble at them, clearly hoping for a morsel of food. The skirts of her rose-colored dress fanned out beneath her, spilling across the green like a giant petal.

"Adara," she said, not looking up at me. She'd styled her sage green hair into a simple plait, and she toyed with the edge of it now as she continued to tease the koi. "It's rude of you to barge into my gardens without an invitation."

Her tone was mild, but I heard the threat beneath her words clear as day. "I didn't mean to disturb you, Lady Mossi," I said, trying to sound apologetic. "But it's been days since I've arrived, and I still haven't received any news regarding my mother. All this waiting has made me a little anxious."

"Anxious?" Lady Mossi lifted her gaze from the pond, a challenge in her eyes. "Are you doubting me, youngling?"

"No, of course not," I rushed out as she rose to her feet.

Though she was shorter than me by a few inches, she somehow managed to tower over me, her presence large and imposing as she stood in the center of the atrium. I swallowed hard as a wave of pure power washed over me, and though her expression was placid, the hairs on my arms stood straight on end.

I might have powerful, rare magic, but we were in Lady Mossi's domain, and everything in this room was a weapon at her disposal. I needed to proceed very carefully.

"I have every reason to think that you want to rescue my mother as much as I do," I said, trying to assuage her. "And I know that as the ruler of this realm, you're not used to being questioned, or answering to anyone other than the king. But you have to understand, it's excruciating, being kept in the dark like this. Not knowing what happened to Mother, where she'd being held, whether Slaugh is torturing her or not. I need to know where she is, what the plan is, and how I can help."

Lady Mossi sighed, her gaze finally lifting from the pond to land on me. Her amber eyes filled with resignation, and her lips flattened as she looked me up and down. "If these were better circumstances, if you were not who you were, I would have been able to tell you the truth from the beginning. But things have been set into motion that cannot be undone, and the best thing you can do, the *only* thing you can do, is remain here and let it play out."

"What is that supposed to mean?" I took a step back as a wave of apprehension rolled through me. Sparks of fire ignited at my fingertips, and I clenched my hand, trying to snuff them out.

Lady Mossi glanced toward my fist, which was now engulfed in flames. "We all know about the prophecy, the one that speaks about the girl of ice and fire." Her face softened as she met my gaze again, something almost apologetic in her expression. "There is no point in fighting fate—you will end up in King

Aolis's hands no matter what you do. But there is no reason for Gelsyne to suffer. I've arranged for her to be returned to me, along with my other granddaughter, in exchange for you."

Betrayal lanced through me, a flaming arrow of outrage and grief that pierced straight through my heart. "You did *what*?"

Lady Mossi raised an arm, and the grass beneath my boots suddenly parted. The soil beneath liquified to mud, and I gasped as my legs sank into the ground. I tried to yank my feet out, but the earth hardened before I could, trapping me in a vise grip.

"Let me go!" I struggled against the earthen bindings, my legs already going numb.

"I can't." Lady Mossi's expression hardened. "Slaugh will be here in less than a day's time with Gelsyne and Avani. I am *this* close to getting them back safely, and I won't let you interfere."

I gritted my teeth, fire igniting in my other fist in response to my fury. "Let me go," I hissed, the flames racing up to engulf my arms. They licked against my skin eagerly, ready to turn their scorching power against an enemy. "Or I'll reduce this entire atrium to ash."

Lady Mossi laughed, then flicked her hand. The earth holding my feet liquified again, and it began swirling up my legs, trying to engulf my entire body. Flexing my legs, I gathered every bit of strength I had and leapt free, diving straight into the pond—the one place in the atrium Lady Mossi's power couldn't easily influence.

"Oh you think you're clever, do you?" she taunted as my head broke the surface of the water. She stood at the edge, her entire body incandescent with a verdant glow. Vines snaked across the ground, drawn from the corners of the atrium to do her bidding, and the air seemed to thicken with all the clashing fragrances, making me feel light-headed. I was certain that some of these had narcoleptic and poisonous effects, and it was only because they were diluted, traveling over such a far distance and mingling with the healing effects of other blossoms, that I hadn't already gone unconscious.

"You can't use your fire magic while you're in there, and you'll have to come out sometime," Lady Mossi said. She twirled her fingertips in the air, and the koi that had scattered to the edges of the pond turned and swam toward me with frightening speed. Their rainbow bodies bumped against me with bruising force, and panic began to claw at my throat as they herded me toward the edge of the pond closest to Lady Mossi. "And once you set foot on solid ground, you're mine."

"Is that what you think?" Fierce determination rose inside me, overtaking the panic and even the rage. I was tired of others thinking I was weak, helpless, easy to manipulate and control. My powers might be new to me, but they were *mine*, and I wasn't about to let others dictate what I should do with them just because they thought they knew better.

This was *my* life, and *I* was in control.

Taking a deep breath, I stopped swimming, then reached for the *other* source of power inside me, the deep, cold pool that sat ready and waiting. It responded eagerly, flowing through pathways that had once been blocked, and I envisioned it turning the pond into a solid layer of ice. The surface of the water began to crystalize, ice rippling out in crackling waves, catching the koi fish in its wake. The ones closest to me fled into the depths of the pond as they sensed what was happening, but the majority ended up encased in the foot-thick layer of ice.

I felt a twinge of guilt for their deaths as I hauled myself onto the frozen surface, then used my power to close off the hole where I'd just been. I hadn't wanted to kill the fish, but there'd been no choice.

"How dare you!" Shock and fury mottled Lady Mossi's features, her lush mouth twisting in a snarl. She raised a hand,

and a small boulder rose from a copse of trees fifty yards away. "You murdered my prized koi!"

She flung an arm in my direction, and the boulder rocketed through the air at lightning speed. Adrenaline surging, I dodged the projectile, and it crashed straight through the ice, leaving a massive hole in its wake. Cracks spread through the surface, and I hastily used my power to repair them before the ice gave way.

Lady Mossi took advantage of the distraction to throw another boulder at me, and I barely dodged it. Soon I was battling against an onslaught as she rained rocks of all shapes and sizes down on me, ripping them from all corners of the atrium. The pond wasn't very big, leaving me very little room to dodge them. Several slammed into my back and my ribs, and I hissed at the pain radiating through me. I was amazed I hadn't broken any bones yet.

"You're going to kill me at this rate!" I yelled, raising my arms over my head to protect my skull.

"Oh don't worry, I'll heal any injuries you sustain," Lady Mossi crooned in a sing-song voice as she hurled a dinner-plate sized rock at me. I dodged it and repaired the hole in the ice it had left behind, but my movements were slower, my breath coming in pants. She was trying to wear me down, and it was working. "After all, I wouldn't want to deliver damaged goods to the king."

She raised her arm again, but before she could fling another rock at me, a huge shape crashed through the ceiling of the atrium. My mouth dropped open in shock as Einar hurtled toward the ground in dragon form, his giant maw open wide to expose arm-length fangs. Lady Mossi shrieked as he unleashed a torrent of fire, and she dropped to the ground, narrowly avoiding the flames. A dome of earth rose around her body, protecting her, but the rest of the arboretum wasn't so lucky.

Several trees caught fire, and I watched in horror as the flames raced through the greenhouse.

It was like the tryouts all over again.

Einar craned his long neck around to face me, his golden eye snagging on me. He tossed back his head and let out a roar, flapping his wings once. The guards rushing toward us flew backward as a gust of wind slammed into them, and I winced as several of them slammed into trees, their heads lolling as they slumped onto the ground.

Hurry up and get on!

Gathering what remained of my strength, I dashed toward Einar. On my way, I veered toward one of the black-trunked trees and snagged a golden apple from between the ruby-red leaves. I wanted to grab a second, but a guard dashed toward me, and I was forced to dodge as he swung a sword my way. I jumped back at the last second, then blasted him with ice magic. A scream ripped from his throat as ice rippled across his chest, encasing his entire body, but the sound cut off abruptly as the ice engulfed his throat and head, leaving a chilling silence in his wake.

I'd just killed a man with my ice magic. For the very first time.

Einar roared again, and I ripped myself from the moment. He thrashed his spiked tail, using it to send guards flying into the trees. There was no time to be shocked, no time for fear or hesitation. I shoved the apple into my boot, then raced toward the massive dragon, taking a flying leap over his tail and scrambling up his back.

The earth rumbled beneath our feet as Lady Mossi, still in her protective dome, tried to use her magic to stop us. But Einar was faster—he leaped into the sky before the earth could suck us down, back through the giant hole he'd made in the atrium. I clung on for dear life as he winged his way into the clouds, pushing higher and higher until I started growing lightheaded.

"Einar," I gasped out, slapping against his hide. "I can't breathe."

He let out a huff, then abruptly dropped through a layer of clouds. I screeched as my stomach shot into my throat, then slammed back down into my abdomen. My vision swam from the sudden rush, and I clung onto the spike in front of me with slippery palms, desperately trying not to fall off.

"You did that on purpose!"

He rumbled in response, not even trying to deny it. It was an angry sound, and I could tell he was furious, although I wasn't sure about what, exactly. I hadn't done anything wrong, and in fact I'd been doing a decent job holding my own against Lady Mossi before he'd come to the rescue.

But I didn't have time to ponder the reasons behind Einar's anger, because a loud screech rent the night air, one that made every single hair on my body stand straight on end. I craned my neck around just in time to see five griffins break through the clouds, winging toward us in V-formation. Their gilded, feathery bodies shone brightly in the moonlight, beaks flashing menacingly, but even worse were the riders on their backs—leather-clad soldiers bearing House Ithir's insignia on their chests. Each one carried a bow, and a sense of foreboding filled me as they nocked their arrows, aiming not for me, but for Einar's flapping wings.

Einar snarled, then flapped his wings harder, propelling us through the night sky at astonishing speed. I held on, tight as I could, as the wind screeched in my ears, the clouds tearing past us. But as fast as Einar was, he wasn't fast enough. The griffins were lighter, and they were closing in, nearly within shooting range now.

Well, two can play that game, I decided. Sucking in a breath, I turned myself on Einar's back until I was facing our pursuers, then raised my hand. Drawing water from the nearby clouds, I used my magic to conjure an array of ice stakes, then swung my arm wide and flung them at the enemy.

The griffins dodged the ice projectiles, scattering in different directions and then rejoining in formation. The bowmen refocused their aim on me this time, and I tensed as they loosed their arrows. Einar swung his tail, knocking the arrows aside, and I launched more ice projectiles, forcing the griffins to scatter once more.

Over and over we kept this up, racing through the skies. I pierced one of the griffin's wings, and Einar smashed another with his spiked tail, sending them both plummeting with pained screeches. But I'd already used a lot of my magic in the fight with Lady Mossi, and my strength was flagging. It took everything I had to stay upright, and my arms shook with every new wave of projectiles I flung.

The remaining griffins drew closer, sensing my weakness. Two of them winged off to attack Einar from either side, leaving me to deal with the one in the middle. I raised a shaking hand, trying to form another set of ice stakes, but the water droplets were sluggish, slow to obey. I managed to fling two more at the rider, but he dodged easily.

I was about to try again when one of the griffins slammed into Einar's side, sending him careening sideways. I screamed as I flew off his back, but before I could go plummeting to the earth, a clawed hand snatched me out of the sky. I winced as the digits clamped around my torso, tight enough that I could only take in shallow breaths through my nose. The other two griffins were attacking Einar's flanks, trying to tear at his hide and wings. From the scent of blood staining the air, I could tell they'd gotten in a few strikes, but Einar kept them at bay, shooting jets of fire and thrashing his tail for all it was worth.

As Einar's strength began to fail, we dropped below the cloud cover. The landscape came into view, and I sucked in a breath at the sight of the Gaoth Aire mountains looming straight ahead. We were approaching the realm of the air fae.

"Einar, head into the mountain range!" I shrieked over the roar of the wind. "The griffin riders can't follow us there!"

Summoning the last of my strength, I flung another ice stake straight at the heart of the griffin on our left. My aim was true, and the griffin's wings snapped wide as the stake plunged into his chest. It spun toward the earth, taking its rider with him, and the other rider fell back. I saw him loose another arrow, heard a roar of pain from Einar, but blackness crept into the edges of my vision, and the sound was faint, as distant as the echo of an old memory.

Please make it, was the last thought that flitted through my mind. I thought we might have plummeted, the wind screeching a warning before we crashed into the mountainside. But the darkness closed around me before I could feel the impact, and I knew no more.

17

Einar

B oom.

The mountainside rumbled as I crashed into it, wings tucked, spine bowed, Adara tucked safely against my chest to shield her from the brunt of the impact. Pain radiated through my side as my left wing crunched into a boulder, but my scream of agony was drowned out as sheets of snow dislodged from the surrounding mountains, building into a deafening roar.

An avalanche, I thought dimly, my mind fogging from the pain. Glancing around, I spotted a cave twenty yards from us, illuminated by a shaft of moonlight that had slipped beneath the heavy cloud cover. My stomach tightened as I gauged the size of the cave entrance—it wasn't wide enough to accommodate my dragon form. I was going to have to shift to make it in there, and judging by the speed at which the snow up ahead was racing down the mountainside, there wasn't time.

You're going to have to ride it out.

Shutting my eyes against the oncoming avalanche, I dug my claws through the snow and into the rough mountain soil below to brace myself against the onslaught. The wave of snow hit us with the force of a hurricane, battering every part of my body and making my injured wing scream in agony. I tucked myself in tighter against the barrage, shielding Adara from the worst of it and praying to the stars for it to be over.

Eventually, the rumbling ceased, and the terrible vibrations melted away. Opening my eyes, I found myself buried in snow nearly up to my eyeballs. The drifts had piled up all around us, blocking the entrance to the cave completely.

Good thing I was a dragon, or we'd be well and truly fucked.

Summoning my remaining strength, I opened my mouth and gently released a stream of fire. The snow encasing my front limbs melted, and I pulled myself to my feet, ignoring the sharp stabs of pain coming from my left wing. Keeping Adara clutched to my chest, I dragged us to the mouth of the cave, clearing a path with my fire as I went, then melting the snow drifts blocking the entrance.

By the time I finished, I was panting with exhaustion, my vision foggy with pain. I wanted to stay in my dragon form, especially since I didn't know what dangers might lurk in the cave. But I needed to heal my wing, and I needed to get us both inside and out of the cold before a storm hit or a predator found us.

Opening my snout as wide as I could, I blasted the inside of the cave with fire, hoping that would kill anything sinister lurking inside. Then I gently put Adara down, just inside the entrance, and shifted.

Sharp, jagged waves of pain ripped through my wing and down my spine as I shrank into my bipedal form, melting away my protective scales, sheathing my claws and fangs and spikes. My entire body shook from the effort, and goosebumps raced across my flesh as cold from the elements scraped against my now-fragile skin.

And to top it all off, my stomach rumbled in hunger.

"Perfect," I muttered to myself, stalking inside the smoking cave. Someone had left kindling behind—there was a small pile of sticks near the back of the cave that had caught fire. A few animal bones, no doubt leftover from someone's kill, were scattered around the cave, and I kicked them away, then picked up Adara's limp body and carried her over to the sorry excuse for a fire.

"Mmpphhh," she mumbled as I set her down. I tried to let her go, but she clutched at my arm in her sleep, holding fast. Bemused, I looked down at the pale fingers curled around my bicep, a stark, yet somehow fitting contrast against my tanned skin. Tenderness welled up inside me, eating away at the sharp edges of my anger. I tried to fight against it, tried to hold on to my enmity for her—what she'd done, confronting Lady Mossi on her own, had been incredibly dangerous and stupid. She should have come to me, should have—

And how exactly was she supposed to come to you for help, when you were busy flying away and pretending to be free?

I shook my head, exasperated with myself. I was constantly torn where Adara was concerned, caught between my desire to protect her and my need to distance my emotions. I didn't want to be mated to a fae, dammit. I didn't want anything to do with this world at all. My loyalty was to my people, and for their sake, I should stay out of this altogether.

And yet, as I stared down at her, watching the way the dim firelight played against Adara's alabaster skin, I realized I was too tired to fight right now. All I wanted was to hold Adara in my arms, and judging by the way she gripped me, she wanted that too, at least subconsciously.

So I ignored every shout and warning my mind threw at me, and laid down with her by the fire.

The moment I pulled her against my chest, everything inside me seemed to settle. Her scent—sweet, salt, and a hint of smoke

—wrapped around me like a comforting blanket, and her curves pressed against me, fitting the planes and hollows of my body like they were made for me.

I braced myself for the usual wave of lust to scorch me, for the overwhelming desire to claim her that I felt whenever she touched me.

But instead I felt a sense of...peace. Of belonging. Like I'd come home.

Adara burrowed into my chest, and exhaustion tugged at my mind, pulling me under. I held her close as I drifted off to sleep, hoping nothing would be foolish enough to attack us in the middle of the night.

Because regardless of my conflicted feelings, I would gladly destroy anything that tried to put her in harm's way.

Adara

The sound of something vibrating against my cheek woke
me from a deep sleep.

Drowsy, I lifted my heavy eyelids with some effort, only to
find that I couldn't see anything. I was in pitch darkness, with
not even a single star to shed any light on my surroundings. A
jumble of confused thoughts hit me at once—where was I?
What happened? How long had I been asleep?

The last thing I remembered was flying at breakneck speed
toward the Gaoth Aire mountains, clutched in Einar's fist. Had
we made it? I knew I'd passed out from using too much magic,
but I thought we'd taken down most of the griffins before that
had happened.

A shard of guilt niggled in my chest as I remembered
watching those magnificent bird-beasts drop from the sky, but I
quickly forgot it when the flat plane against my cheek vibrated
again. Blinking, I reached a hand up to feel what I was lying
against, and jolted rippled through me when I met soft linen
fabric and hard muscle.

Einar. It was Einar I was lying on top of.

My heart pounded at the realization, but I didn't move. He had one arm thrown around my waist, as if to hold me against him, and one of his hands was loosely tangled in my hair. As if on cue, his fingers scraped against my scalp in a gentle massage, sending tingles down my spine. I shivered a little, and his arm tightened around me, as if he were afraid I might try to get up.

I really *should* try to get up.

But there was something comforting about being in his embrace, enveloped by his masculine scent. He smelled like wood smoke and starlight, like a blazing campfire beneath a brilliant night sky, crisp and sharp and full of promise. Something stirred inside me as I inhaled his scent, something that made me want to spread imaginary wings of my own and fly, fly, fly.

Against my better judgment, I slid my hand up his chest. That steady rumble wasn't just breathing—it was almost like a purr, a subconscious resonance of satisfaction. As if holding me in his arms brought him peace.

But how could that be, when he hated me and my kind as much as he claimed?

My fingers trailed higher, over his Adam's apple, along the edge of his jaw, across his chin. I was mapping his face with my fingertips, like a blind person might when trying to imagine what someone looked like. My forefinger sank into his pillowy lower lip, and the tip of his hot tongue brushed against my skin.

The intimate contact sent a flood of warmth rushing through my body, and I snatched my hand back, heart pounding with mortification and exhilaration. Einar's eyes blinked open, and my breath stuttered to a halt in my chest. There was something different about his gaze as he stared at me through heavy-lidded eyes—his irises, golden once more, were the same, but the pupils had narrowed to vertical slits, giving them the same reptilian shape they had when he was in dragon form.

"Einar?" I asked hesitantly, not entirely sure if he was awake.

He gave another deep rumble in response, then slid his hand up the back of my neck. I gasped as he buried his fingers in my nape and tilted my head back, and before I knew what was happening, his mouth slanted over mine.

The press of his mouth—soft, warm, inviting—sent sparks skipping through me, and I instinctively dug my fingers into his shoulders before I remembered myself. Chagrined, I opened my mouth to protest, but he took advantage immediately, slipping his tongue in to stroke against mine.

He kissed me with the hunger of a raging firestorm, illuminating the night with its brilliance and devouring everything in its path. I felt like a pile of kindling struck by lightning— abruptly alive and burning with a fierce flame that threatened to consume me whole.

And yet, I didn't want to let go. I wanted to kiss him back, to *let* him consume me until there was nothing left of my pain but ashes.

The moment I thought that, the memory of the *last* time I'd been kissed reared up in my head, like a viper waiting in the recesses of my mind for this exact moment to strike. The pitying look on Dune's face when he told me we couldn't be together, that he would never marry me, was like a punch to the gut, and I jerked back, breaking the kiss.

"*No,*" Einar growled, yanking me back into him. "You're *mine.*"

The voice that rumbled up from his chest sounded different, more guttural, as if it had come from the deep bowels of some predatory beast. He tried to kiss me again, but this time I shoved him with all my strength, sending him skidding across the floor. Heart pounding, I leapt to my feet, a flame erupting in the palm of my hand to cast a flickering glow against the pitch dark shadows.

"What in the blazes?" Einar snapped, sitting up. He shoved a hand into the tangled mass of his shoulder-length brown hair as he blinked up at me, his eyes adjusting to the dim light. My heart galloped in my chest as I stared at him, my entire body trembling from the rush. "Why did you wake me, Adara? Did something happen?"

"Yeah, you kissed me!" I jabbed a finger at him, as though I were accusing him of a terrible crime. "I woke up to find you in my arms, and then when I tried to get up you pulled me into your chest and shoved your tongue inside my mouth!"

"I—" he sputtered in disbelief, his entire face reddening with embarrassment. It might have been comical if I hadn't been so shaken by the encounter. "That's impossible. You must have been dreaming."

"I'm sorry to disappoint you, but I don't fantasize about sloppy dragon kisses when I close my eyes at night," I shot back, my own cheeks heating. I knew I hadn't been entirely truthful with my portrayal of what had happened, but I couldn't admit to him that I'd enjoyed being in his arms, that I'd touched his face and run a finger over his luscious mouth. "It's bad enough that I have to deal with you while I'm awake."

Einar stilled at my words. "Is that so?" he said, his eyes narrowing. I noticed his pupils had returned to normal, but I didn't have time to wonder about the change. "Well in that case, maybe I should have left you at Lady Mossi's mercy instead of flying in to rescue you."

"I was handling that—" I said hotly, though a twinge of guilt pricked me as I remembered that he had, in fact, rescued me—

"Or maybe I should have left you earlier, when your own villagers turned on you. Or when the dire wolves were about to rip you to shreds." The scathing tone in Einar's voice tore at me as he got to his feet, his white teeth flashing in the low light as he bared them in a snarl. "Don't worry Adara, you won't have to *deal* with me any longer. Since you can handle yourself just fine on your own, I'll be going."

He stalked out of the cave, spine rigid, fists balled at his sides. The twinge of guilt became a sharp stab, and my stomach dropped into my shoes as he disappeared into the snowy expanse.

Giant's teeth, what had I been thinking, saying something so awful? Tears of shame flooded my eyes as I realized how petulant I'd been, and I rushed out of the cave after him, wanting to make it right. The horizon was already lightening, heralding the coming dawn, and I could just make out his silhouette.

"Einar!" I shouted, rushing after him, but he was too far ahead, his long-legged stride eating up the ground. Before I could even try to close the distance, wings sprouted from his back, ripping through his already-tattered shirt. My jaw dropped as he took a running start and leaped off the mountainside, then caught an updraft and soared away.

"Einar, wait!" I screamed as he disappeared into the clouds, but the wind snatched my voice away, fettering it to the cold and unfeeling valleys plunging below. My heart sank as the sun crested the horizon, gilding the snowy peaks of the surrounding mountains. But even its tentative warmth could do nothing for the desolate feeling that weighed heavily on my chest.

He'd really, truly left me this time.

"Einar!" I yelled again, stumbling down the mountainside. I called his name again and again, desperately hoping he hadn't flown too far away, that he was still close enough to hear me. We'd gotten into fights before, but we'd always been able to put aside our differences. He would come back, right? He had to.

And why, exactly, does he have to? A doubting voice in my head asked. *There isn't anything in this quest for him, not really. Yes,*

Mother will make him the sleeping draught when you rescue her, but she isn't the only other healer in Ediria. He could find someone else.

"Einar, please!" I shouted again. "I didn't mean what I said! I do need you. I'm sorry I said those things. You did nothing wrong. Please, come back!"

A shadow passed overhead, eclipsing me, and I jerked my head up, heart leaping as I looked for Einar.

But while the creature hovering above me certainly could fly, she looked absolutely nothing like a dragon.

"Oooh, lookie here," she said, flashing sharp rows of teeth at me. "Looks like I've found breakfast for the eyrie this morning."

The winged creature uttered a sharp, bird-like call, and two more of them dove from the cloud cover to hover next to her. My stomach sank as I took them in—they were caught halfway between bird and fae, feathered crests sprouting from the tops of their heads in lieu of hair, their arms blending seamlessly into their wings. Their legs were avian, feathers starting from the tops of their hips and ending in clawed feet with talons. Leather armor covered their torsos, and skulls adorned each of their shoulders. Fanged necklaces rested on their bare necks, and they each carried a different weapon.

These females were no fae. They were harpies, and they weren't joking about having me for breakfast.

19

Einar

"E inar, wait!"

The sound of Adara's pleading voice tore at my heart as I flew away, making my wings slow their beat for a fraction of a second. Every fiber of my being wanted to turn around, to heed that call and race back to her side.

But I knew that was just the mate bond talking, so I gritted my teeth against the urge and forced my wings to beat faster and push me higher into the sky.

Frigid winds whipped around my face, slapping at my cheeks and tugging harshly at my hair. I knew I would be more comfortable if I was in dragon form, but I couldn't risk shifting in broad daylight, so I pushed on, heedless of the cold. Tears slipped down my cheeks, and I told myself it was just from the wind, that it had nothing to do with Adara's harsh words from earlier.

After all, why would I cry over a fae female I didn't even *like*?

That's not true, a voice in my head argued, but I shut it down immediately, refusing to entertain the thought. I *didn't* like Adara.

Yes, she was beautiful, and courageous, and she wielded amazing power, but she was also headstrong, stubborn, and a pain in the ass. She'd run headlong into danger several times without a backup plan or consulting with me, and even though I'd saved her life more than once, she wasn't even remotely grateful.

I swallowed against a sudden lump in my throat, and that's when I realized there was a foreign taste in my mouth. Lavender and sea salt, with just a hint of sweetness. My lips tingled, and my heart sank as I realized it was Adara's taste on my tongue.

She hadn't been lying. I *had* kissed her.

Dammit. I swiped at my mouth, swearing under my breath. I had no recollection of kissing her, and I hated that a part of me wished that I did remember. My inner beast must have been in control at that moment—the raging animal inside me that wanted nothing but to claim her.

It had been stupid of me to let my guard down like that, to fall asleep with her in my arms. If she'd been willing, if she'd given into my primal urges, I would have woken up mated to her. And once a mating bond was sealed, it could not be broken.

Not even by death itself.

As if summoned by my thoughts, the mating bond tugged at my chest, insisting that I return to Adara. I scowled, wanting to ignore it. After all, it was clear that Adara didn't want me. She'd rebuffed my advances twice now. The best thing to do was tell her about the mating bond now that I was sure she despised me, so she could formally reject me.

Doing so would be agonizing, but at least the bond would be severed, and we could go our separate ways.

But first, I needed to find her.

Sighing, I winged my way back toward the cave, intending to end this once and for all. But as I drew closer, I heard the sounds of fighting—screeching, yelling, scuffling. My heart kicked into a gallop, and I angled myself downward, breaking through the cloud cover so I could see what was going on.

My eyes widened at the sight below—Adara, facing off against three harpies. The winged females were dive-bombing her, and Adara flung ice stakes as she dodged them, trying to keep them at bay. Her stakes were missing their mark, flying past the harpies or losing momentum before they could reach their target, but they were at least keeping the harpies back—for now. Her cornflower-blue eyes were wide with fear, and even from here I could see the beads of sweat gathering on her alabaster forehead. Even with her impressive speed, she wouldn't be able to hold out much longer, not on her own. Not when she'd spent so much of her own magic last night.

I didn't have enough power left to shift into my dragon form, so I tucked my wings and dove for the harpy closest to me. Sensing the danger, she twisted midair and flung a throwing knife at me, but I knocked it aside easily with my scale-armored forearm. Turning my body, I slammed into her with the brunt of my shoulder, sending her flying.

"Who is this?" the harpy screeched, drawing the attention of the other two. They halted in their assault on Adara and turned to face me, their eyes narrowing with assessment.

"You are like no creature I have seen," the tallest one remarked. She pulled a short hunting bow from her back, then nocked an arrow from the quiver strapped behind her hips. Her feathers were the color of sea glass, blue stars adorned the foreheads of the skulls adorning her shoulders, and she carried three fangs on the cord around her neck. "Wings like a bat, scales like a lizard, and claws like a harpy."

Adara flung an ice stake at one of the harpies' backs, but a gust of wind intercepted it and it flew wide. Irritated, the harpy whirled and fired an arrow at Adara, who ducked again. A spark of rage burst to life inside me, and I blasted the harpy with a fire-ball, intent on incinerating her.

But before the fireball could even reach her, the wind whisked it away.

"What is going on here?" I roared, frustration getting the better of me. The very winds seemed to be determined to thwart us. "Harpies don't have the power to control the winds!"

"Maybe the winds favor us." Another of the harpies, this one shorter and more curvaceous than her fellow warriors, smirked at us. Her feathers were bright yellow, like a canary's, giving her a cheerful appearance that was completely at odds with the vicious smile on her face. She pulled three throwing knives from the pouch at her hip and clutched them between her knuckles. "Either way, it looks like we'll have meat to last us for weeks between the two of them, wouldn't you say, Eleerie?"

The taller harpy shook her head. "No, Wynna. The queen will want him alive."

"What about the other one?" The third harpy, a purple feath-ered female, demanded. "There's nothing special about *her*."

"I'm right here, you know," Adara called up, her voice heavy with sarcasm. Her expression was full of false bravado, but as our gazes met, I caught a flash of gratitude and relief in her eyes.

She's glad to see me.

Something lightened inside me at that realization, but the moment was interrupted as the leader—Eleerie—turned back to Adara. "Yes, how rude of me to keep you waiting." She bared her shark-like teeth at Adara as she knocked her bow. "Sisters, let's finish them off, shall we?"

But before she could fire the arrow, something in the air shifted. A dark cloud rolled across the early morning sun, casting a shadow across the mountain, and an icy wind whipped through the air, making even the harpies shiver. The sound of dozens of beating wings filled the sky, and I turned toward the noise just in time to see a flock of large, black birds cresting a mountain just three peaks away.

"Skies above," Wynna hissed. "A shadow swarm!"

Dread gripped my throat as the flock winged their way toward us, and a sudden flashback hit me. Of Aolis storming into Hearthfyre with that terrible spear of his, pulsing with the same insidious magic that flowed through these birds' veins. The shadows had caressed him like a jealous lover, weaving into his hair, his armor, his very skin, bleeding from him to snake across the ground like venomous vipers. Even our dragon hide had not been strong enough to protect us from that spear, and one by one, he had corrupted us, turning dragon against dragon until we were tearing each other apart to stay alive.

I'd been forced to slay my own mother that day, and my last remaining sister. It had been kill or be killed, and while I would have laid down my own life for theirs, I couldn't allow them to live the rest of their lives out as mindless monsters, corrupted by the new fae king's will.

"Einar!"

Adara's voice snapped me out of the memory, and I shook my head violently, trying to clear it. This was no time to be caught up in the past. We needed to act now.

"We're going to have to work together to defeat them," I said, summoning more fire to my palms. My arms shook from the effort, and I clenched my jaw against the strain. "If two of you can flank them and drive them toward me, I can incinerate them with one blast."

"That won't be necessary," a cheerful voice called. "I've got this."

The four of us turned toward the sound in time to see a fae child zip down from the clouds. I stared at the sight of him—he was maybe five feet tall, with a thick head of white hair that stood straight up from his head, and storm grey eyes that glinted with mischief. He wore a black vest, loose white pants, and lace-up boots. A pair of brass goggles rested on his forehead, perched just at the beginning of his hairline.

He was also standing on a cloud, which seemed to be fully supporting his weight.

"An air fae," I spat, realization crashing over me. "You're the one who's been intercepting my and Adara's magical attacks!"

"Of course." He looked at me as though I'd grown a second head. "I couldn't let you hurt my friends."

"You're friends with the harpies?" Adara shouted from the ground, an incredulous look on her face. "But they eat fae!"

"Yeah, we've been working on that," the air fae said with a wince. He scratched the back of his head as he looked at the harpies. "I was pushing you guys back, too," he admitted. "I didn't want you to kill them."

"What?" Wynna shrieked, looking outraged.

"We don't have time for this," Eleerie snapped at them both. "The shadow birds are nearly upon us, Leap!"

"Oh! Right." Leap gave Eleerie a sheepish look. "Let me try to thin them out a bit."

He zipped off toward the birds, legs spread wide, lifting his arms to the sky, palms up. The clouds rumbled ominously, drawing together, and a bolt of lightning arced through the air, ripping through the flock. Seven of them dropped from the sky instantly, while the others scattered, their angry caws ricocheting off the mountains.

This boy wasn't just an air fae. He was a lightning rider. One of the rare, famed air fae warriors who could harness the electricity in the sky and use it as a weapon.

The shadow birds reformed into a handful of smaller groups, splitting off in different directions to attack us individually. The same fear I'd felt before tried to grip me once more, but

I pushed it aside and blasted them with a huge gout of flame. The birds shrieked in agony as I incinerated them, and I immediately winged my way toward Adara, intent on helping her next.

But Adara was holding her own, using a fire whip to knock the birds out of the air before they could reach her. I couldn't help but be impressed by the level of control she'd mastered— rather than blasting them with raw energy, since her magic reserves were low, she'd chosen to concentrate her fire magic into a weaponized form instead. Pride swelled in my chest as she valiantly fought the shadow creatures off, sweat dripping down her face, hair whipping in the wind, feet planted like the roots of a strong, stubborn oak.

I'd never seen anything more beautiful in my life.

One of the harpies let out a blood-curdling shriek, and I turned just in time to see one of the birds sink sharp talons into her exposed bicep. Black magic bled from the tips of its claws, spreading across her skin, and my insides froze with horror as I realized she was being corrupted, being turned into a shadow creature herself.

"Nooooooo!" The air fae boy cried, hurtling toward her. He called more lightning down from the sky, channeling it into the tip of his finger and aiming it toward the shadow creatures. The lightning shot through the air like a javelin, striking the birds dead in the sky.

But it also struck the harpy, too.

"Aria!" Eleerie wailed as the infected harpy's back arched, body vibrating as the electricity seared her from the inside out. She sped through the air faster than any arrow bolt, catching her fatally struck comrade before she could fall.

"No," the other harpy, Wynna, choked out. The rest of the birds were dead, the remnants of their bodies littering the otherwise pristine snowy landscape, like streaks of soot on a maiden's gown. She and Eleerie gently brought Aria to the ground, and Leap and I followed somberly behind her.

We might have been enemies, but I knew these harpies' pain all too well.

Adara let her fire whip disappear and came running over as the harpies laid their comrade down. "Is she still breathing?" Adara demanded, skidding to her knees at the harpy's side.

"Yes, but it doesn't matter," Eleerie said in a harsh voice. She pointed a shaking finger at Aria's arm, where the blackness was spreading down to her fingers. "Aria's already infected. We have to kill her now, or she'll end up like...like..." her voice broke.

"Like a shadow creature," Leap said in a small voice. He'd hopped off his cloud and came to stand next to us, his storm grey eyes filled with tears. "This is my fault, Eleerie. I shouldn't have gotten so distracted."

Wynna put her arm around Leap's shoulder, pulling him in close. "It's not your fault. Aria is a capable warrior, just like the rest of us. She fought well."

Sympathy welled inside me as I looked at the harpies and the air fae child. The four of them seemed like a family, like many families I'd witnessed who'd been torn apart by war and strife. Even though they'd tried to capture me and kill Adara, and I would have gladly killed them in self-defense, I didn't want to see one of their own die at the hands of shadow magic.

I glanced at Adara, who was also looking at Leap and the harpies. She seemed to be having an internal debate, her body poised as if she were on the brink of a major decision, and after a minute, she puffed out a sharp sigh.

"Your friend doesn't have to die today. I can save her."

The harpies' heads snapped in Adara's direction as she pulled something out of her boot. My eyes widened at the sight of the golden apple resting in her palm—one of the apples I'd seen in Lady Mossi's arboretum.

Leap's eyes nearly bugged out of his skull. "Is that an Ithir apple?" he asked, his voice echoing with disbelief.

"Yes," Adara said, holding out her free hand impatiently. "Someone, please, give me a knife."

Wynna pulled one of her throwing knives out of her pouch, but hesitated. "How do we know you won't—"

"Try to kill her?" Adara asked sarcastically. "Isn't that what you guys were already planning on doing anyway?"

Wynna's cheeks flushed angrily, but she handed Adara the knife.

"I need one of you to hold her down, and the other to pry her mouth open," Adara instructed the harpies. "Hurry, we don't have much time. You there, keep a look out, make sure nothing else tries to attack." She jabbed a finger at Leap.

Leap nodded and hopped back onto his cloud, which whisked him off to a spot about thirty feet in the air. Close enough to see what was going on while giving him a bird's-eye view of their surroundings. Not wanting to stand by uselessly, I grabbed Aria's legs while Eleerie gripped her shoulders and Wynna pulled her mouth open.

Adara used the knife to slice off a piece of the apple. Immediately, a thick, golden syrup began to drip from the fruit, and Adara held it over Aria's skin while she shoved the first piece of apple into the harpy's mouth. The harpy's hips bucked immediately, but Wynna worked her jaw open and closed as Eleerie held her down, forcing Aria to chew and swallow.

Black steam began to rise from Aria's body, and she twisted and sobbed as Adara force fed her the apple piece by piece. The corruption stained the ground, spreading through the snow like a bottle of spilled ink on parchment. My skin crawled as the stench of shadow magic filled the air, but I held fast to Aria's legs, holding her tight as Adara and Wynna made sure she consumed the entire apple.

When it was done, we lifted her from the tainted patch of snow and carefully set her down in a clean spot, free of bird carcasses and magical corruption.

At first, nothing happened as the last bits of black steam curled away from her skin. But a few seconds later, Aria sucked in a full breath and bolted upright, her yellow eyes flying wide as she clutched her arm.

"Wha—what happened?" she sputtered, looking around. "I—I was in the sky, fighting the shadow creatures and then..."

"You were infected," Eleerie said gently, placing a soothing hand on Aria's shoulder. She pointed at Aria's bicep, which was now pristine, as if the taint had never touched her. "This fae fed you a magic apple, and it cured you. It's a miracle."

"It's not a miracle." Leap hopped down from his cloud, landing lightly in a crouch despite the thirty-foot jump. He stared at Adara in open fascination. "Though it might as well be, considering how difficult it is to get hold of Ithir apples. How did you get one?"

Adara gave him a wry grin. "I stole it from Lady Mossi's arboretum."

Leap's eyes bugged out. "No way! How did you manage it without getting caught?" The boy looked seriously impressed.

I snorted. "She had a distraction," I said, thinking of how I'd smashed through the windows in dragon form and thrown the arboretum into chaos. Was I going to get any credit for *my* contribution?

"So these apples are rare, then?" Aria demanded, glancing between Adara and Leap. "And yet you gave it to me? Why?"

Adara shrugged, looking a little uncomfortable. "My mother is a healer. I've been helping her treat the sick and wounded since I was old enough to learn how to wrap wounds. It just... didn't seem right, leaving you that way. Not when I've already seen what shadow sickness does to a person."

Wynna huffed out an exasperated breath. "Well, we can't eat her now," she said, sounding thoroughly put out. "Not when we owe her a blood debt."

"Technically I'm the only one who owes her a blood debt," Aria said thoughtfully. "The rest of you could still eat her."

"Still sitting *right* here," Adara said, though she sounded more weary than annoyed. Now that the excitement from the battle was wearing off, exhaustion began to settle into my own bones.

"We won't be eating her, but we will take her to the queen all the same." Eleerie arched an eyebrow at Adara before looking at me. "She will be very interested to learn about a fae female who can use fire and ice magic, and her dragon companion."

Adara winced, and I sighed—it was only a matter of time before they figured it out. "A dragon?" Leap squeaked. He stared at me, his expression caught somewhere between terror and delight as he took in my wings, scales, and claws. "I thought there weren't any more of you left!"

"And yet here I am." I sketched a sardonic bow, then turned back to Eleerie. "What if we don't want to come with you?"

Eleerie gave me a wry smile. "You can refuse, but I don't think you're in any condition to resist. Besides, you're dead on your feet, and the eyrie has warm and comfortable beds. The least we can do is feed you and offer you some rest."

Adara and I exchanged a glance before she rose to her feet. "We will take you up on your offer," she said, dusting the snow off her knees with a smile. "After all, few fae have seen the inside of a harpy's eyrie and lived to tell about it. I'd love to be an exception."

20

Adara

"So, how exactly does this cloud thing work?"

Leap rolled his eyes at me as we sailed through the air, following the harpies to their eyrie. Since Einar couldn't shift right now and we were too heavy for the harpies to carry, Leap had offered to give us a ride on his cloud. I'd been skeptical initially, since it only seemed wide enough to hold Leap by himself, but the puffy cloud had drawn a few larger tufts from the other clouds to itself, expanding until it was wide enough to seat all three of us.

"She's not a *cloud thing*," Leap said as we soared past a herd of mountain goats. I stared in amazement as the shaggy-haired animals hung vertically on the cliff-side, grazing from the leafy plants that clung to the rocky soil. "Her name is Cirra, and she's my cloud familiar."

"Cloud familiar?" I glanced down at the puffy cloud below us, noticing for the first time that it was a little different from the other clouds. Not just because it was puffier and dense enough to hold our weight, but because the vapor had a faint gold tinge to it, like something had dipped it in sunshine many, many years ago. "What is that?"

"They're cloud spirits," Einar grumbled from behind us. He sat cross-legged with his arms folded over his broad chest, a sullen look on his handsome face. He was clearly unhappy with the current arrangement, and I suspected that under other circumstances he would have rather died than accept a cloud ride from an air fae. "The air fae's lightning riders use them instead of wings to fly. They have minds of their own and are impossible to destroy, even with fire. I've tried evaporating one and the damned thing just reformed again and caught its rider before I could kill him."

The cloud vibrated angrily at this, and Leap glanced over his shoulder at Einar. "It's probably better if you don't talk about trying to kill cloud spirits while you're riding one," he said. "Cirra has been known to burst into rain when her feelings are hurt." He stroked a hand along the edge of the cloud and crooned, "There, there, Cirra. He's just a crotchety old dragon reliving his glory days. You don't need to pay him any mind."

"I am *not* a crotchety old dragon," Einar growled, and Leap and I both suppressed our snickers.

We crested a mountain ridge, and the eyrie came into view. A stone building that looked like a cluster of towers tucked into the side of a verdant mountain, it was built of rough, moss-covered stone that blended seamlessly into its surroundings. I spotted several harpies perched on the roof ledges and battlements, their hawk-like eyes pinned on us as we approached. They gave us suspicious looks, but said nothing as we followed the three harpies escorting us through one of the many large, arched windows set at intervals along the length of the towers.

We landed inside what looked like the entrance to a communal hall, with a huge, roaring hearth, furs on the floors, and rough-hewn wooden tables scattered throughout. Several harpies were sitting at the tables drinking from tankards, and they looked over at us in unison as we walked in.

"Eleerie," one of them said, getting to her taloned feet. Her pitch-black feathers were a sharp contrast against her bluish-white skin, and the skulls on her shoulders had black daggers painted on their cheekbones. A scowl pinched her angular features as she approached us. "Why are you bringing more fae pets into the eyrie? Don't we have enough extra mouths to feed?"

She shot Leap a dirty look, who stuck his tongue out at her in retaliation. "Hey," he protested. "I earn my keep around here."

"These are honored guests, Rachis," Eleerie said sternly. "These two helped us fight off a shadow creature attack, and they saved Aria's life."

Rachis tossed her feathered head, looking thoroughly unimpressed. "Even so, we are not a fae sanctuary. The fae are our enemy, and have been since the beginning of our history. This one should be dinner, and this one..." she licked her lips as she looked Einar up and down, a lustful gaze lighting her yellow eyes. "Well, I've already raised my hatchlings, but I have a daughter who would love to take him." She glanced over her shoulder at a harpy sitting at the table with pearl-grey feathers, who was staring at Einar with a ravenous look on her face.

A surge of jealousy reared up inside me, and I found myself stepping in front of Einar before I could stop myself. "You can't have him."

Einar choked.

"And you think a scrawny hatchling like yourself can stop me?" Rachis smirked at me, folding her arms across her chest. She was broad in the shoulders and chest, and towered over me by at least a foot. I think she might have even been taller than Einar. A hefty sword hung from her hip, and I had no doubt she could cleave me in two with it.

"I..." I hesitated. What did I even care anyway, if Einar

wanted to have sex with a harpy? He certainly wasn't mine, and I didn't want him, either.

"I'm flattered by the offer," Einar said smoothly, saving me from having to finish the sentence. He'd shifted out of his half-dragon form, wings and claws tucked away so that he looked like a fae once more, minus the pointed ears. He gave Rachis a flirtatious wink that made the jealousy monster in my chest snap her vicious teeth, and I scowled, annoyed at my internal reaction. "But if I remember correctly, harpies kill their mates when they finish with them, and I, unfortunately, would like live."

"Oh, I don't know," Rachis purred, her lips curving into a lascivious smile. "You look like you might have enough stamina to live through at least one mating season."

My mouth dropped open as my mother's tales about the harpies came rushing back. "I remember why the air fae hate you so much. You raid their villages once a year and steal their young males, then force them to mate with you over and over until they die from exhaustion!" The harpies secreted a special pheromone that drove fae males wild, forcing them to copulate repeatedly until their hearts gave out. I remembered how horrified I'd been when my mother had told me about it.

Rachis shrugged. "It takes a lot of seed to fertilize harpy eggs," she said. "And the males do enjoy it, despite the terror of their impending death." A regretful look crossed her face as she turned her head and stroked the cheek of the skull perched on her left shoulder. "I do miss this one though, sometimes. His cock had the most amazing shape, hit just the right—"

"Eww, gross." Leap interrupted, his face screwed up in an expression of distaste. "Can you not talk about screwing my fellow air fae to death while I'm standing right here?"

"Careful, hatchling," Rachis sneered. "The only reason we haven't done the same to you is because the queen has a soft spot for you."

"And because he hasn't entered manhood yet," Aria pointed out.

"*And* because we do not harm *hatchlings*," Eleerie reminded them sharply, glaring at both Aria and Rachis.

"Wait...those are the skulls of *your dead mates*?" My gut curdled as I spun around to stare at the three harpies, looking at the skulls mounted on their shoulders in an entirely new light. *"All of them?"*

"Of course." Aria patted the skull on her right shoulder fondly, which sported a crown of tiny roses painted around the base of its scalp. "We honor the sacrifices of our mates by wearing them proudly into battle."

"That's...barbaric." I said.

I glanced at Einar to see his reaction, whose expression was surprisingly thoughtful. "It's terrible, kidnapping males against their wills and forcing them to sacrifice their lives for the sake of your offspring," he said eventually. "But I respect the way you choose to pay tribute to them."

I shook my head. "Unbelievable." I looked over Einar's shoulder at Leap, who was sitting cross-legged on his cloud. "How can you live with them, when they prey on your own kind?"

Leap looked away, his shoulders hunching in. "They took me in during a rough time."

The unexpected flash of vulnerability in his eyes made me feel a little guilty for being so judgmental. Leap was just a child —the fact that he was out here, living with the harpies, meant that some tragedy had separated him from his parents.

"I'm sorry," I said. "I didn't mean to judge you."

"I've had enough of this conversation," Eleerie declared. She raised her voice so that the rest of the harpies in the room could hear her. "The queen needs to meet these fae, so they are not to be harmed during their stay here." She turned to Wynna. "Show them where they can wash up, and fetch some food for them while I find the queen. They must be starving."

Despite our less than welcoming reception from the harpies, Einar and I were treated well. The harpies showed us to a communal bathing chamber so we could wash, gave freshly roasted meat and root vegetables to eat, and even tankards of ale to wash it down.

After we bathed and ate, Wynna escorted us to the queen's throne room at the top of the tower. It was a large, circular room with round glass windows set at six-foot intervals in the walls, allowing sunlight to stream in from all angles. Pairs of preserved harpy wings in a variety of colors were mounted between the windows, and a throne cobbled together from what I strongly suspected were either fae or harpy bones sat near the back of the room. Eleerie and Aria were already waiting in front of the throne, their winged arms folded behind their backs, heads raised, shoulders back and proud, and several guards were stationed along the walls, ready to defend their queen at a moment's notice.

Perched on the bone throne was a muscular harpy with white-tipped golden feathers. Her leather armor was gold and white to match, and even the skulls adorning her shoulders were painted with golden starbursts. A crown of jagged opals sat on her feathered head, and resting in a holder to the right of her throne was a long alabaster staff, with a pure white stone set into the top. A faint spark glittered in the center, and I narrowed my eyes as I recognized that familiar glint—a primal stone.

"You are in the presence of Makani Windrider, Queen of the Harpies," Wynna informed us. She stopped in front of the throne and bowed. "My queen, this is Adara and Einar, the tres-passers we found in our territory."

I sensed Einar stiffen next to me, and my stomach tensed. She was introducing us as intruders? This wasn't good.

"Trespassers?" The queen's golden eyebrows darted up her prominent forehead. She has narrow, almond-shaped eyes, a hooked, beak-like nose, and a wide mouth with full lips. Hints of crow's feet at the corners of her eyes were the only indicator of her age—and considering how brutal harpy lives were, any sign of age was a testament to her strength and wiliness. "There must be something unusual about them if you brought them to me alive."

"They healed Aria from an infected shadow creature wound," Eleerie said, drawing the harpy queen's attention to her. "But also...the male is a dragon, and the female can use fire magic."

"A dragon and a fire fae?" the queen's eyes widened, and she studied us more closely. A dubious look came over her face as she took in my features. "You look like a water fae. Everyone knows water fae can't use fire magic."

I shrugged. "This one can." I snapped my fingers, and a flame sprang to life along the edge of my forefinger. A gasp flew from the queen's mouth, and steel rang through the room as the guards drew their weapons.

"Relax, relax!" I held up my hands, the fire snuffing out immediately. "I was just giving a demonstration. I mean you no harm."

The harpy queen lifted a finger, and the guards reluctantly sheathed their swords. "Very interesting," she said, a calculating gleam in her eyes. "You can use both water and fire magic?"

"Yes." I wasn't sure if I should mention that I couldn't use either just a few days ago, so I said nothing else.

"And a living, breathing dragon." The harpy queen licked

her lips as she turned her gaze to Einar, her yellow gaze turning predatory with lust. "I've always thought it was a shame that harpies and dragons never mated. We both lay eggs, so I'm certain we would be very compatible. And you look like you would make powerful warrior babies," she purred, leaning forward a little. The position put her generous cleavage on full display, and I clamped down as a fresh wave of jealousy surged inside me.

Einar laughed, a deep, rich sound that spoke of dark nights and wicked promises. "You aren't the first one to make that offer since I've arrived," he said, and I wanted to claw his face off right then and there. "But as I mentioned to the others, I'd like to watch my children grow up, if I should ever be lucky enough to have any."

A hint of sadness tinged his voice, and the green monster eased away. I hadn't considered the fact that Einar had once had hopes and dreams of a future, a family, a life, before King Aolis had destroyed his people. Had he had a lover before they'd all been killed? Someone he'd planned to marry and settle down with?

The harpy queen shrugged. "Better to pass on your seed with a strong female than not pass it on at all," she said. "Unless you were planning on planting it in a different womb?" She glanced between us, an obvious question in her eyes.

My face flamed at the implication, and Einar's entire body went rigid. "I would never," he hissed, and the words were a slap to the face after the steamy kiss we'd shared. "Not after what the fae did to my people."

"Hmm." The harpy queen didn't seem convinced. She leaned back on her throne and tapped a chin as she considered us. "Still, the fact that the two of you are even together is an oddity in and of itself. Why are you traveling with a fae if you hate them so much?"

"We have an arrangement," I said stiffly, thankful for the change in subject. "He's helping me rescue my mother from the king."

"The king has taken your mother? Why?"

I gave the harpy queen an extremely abridged version of what happened, telling her about the appearance of my fire magic, General Slaugh's attempted capture, and the recent battle with Lady Mossi. By the time I was done, the queen was staring at me as though I were a fascinating puzzle.

"This entire tale smacks of fate and destiny," she said, drumming her fingers against the arm of her chair. "You said this General Slaugh spoke of a prophecy, didn't you?"

"Yes," I said hesitantly, not sure where she was going with this.

"It's too much of a coincidence that the same night your fire magic awakened, you also awakened the last living dragon in Ediria," the harpy queen said, glancing at Einar again. "You're rushing in headlong to rescue your mother, but you have no knowledge of what the enemy truly wants from you, or *why*. Unless you find out more information about this prophecy, I doubt you will succeed."

"Find out about the prophecy?" I bit my lip, thinking of my mother again. How was she holding up in the king's dungeons? And if they were torturing her, how long did she have? "But I don't know where I'd look, or who to ask."

"Oh, that's easy." Leap piped up for the first time. He'd been perched on one of the window ledges this entire time, swinging his short legs as he listened to us talk. "You need to go see the Oracle in Wynth."

"The Oracle?" Einar scoffed. "You mean that charlatan who sits cloistered in that temple of hers, shut off from the rest of the world? Yes, I'm sure she gives wonderful advice."

Leap rolled his eyes. "I can assure you that Quye isn't as sheltered as everyone wants to believe," he said. "And that she's the real deal. She used to love—" his eyes widened, and he abruptly snapped his mouth shut.

I raised my eyebrows at him. "Sounds like you know her pretty well, Leap."

He shrugged. "I know a lot of people," he mumbled, turning his head away. The sullen look on his face made it apparent that his past was a touchy subject, and I made a mental note to lay off...for now. After all, I needed him to tell us more.

"Okay fine." I held my hands up, indicating that I was dropping the subject. "So we need to go to Wynth? How do we get there?"

"It'll take you a week to get there on foot," Eleerie remarked. "Unless your dragon flies, but I don't recommend that. We aren't the only harpy clan living in these mountains, and then there are the air fae themselves to contend with. They are annoyingly diligent about patrolling the skies and preparing for air attacks. You'll be seen, even at night."

I shook my head. "We don't have time for that. My mother could be dead by then."

"I'll take you," Leap said.

Everyone in the room went still, except for the harpy queen as she whipped her head around to face Leap. "You will do no such thing," she snapped. "Not while you are under my protection."

"How do we even know we can trust you?" Einar asked, his tone rife with suspicion. He crossed his arms over his chest and glared down at Leap as though he could intimidate the boy into revealing all his secrets. "Not only are you an air fae, but you're consorting with a race that kills and eats your own kind. You don't exactly strike me as trustworthy."

But Leap smiled, unbothered by Einar's enmity. "The harpies might be brutal and bloodthirsty, but they took me in when I had no one." His expression softened as he looked over at the harpy queen, a tender note of gratitude in his voice. "Queen Makani found me alone in the mountains, starving, too weak to use my magic or hunt for food. She took me in and nursed me back to health, then gave me a place to stay. The only thing she asked in return is that I use my lighting magic to protect the eyrie, and I'm happy to do it." A regretful look crossed his face. "But I have to help them, Queen Makani. I'm the only one who can, and I know what it's like to lose your parents. If I can help Adara get hers back, I'd like to."

Tears burned at the corners of my eyes, and even Einar seemed moved by Leap's declaration. "Oh very well," the queen huffed, sounding both annoyed and resigned. "But you must return to the eyrie when you've finished."

"I will," Leap said. He hopped down from the ledge and propped his hands on his hips, a wide grin spreading across his face as he looked between me and Einar. "A dragon, a lightning rider, and a fire fae sneaking into Wynth to visit the Oracle. This is going to be fun!"

21

Adara

After some heartfelt goodbyes for Leap—the most emotional coming from Rachis, much to our surprise—we zoomed off to Wynth on top of Leap's cloud, Cirra. The harpies had equipped us with hooded fur cloaks to wear during our travels as thanks for rescuing Aria, and while the cold didn't bother me, I was grateful for a buffer to protect my skin from the harsh winds.

It was a long flight, and Leap had a short attention span, so he quickly roped an unwilling Einar into playing a variety of games with him—rock-paper-scissors, the yes-no game, and something called Would You Rather.

I wished I could get into the spirit of things with them, but my mind was too heavily weighed down with thoughts, and I let it wander as I absently took in the verdant, rocky landscapes we passed over.

I knew the harpy queen was right, that finding out more about what the king wanted was the smart thing to do. It would be nice if I could charge into Kaipei Castle, whisk my mother out of the dungeons, and run off into the sunset with her, but that was unrealistic. The king would search every corner of the kingdom to find me. I needed to know what he wanted from me, and if there was a way to leverage that to my advantage.

"Would you rather have no elbows or no knees?" Leap asked Einar.

Einar wrinkled his nose. "What kind of dumb question is that?"

Leap grinned. "Just answer the question, grandpa."

"Quit calling me that!"

Einar swatted at Leap, then yelped as the section of cloud beneath him began to evaporate, causing him to sink nearly all the way through. "I'm sorry!" he shouted, and Leap fell back, cackling madly. The cloud solidified beneath Einar again, who scowled. "I would rather have my elbows. I would tell you why, except I fear Cirra will try to murder me again."

Leap snickered. "Oh, stop being dramatic. I've seen your wings, you can fly."

"That isn't the only thing I can do," Einar said, a threatening tone in his voice.

"Leap," I said, interrupting thembefore Einar could upset Cirra again, "aren't the Gaoth Aire cities heavily fortified to keep out shadow creature attacks? How are we going to get in without being seen by the guards? I'm wanted by the king, so word is going to get out about me eventually. I can't assume they haven't been told to look out for me already."

"Yeah, I figured that," Leap said with a nod. "The city of Wynth is fortified with a domed electrical field that zaps anything that tries to fly in or out without going through the official entrances and exits. But I can use my own lighting magic to open up a path for us."

"Are you sure?" Einar asked, sounding dubious. "It's one thing to use your lightning to strike down a few shadow creatures, but using it to manipulate an electrical field large enough to protect an entire city is quite a feat. And you *are* still a youngling."

Leap rolled his eyes. "I'm thirteen, only three years away from my majority. Which means I can run circles around you, grandpa." He waggled his tongue at Einar, who growled. "There's a weak spot in the force field I've used before. We just need to wait until it's dark to get in."

"The fact that you even know about this weak spot means that you've snuck in and out of the city before," I pointed out. "Why would you need to do that?"

"That's for me to know, and you to wonder about."

I raised an eyebrow at him. "You're pretty secretive."

"I'm a male of mystery. Makes me more attractive to the ladies." He winked at me, and Einar and I both snorted in unison. We caught each other's eyes, and I thought I saw the corners of his mouth twitched before I looked away.

I wished things weren't so confusing between us. That he didn't make me feel both safe and vulnerable, that he didn't light me up with his touch, that we'd never shared that kiss. My core pulsed as my body remembered the taste of him, the way he'd sunk his hands into my hair and held me tight, and a wash of heat stung my cheeks.

He didn't even remember the damn kiss, and here I was, getting all hot and bothered over it!

Huffing out a breath, I curled up in my spot on the cloud, turned my back to Einar, and put all thoughts of males and kisses out of my mind. I hadn't slept much last night, and I needed to keep up my strength for the challenges ahead.

"Adara, wake up."

I stirred groggily at the sound of Einar's voice. His warm breath ghosted across the shell of my pointed ear, and every fiber in my body came alive as his hand curled around my shoulder to shake me gently. I could feel the leashed strength in his palm, and the warmth of his hand seeped through my clothes and skin and all the way into my bones, making me want to curl into him.

Instead, I pushed his hand off me and sat up, rubbing at my eyes. "I'm up," I said, glancing around. Shades of red, gold, and lavender streaked across the sky, and I had to squint against the harsh glare of the dying sun. "Where are we?"

"Shhhh," Leap said, his voice barely above a whisper. "The winds carry here."

He pointed, and I followed the direction of his hand. Just ahead, built at the very top of the mountain in front of us, was a gleaming walled city that seemed to be carved entirely from a bluish-white stone, no doubt quarried from the mountain itself. Battlements and rounded towers surrounded the city, and pristine stone buildings staggered at intervals along the steep mountain peak. Perched at the very top, right in the center of the city, was a pagoda-style temple. A narrow, spindle-like tower jutted from the top, with four smaller spires clustered at the base, and below that, four terraces that spilled out from a cube-like platform. Bluish-white light burned from the tips of the spires and the tower, like stars that had been speared from the sky and brought down to live amongst mortals.

Similar lights topped each of the turrets placed at intervals along the city walls, and I wondered at their purpose.

"Where is the electrical field?" I asked Leap, leaning in so that I could pitch my voice as low as possible. It was hard to believe the guards patrolling the walls could hear us when we were still a good half-mile away, but I wasn't about to doubt Leap. "Does it have something to do with those lights?"

He nodded. "They generate the field's power," he said. "Each one is a powered by a primal stone. You don't see the field, but as you approach, you can hear it humming, and if something hits it..." he sucked in a breath. "Well, actually, you're about to see what happens when something hits it."

He pointed, and I sucked in a breath of my own as I caught sight of a flock of shadow creatures approaching from the west. They looked like large bats, with thin, leathery wings, and the screeches they emitted were so piercing that even at this distance, I had to clap my hands over my ears at the hair-raising sound.

I braced myself, ready for a fight, but the shadow creatures dove for the city. The moment they came within range, the force field flared to life, a dome of bluish-white energy that crackled and zig-zagged across the sky, frying every single creature that tried to penetrate it. The bodies were incinerated; the ashes whisked away by the brisk winds. I caught a whiff and a full body shudder wracked me as I smelled burnt hair, flesh, and the faint stench of black magic.

"I *really* hope you're right about that weak spot," Einar muttered darkly.

Leap huffed. "Oh ye of little faith," he said, but I couldn't exactly blame Einar. I *really* did not want to be fried to a crisp.

Studying the city again, I noticed that there was no road leading to the main gate. Instead, there was a platform built just outside the gates, that looked like it was meant for landings.

"How do you get in normally?" I asked Leap. "You know, if you're not a criminal?"

"You have to ride the wind path," Leap said. He pointed to what I could only assume was an air current, invisible to the naked eye. "Which only air fae can do. If you're not an air fae, you have to be accompanied by one to even make it to the city gates."

"Or you have to be a dragon," Einar murmured.

"Yeah, but I don't think we let you guys waltz through the door," Leap said dryly.

"Definitely not." Einar snorted. "We had to take out the towers anytime we attacked one of your cities, and you hardly have any natural resources of your own, which made it more trouble than it was worth most of the time. Domhain and Lochanlee were far more lucrative to plunder."

"I don't suppose your people ever considered *not* resorting to piracy?" I asked sardonically.

Einar arched an eyebrow. "We might have, if your people didn't refuse to trade with us. No, instead they sent air and earth fae into Hearthfyre's mines so they could *steal* the primal stones and precious metals they used to barter with the fire fae for. We simply returned the favor."

I opened my mouth, then shut it again. Einar was right. We could have traded with the dragons for what we needed. Of course, that would have required ignoring the fact that they'd genocided an entire portion of our race, but bringing that up would only start another fight, and we needed to stay focused.

We waited in silence until the sun set, and complete darkness descended upon the mountainside. The primal stones powering the electrical field blazed even brighter now that they were no longer competing with the sun, and I could now see the faint, glowing dome that protected the city.

"All right," Leap said. "Let's do this."

He gave Cirra a pat, and she slowly glided forward, moving at the speed of a regular cloud so as not to draw attention. The three of us lay flat on her back as she puttered along, holding our breaths as we drew closer to the city. When we were about fifty yards away, I began to sense the low hum of the electrical field, and could feel the energy buzzing along my skin. The hairs on my arms raised in warning, and every muscle in my body tensed as they sensed the inherent danger.

We were nearly within range when I caught a flutter of movement to my left. "Something's flying toward us," I hissed in Leap's ear. My heart pounded as it winged toward us—another shadow creature?

Leap glanced toward the flying intruder, and I saw the whites of his eyes grow wide in the darkness. "Faster, Cirra," he urged. "We can't risk using lightning or fire this close. The guards will spot us."

I glanced toward the city to see a guard posted at the nearest tower, just twenty yards off from where Leap intended to land. He was looking into the distance, but if he glanced to his left, he would see us.

But the shadow creature was closing in, fast. It was an enormous bird, with a wingspan of at least twelve feet, and large talons that looked wicked sharp. It was more than capable of knocking us off the cloud, and we couldn't afford another aerial battle. Not now.

Thinking fast, I conjured two ice stakes, drawing from some of Cirra's moisture to make them. The cloud vibrated in protest, but I ignored her and flung the stakes in the flying monster's direction. The creature let out a piercing shriek as the ice stakes plunged into its wings, loud enough to reverberate off the nearby mountains, and it tumbled from the sky.

The guards on the wall immediately snapped to attention, swinging their bows toward the sound and away from us. Cursing under his breath, Leap jumped off the cloud and caught an air current that carried him into the force field. He extended his arms and pulled the energy toward him, then made a ripping motion with his hands as if he were tearing a piece of cloth in half.

The energy field parted, and we darted through the opening on Cirra's back.

"Come on," Leap hissed, already running along the narrow path between the wall and the force field. We followed him to a section of wall that looked exactly the same as the others, and watched in bemusement as he rapped three times on a brick that looked slightly smaller than the others. The brick Leap tapped on receded into the wall, and several dozen others followed suit, creating an opening that revealed a dark staircase leading into what I could only imagine was an underground tunnel.

"What the name of the Radiants is this?" Einar asked, sounding as bewildered as I felt.

"A secret passage, duh." Leap stepped through the entrance without looking back. "Come on, grandpa, before someone catches us."

Einar and I exchanged dubious glances, but we followed Leap, seeing no other options. The bricks closed up behind us as we descended, leaving us in total darkness, and I snapped my fingers, lighting another flame at my fingertip so I could see where we were going.

The scent of damp water and sewage reached my nose before we reached the bottom of the stairs, and I wrinkled my nose. "I knew it," I said as we stepped through a door at the bottom and into a sewer. Slime squelched beneath my feet, and my skin crawled as I heard rats scurrying around. A river of filthy water sluggishly meandered through the tunnel, and I was thankful it was dark so I didn't have to see what might be floating in it. "This place is disgusting."

"Which is why no one ever comes down here," Leap said with far too much cheer considering the circumstances. He led us up the path and to a ladder a few yards away, and I followed, trying to ignore the sound of small bones crunching beneath my feet. "Up this way."

He scampered up the ladder, nimble as a monkey, and Einar and I did the same. There was a low scraping sound as Leap pushed aside what I assumed was a sewer hole cover, and the next thing I knew, we were climbing out of the sewer and into a dim alleyway.

"Oi!" a voice said, and I nearly jumped out of my skin. Sitting on top of a dumpster was another air fae child, a female dressed in loose canvas pants, sturdy boots, and a long, double-breasted coat with many pockets. Her bright purple hair was pulled back into corkscrew pigtails, and while she had an innocent-looking face with chubby, pink cheeks and a wide mouth meant for smiling, her silver eyes were narrowed on Leap.

"Elra," Leap said in a resigned voice. "I should have known you'd be here."

"Well of course I'm here. It's my turn to watch the alleyway." She hopped off the dumpster and came to stand in front of us, arms crossed over her flat chest. She was taller than Leap by at least six inches, and looked about a year older than him. "What are you doing back in Wynth? I thought you'd left for good."

Leap swept a hand toward me and Einar standing behind him. "I'm playing tour guide for a few of my friends," he said with a smirk. "They wanted to see the underbelly of Wynth up close and personal."

Elra snorted. "And you're not going to pick their pockets?" She eyed us up and down as if we were marks. "Not that they look like they've got much on them."

"Gee, thanks," I said.

Einar huffed. "Never thought I'd be standing in a stinking alley listening to a street urchin insult me, but here we are."

Elra ignored us both, turning her attention back to Leap. "Storm isn't going to be happy you're here, you know."

Leap narrowed his eyes. "I don't care. Storm doesn't own the city, and I'm not here to interfere with his business." He raised a hand, and a chill wind whipped through the alleyway, tugging at Elra's pigtails. "Are you going to stand in my way, Elra, or are you going to let us pass?"

Elra sighed. "No. But I wish the two of you would make up. I don't like this rift."

Leap shrugged, but his expression softened a little. "We can't always change which way the winds blow," he said softly.

"I know." She stepped aside, then clapped him on the shoulder. "Be careful."

We filed past Elra and out of the alley, into a wide street lined with shops and restaurants. The street was filled with working class fae coming and going, and we fell into step easily with the crowds. Lamp posts lined the sidewalks, and there were festive-looking garlands strung between them made of colorful paper cranes.

"What was that all about?" Einar asked as we followed Leap, keeping our hoods up to hide our features. "Are you involved in some kind of street gang?"

"Nope," Leap said brightly as he led the way. But there was a bounce in his step that seemed a little too deliberate, and the stiff set of his shoulders told a different story. "Just a little argument between old friends. Shouldn't affect us at all."

"Uh huh." I didn't believe him one bit. "Is that why that girl mentioned a fae that doesn't want you in the city?"

Leap shrugged. "It's not my fault that not everyone loves my winning personality." He winked at me. "Relax, fire girl. I'm not about to get you involved in a gang war."

"Fine." I huffed out a breath. "So how do we see the Oracle? Do we make an appointment?"

"Nah," Leap said, stopping by a cart filled with fresh steamed buns. He snatched up three of them, then flipped the vendor a coin from his belt pouch. "The only people who can make an appointment with the Oracle are royals or fae wealthy enough to make a substantial donation to the temple. Everyone else has to wait until their coming of age ritual. Fae from all over the Gaoth Aire travel to Wynth to present their sons and daughters to the Oracle for the one and only time when she'll read their future."

"Where did you get that money pouch?" Einar asked suspiciously as Leap handed each of us a steamed bun. "You weren't carrying that when we entered the city."

"Or was I?" Leap winked at him, then bit into the bun. "You should try these. They're really good."

Einar scowled, then took a bite. A look of rapture slowly spread across his face, his grumpy countenance vanishing. "This is delicious," he groaned.

I took a bite, and had to bite back a groan myself as the taste of spiced meat and savory dough melted into my tongue. "This may be the best thing I've ever eaten," I said.

Leap grinned around a mouthful of bun. "I know. I used to eat these almost every day. I missed them." A wistful look crossed his face briefly before he shoved the rest of the treat into his mouth.

I took another bite, chewing thoughtfully. "I've never had a coming of age ritual," I said to Leap. "Any chance we could fake one for me so I can get a reading?"

Leap shook his head. "It's only done for the Gaoth Aire people, and you are very obviously *not* an air fae." He playfully tugged the end of my lavender blue braid.

I frowned. "I could change my hair color, try to blend in."

"Even if you did that, parents have to reserve readings at least a year in advance." Leap glanced toward the temple, its spires glittering in the distance. "Sneaking into the temple is our best hope."

"That's a terrible plan," Einar protested. "The Oracle will call her guards once she sees us. We can't force her to tell us the prophecy."

"Oh, we won't have to force her," Leap said with a chuckle. "Quye loves visitors, and she rewards courage and guile. If we can make it past the guards and the temple defenses, she'll tell us what we want to know. But first, we need to get some sleep."

We stopped outside a quaint-looking inn, and Leap led us inside and to the counter, where he ordered a room with two beds. "Don't worry," he said, tossing a wink over his shoulder at me. "You don't need to share a mattress with gramps over there. You can sleep with me instead."

I choked back a laugh, and Einar growled. "How about you two share a bed, and I'll take one for myself." The idea of sharing a bed with Einar after what happened, even with Leap in the room, was almost more than I could bear, but I wouldn't put it past a thirteen-year-old boy to get a little handsy in his sleep, either.

Leap waggled his eyebrows. "What, you don't trust me with your maidenly virtue?"

"Not even remotely." I stuck my tongue out at him, and he snickered.

The innkeeper gave Leap a key, and we made our way up the stairs and to a room down the hall. "The Twelve Winds festival is the day after tomorrow night," he explained in a low voice as he unlocked the door and stepped inside. "That's what all those crane garlands were about, and it's actually perfect timing for us as everyone will be caught up in the festivities—"

He came to an abrupt halt, and Einar and I nearly crashed into him. I opened my mouth to ask what the big deal was, then froze as I caught sight of another fae child sitting on the sill of the open window across the room. He had silver hair that was shorn on the sides and grew long on top, a wicked smile, and he wore a fancy blue and gold tunic and pants that looked two sizes too big for him

He was also holding a loaded crossbow, the bolt aimed straight at Leap's chest.

"Well, well," the boy said, a smirk curling the corners of his mouth. "If it isn't the prodigal son, returned to repent for his sins. Why don't you have a seat, Leap, and tell me what the fuck you're doing in my city after what you've done?"

22

Einar

The fae child smirked as he held the crossbow on Leap. His gaze was rock steady, his aim true, and I knew without a shadow of a doubt that if we didn't do exactly as he asked, the boy would shoot Leap.

Still, I expected Leap to do something. Use his wind magic to knock the crossbow out of the other air fae's grasp, or shoot him with a bolt of lightning. Instead, he raised both of his hands slowly, palms up, a clear gesture of surrender.

"It's all right," he said to me and Adara, though he didn't take his eyes off the intruder. "Storm won't hurt us."

Storm snorted. "Don't bet on it." His eyes narrowed, lips thinning with obvious loathing. "I nearly killed you before you fled the city, remember?"

"But you didn't," Leap shot back. "Because Skye wouldn't have wanted that."

"Oh, that is *it*." Adara stomped her foot, and both boys turned to look at her in surprise. "We've given you a lot of leeway with your secrets, Leap, but now they're getting in the way of our quest, and I'm tired of being kept in the dark. *What* is going on here?"

"Oh, he hasn't told you?" Storm chuckled darkly. "Leap here used to be a member of my gang, the Gliders. We run rackets here in Wynth and take on the odd—"

"—it isn't *your* gang," Leap interrupted crossly. "We're a democracy—"

"—that you aren't a part of anymore," Storm finished smoothly, and Leap flinched. "Anyway, as I was saying, we sometimes take on the odd thieving job, depending on who the mark is and how much the payoff is. We'd never steal from the less fortunate, but as far as the rich are concerned..." he trailed off with a wink. "Well, you get the idea. Anyway, Leap here signed us up for a job that he didn't do his due diligence on, and we got double-crossed. Buyer's remorse, I suppose," he added with a shrug, but his lip curled as he looked back at Leap. "One of our group, Skye, was killed while we were trying to escape. We had to leave her body behind, and the guards strung her up outside the gates of the city hall, as they do with all thieves and criminals who get caught. I had to sneak up there at night to cut her down so we could burn her and scatter her ashes on the north wind."

Storm's eyes glittered with outright hatred, and I caught the sheen of tears before he blinked them away. I couldn't see Leap's face, but judging by his slumped shoulders, I could see that the guilt of Skye's death weighed heavily on him.

"Even the best laid plans go awry," I found myself saying. I was a little surprised that I was defending the twerp, but I'd lost plenty of friends in battle and I'd tortured myself for years second guessing whether there was something we could have done differently, if there was anything I could have done to save them. If anyone here understood how Leap felt, it was me. "If your gang is truly a democracy, then you are all equally responsible for the outcome of the heist. Leap can't be blamed alone."

Storm switched his aim from Leap to me in the blink of an eye. "I don't remember asking you for your opinion, outsider." He raked me up and down with a scathing look. "Who even are you, anyway? You don't look like a—"

I moved in a blur, closing the distance between us before Storm could even finish his sentence. Yanking the crossbow from his hands, I tossed it out of the open window. The room grew dead silent, the only sound coming from the crossbow as it clattered down the side of the roof and landed in the alley below.

"Anything else you'd like to say about me, *youngling*?" I asked, looming over him threateningly. The boy looked up at me with wide eyes, but even as he cowered, I could see him reaching for the knife at his belt. "I wouldn't do that if I were you, unless you'd like me to toss that out the window, too."

"Einar." Adara grabbed my arm, but even her touch wouldn't dissuade me. This little brat might have pulled the crossbow on her instead of me, and that was a threat I couldn't abide. "He's just a child."

"He's clearly not *just* a child, since he makes his living from stealing and racketeering," I said, refusing to take my eyes off him. "Give me one good reason I shouldn't toss him out the window, too."

"Well, for one, I'll just glide right back in, so that won't work," Storm said sarcastically. "And for another, if you try to harm me, I've ordered my team to go to the authorities and give them your description." He smirked up at me, and I sensed Adara and Leap stiffen behind me. "The fact that Leap snuck you in means that you're trying to keep a low profile. I don't know why, but I'm sure it wouldn't be too hard to find out."

"You little shit," Adara growled, and I couldn't have agreed with the sentiment more.

"All right, all right!" Leap shouted, his voice pitched high in exasperation. "Einar, can you please just...take a step back? And Storm, can you tell us what in the devil winds you want from us? You didn't come here to kill me, that much I know."

Storm rolled his eyes. "Even if I had, I wouldn't be able to now." Huffing, he plopped onto one of the beds and assumed a lounging position, then fixed Leap with a gimlet stare. Even mostly disarmed, he still acted like he owned the place. "I want you to steal Onche's Fan during the Twelve Winds Festival."

Leap scowled. "Onche's Fan? No one knows where that artifact is kept. I don't even think it's been seen in the last five hundred years!"

"Oh it has been," Storm said with a toothy grin. "Madame Gale, one of Wynth's biggest financiers, has had it in her grubby hands for the past few years, and she'll have it with her at the air temple festival gala. And wouldn't you know it, but I have several invitations." He pulled three cream envelopes with silver wax seals from the inside of his breast pocket and dangled it in front of our eyes. "You'll need appropriate costumes, of course, but these should get you in."

"Onche's Fan is a priceless artifact," Leap said, his eyes narrowed with suspicion. "Why are you trusting me, of all people, to steal it for you, after everything that's happened?"

Storm curled his lip, that look of loathing back on his face again. "Because even with disguises it's going to be hard for any of us to pass as adults," he said. "You have two with you, so the three of you can pose as a family, and since it's a masked ball, you won't run into any issues being recognized."

Adara, Leap, and I exchanged veiled looks. On the one hand, I loathed the idea of being forced to do this shrimp's dirty work, but on the other hand, these invitations provided us an easy in to the temple. We could kill two fae with one fireball, so to speak.

"All right," Leap agreed. "We'll do it."

"Excellent." Storm sat up, rubbing his hands together gleefully. He gave Leap the invitations, along with a scribbled note with instructions. "Be there no later than seven o'clock," he warned. "If you fail to check in at the appropriate time, I won't just rat your friends out. I'll send word to your uncle, too."

Leap's face turned white. "You wouldn't."

"It's the least you deserve," Storm sneered, hopping off the bed. He moseyed over to the window, then turned back to wink at me and Adara. "Nice meeting you both. Welcome to Wynth."

And with that, he jumped out the window and disappeared into the night.

"All right," Adara said once we'd shut the window behind Storm and inspected the room for any other unpleasant surprises that might be lurking. Her expression was like a thundercloud as she rounded on Leap, and she looked as if she would strike him down with a lightning bolt if she had the power. "It's time for you to tell us the whole story."

She sat down on the edge of the bed furthest from the window and stared pointedly at Leap, who started fidgeting. Hands behind his back, feet shifting from side to side, he looked like a child who'd been called to the front of the class.

"I guess you want me to start from the beginning," he said, not quite meeting Adara's eyes.

"Normally, yes," she said. "But first, I want to know what this fan is, and why Storm wants it."

"It's a royal heirloom that was commissioned by Ythor, one of

House Reatha's earliest rulers," Leap said. "He felt that the other members of his house were a little too free-thinking, so he had the witchlings enchant him a fan that would allow him to influence people. All you have to do is give it a little wave, and the person you're talking to becomes *very* suggestible." A wistful look came over Leap's eyes. "It would actually be a really handy tool to have as a thief."

"Or a politician," Einar said dryly. "I imagine that this Madame Gale moves in elevated circles, and that this fan helped her get there."

I shook my head. "How do you even know all this?" I asked Leap.

Leap smirked. "It's my business to know these things."

"Leap..." Adara said in a warning tone. "We said no more secrets."

Leap huffed. "It *is* my business to know these things," he protested. "I was part of a gang that traded in stolen goods and information."

"Fine," Adara said, waving her hand impatiently. "But what's this grudge between you and Storm about? Who is Skye?"

Leap's face fell at the mention of Skye's name. "She was an air fae orphan, like the rest of us," he said sadly. "Storm and I both had a crush on Skye. We used to compete for her attention all the time, even though outside of missions she wouldn't give us the time of day. She was the safecracker of our group—she could pick any lock, open any door, no matter how complex the combination. But during that last job..." he heaved out a sigh. "We were stealing a priceless necklace from a merchant's vault, but the guard I blackmailed to look the other way betrayed us, and the guards caught us on the roof on our way out. The rest of us managed to escape, but Skye took an arrow straight through the eye. I didn't even have time to catch her before she tumbled off the roof."

"Oh Leap," Adara said as Leap's face crumpled. My own heart twisted with sympathy as the boy raked a hand through his wild, silver-white hair, his face stark with anguish. "I'm so sorry."

"Why did the guard double-cross you?" I asked. "Was your blackmail threat not strong enough?"

"I guess not," Leap scrubbed a hand over his face, a haunted look in his eyes. "I told the guard that I'd tell his wife about the midnight trysts he was having with the merchant's missus. Seems he decided his job was more important, or maybe he just knew the merchant's wife loved that necklace and didn't want to see her upset. So I made good on that promise, and sent a note to the merchant too, for good measure."

"So the guard ended up losing his job after all," Adara said. "I guess that's some consolation."

Leap sneered. "Yeah, *that* seems like a fair trade for Skye's life."

I sighed. "So Storm blames you for Skye's death, and this is his way of making you atone."

"Seems that way." Leap hopped off the bed. "Much as I'd love to continue this discussion, we're going to have to put it on hold. It's not safe to stay here now that this location is compromised."

"What? But we already paid," Adara protested as Leap moved to the door. "Where are we supposed to go? If Storm can break into a hotel room on the second story simply by flying in through a window, then he can break in anywhere."

"Yep," Leap said, opening the door and stepping out into the hallway. "That's why we have to go somewhere he doesn't expect."

I scowled as we followed Leap out of the inn. "I don't like the sound of this," I said as we walked through the crowded streets. I had to lengthen my stride to keep up with Leap as he led us out of the lower city, higher up the mountain into an upper middle-class neighborhood, the houses here are five times the size of even the largest in my village, many of them multi-storied and with well-kept front gardens. The child was half my height, but he zipped through the streets as if on winged feet, and I suspected he was using his air magic to propel himself faster than his shorter legs could ordinarily carry him.

"What are we doing here, Leap?" Adara asked as we stopped outside a two-story house sporting multiple turrets and a hipped roofline. Statues of winged horses decorated the well-kept front yard, and a few mountain roses still bloomed from the bushes, adding color to the house's bluish-grey countenance. "This doesn't look like a place we can lie low. There's a family inside!"

"I know," Leap grumbled, a scowl on his face. "This is one of several houses in this neighborhood that are used as second homes by families who come to Wynth on holiday. They must have come for the Twelve Winds Festival."

"That was your idea?" Adara asked, aghast. "To break into someone's home?"

"It's actually not a bad one," I said, keeping my voice pitched low so the inhabitants wouldn't overhear. "Are there any others in the area we might try?" I was keen to get out of the open so we could discuss our plan for getting into the temple in private.

"You can't seriously be siding with him, Einar," Adara hissed, narrowing her eyes on me. Even shadowed by her hood, the angry glint in her cornflower blue eyes would have been enough to make a lesser male take a step back. "Can you imagine if we were caught?"

"We would have to be careful," I acknowledged, "but staying in an empty house means we won't have to worry about eaves-droppers or potential enemies."

"Exactly," Leap beamed. "Glad to see you agree with me, gramps."

I glowered at Leap, but before I could come up with a retort, I caught a flicker of movement from the corner of my eye. We all turned our heads to see someone move a window curtain aside from inside the house. A flicker of recognition lit inside me as a familiar face peered out—long auburn hair, nut brown skin, forest green eyes, and a sassy mouth.

"Mavlyn?" Adara shrieked, and I winced as her voice ricocheted through the quiet neighborhood like a banshee wail. *"Is that you?"*

23

Adara

The sight of Mavlyn's face in the window was a balm to my soul after so many nights in hostile territory. Ignoring Leap's shouts, I vaulted over the fence and raced up the path to the porch.

The front door swung open as my foot hit the first step, and I faltered as a tall, imposing-looking air fae stepped out onto the porch. "Who are you?" she demanded, her almond-shaped eyes glinting with suspicion. She had long, ivory hair that was bound into a sleek bun at the top of her head, leaving the elegant bones of her pale face unframed. A long, cerulean gown made of layers of wispy fabric floated around her willowy form, and though she was slight of frame, I could sense the immense power humming in the air around her.

There was no doubt about it. She was a Greater Fae.

Realizing my hood was still up, I hastily lowered it. "Sorry," I said, my cheeks growing pink with embarrassment. This fae was clearly the epitome of poise and grace, while I looked like a disheveled vagrant. I sensed Einar and Leap come up to stand beside me, and I gestured to them. "My name is Adara, and these are my friends, Einar and Leap."

I motioned impatiently for them to remove their hoods, and they reluctantly did so. The air fae looked like she was about to question us further, but before she could, Mavlyn burst through the doorway behind her.

"Adara!" my best friend cried, her face beaming with joy. She raced past the air fae and caught me up in a fierce hug. A torrent of relief gushed through me, and I hugged her back hard, taking in her familiar scent of pine, maple, and rich, loamy earth. "I was hoping we would find you here!"

"You came looking for me?" I pulled back to look at Mavlyn, and then the fae behind her. "How did you know I would be here?"

"Mother and I went to Talamh to find you, and we managed to get the story out of Lady Mossi. Or at least a version of it." Mavlyn raked a hand through her hair with a sigh. "She claims that you and Einar attacked her and then fled into the Gaoth Aire mountains, but I had a feeling your side of the story was different." She glanced over her shoulder at the air fae woman with a grin. "Mother couldn't come with me to find you, but Mrs. Aeolan was happy to oblige. She's a friend of my mother's, and a professor at Talamh University."

"Oh." I turned my attention to Mavlyn's aunt, feeling incredibly awkward. "Pleased to meet you, Mrs. Aeolan."

"Likewise," the air fae said. Her expression had softened fractionally, and something almost like a smile played at the corners of her thin mouth. "Why don't you all come inside and get out of the cold. You can tell us how you came to Wynth, and why you were casing my house from the street."

I stammered, caught off guard by Mrs. Aeolan's disconcertingly astute observation, but Leap stepped forward with a charming grin, saving me from having to come up with a response. "Pleased to meet you, Mrs. Aeolan," he said, bowing with a flourish. "You've got such a lovely house we couldn't help but stop for a few minutes to admire it. I promise we meant no offense."

Mrs. Aeolan arched an ivory eyebrow, clearly unmoved by Leap's gallantry. "I am not a fan of silver tongues," she said, stepping aside and making a shooing motion toward the door. "Now get inside. You're letting in the cold."

"Don't have to tell me twice." Leap skipped past her cheerfully, and I slunk in after him, my gut squirming with guilt. Mavlyn grabbed my hand and led me through the hall and into a parlor room, Einar and Mrs. Aeolan following close behind. There was already a tea service waiting on the low table, as well as a plate piled with sandwiches. My stomach rumbled pitifully, and I remembered that aside from that steamed bun Leap gave me, I hadn't eaten anything since the harpies had fed us breakfast.

Had it really been less than a day ago that we'd been eating and parlaying with the harpies in their stronghold? My head spun as I tried to recollect everything that had happened since the tryouts. It seemed impossible that so many life-altering events could have occurred over the last few days, and yet...

"Mrs. Aeolan and I were having tea when she heard you talking outside," Mavlyn said as she ushered us into the seats. There was a fire roaring cheerfully in the hearth, and I heard Einar sigh in pleasure as he sat down in the chair nearest to the flames. He probably wasn't used to the cold—I'd never been to Hearthfyre, but I imagined it didn't get very cold with all the volcanoes and deserts and magma lakes out there. "She's very good at catching conversations on the wind, especially the ones you don't want her to overhear."

"Yes, very interesting conversation, that was." Mrs. Aeolan's gaze cut to Leap and Einar, her silver-blue eyes sharpening.

"The two of you seemed to be discussing the merits of squatting in my house."

Einar had the sense to blush, but Leap merely shrugged. "We would have taken good care of it, Mrs. Aeolan," he said, unrepentant. "Done the dishes, swept the floors, dusted the counters. Maybe even shined that mirror over there for you," he said, pointing to the gilt-framed silver rectangle hanging on the wall behind her. "Looks like it could use a good polish."

Mrs. Aeolan huffed. "I doubt cleaning was what you were planning on doing with the mirror," she said, but her lips twitched a little. She turned her attention to me, and her gaze softened. "But I do understand your desire to lie low. General Slaugh is relentless, and a formidable foe. It will not be easy for you to evade him."

"Clearly not, since it was so easy for you to track us here," Einar said with a glower. "How did you know we would be in Wynth?"

"We didn't," Mrs. Aeolan said with a delicate shrug. "But since you fled into the Gaoth Aire mountains, it only stands to reason you would have to pass through Wynth to get to Kaipei, where Adara's mother is being held." She gave Einar an assessing look, and Einar stared back, his expression revealing nothing. "I'd like to know what interest you and this youngling have in helping Adara with her quest," she said after a moment.

"I'm madly in love with her," Einar said without missing a beat, and I nearly choked. "Who could possibly resist a maiden in distress?"

"Hmm." Mrs. Aeolan didn't seem convinced. "Remove your cloak and tunic."

Einar stiffened, and this time I really *did* choke. "Oh boy," Leap chortled. "Looks like professor wants a show."

"Mrs. Aeolan?" Mavlyn asked, her voice thick with confusion. "What are you doing?"

"Confirming my suspicions." Mrs. Aeolan's gaze didn't waver from Einar's face, and my heart dropped a little as I remembered that the eye-color changing potion I'd given him had finally worn off. No fae had golden eyes like that, and Mrs. Aeolan was definitely old enough to have been alive during the war. "Take them off. Now."

"And if I don't?" Einar asked, not moving a single muscle. His voice was soft, but the deadly intent behind each word sent shivers up my spine. Power hummed in the air between the dragon and the air fae, an invisible current that made gooseflesh ripple across my arms, and I sensed that one wrong word or move would ignite it.

"Then you and I are going to have a problem," Mrs. Aeolan said, just as softly.

The two of them stared at each other in silence for a long, fraught moment. Then, slowly, Einar got to his feet. He unclasped his cloak and draped it gently over the back of his chair, then grasped the edge of his tunic and dragged it upward with painstaking slowness.

The room suddenly seemed too hot, too small, my pulse beating faster in my throat as Einar removed his tunic. Inch by torturous inch, the fabric crept up his abdomen, revealing smooth tanned skin and rippling muscles that glowed like honey in the firelight. I'd seen him without his shirt before, but after everything that had passed between us, after feeling that hard body against mine and tasting that wicked, sensuous mouth, this somehow felt intimate, forbidden.

I was beyond grateful that everyone else in the room was also staring at Einar—I could feel my cheeks flaming hot, nearly as hot as the fire spreading through my loins. Gritting my teeth, I clenched my legs together, but regretted it immediately when my core throbbed in response.

What was wrong with me? Why was I having such an

intense reaction to a little bit of skin? It wasn't as if I'd never seen a shirtless male before—on the contrary I'd seen plenty back in Fenwood, out working in the fields or sparring during training sessions. Even Dune had never inspired such an intense wave of lust.

"Ahh, and there it is," Mrs. Aeolan as Einar's tattoos were slowly revealed. "The Umnar. A dragon warrior's holy tattoos, etched into them with their own blood when he or she reaches adolescence."

Einar's gaze sharpened on her as he finished pulling his tunic over his head. He stood tall and proud, the swirling flames covering the left side of his chest and arm on full display. I'd never appreciated how beautiful the intricate tattoos were, and they seemed to move in the flickering firelight, almost as if the flames were real.

"Not many fae know of the Umnar," he said. "They think these are mere ink tattoos."

Mrs. Aeolan smiled. "I'm a scholar, dragon," she said. "And as my people have faced yours in the air many times over the millennia, I have always found dragons fascinating. Your kind lay eggs, but you hatch out of them in your bipedal forms rather than your reptilian ones. The tattoos awaken your dragon forms, and you etch them into your skin yourselves, guided purely by instinct. No two dragon warriors have the same design, and they aren't always in the same place, either."

I stared at the tattoos, even more fascinated now. "You had to ink those yourself?" I whispered, not quite realizing I was speaking aloud. "How long did that take?"

"Three days," Einar said, his gaze clouded with memory as he stared off into the middle distance. Absently, he traced over the whorls of flame with his fingertip, and my own fingers twitched with the urge to do the same. Thankfully there were others in the room, or I might have followed through on that impulse. "I was given a special herb to smoke that put me in a trance of sorts, and sent to the top of Mount Furian to meditate. The design came to me in a vision, and I worked on it feverishly. The pain was a spiritual experience that defies description. With each puncture of the needle, I could feel the beast inside me unfurling, awakening, until…"

He trailed off, and then cleared his throat, as if realizing he'd said too much. "Are you satisfied, then?" he asked Mrs. Aeolan brusquely.

"Not even *close*," Mavlyn said, the words exploding from her mouth and shattering the tension in her room. She leapt to her feet, mouth gaping, finger pointing straight at Einar's chest as she rounded on me. "Giant's teeth, Adara, when were you going to tell me your new friend was a *dragon?*"

I winced as Mavlyn's voice rose to a fever pitch. "There wasn't exactly time, the last time we met," I pointed out. "We only had a few minutes to talk before Dune and his father tried to capture me."

"True, but it didn't look like you were planning to tell us this time around," Mavlyn pointed out. She swung around to stare at Einar again. "By the Radiants," she swore under her breath. "How did you find him, and why hasn't he eaten you yet?"

Einar screwed up his face in distaste. "I would never defile my body by consuming a fae."

Mavlyn waggled her eyebrows. "I can think of much better ways to defile your body," she purred.

Einar's eyebrows winged up, and I had to lock down every single muscle in my body as a fresh wave of jealousy hit me. The urge to grab Mavlyn by the hair and drag her as far away from Einar as possible seized me, and I shook my head *hard*, trying to clear the vicious thought away. Mavlyn was my *friend*—I'd never do that, and besides, there was no reason for me to be jealous at all. I didn't want Einar. He was a dragon, for Radiant's sake.

Keep telling yourself that, a voice in my head muttered sarcastically. I ignored it.

"Ugh. First the harpies, and now you," Leap said, his voice filled with disgust. "Can you put your tunic back on, Einar, before we all end up swimming in drool?"

"Wait a minute. Harpies?" Mavlyn asked. "You were flirting with harpies?"

Einar shrugged as he pulled his tunic back over his head. "What can I say? I'm popular with females of all races, it seems."

"I think you'd better tell us the rest of this story, before your dragon friend's head explodes from his swelling ego," Mrs. Aeolan said primly. There was not even the slightest hint of a blush in her pale cheeks—her interest in Einar's tattoos had been purely professional, it seemed.

"So...you're not going to report Einar to the authorities?" I asked cautiously.

"Radiants, no," Mrs. Aeolan huffed. "That would bring the wrong kind of attention our way. But it seems you've gotten yourself into quite the debacle, teaming up with a dragon of all creatures and going on the run. Mavlyn and I won't be able to help you if you don't tell us what happened."

"All right. But I'm going to need something a little stronger than tea."

Mrs. Aeolan went to a small side cabinet and fetched a bottle of violet liquor. She poured me three fingers from a crystal glass, and one for Einar as well. "None for you," she said sternly to Leap, holding the bottle out of his reach. "Just because you're a delinquent doesn't mean I'm going to allow you to behave as one while you're under my roof."

"Squalls," Leap muttered, kicking at the carpet with his boot.

"And there will be no swearing, either," she added.

He scowled, but kept his mouth shut this time.

I took a fortifying sip of the liquor, which burned its way

down my throat and pooled in my stomach. The warmth eased some of the tension in my limbs, allowing me to steady myself and get my thoughts in order. Over the next hour, I told Mrs. Aeolan and Mavlyn everything, with Einar and Leap chiming in at pertinent moments to fill in their portions of the adventure.

"Fascinating," Mrs. Aeolan said. Her silver-blue eyes were on Leap now. "So you've managed to get these two into even more trouble, under the guise of helping them."

"There is no guise," Leap said indignantly, sitting up straight from his perch on the couch. "I'm helping them out of the good-ness of my heart! Well, and because they saved Aria," he added. "But anyway, I definitely wasn't counting on Storm roping me into a heist. I'm being forced to do this against my will. I'm not even going to see any profit from it!"

Mrs. Aeolan shook her head. "Normally I wouldn't condone thievery, but Madame Gale is a despicable person, and the fact that she's been using Onche's Fan to manipulate things to her advantage really cannot be borne. And aside from that, it is imperative that you see the Oracle, Adara." She turned to look at me, her expression grave. "We Greater Fae have long been aware that King Aolis has been searching for a child of ice and fire, but we've never known why. It is important that you discover the truth about your fate, and whatever role you must play in the future of our kingdom." She sighed, smoothing the skirts in her lap. "If we had time, I would simply make an appointment to see Quye, but she is booked out months in advance."

Leap huffed. "That's cause she only sees one person a week," he said. "They say its cause they don't want her to overwork her inner eye, but she's really just lazy."

"Hush your mouth, child," Mrs. Aeolan said. "It's disre-spectful to speak of the Oracle in such a familiar manner, and it gains us nothing, in any case. I have heard that the Oracle is a capricious sort, and if you can gain access to her during the festival, she might grant you an audience. It is certainly worth a try."

"Will the Oracle be at the ball the temple is hosting?" I asked.

"She will make an appearance to make her predictions for the year," Mrs. Aeolan confirmed. "Invitations are coveted, and very limited, so I suppose it is lucky your hoodlum friend here has a few in his possession. I am issued a single invitation every year as a courtesy to my family, which I can give to Mavlyn if she wishes to attend."

"Of course I want to come," Mavlyn exclaimed. "The Twelve Winds festival is famous! And I want to be there as backup in case you need my help," she added to me. "It's not going to be an easy feat to steal the fan *and* coerce an audience with the Oracle."

"Indeed it won't be." Mrs. Aeolan said. She rose from her chair and went to a side table, where she fetched a leather-bound book, quill, and ink. Perching a pair of silver-rimmed spectacles on her nose, she resumed her seat and crossed her legs, book open and quill ready to go. "Now let's get to work. We have forty-eight hours to come up with a plan and get you four costumes, and I won't have you showing up to the festival looking anything less than your absolute best."

24

Einar

"Hold still," Mrs. Aeolan ordered. "If you keep fidgeting, I'm going to stick you with one of these pins."

"You've already done that twice," I groused as I stood atop a crate barely sturdy enough to hold my weight. I was wearing an outrageous pair of golden pantaloons and a matching red and gold vest over a puffy-sleeved silk shirt. Apparently this outfit had been standard air court fashion nearly a millennium ago—just old enough to be considered a historical costume now—and had remained remarkably well-preserved in Mrs. Aeolan's attic ever since the family had retired it from daily wear.

"My point exactly." Mrs. Aeolan removed a pin from the clutch she held pressed between her lips—how she managed to speak while holding them there, I would never know—and slid it through the hem by my left ankle. "The masquerade ball is tomorrow night, and you don't want to show up looking like a porcupine attacked you. Stop moving, and let me finish here so I can hem these."

I gritted my teeth as she plucked another pin from her

mouth. Out of the corner of my eye, I could see Adara and Mavlyn at a nearby worktable they'd set up in an attic, working diligently at sewing and decorating the masks we would wear. Leap was nowhere to be found—he was out and about, gathering supplies and information for our venture tomorrow night.

"I am not used to being in such proximity to an air fae," I said tersely. "At least, not one who wasn't trying to maim my wings or ground me in some other way so I could be killed."

"And I've never been so close to a dragon who wasn't trying to burn me into a crisp," Mrs. Aeolan said matter-of-factly. "I fought in the dragon-fae wars, same as every able-bodied fae back in those days. I've shed dragon blood, and watched dragons tear my fellow air fae apart."

A thick silence descended upon the room, and I could feel Adara and Mavlyn's eyes on us as they watched the exchange. Memories of being ambushed in the air by lightning riders, darting through the air they called wind and lightning to their fingertips, clouded my mind. I could smell the ozone in the air, feel the rage and fear as I watched them strike at the other dragons in my unit. Our iron hide was impervious to fae magic, but the thin membranes of our wings were a weak spot the air fae had exploited ruthlessly. The cloud familiars they rode were fast and wily, able to avoid our flames almost before we even shot them from our throats, and if more than three riders converged on any one dragon, it was usually a death sentence.

The only way to survive an ambush was to close ranks and keep them from isolating us. But even then, they would always catch at least one of us. I'd lost count of how many dragons I'd seen brought down by an air fae, wings mangled, forced to land on the ground for waiting earth fae soldiers to finish the job.

"I suppose you take great pride in having gotten your pound of dragon flesh back in the day," I said woodenly as Mrs. Aeolan continued to fuss around my legs.

The air fae noble paused. "No," she said, her voice grave as she looked up at me. "I always thought it a great travesty, that our two races were trapped into such a vicious cycle. You dragons are a magnificent race, and I hated that we were forced to kill so many of you."

My gaze snapped to hers, and I was both surprised and incensed to see sadness welling in the depths of her silvery eyes. "Forced?" I echoed, my voice vibrating with anger. "You could have put down your weapons any time."

"We tried," Mrs. Aeolan said curtly. "We offered our princess to you in exchange for peace."

"And we offered our prince, and instead you *killed* him." Beyond furious, I ripped my leg from Mrs. Aeolan's grasp and jumped off the makeshift stool. "You may sound like a dragon sympathizer, but you view us as curiosities, exotic beasts, and in the end you still didn't hesitate to kill us."

Mrs. Aeolan looked taken aback by my outburst. "Do you really hold it against me for not speaking up?" she asked. "If I had been alive when the wars had first started, I might have championed for peace, but after three millennia of war crimes committed on both sides, nothing I could have done or said would have stopped the fighting. Your people were taking more and more of our territory, stealing resources, killing any fae who crossed your path!"

"We were just trying to survive," I snarled. Survive in a hostile land we'd been trapped in for centuries, through no fault or choice of our own. The fae have never once tried to understand our position. "Princess Olette was the only fae who *ever* spoke up in defense of my people, and if she hadn't been mated to one of us, I doubted even that would have happened."

"Yes, and look what she had to show for it in the end," Mrs. Aeolan said harshly. "Death and ruin and the end of her family line!"

I spat on the ground at Mrs. Aeolan's feet, then turned on my heel and stormed out of the attic. Anger clouded my vision as I took the stairs two steps at a time, then burst through the rear entrance and into the back garden. Chest heaving, I sucked in gulps of cold mountain air, trying to get hold of my emotions. A firestorm churned in my gut, begging to be released, for me to spew fire and ash all over this peaceful plot of land, to incinerate the lovely mountain roses and reddish-gold paintbrush plants that added touches of color to the otherwise dormant garden. I paced in front of the small fountain in the center, listening to the soothing burble as I ignored the stone benches waiting patiently nearby.

What had I been thinking, coming to city filled with air fae?

"Einar." Adara's voice cut through the fog of anger, like a fresh rainfall clearing away a haze of ash. I turned to see her walking up the path, gravel crunching beneath her shoes as her hips swayed gently. She wore a simple white cotton dress, tight in the bust and waist, flowing from the hips to the ankles, her hair plaited in its usual fishtail braid. She looked pure as a fresh snowfall, and the beast inside me, already agitated, rumbled with carnal hunger. It wanted to defile that virginal sweetness, to stain it with our scent and seed so that there would be no doubt in anyone's mind that she belonged to us. To *me*.

"Leave me alone," I snarled, turning my back to her. I was in no mood to fight my inner beast. It was taking everything I had not to shift into dragon form and fly as fast and as far away from here as I could.

Adara sighed, and I heard her step falter for just a second before she continued. I thought she might try to touch me, but instead she sat down on the edge of the fountain, just a little off to my right.

"You *have* been left alone," she said, matter-of-factly. "For over twenty years."

She held my gaze, her cornflower blue eyes steady even as I bared my teeth at her. She showed no fear, no pity, no anger or frustration. Just looked at me, taking me in as I was, waiting for me to say something.

The beast inside me grumbled a little, then settled down. My shoulders slumped as its sharp claws retracted from inside my chest, and my next breath came softer, easier.

"You don't know what it was like, knowing I was the last dragon left in Ediria," I said, my voice as soft as the breeze gently playing with a few loose strands of Adara's hair. I wanted to reach back and smooth them from her face, but instead I sat down next to her on the lip of the fountain, gripping the edges of the stone basin. Water lapped at my fingertips, the icy liquid bringing a rush of clarity to my brain. "I'd just lost my family, my best friend, my people, my homeland filled with the scent of death and ash shadow magic. There was nowhere I could go that was safe, nowhere I could live where I wouldn't be surrounded by people whose hands were stained with dragon blood. Being put to sleep was the only way to escape the pain."

"Who did it?" she asked. "Who put the sleeping spell on you?"

I fiddled with the cuff on my wrist as I pondered whether to answer that question, allowing the deep red stone to catch and reflect the light. Did I tell Adara about the Radiant who had opened a portal to a new realm for my people, who had used my blood and life force to seal it off so none could follow? Who had put me into the enchanted slumber afterward as a kindness, the one thing he could do to ease my pain since taking my own life was not an option?

"I can't tell you that," I finally said.

Hurt flashed in Adara's eyes, but she nodded. "You don't trust me," she said in a resigned voice.

"No." My throat tightened, a lump of longing and sadness swelling, threatening to cut off my voice. "But I wish I could."

Adara turned away, her gaze fastening onto a pair of hummingbirds fluttering around a feeder hanging from a nearby tree. Their wings moved faster than the eye could follow, filling the air with a pleasant buzzing sound as they sipped from the well of nectar, their green and orange plumage adding a splash of color to the bluish-green mountain landscape. I wondered if the two of them were mates, if they had a nest somewhere waiting to be filled with tiny eggs in the coming springtime, and my heart ached a little at the thought.

"There was an old fae who lived in my village," she said after a minute. "He, like many others, fought in the war, but unlike the other elder warriors who had retired to live out their days, the ghosts of his comrades haunted him. We often found him at the pub, drowning his memories in the bottom of a tankard. Mother used to make him a special draught that would numb the pain, make his days a little more bearable. She tried to get him to open up about the past, but he refused to talk about it, and the memories festered inside him until one night, he drank an entire bottle of the draught, then laid down to sleep and never woke up again."

She turned to look up at me, and my breath caught in my throat at the soft, almost tender look in her eyes. "I can't pretend to understand your pain," she said quietly. "But I have seen where the road you're on ends, and I don't want that for you, Einar. You're going to have to let somebody in someday. Everyone needs someone to talk to."

I opened my mouth, then shut it, unsure of what to say. There was no one I could talk to, no dragon elders or fellow warriors I could feel safe to share my pain with. No fae would sympathize, except perhaps for Adara, and I couldn't pour my heart out to her. We were already growing far too close, too intimate. Even now she tested the barriers erected around my heart, that open, honest gaze beseeching me to let her in, her lavender and sea salt scent enticing me to pull her into my arms and inhale until my heart settled and my inner beast purred with contentment.

But she was *fae*. And as much as my inner dragon wanted her, I couldn't allow it. If Daryan and Olette's fate had taught me anything, it was that a union between a dragon and a fae was impossible. Even if we tried to create a future, it would only be a matter of time before someone targeted us and tore us apart. That was the natural order of things.

Dragon and fae were destined to be enemies. Never lovers, or friends.

"I appreciate the advice, but it doesn't matter," I said curtly. "When we find your mother, she'll put me back to sleep."

Adara snorted. "Right. I forgot about that. You'll just go back to your enchanted oblivion. Problem solved."

I shrugged. "It's worked well enough for the last twenty years."

Adara huffed out a breath and popped to her feet, planting her hands on her hips. "You—" she started, but whatever tirade she was about to embark on was interrupted as the back door flew open with a bang.

"Oi!" Leap yelled, waving at us. His goggles were askew atop his nest of white hair, and there were smudges of dirt on his face. "Stop necking, lovebirds, and come inside. It's time to go over the plan for tomorrow night!"

25

Adara

"I look ridiculous," Einar grumbled as we rode in Mrs. Aeolan's family carriage. He sat on the bench across from me next to Leap, looking very uncomfortable in his court finery. I had to admit he had a point--the pantaloons bloomed around his thighs like a short, puffy skirt, and the puffy sleeves of his silk shirt didn't make it any better. The only saving grace was the vest, which fit him like a glove and accentuated his broad chest and shoulders. It was an odd combination of masculine and effeminate, something a simpering courtier of old would wear, not a dragon warrior.

Which was exactly why I thought it was perfect.

"Oh relax," Mavlyn said, waving a hand at him. She was loosely dressed like a peacock, with long peacock feathers placed strategically along her skirt and bodice, and a lone feather perched on the corner of her mask. "At least you don't look like a bird."

"You *chose* to look like a bird," Einar pointed out. "I saw the look of glee on your face when you pulled that peacock feather fan out of that box yesterday."

I swallowed a sigh as the two of them bickered and glanced down at my lap, running a hand over the fabric of my own costume. The shimmering sea blue gown I'd found in the attic had reminded me of the old tales I'd heard of sirens—undersea creatures that looked like fae from the torso up, but fish from the waist down, and whose unearthly beautiful voices had lured many a male to their deaths. The dress was sleeveless and strapless, form-fitting from the top of the heart-shaped bodice down to mid-thigh before flaring out in a short train that looked remarkably like a siren's tail. Mavlyn had embellished parts of the skirt with large, glittering sequins to make them look like clusters of scales, and she'd added fins to the sides of my mask to complete the look. Mrs. Aeolan had loosely piled my hair on top of my head and secured it with pearl-topped pins, leaving a few tendrils to hang down and frame my face.

I'd never worn anything so fine in my life, and even though I knew there was no prince waiting at the ball to sweep me off my feet, I felt like a princess nonetheless.

"Don't whine so much, gramps," Leap said, pulling me away from my thoughts. He wore a black and white court jester costume, his white hair stuffed beneath a ridiculous hat with multiple bells that jangled with each bump and jostle of the carriage. "You're only going to have to wear that thing for an hour or two. Once I get the fan, we're out of there."

"If you keep on calling me gramps, I'm not going to help you steal anything," Einar said. He reached out and flicked Leap on the nose. "After all, it's not like we'll need you once we're inside the temple."

"Oww!" Leap rubbed the tip of his nose, scowling. "You better not mean that, fire breather."

"Of course he doesn't," I said in a soothing voice. "You've been invaluable in helping us so far, Leap. We wouldn't betray you like that."

I shot Einar a warning look, who rolled his eyes. "I've done many questionable things in my life, but I'm no traitor," he said with a huff, leaning back in his seat. "I won't abandon you, Leap."

I peeked out the carriage window to see that we were rounding a narrow bend in the mountain just below the temple. Anxiety crawled along my skin as I looked over the edge of the road—there was a sheer drop just below, and with night having fallen already, I had no idea how far a drop it was.

"We'd definitely die if the carriage tipped over right now," Mavlyn declared, reading my thoughts perfectly.

Leap rolled his eyes. "No we wouldn't," he said, jabbing at his chest. "Air fae, remember?"

"Are you really powerful enough to summon a wind current strong enough to catch a carriage?" Mavlyn asked dubiously.

"Not yet," Leap admitted, "but I can definitely use the wind to slow our descent so that we're not smashed into a million pieces."

I frowned. Leap was already very talented for such a young fae, and the fact that he was a lightning rider meant he was a Greater Fae. His parents must have been important people, likely celebrated lightning rider warriors themselves. How did such a child end up orphaned in a big city like this, running with criminals on the streets?

The carriage slowed, and my heart started beating faster as I realized we were arriving. "Speaking of the wind," Leap said as we came to a halt, "it's time to head into the vortex."

Our driver opened the door, and Leap hopped out, followed by Einar. I got to my feet and braced my hand against the door frame, intending to climb out myself. But a strong, warm hand clasped my free hand, and before I could quite comprehend what was happening, Einar was helping me down the steps.

"That's awfully gallant of you," I said as my slippers alighted on the gravel road. I looked up into his masked face, trying to catch a glimpse of his golden eyes. He looked more civilized than I'd ever seen him, freshly bathed and shaved, his shoulder-length chestnut hair pulled back into a neat tail at the nape of his neck. A rakish hat, perched on his head, completed the look while also drawing attention away from his lack of pointed ears, and Mrs. Aeolan had decided it was okay to leave his eyes as-is, since dyeing hair and eyes wasn't unusual at an event like this anyway. The costume, as outlandish as it was, still managed to flatter him, the vest accentuating his broad shoulders and chest, the tight hose showcasing his powerful calf muscles. The puffy sleeves and pantaloons I could have done without, but he was so insufferably handsome already it was nice to see him taken down a peg.

"Well, you are supposed to be my wife for the evening," Einar said. Was it just me, or did I imagine the low, smoky note in his voice? His golden eyes gleamed like a dire wolf scenting a predator as he trailed them down my body, and my skin warmed in response. He was still holding my hand, I realized, his fingers curled almost possessively around mine. Something about it felt...right.

Wordlessly, Einar tucked my arm around his, and we followed Leap to a large, circular stone platform a few yards away, tucked right at the base of a sheer cliff. The temple loomed over us, its spires glittering like diamond tips, golden light spilling from the hundreds of open doors and windows to bathe us in a warm, welcoming glow. A swirling vortex of wind spun in the center of the platform, whirling far too quickly for my comfort.

"We're supposed to ride that to the top?" Mavlyn hissed at Leap. "We'll be flung into the abyss!"

"Shhhh," Leap said. "Watch." He jerked his head at the air fae couple who had alighted from the carriage ahead of us, who were walking toward the vortex now. I watched as the fae on the left raised her hand and made a counterclockwise motion with her index finger, the opposite direction in which the vortex was spinning. Immediately, the tunnel of air slowed, and the two of them stepped into it, hands clasped.

"Amazing," I murmured as the couple slowly twirled to the top, alighting safely in a rustle of pink and silver skirts. They were wearing matching dresses, and I wondered if they were sisters or lovers. It was hard to tell since they were wearing masks.

"See? Perfectly safe...as long as you have an air fae to accompany you." Leap winked, holding out a hand to Mavlyn. "If you wouldn't mind, milady."

"I would be honored." Grinning, Mavlyn took the boy's hand and allowed him to lead her to the platform. Einar and I followed very closely behind as Leap made the same twirling motion with his finger, forcing the vortex to slow. He and Mavlyn stepped into the current first, and before I had a chance to think twice about it, Einar pulled me after them with a tug.

I let out a little whoop of delight as the current whisked us upward, faster than I expected. A wave of giddiness raced through me, and I clutched at Einar's arm for balance even though I wasn't standing on anything. A grin tugged at my lips— I hadn't felt this way since I was a child, soaring through the air on the rope swing that hung in Mavlyn's back yard.

But in no time it was over, and my feet touched down. I stumbled a little, surprised at the sudden feeling of earth beneath my feet, and Einar's hand came around my waist to steady me.

268 | JASMINE WALT

"Are you all right?" he asked.

I glanced up into his face, and my breath caught as I realized how close we were. His lips were only a few inches from mine— if I leaned up on my tiptoes, even a little, they would touch, and I could taste him again.

"Oi, hurry up!" Leap called, shattering the moment between us. I almost leaped away from Einar before I remembered we were supposed to be a couple, but thankfully his wits were still about him, and he tucked my arm firmly into his once more before guiding me up the well-lit staircase carved into the terraces that led up to the main temple platform.

"Are these statues supposed to represent the twelve winds?" Einar asked as we passed the marble figures that lined the stairs. Both males and females were represented, clad in swirling robes and dresses, each holding a different figurine to signify their individual aspects. A female with long, flowing hair held an olive branch between her fingers, symbolizing what I assumed to be peace, while others held flaming torches, delicate flowers, and various tools and weapons.

"Yes," Leap said. "Twelve is a pretty prominent number around here. Twelve spires, twelve statues, twelve pillars—it goes on. The winds are a pretty important part of our culture."

"I'll say," Mavlyn said as we passed through the arched entryway and into a cavernous, grand hall. A guard patted us down for weapons, but I barely noticed his hands, too busy staring. As Leap had mentioned, twelve massive pillars separated the space, each of them carved to look like swirling wind tunnels. A massive fresco decorated the ceiling, depicting each personification of the twelve winds as they danced through a pearly blue sky dotted with wispy clouds. The floor was black marble, and in the center, beneath the swishing skirts and booted feet of guests dancing to the lively music, I could just make out the painted design of a golden compass rose.

"I imagine the Oracle will be up there somewhere," Einar said, his head tilted up. I followed his gaze to the second level, where I could see more guests and revelers watching from behind the ornate balcony railings that ran around the entire space. Directly in front was a smaller platform with throne-like chairs. A pair of fae I assumed were the head priest and priestess sat in two of them, dressed in ornate, flowing robes of white and gold. Their heads were shaved, and I could just make out what looked like blue swirls tattooed into the skin where their hair should be. A third chair sat empty between them, slightly lower on the platform, which I imagined was for the Oracle.

"How am I supposed to get up there to see her?" I hissed in Leap's ear. "There's no way I'll be able to get a private audience if she's sitting on that throne, surrounded by guards and courtiers and who knows who else!"

"Oh, Quye won't be up there until she absolutely has to," Leap said with a chuckle. "She's either still hiding out in the upper section of the temple, where she and the monks live, or she's down here somewhere in disguise, rubbing elbows with unsuspecting guests. She enjoys pretending to be one of the common people."

Mavlyn snorted. "There's no one here who looks like a common person," she said, eyeing the guests in all their finery. "A single one of these gowns could feed the inhabitants of my village for at least a month."

Leap shrugged. "Just look for a female with curly white hair and a star-shaped birthmark on her right cheekbone," he said to me. "I don't see Madame Gale on this floor, so I'm going to have a look upstairs and see if she's arrived yet. In the meantime, have fun and try to blend in."

He disappeared into the crowd, leaving me, Einar, and Mavlyn standing off to the side.

"I think I'm gonna go get something to eat," Mavlyn said after a beat. "You two want anything?"

I shook my head. "I don't think I could keep food down right now," I admitted. My stomach was churning with nerves now that we were here.

"Gotcha." Mavlyn gave my shoulder a sympathetic squeeze, then left us, heading for the row of tables laden with food toward the left side of the hall.

The seconds ticked by as Einar and I stood silently together, and the churning in my stomach only became worse. I knew we should mingle, but I was too caught up in my worries to even think about approaching anyone. Sweat pooled at the base of my spine, and my left foot started jiggling. There were so many things that could go wrong tonight. Leap could be caught. The Oracle could refuse to help me, or worse, turn me in to the king.

I needed a distraction. Any distraction.

"Do you want to dance with me?" I blurted at Einar.

"What?" His golden gaze snapped to mine, wide with obvious surprise.

"Dance," I repeated. Nerves of a different kind skittered across my skin, and I could feel my cheeks flush with embarrassment. The last time I'd asked a boy to dance was when I'd been six years old at the spring festival, and he'd turned me down. Now here I was, doing it again, but this time with an ornery dragon I had complicated feelings for.

What was I thinking?

"Never mind," I muttered, turning away. I really should be mingling with the crowd anyway, trying to spot the Oracle, if she was even here. Einar could—

A strong, warm hand closed around my wrist, rooting me to the spot. Shocked, I looked over my shoulder to see Einar staring down at me. His golden gaze was unreadable, but there was no mistaking the electric current running between us, lighting me up from the inside and making me feel as though I'd been caught in the center of a wild storm.

"Yes," he said, and the dark rumble of his voice sent a shiver through me. "I'll dance with you."

26

Einar

My heart pounded in my chest as Adara stared up at me, the shock in her cornflower blue eyes mirroring my own.

I hadn't intended to say yes when she asked me to dance with her. Just walking arm in arm with Adara, the curve of her breast lightly brushing against my arm, her beguiling scent wrapping its tendrils around my heart, was torturous enough. Taking her into my arms for a dance wasn't just tempting, it was downright dangerous.

But when I'd seen the hurt look in her eyes as she'd turned away, I hadn't been able to say no. I could feel the fear and anxiety coming off her in waves, and my inner beast demanded I do something, anything, to soothe her.

When Adara didn't try to pull out of my grasp, I slid my hand down her wrist and laced my fingers with hers. The gesture was somehow more intimate than anything we'd done so far, and my heart tripped when she gently squeezed my hand.

"Thank you," she whispered.

I said nothing as I led her onto the dance floor, joining the other guests as they moved to the rhythm of the music. The lively music dancing through the air changed to something softer, slower, and I sighed a little. This would have been easier if I could have twirled her around, keeping her at arm's length and moving fast enough that my gaze wouldn't have time to linger on her.

Instead, I settled my free hand at her waist, and brought our interlaced fingers up so I could lead her into the slow, rhythmic dance. Her left hand settled on my shoulder, and she gazed at a point just beyond it as we moved. Her body was stiff beneath my hands, her eyes crowded with far too many thoughts, and I could feel the tension coiled in her back.

"Relax," I murmured, gently caressing her lower back with my thumb. Her sharp intake of breath made my inner beast lift its head, but I did my best to keep my thoughts focused on Adara, and what she needed. "Breathe, and let those thoughts go. Just for a moment."

I felt, rather than heard, her slow exhale, and her body relaxed incrementally. The pace of the song picked up a bit, and she relaxed further as we moved faster, gliding effortlessly between the other couples on the dance floor.

"You're a good dancer," Adara said, her gaze still not on me. I wished she would look at me, but I knew she was scanning the crowd, searching for the Oracle. "I wasn't expecting that."

I smirked. "You might think I'm a mere dragon brute, but I was a member of high society within my race," I murmured in Adara's ear. I allowed the barest brush of my lips against her earlobe, and my inner beast rumbled with satisfaction when she shivered in my arms. "I assure you I am more than capable of rubbing elbows with the hoitiest of the toitiest."

A surprised laugh burst from Adara's lips, and a grin tug at my lips at the bright sound, like golden champagne bubbles dancing in a freshly-poured flute. Her eyes sparkled as she met my gaze, and that tender feeling inside me spread just a little more, testing the cracks in my armored heart.

Unable to resist, I pulled her in a little closer and ran my hand up her spine. My lips dropped to her shoulder, and I let them hover over her skin as I inhaled her addictive scent. Images of a sparkling ocean, of holding hands on a sandy beach as the surf crashed over our toes, danced in my mind, and suddenly I wished things were different. That I could take her to this place, wherever it was, and make her body sing for me beneath that starry, moonlit shore.

I'm falling in love with her, I realized dimly. Despite my better judgment, despite fighting the mating bond tooth and nail. I was falling in love with a fae.

Why didn't that terrify me?

"Einar," Adara said. Her voice was a throaty murmur, and I lifted my head to see a flush staining her pale, delicate cheeks. It faded into a pink glow that crept down her neck and over the expanse of skin exposed by the v-cut of her gown, and I wanted to follow it with my tongue, to see what secrets might be hiding beneath that shimmering silver-blue fabric. "I—"

"Hey." A tug at my sleeve broke the spell between us, and I turned my head to scowl at Leap, who'd appeared at my elbow. "It's showtime."

He jerked his head toward the entrance, and I followed his gaze to a heavy-set fae gliding through the crowd. She wore an off the shoulder gown that made the most of an admittedly impressive bust, but with wide, multi-tiered skirts that made her look like a badly layered cake. Her silver hair was piled atop her head and threaded with gaudy jewels that matched the heavy gold necklace resting on her chest, and dangling from her wrist was a silver fan with a deep blue gemstone set into the handle.

Madame Gale had arrived.

"It's all right," Adara said, drawing my gaze back to her. Sadness filled her blue eyes, making me want to tug her closer, but she pulled out of my grasp. "I need to look for the Oracle, anyway. Good luck, you two... and thanks for the dance."

She drifted away, and I cursed under my breath, torn between the desire to follow and the need to let her go. I wanted to know what she'd been about to say, if she'd been thinking the same thing I had been, which was obviously a clear mark of my insanity.

It shouldn't matter to me what she thought, what she wanted. These ridiculous feelings were clouding my judgment, skewing my priorities. Shoving away all thoughts of Adara, I put on my most disarming smile, and made my way through the crowd toward the aging dame. There was only one female I was supposed to charm tonight, and I had a feeling she smelled nothing like moonlit beaches or lavender dreams.

27

Adara

"Well, that definitely wasn't the Oracle," Mavlyn said as we walked away from yet another white-haired female. "I was ready to stab my eyes out listening to her talk about the difficulties of importing fresh seafood for her cocktail parties."

I sighed a little as I scanned the crowd, looking for another fae who might fit the description. "Maybe the Oracle is a boring person," I said. With the masks on, it was hard to tell if any of them had the star-shaped birthmark Leap mentioned, but there were a number of curly haired fae among the guests.

"Don't be ridiculous," Mavlyn said. "There's no way someone who can see the future would be that boring to talk to. And the way Leap described her, she sounds like the type who might even enjoy causing a little mischief. I could see her toying with guests, pretending she doesn't know their little secrets and leading them into all kinds of conversational pitfalls."

I raised an eyebrow. "Sounds like you're really looking forward to meeting her," I said.

"Are you kidding?" Mavlyn said, and there was no missing the excitement in her voice. Her green eyes sparkled, and a rosy glow lit her nut-brown skin from within as she grinned at me. "Having your fortune told by the Oracle is an honor usually only reserved for air fae. I'm not saying that she's going to tell me mine, but even getting to meet her is going to be a huge feather in my cap when I get back home."

Home. A pang hit my chest as I thought of Fenwood, of the cozy little cabin my mother and I had lived in for the last eighteen years. What I wouldn't give to be back there now, chopping ingredients and listening to her chatter about the properties of bloodroot and wyrmwood. No, our life hadn't been perfect, but we'd been safe and comfortable, and we'd had each other. I couldn't believe how stupid I'd been to take that for granted and risk it for the sake of a little adventure.

If—no, when—I got my mother back, we were going straight back to Fenwood, and we would never leave again.

Turning away from Mavlyn, I leaned over the balcony railing and scanned the crowd, looking for anyone who might be the Oracle. Mavlyn and I had spent over an hour down there before we'd moved our search upstairs, to no avail. My gaze snagged on Einar—it looked like he was finally getting his audience with Madame Gale. A group of fae had swarmed her before she'd made it more than ten steps into the hall, and Einar had been forced to hang back while she socialized.

I couldn't blame him for taking his time approaching her—it wouldn't be a good idea for Leap to try and steal the fan while Madame Gale had so many eyes on her. The two of them were standing off to the side, a glass of wine clutched between Madame Gale's meaty fingers as Einar flirted with her. She threw her head back and laughed at something he said, and as Einar ducked his head to whisper something in her ear, a streak of red-hot jealousy ricocheted through me. I gripped the railing hard, seized by the sudden desire to rip that fan off her wrist and beat her with it.

"Hey." Mavlyn's hand landed on my arm, bringing me back to reality. "Are you okay, Adara?"

I blew out a frustrated breath. "I'm fine. I just...really want to get this whole Oracle thing over with."

"Well, she should come out soon to make her yearly predictions," Mavlyn said. She nodded to the dance floor, which had been cleared of guests. Monks in gauzy, flowing white costumes that streamed out from their limbs like ribbons whirled and leaped across the floor. Their movements were mesmerizing—it looked like they were floating on the wind as they performed their acrobatic moves, and considering that they were air fae, they probably were. "Apparently, this is the traditional yearly dance the monks perform to honor the twelve winds. I'm a little surprised the Oracle isn't already here."

I listened to Mavlyn with half an ear, my attention on what was happening below. While Einar whispered in Madame Gale's ear, I watched Leap sidle out from behind a pillar. In one smooth motion, he slipped the fan off the air fae's wrist, then tucked it away into a pocket and kept walking, blending seamlessly into the crowd. It had been the perfect snatch—with Einar keeping Madame Gale occupied, and the crowd's attention captured by the dancers, no one had noticed the theft.

"That was pretty impressive, wasn't it?" a bright voice said in my ear, and I jumped. Heart thundering in my chest, I spun around to see a female with a riotous mane of hair. Her curls were the color of fresh milk, and blue-grey eyes twinkled with mischief behind an iridescent teal butterfly mask. "How long do you think it'll take for Madame Gale to notice her fan is missing?"

"Y-you!" I stuttered, taking an involuntary step back. With a little space between us, I was able to take the fae in fully—she was at least four inches taller than me, her slender body clad in a flowing, empire-waist gown with butterflies sewn into her skirt that matched her mask. Just below that mask, on the edge of her cheekbone, I spotted a birthmark in the unmistakable shape of a star. "You're the Oracle!"

"The Oracle?" The fae placed a hand against her chest as if wounded. "How dare you! I'm dressed as Oirtha, can't you tell?"

She twirled, and the butterflies on her skirt fluttered with the movement. Dimly, I recalled one of the statues outside had depicted a female with several large butterflies perched on her shoulder, her forearm, and one outstretched finger.

"You mean the wind spirit?" I asked dumbly.

"Oooh, so you do know something of our customs after all!" The Oracle tapped me on the nose. "That's impressive, considering that you've spent your entire life sheltered in that tiny backwoods earth village."

I scowled. "I can't imagine you've lived a worldly life yourself, shut up in this temple your whole life," I said, unable to keep the defensive tone from my voice.

Quye laughed, a light, tinkling sound that seemed to swirl through the air. "Oh, trust me, while I have left the sanctity of the temple more times than my caretakers would like to admit, I don't need to. The winds bring everything important that happens in the world to me. How do you think I know who you are, Adara, or that I'd find you here?"

A chill ran up my spine, but before I could come up with an answer to that, Mavlyn tapped me on the shoulder. "Don't look now, but I think Einar and Leap are being arrested."

Whirling, I leaned over the balcony to see Leap and Einar being subdued by two pairs of guards. A small circle had formed around them as the crowd watched the commotion, and I saw Madame Gale standing just a few feet away, looking as though she were about to faint. A third guard was at her elbow, trying to reassure her and keep her calm.

"Giant's teeth," I swore, gripping the railing. "We have to help them!"

"Help them how?" Mavlyn asked as the guards pulled Einar's wrists behind his back and secured them with heavy cuffs. His face contorted with fury, and he looked like he was seconds away from torching the entire ballroom. I strongly suspected the knowledge that his cover would be blown to smithereens was the only reason he hadn't done so yet.

"Oh, I think I can help with that," Quye said. We turned around to see her smiling brightly at us. "Why don't you two come downstairs with me, so we can get in on the action?"

28

Einar

"So how long will you be visiting from the earth kingdom, Mr. Fahar?" Madame Gale purred as she plucked a third glass of wine off a passing server's tray.

I fought the urge to grit my teeth as she slid her free hand up my shoulder, her meaty fingers squeezing the way a farmer might squeeze the flesh of a stallion he was hoping to buy. I'd love nothing more than to rip that hand from her body and beat her over her overly done up head with it.

Instead, I gave her an enigmatic smile and took a sip of my own drink. "Just for a few days," I said as the alcohol burned down my throat. "I've got a few meetings, and then I'll be heading back home to Talamh and my business."

Drinking on the job wasn't the smartest thing, but after ten minutes of dealing with this insufferable hag, I'd decided the only way I would make it through this was by switching out my glass of water for something stronger. If I was being completely honest, though, the wine was hitting me a little harder than it should have.

When was the last time I've had a drink? I wondered dimly to myself. At Daryan and Olette's wedding feast? That had been over twenty years ago. The memories from that horrible day threatened to surface, and I shoved them back firmly. This was no time to get caught up in the ghosts of the past.

"Well, it's very brave of you to travel all this way just to buy starsilk," Madame Gale said. "I've heard reports that the number of shadow creature attacks in Domhain is rising. It's a dangerous time to be traveling."

"Yes, but my customers love starsilk garments, and I can't bear to disappoint them." I'd told Madame Gale that I owned a chain of tailor shops in Talamh, and that I'd come to find a new starsilk supplier since my old one had raised his prices too much. Starsilk was extremely rare, and the caterpillars that spun the light, shimmery thread could only be found in the Gaoth Aire mountains, which meant it had to be imported. "But you're right, the journey here was treacherous, and I'm in no hurry to get back on the road." I leaned in to brush a curl of hair behind her ear, and whispered, "Perhaps I might find a reason to stay a few days longer."

Madame Gale let out a girlish giggle, and I nearly gagged at the scent of her cloying perfume. I wanted nothing more than to pull away, but I could sense Leap approaching, so I gently caught her jaw between my fingers and nuzzled her neck. I hated debasing myself like this, but I had promised to help in exchange for getting us in here, and I wouldn't go back on my word.

"What do you think?" I murmured. "Are there any...attractions...in this town, that might keep me occupied for a little while?"

"Oh, I think I could find something to grab your attention." She clasped my hand in a surprisingly strong grip and brought it down to rest against her exposed cleavage. I noticed the fan was no longer dangling from her grip, and my heartbeat picked up a bit. It was only a matter of time until she noticed it was missing, and I needed to make myself scarce before that happened.

"Your glass is empty," I said in a husky voice, reaching for the wine glass dangling between her fingers "Would you like me to get you another?"

"I would," she said, but instead of letting me take the glass, she closed her free hand around my wrist in a vise-like grip. "But before you do, I'm going to have to insist you give my fan back."

"What?" I blinked, keeping my expression politely confused even as sweat broke out along my spine.

"You heard me." Her short, stubby fingernails dug into my skin, and her flirtatious smile turned mean. "I felt your little friend take the fan while you were whispering sweet nothings in my ear. I have to admit it was a slick job—if a guard hadn't tipped me off, I'm not sure I would have noticed until it was too late."

Icy dread pooled in my stomach, and I glanced over Madame Gale's shoulder as a commotion snagged my attention. It was Leap, struggling against two guards as they fought to subdue him. His mask had come free, revealing the shocked, furious expression on his face, and I could feel the stirrings of anger in my own heart.

Had we been betrayed?

I tried to push past Madame Gale to help Leap, but before I could, something hard cracked across the back of my skull. Stars swam in my vision, and I fought to stay focused as I spun around to face my attackers. Two more guards were there, holding clubs, and I ducked as one of them swung his weapon toward my head, barely dodging the blow. Furious, I ripped the second guard's club from his grip and smashed it into his head. Several people in the crowd screamed as the guard went down, and it was then that I realized we had quite an audience.

Was it really worth it to engage in an all-out brawl now, when it would be impossible to get away? Or was it better to wait until we were in a more private space, and I could use my abilities without fear of too many witnesses?

Knowing the answer, I relaxed my posture and held up my hands, surrendering. In response, the guards rudely yanked my hands behind my head and secured them with manacles. I scanned the crowd as they led me and Leap away, trying to find Adara and Mavlyn, but they were nowhere to be seen. Did they know what was happening?

Hopefully they're just preoccupied with the Oracle, I thought as they hustled us down a dark hallway and up a narrow staircase barely wide enough for my frame. The guards unceremoniously shoved us into a drawing room, and kicked the backs of our knees, forcing us to drop to the hard floorboards.

"You," Leap spat, glaring at one of the guards as the door slammed behind us. "I recognize your face. You're friends with Storm, aren't you?"

"Storm?" The guard pretended to look puzzled. "Oh, you mean the kid that told me you'd be here trying to steal the fan tonight? I don't know him, but we sure do appreciate the tip." He winked.

Snarling, I called on my power, willing fire to spring to my fingertips so I could melt the cuffs and tear this smarmy bastard's limbs from his body.

But nothing happened. I couldn't feel anything, not even a spark.

"They used enchanted cuffs," Leap grumbled. "Magic won't work here."

"What?" I scowled, craning my head over my shoulder and lifting my bound hands to get a better look. In the dim firelight, I could just make out the glint of tiny primal stones set into the metal. "Blast it." I hadn't realized the fae had these—it wasn't as though they'd released any of the dragons they'd taken prisoner during the war.

The door opened, and Madame Gale sauntered in, a pouting look on her face. The flickering flames from the fireplace cast ugly shadows across her heavyset face, and my stomach soured as she turned and locked the door behind her.

"Well, well, well," she said, sashaying up to me. She gripped my chin in her meaty hand, and a shiver of revulsion rippled through me as she slid her thumb across my lower lip. "I didn't know thieves could look so pretty. I was going to have you both killed, but I think I might keep this one for myself. The boy will have to go though—I can't abide younglings."

Leap scoffed. "Right, because kids are just lining up to hang out with *you*."

Madame Gale released me—not a second too soon, as I was about to give in to the urge to bite her finger clean off—and turned her attention on Leap. "Any street rat would be lucky to have a home with me," she said archly. "I have more wealth and connections than most of the air fae here—even those in House Reatha. It's too bad you tried to steal from me, boy; I could use someone with your talents."

Leap looked her up and down with a sneer. "As if I would ever work for a hag like you."

Madame Gale scowled and turned to the guards. "Did you retrieve the fan from him?" she demanded, addressing the one who'd betrayed us.

"No, not yet," he said, his cheeks coloring a little. He took a step toward Leap, but before he could search him, the door opened.

"Who—" Madame Gale snarled, turning toward the door, but the words on her lips died as a white-robed figure glided into the room. A gauzy veil completely obscured her hair and features, and if her outfit and the serene way she moved hadn't been enough, the sight of Adara and Mavlyn following warily behind her was enough to confirm her identity.

"Quye," Leap said dryly. "Impeccable timing."

The guards immediately saluted, and Madame Gale executed a hasty curtsy. "Oracle," she stuttered. "It's an honor to be graced by your presence."

"Rise, child," the Oracle said in a dreamy voice, and Leap snorted loudly. I raised my eyebrows at his irreverent attitude, but if anyone else noticed it, they kept it to themselves. "I apologize if I've interrupted you, but I'm afraid I'm going to need this room."

"Oh," Madame Gale said, a pained note in her voice. Her eyes darted toward Adara and Mavlyn, obviously wondering what business they had with the Oracle, but she wisely decided not to ask. "Certainly, we can find another room. Just give us a moment."

She gestured for the guards to grab us, but before they could obey, the Oracle held up her hand. "These two need to stay behind as well."

The guards froze. "Happily," Madame Gale said stiffly after a very protracted silence. "I'll just need to collect an item of mine from one the boy. He stole something from me, you see."

"Yes, I know," the Oracle said, and though her tone remained serene, I could hear the sharp smile in her voice. "That's one of the reasons I came down here. I'm in need of a new fan, you see."

There was another long silence, and if looks could kill, the look in Madame Gale's eyes would have struck the Oracle dead. "There are a number of fans available for purchase," she said, looking like she'd swallowed a poisonous toad.

"Yes, but not too many of them can be used to manipulate and control the decisions of others," the Oracle said. A thread of steel entered her voice now, and power hummed in the air surrounding her. Just a hint, but the hairs on my arms stiffened, and the guards shifted uneasily on their feet. "The winds have told me all about the many exploits you've made with that fan, Madame Gale. I could easily pen a letter to Lord Oren several pages long informing him of them...or, I could let you leave this room unscathed, with him none the wiser. Providing that none of you mention anything that happened here tonight, of course."

All the blood drained out of Madame Gale's face, leaving her looking like a fresh corpse left to rot on a snowy mountainside. "Yes, Oracle," she said quickly, dipping into another hasty curtsy. "Have a good evening."

She fled from the room as if she were being chased by harpies, rudely jostling Adara as she did so. An annoyed look flashed across Adara's face before she met my gaze, and something inside me warmed as she gave me a relieved smile.

So, she had noticed we'd been taken. And it seemed she'd convinced the Oracle to save us.

"You there," the Oracle said, pointing at one of the guards. "Release these two, and then clear the room, please."

The guard hesitated. "Are you certain, Oracle? They are criminals—"

"I know very well who they are," she said calmly. "Now release them."

The guard sighed, then fished a key out of his pocket. He undid Leap's cuffs first, then approached me more warily, clearly nervous that I would harm him if he set me free. I wanted to, but there were more important things to worry about than beating up a guard who was just trying to do his job, so instead I held still and allowed him to unlock the cuffs. I sighed in relief as I felt my magic rush back into my fingertips, and the guard leaped back as flames blossomed to life in my hands. Quickly, I shook them out before I accidentally set him on fire.

"You didn't see that," I said, glaring at him.

He nodded in wide-eyed agreement, then rushed out of the room, the other guards following suit. The door slammed shut behind him, leaving the five of us alone.

"Well, that was the most excitement I've had in months!" the Oracle exclaimed, plopping unceremoniously into a chair. She ripped off her veil, revealing a heart-shaped face with ice-blue eyes, a pert nose, and a wide mouth that was made for smiling. I had a feeling that despite the serene act from earlier, her spirit was just as wild as the mane of white curls cascading over her shoulders.

"All right, let's get to it," she said, snagging one of those curls and twining it around her forefinger as her mouth widened in a mischievous grin. "Which one of you poor fools wants to hear how you die first?"

Adara

"What?" I blurted as Quye's question echoed through the drawing room. A shiver skated over my skin, and I resisted the sudden urge to hug myself. "That isn't what I came here for. I don't want to know how I die!"

"I second that," Mavlyn said, raising her forefinger into the air. "As far as I'm concerned, I'm immortal. In fact, I'm far more interested in hearing about how *you're* going to die," she said, smirking at the Oracle.

The Oracle gave a breathy sigh, throwing her head back and pressing the back of her hand dramatically against her forehead. "Alas, it is the curse of the Oracle to never be allowed to see her own future," she said. "Not that I think my death will be especially exciting or anything. I'll either be devoured by shadow creatures, or I'll die of boredom and old age in my fluffy feather bed. Depends on the choices you two make, really."

She nodded at me, and then at Einar, making me frown. "Us two?" I asked.

"Oh yes," Quye said, nodding sagely. "Your fates are intertwined. There's no use fighting it," she added when Einar opened his mouth, looking as though he wanted to argue. "You of all people should know that." She gave him a pointed look.

"And just what is that supposed to mean?" I propped my hands on my hips as I looked back and forth between them. "Is there something you know that I don't, Einar?"

"Not a damn thing," he said stonily, but he wouldn't quite meet my gaze.

I growled, seized by the urge to storm over to him and shake him until whatever secrets he was hiding spilled from his mouth. I'd been so worried when I'd rushed down here with Mavlyn and the Oracle, but Einar barely seemed grateful that we'd come to his rescue. Insufferable male!

"I'd tell you what it is," Quye said, drawing my attention back to her, "but that would really take the fun out of things, so I'll leave it up to you to pry the truth out of Einar later." She winked at me. "I can, however, tell you about the prophecy. That is what you came here to speak to me about, yes?"

"Umm. Yeah. Right." I blinked, trying to get my mind back on track. Of course that was what I came here for. A tingling awareness spread through my veins, and my heart was about to beat faster. I'd been waiting for days for this moment, and now that we were finally here, I was thinking about Einar. What was wrong with me? "Yes, I'd love to hear the prophecy."

"Okay, okay, but hang on." Quye shook out her sleeves and cleared her throat. "I've got to use my prophecy voice."

She tilted her head to the ceiling, and her eyes turned milky white. The air in the room grew thick with power, and shivers raced up and down my limbs as she spoke in a deep, resonant voice that was absolutely nothing like the light, airy tone she usually spoke with.

· · ·

There comes a girl of fire and ice
  Born of two worlds, with the power of light
  To save Ediria, she must awaken the beast
  And defeat the shadows that live in the east
  Her enemy lives inside one she holds most dear
  He thrives on darkness, and feeds off fear
  She must conquer his chaos and trust in her heart
  Or all she loves will be lost to the dark

Quye's voice faded as she finished the prophecy, and her eyes returned to their normal color. "Phewweeee," she said, rolling her neck on her shoulders until it popped. "It's been a while since I went into trance mode. What did you all think? Did I live up to your expectations?"

"I don't understand," I said, digging a hand into my hair as I tried to process her words. Several pins clattered to the ground, and I winced as I remembered I was wearing a fancy updo. "The power of light? Saving Ediria? You're making me sound like some kind of savior!"

Quye shrugged. "I don't make up the prophecies. I just deliver them."

"Well, you've definitely awakened the beast," Mavlyn said, gesturing to Einar. He scowled, but didn't contradict her. "But so far I haven't seen any evidence that you can wield light magic, Adara."

"That's because no fae can wield light magic," Leap said with a huff. "Only the Radiants have that power."

"That's actually not true," Mavlyn piped up. "Don't you remember the stories we were told?"

"Ooohhhh..." Quye said, sitting up straighter. "Someone who remembers the history of the champions! I think I might be in love," she declared, clapping a hand over her heart.

"I didn't know the Oracle was such an outrageous flirt," Mavlyn said, grinning. Was that a trick of the light, or was she blushing?

"What can I say?" Quye winked. "I'm a sucker for brains and beauty."

"Excuse me," Einar interrupted, "but what are you two talking about? What champions?"

"Every thousand years or so, the Radiants appear to a worthy fae and ask him to be their champion," Mavlyn said. "If he accepts, they bestow on him—or her—the power of light magic, in addition to whatever fae abilities they already have. Light magic is very powerful, and amongst other things, can alter perception and reality itself. Champions always end up in powerful positions, usually as kings, but sometimes generals or other people of influence, so the Radiants try to pick someone they think will do the most good."

"That's all well and good," I said, remembering the stories Mother had told me about the champions when I was a little girl, "but the champions were always Greater Fae who were approached during their coming of age ceremonies. That's not me."

"Not *yet* you," Quye corrected, and I went still. "You haven't had your coming of age ceremony yet."

"I..." I opened my mouth to argue, but the words died on my lips. Of course I'd never had a coming of age ceremony—I'd always thought I was a lesser fae. Coming of age ceremonies were a ritual of the Greater Fae, done when a fae turned sixteen to unlock the beast form that lived within each of them. Lesser fae didn't have beast forms, so when we reached adulthood we just had regular celebrations. Mine had been held by Lake Fenwood, with Mavlyn and my mother in attendance. We'd eaten cake and swam in the lake. That was it.

"So you're saying that if Adara does the coming of age ritual, the Radiants will bestow her with light magic?" Einar demanded. "And she'll be able to defeat the shadows?"

"Hang on now," Quye said, holding up a hand. "I didn't say any of that."

"Oh come on, Quye," Leap complained. "Do you have to be so cryptic all the time? Just tell Adara what she needs to do to get her mother back!"

Quye sighed, turning in her chair to face Leap. "You know I can't do that, cousin," she said. "I can't give specific details about the future beyond what the prophecies say, not without betraying the winds. They'll stop whispering to me if I do that, and then where will we be? But I *can* say that regardless of anything, Adara is way past due for her coming of age ritual, and in *my* opinion, it should be her *first* priority."

She winked at me, but I was barely listening, my attention still snagged on her first sentence. "Cousin?" I repeated, glaring at Leap. "The two of you are *cousins*?"

Leap swore, and Quye batted her eyelashes. "Oh, you didn't know?" she asked in a voice that was pure innocence. "I thought Leap would have told you."

"You know damn well I didn't tell them," Leap snapped. "Why would you out me like that!"

"Well, that explains why you seemed to know so much about Quye," Mavlyn said with an arched eyebrow. "And if you're related to her, that means your parents were members of the nobility."

"I thought we agreed on no more secrets!" I threw up my hands, more than a little incensed. "How could you hide something so important from us, Leap?"

"And just what makes you think you have the right to my secrets?" Leap snapped. Suddenly, he was in my face, his storm grey eyes crackling with lightning, his teeth bared in a snarl. I took a step back, startled—I'd never seen him so angry. "Why do you think you deserve to know about my past, about my life? I agreed to help you get into the city, to see the Oracle, and I've fulfilled my end of the bargain! You don't get more than that!"

He turned to storm out of the room, but before he could, Quye snatched him by the wrist. "Not so fast, Leap. You have something I want."

He spun around to face Quye, his gaze furious. "You can't have the fan. I need to give it to Storm, so that he doesn't tell—" he snapped his mouth shut with a click of his teeth and pressed his lips together.

Quye rolled her eyes. "Why do you think I came in to rescue your sorry tails?" she said, crossing her arms. "I've been watching Madame Gale use that fan to spread corruption and manipulate our economy for years, and I decided something needed to be done about it. I knew she would be here with the fan tonight, and the opportunity to relieve her of it would arrive, so I made sure I would be in the right place at the right time to take it. Besides," she added, "Storm expected you to fail, anyway. He's the one who bribed that guard to betray you."

"I figured as much," Leap said tightly, "but once he hears I've escaped, he'll tell Uncle Oren about me, anyway."

"Uncle Oren?" Mavlyn said, aghast. "As in, Lord Oren of House Reatha? Ruler of the Gaoth Aire?"

"Yes," Leap said with a sigh, dragging a hand across his face. "Lord Oren is my uncle."

Einar snorted. "He must be a terrible uncle, if you prefer living on the streets and running around with cutthroats to living in a lavish palace in the air mountains and being waited on hand and foot," he said.

Leap shot him a glare. "Being a member of the nobility isn't all that it's cracked up to be. I'd rather sleep in a ditch than spend a night under Uncle Oren's roof."

"Anyway," Quye said in a pointed tone, "my point is that

Storm was never expecting you to show up with the fan. So as long as you make yourself scarce from Wynth after tonight, you should be fine."

"And what if I don't want to make myself scarce from Wynth?" Leap challenged. "What if I want to stay here and take back my position from Storm?"

Quye smiled. "We both know you're not going to do that, Leap."

She held out an expectant hand to Leap, and he let out a defeated sigh. "Why can't I just keep it?" he groused as he pulled the fan out of his pocket and handed it to her.

"Because I don't trust you with it," she said archly, tucking it up a sleeve. "As the Oracle, I'm the only person who doesn't need the fan to get people to do what I want. Therefore, I'm the only responsible choice as the fan's custodian."

"I'm not sure your Uncle Oren would agree with that logic," Mavlyn said with a chuckle.

The Oracle grinned. "Yes, well, I think my cousin here would agree that what Uncle Oren doesn't know won't hurt him, right?"

Quye winked at Leap, who rolled his eyes, but I thought I saw a small smile twitching at his lips. "Now you..." she turned to Einar, looking him up and down slowly. "I don't need to tell you where your place is or what you should be doing. Your heart already knows where you belong, it's just up to your mind to accept it. As long as you keep fighting your destiny, you will never find happiness."

"I don't want happiness," Einar growled. "Only sleep."

"That might have been true, once," the Oracle agreed. "But there's no use in lying to me, Einar. I see everything. And the question you should really ask yourself is, what would Daryan say if he could see you now, holding so tightly onto the hatred in your heart?"

I glanced at Einar, curious at the stricken look on his face. It quickly morphed to fury, though, and he clenched his fists at his side. "How dare you speak his name," he growled, a muscle twitching in his jaw. "It's not fit to touch any fae's lips, least of all an air fae's."

Quye shrugged, then turned to Mavlyn. "Your loyalty will be severely tested," she told her. "My only advice to you is that in your hour of need, seek out the Traveler's Grove. You'll find that which you've been searching for."

"The Traveler's Grove?" Mavlyn's eyes widened. "I thought that was just a myth!"

I opened my mouth to ask what they were talking about, but before I could, the door banged open, and an irate monk in ornate robes stormed in.

"Quye!" His eyes widened with scandalized outrage when he saw the Oracle lounging by the fire. "What are you doing amongst these strangers, with your face unveiled!" He snatched Quye's veil from the floor, where she'd let it fall carelessly, then hastily draped it over her hair. "We've been looking everywhere for you—you're supposed to be in the ballroom, making the predictions!"

"Alas, duty calls," Quye said with a sigh. She stood up and allowed the monk to drag her from the room, waving a hand at us in farewell. "Good luck, Adara and company. The fate of the world depends on you all, or something like that!"

The door slammed shut behind her, leaving us with far more questions than answers.

30

Einar

"Well?" Mrs. Aeolan asked as we entered the breakfast room the next morning. She put down the paper she was reading, adjusted the spectacles on her pert nose, and gave us an expectant look. "How did it go?"

I glanced over at Adara, who shook her head wearily. The shadows under her eyes told me she'd gotten about as much sleep as I had after we'd crawled into bed in the early hours of the morning. She'd pulled her lavender hair into a messy bun on top of her head, and there were still traces of makeup smudged around the corners of her mouth and eyes. She probably hadn't even looked in the mirror before she'd thrown on that dressing gown.

And yet, despite her disheveled appearance, my heart tugged every time I looked into those cornflower blue eyes of hers. It defied all logic, all rational explanation.

Your heart already knows where you belong. It's up to your mind to accept it.

"Nothing like we expected," Adara said as Quye's words

echoed back at me from last night. She pulled out a chair and sat down at the breakfast table, and I followed suit. Platters of cold meats, cheeses, and breads sat on the table, and she reached past them for the pot of tea to pour herself a cup. "Almost nothing went according to plan."

"We did get to meet the Oracle, though," Mavlyn said, yawning as she entered the room. She'd left her auburn hair hanging in rumpled waves around her shoulders, her dressing gown haphazardly tied around her waist. "Also, we found out Leap is Lord Oren's nephew?"

"Are you going to tell *everyone*?" Leap hissed as he followed in behind her. Of the four of us, he was the only one dressed, though he looked just as bedraggled and tired as everyone else. "Why don't you just climb up to the rooftops and shout my name for all of Wynth to hear!"

"I suspected as much," Mrs. Aeolan said, surprising us all. At Leap's bewildered look, she added, "You look a great deal like your mother, Lady Orla. I knew her and your father, back when they still served in the Lightning Rider Force. They were fierce, courageous warriors."

A barb sprang to my tongue—I had nothing good to say about air fae warriors—but I swallowed it at the stricken look on Leap's face. "I didn't know you were friends with my parents," he said in a quiet voice.

"I would have called them acquaintances more than friends," Mrs. Aeolan corrected him gently. "But they were greatly admired at court, and you were their pride and joy. I can't blame you for wanting to go back to Wynth, since this is where they lived and cared for you. I can imagine that living under Lord Oren's roof wasn't easy."

Leap swallowed. "I don't really want to talk about it," he said. He took a seat and snatched up two rolls, but despite his words, I noticed that he'd chosen to sit directly next to Mrs. Aeolan.

The air fae nodded once, as if she understood his recalcitrance, then turned to Adara. "What did the Oracle tell you?"

As Adara recited the prophecy Quye had given us, the Oracle's words to me echoed in my head again. *What would Daryan say if he could see you now,* she'd accused, a knowing look in her eyes, *holding so tightly onto the hatred in your heart?*

Those words had haunted me all night, leaving me to toss and turn as I replayed them over and over. Because I knew exactly what Daryan would have said. I touched the cuff at my wrist, and one of our final conversations began to replay in my mind, fresh as though it had happened yesterday.

"I don't understand," I'd told him as we'd stood on the balcony outside his rooms, overlooking the Dragon Vale. "How can you marry a fae, Daryan? To share a bed with a female whose hands are stained with the blood of our people?"

Daryan sighed, placing a hand on the banister as he gazed at our lands. From our vantage point, we had a crystal clear view of Mount Furian, unmarred by even a single cloud in the clear blue sky. Standing there, dressed in a simple leather jerkin and trousers, his crown conspicuously absent from his mop of curly russet hair, he didn't look like the commanding dragon prince who had fearlessly led us into battle dozens upon dozens of times.

Today, he was just a dragon. My best friend, my confidant, my brother in all but name only. And it was here, in these quiet moments unsoiled by duty and obligation, that we could be frank with each other.

"I could tell you it's because of the mating bond," he said after a long moment, finally turning to face me. His golden eyes, flecked with bits of ruby, glowed, and it was not just the sunlight that lit them from within like that. He always looked this way when he spoke of the fae princess, as if he were overflowing with joy. "I could tell you it's because Olette's unconditional love has transformed me, healing the bitterness in my heart and making me see hope for the first time since

my father put a sword in my hands and told me I would have to fight for my very right to exist."

I stared at him, unsure of where he was going with this. I thought that was exactly what he would say—that the mating bond was compelling him, that he couldn't live without Olette, that their love would be enough to heal the great divide between our people.

"But truthfully," he said, turning back to face the vale again, "I'm not doing this because of the mating bond. Or at least, not only because of the mating bond. I'm doing it because I'm tired of holding onto this hatred in my heart. It's a slow, insidious poison, driving us all to an early death swifter and surer than any fae blade could."

"I don't understand what you mean," I said. My fingers dug into the stone railing, trying to find purchase as stormy waves of confusion pitched my brain back and forth. "The fae have been murdering us for eons. They've earned our hatred!"

"Maybe they have," Daryan agreed. "But in their eyes, we have earned their hatred as well."

"Why, because of that bullcock story about us killing off the fire fae?" I spat. Anger vibrated through my body, forcing me into motion, and I paced restlessly outside the double doors leading into Daryan's rooms. "We never touched the fire fae—they were gone before we got here!" The remains of fire fae civilization were buried beneath thousands of years of ash and stone, the truth of their demise lost to death and time.

"Yes, yes," Daryan said, waving an impatient hand. The cuff on his wrist glinted, the deep red primal stone set into the center flashing in the bright daylight as it moved. "And dragons and fae can continue going in circles, fingering the blame at one another and killing each other in retaliation for crimes both real and imagined. We can continue to let the hatred in our hearts fester until both of our races are mere bone dust floating on the winds, memories whisked away so that nothing remains of our once great legacies."

I scowled. "What makes you so sure that will happen? That drag-onkind won't eventually prevail?"

"Because in three-thousand years, we have never come close!" Daryan whirled to face me, his golden eyes flashing in a rare show of temper. I took a shocked step back as he stalked toward me and fisted a hand in my tunic—of the two of us, he was always the calm, collected one, and rarely lost control of his emotions. "All we have succeeded in doing is maintaining our borders, and harrying the fae by stealing their resources. Rarely have we ever kept any territory we've managed to take, and the fae continue to outnumber us. If our iron hide didn't protect us from their magic, they would have eradicated us long ago."

He released a long, slow breath, his fingers uncurling from my tunic as he looked away from me again. "We cannot go on like this," he said quietly, taking a step back. "We cannot allow hatred to blind us, for pride to hold us back. My marriage to Olette may not solve things overnight, but it is a first step. An invitation for more dragons and fae to join hands, to put aside old hurts and grudges, and start anew. Only by doing so can we purge the poison from our hearts, and end this cycle of destruction."

I shook my head, running a hand through my hair. "I don't know, Daryan. It seems to me that there is a lot of trust involved here. You're expecting the fae to honor this marriage, honor this treaty. How do you know they won't backstab us at the first opportunity?"

"There are no guarantees," Daryan agreed. "But while the fae might try to betray me, I know Olette never will. And someone has to extend a hand first before trust can be formed. If I don't take this chance to do it now, we may never get another one. How can you expect me to do anything less?"

"Einar?" Adara's voice cut through the memory, snapping me back to the present. I blinked to see that everyone at the table was staring at me. "Have you been listening to a word we've been saying?"

"Sorry." I shook my head, trying to clear the cobwebs of the past away. "I was...thinking."

"More like daydreaming," Leap snarked around a mouthful of bread. I raised an eyebrow as I noticed half the platter of rolls had disappeared, then quickly grabbed two. At the rate Leap was going, they'd all be gone by the next time I blinked. "We were talking about Adara's coming of age ritual, and whether we should try to get it done before rescuing her mother from King Aolis's clutches."

"How does the ritual work?" I asked, buttering one of my rolls. "Is it something that can be done quickly?"

"Absolutely not," Mrs. Aeolan said primly. "A ten day fast is required beforehand, followed by a journey to your house's most sacred temple where your head of house will perform the rite. As a water fae, that would be the Eldoris Temple, which is at the bottom of the Shardian Sea."

I frowned. "But how do we know that's the right place? As a fire fae, wouldn't it make more sense for Adara to do the ritual at Mount Furian instead?"

There was a very pregnant pause before everyone spoke all at once. "That's insane—out of your mind—too dangerous—how would it even work—!"

"Enough!" Mrs. Aeolan snapped, and the room quieted. "Even if Adara could fight through the hordes of shadow creatures guarding Mount Furian, there are no fire fae alive who can perform the rite. It has to be Lady Axlya, Usige House's matriarch."

"Well that'll have to wait," Adara said firmly. "I don't have time to fast for ten days. Mother's already been in King Aolis's dungeon for a week now. She might not be alive if I make her wait that long."

"Don't be silly, girl," Mrs. Aeolan admonished. "King Aolis is a formidable foe all on his own, never mind the hundreds of fae warriors he has at his disposal in Kapei Castle. Light magic may be the only chance you have at defeating him."

"But I don't need to defeat him," Adara argued. "I just need—"

A loud, splintering crash cut Adara off mid-sentence. I jumped to my feet, fire already springing to my fingertips at the sound of heavily booted footsteps, and snarled as a hulking, black-armored fae stepped into the dining room. I'd recognize that grotesque, half-melted face anywhere.

"Slaugh!" I hurled a fireball at his head, but he was ready for it. Raising his hand, which was haloed with dark, crackling energy, he sliced through the flames as though they were as inconsequential as a snowball.

"Tsk, tsk." Slaugh wagged a finger at me as a dozen soldiers, all clad in similar armor to his, rushed in, surrounding the table before any of us could take more than a few steps away from it. He grabbed Adara by the upper arm, and she tried to wrench away, but his grip held fast. "I've a score to settle with you, Einar, but not today. It's time to take this little princess home, where she belongs."

A swirling vortex of darkness manifested directly behind him, and everyone in the room froze as the hum of dark magic filled the air. Before I could recover, Slaugh took a step back, pulling Adara along with him.

"No!" I shouted, vaulting over the table. But the vortex collapsed before I could reach it, and my hands only met air.

Adara was gone.

31

Adara

I opened my mouth to scream as the darkness closed around me, but no sound came out. The inky blackness that surrounded me seemed to fill every part of my body, slithering up my nostrils, into my ears, and down my throat. It cut off all my senses—sight, sound, taste, touch, smell—leaving me only with that pervading sense of *wrongness*. Even General Slaugh's vise-grip on my arm faded to nothing.

Was this what death was like? Was my soul being consumed by the shadows, my body and mind already eaten away? Would my entire identity be swallowed up, until there was not even a stain or a smudge of residue to mark my existence in this world?

But just when I thought that might happen, that I might really cease to exist once and for all, the darkness spat me out again. I stumbled as my feet slammed into damp stone, blinked as my eyes struggled to adjust to the darkness. The air smelled of moldy straw and blood, the only light coming from flickering torches set into the walls.

"You really must be the girl from the prophecy, then," Slaugh said, a curious note in his voice. The sensation of his fingers digging into my arm came back, and with it, a rush of awareness that he was still with me. "Any other fae I've tried to shadow travel with has always died of shadow sickness afterward, but you're untouched."

That single statement alone carried so many questions with it, but those would have to wait. Allowing my rage to run unchecked, I twisted out of Slaugh's grip and swung a flaming fist at his face. Slaugh dodged the fiery punch, and I cried out in pain as my fist connected with the stone wall instead.

"Not so fast, princess." Before I could recover, Slaugh whipped my hands around my back. I swore as cold, heavy manacles clamped around my wrists, and dread spread through my stomach as I felt my magic drain away. "Can't have you burning off the good side of my face."

"It's the least you deserve," I fumed, kicking and struggling against him as he hauled me into a room that was only marginally more well lit than the hallway. It was no use though—he was stronger than me, and without my magic, there was nothing I could do. "You won't get away with this, you know. My friends will come for me." But even as I spoke the words, doubt filled me. I knew Mavlyn would come, but would Leap? Would Einar?

Slaugh snorted. "I'm hardly concerned about your little ragtag band of rebels," he said. "And if your dragon friend tries to come and rescue you, he'll meet the same fate the rest of his kind did at King Aolis's hands."

My stomach dropped as I got a good look at the room—a rusted metal table, chains, a shelf full of wicked looking torture instruments. "What are you doing?" I asked, trying to keep my voice steady, but my breaths were coming too fast, too sharp. "Did King Aolis tell you to torture me?"

Slaugh snorted. "Of course not. You're his precious savior." He dragged me over to the chains dangling from the wall and fastened them to my wrists, holding me in place. I tried to kick him as he moved back, but he was too fast. "I just want to ask you a few questions, before I present you to him."

"What questions?" I narrowed my eyes as I forced my body to go still. There was no sense in wasting energy, not if Slaugh wasn't going to kill me. "And where is my mother?"

"Do you know who your parents are?" Slaugh asked, ignoring my question.

I scowled. "Of course I do. My mother is Chaya—er, I mean Gelsyne, I guess," I corrected lamely, feeling slightly ashamed. How could I have lived with my mother my entire life without knowing her real name? "My father was Caol, a water fae."

"Hmm." General Slaugh didn't seem impressed with my answer. He pulled a chain from his pocket, and my heart beat faster as I recognized the pendant dangling from the end. "I researched the origins of this talisman. It's an ancient primal stone, specifically spelled to nullify fire magic. It seems that it weakened your water magic to a degree as well, which I'm sure your *mother* did not intend when she put it around your neck as a babe." He said the word *mother* with a heavy dose of sarcasm.

I pressed my lips together, the tips of my ears burning with embarrassment. "I'm not sure what the point of this interrogation is," I said in a scathing tone. "You're asking questions you already know the answers to, and you aren't telling me anything I don't know already."

Slaugh ignored that. "Where did you find the dragon? And why is he helping you?"

I ran my tongue over my teeth, trying to decide how much to tell him. "I found him in an abandoned tower, turned to stone, and woke him up accidentally. He nearly killed me, but I convinced him to help me. Apparently he's more interested in seeking vengeance against the fae who actually killed his people than some girl."

"A girl who can use fire magic would be of great interest to a dragon." Slaugh searched my face with a suspicious glint in his eye, as if trying to detect whether I was being truthful. "It's hard to believe that you're as ignorant as you claim to be," he said after a long moment. "But perhaps that explains why you stayed in that backwoods village for as long as you did."

I lifted my chin and glared at him. "If I'm so ignorant," I told him, "then why don't you do me a favor and enlighten me?"

He shook his head and stepped forward, digging something out of his pouch. "In time," he told me, pressing a cloth against my mouth. I held my breath as a sickly sweet stench hit my nose, but eventually I was forced to breathe the sleeping potion in. Blackness crept in at the edges of my vision, and I sagged in my chains as I succumbed to the effects, leaving myself at the general's mercy.

When I woke, I wasn't in the dungeon, as I expected to be. Instead, I was lying on a feathery mattress, a down comforter pulled up to my chin. The soft, dreamy notes of a harp floated in the air, nearly lulling me back to sleep.

But the harp meant I wasn't alone in the room. There was someone else here, playing. Watching me.

I bolted upright, wincing as my head pounded with the motion. Whatever potion was in that rag had been potent stuff. Clutching my head, I noticed the manacles were still locked around my wrists, but the chain between them had been removed. The tiny primal stones set into the metal winked mockingly, and I scowled back at them. I was free to move my wrists, just not my magic. A prisoner in a pretty cage.

"Ahh, you're awake." I swung my head toward the sound to

see a pretty earth female lounging on the bed next to mine. She wore a gauzy emerald silk dress, her leaf-green hair left to hang around her shoulders in loose waves. Horror caused my heart to stutter in my chest as my gaze snagged on her face—there were delicate black veins creeping beneath her rust-colored skin, feathering the edges of her jaw and cheeks. A similar taint bled outward from her pupils, nearly swallowing her moss-colored eyes entirely.

This girl wasn't just a captive. She was shadow tainted.

"Who are you??" I asked carefully, studying her features. She wore a placid expression, as though she was simply enjoying a lazy day instead of being held captive in Castle Kaipei, her soul slowly rotting away with shadow sickness.

"I'm Lady Avani." Avani smiled, setting the book in her lap aside. I blinked, realizing that she wasn't playing the harp, and glanced around the room, looking for the source. I found the instrument in the corner, an ornate, gilded thing around four feet tall, its strings vibrating of their own accord. It must have been enchanted by witchlings. "General Slaugh told me to help you get settled in."

I nodded absently, still looking around the space. We were in a large, well-appointed tower room, done up in varying earth tones, possibly at Lady Avani's request. Disappointment filled me as I realized there wasn't a single thing in here that could be used as a weapon.

"Are all the other hostages shado—" I was about to say shadow sick, then trailed off in shock as I looked at Avani's face again. The lines marring her skin had disappeared, along with the blackness tainting her irises. "What happened to your face?"

Avani lifted a hand to touch her cheek, a frown gathering between her eyebrows. "What do you see?"

"I...well, you had these black veins, before," I said lamely, feeling ten kinds of foolish.

Had I just imagined it? Perhaps the effects of the sleeping potion were still wearing off, and I wasn't fully awake yet. "But you look great now. Your skin is perfect."

Lady Avani sighed, but not in relief. "It's the shadow taint," she said, her gaze heavy with sadness. "We all take everbright potion daily to ward off the effects of living here, but it's not quite enough to keep it at bay all the time."

"We?" I glanced around. "Are there others living here?"

Avani nodded. "Lady Cascada, and Lady Tempest, the other two hostages from the water and air realms. King Aolis keeps us here to keep our houses in line, and make sure the other realms don't rise against him." She cocked a head at me. "Cascada will be especially curious to know why you're here, since there's no reason for Lady Axlya to send a second hostage."

"I'm not—" I cut myself off, unsure how much to reveal. Clearly General Slaugh didn't tell Avani the truth about me, and I wasn't sure if that was good or bad. I was still trying to wrap my mind around the fact that Aolis was keeping the other houses in line with hostages. Were the other realms really so malcontent with his rule that this was necessary? "I'm not allowed to talk about it," I decided on.

"I see." Avani looked disappointed, but she quickly brightened. "Are you hungry? They should be serving dinner soon downstairs."

I glanced around the room again, noting the door. There were bars on the windows, but the door itself didn't seem to be anything special. I could probably knock it down with a well-placed kick. "Are we allowed to leave?" I asked dubiously.

Avani laughed, hopping lightly off the bed. The rose vines on her dress moved as she did, and I realized with a start that they were real. "Of course we are," she said, gliding toward the door. "We might be hostages, but we're still nobility. King Aolis has to give us some comforts." She glanced back at me, then frowned. "Although first, we should probably get you dressed."

I looked down at myself, realizing for the first time that I wore a simple white nightgown. "Is there anything for me to wear?" I asked, glancing at the closet on my side of the room.

Avani strode toward the closet doors and flung them open. It was filled with gowns in all imaginable shades of blue and red, some of them a blend of both colors. "I was a bit confused when I saw them bring up both fire and water colors," Avani said, eyeing me curiously, and I realized then that while she might not know anything, she had her suspicions. "Could they have made some kind of mistake, perhaps?"

"Possibly," I agreed, approaching the closet. I selected a practical gown with long sleeves and a simple, A-line skirt with minimal layers. If I needed to run or fight, I wanted as little fabric to get in the way as possible.

I changed into the gown and matching slippers, then followed Avani down the stairs to meet my fellow prisoners. We passed through a sitting room with wide, rectangular windows overlooking the courtyard, and I paused to look through the bars at the view down below.

"It's so...desolate," I said, taking in the gardens. I knew winter was around the corner, but I still expected to see some plant life. Instead, the trees and shrubs were stripped bare, branches gnarled and twisted, trunks hunched in and shriveled into husks of their former selves. The flower beds were barren, not so much as a single shoot popping up from the dry-looking soil. Fountains stood here and there, but they were dry, and I couldn't see a single sign of animal life.

"I know," Avani said sadly. "It's the shadow taint. Nothing will grow in those gardens, no matter how much work is put into them. I myself have tried to cultivate flowers over the summers, but they never take root. The earth itself has been corrupted."

I turned away from the depressing scene outside, and followed Avani into a small dining room. Two fae sat at the table already, delicately spooning some kind of creamy soup from the bowls in front of them—a water fae in a diaphanous blue gown, and an air fae dressed in pure white. The air fae's mass of curly hair reminded me of Quye, except her curls were cropped short to form a halo around her head, and the water fae had cornflower blue eyes remarkably similar to mine.

"Cascada, Tempest," Avani said by way of greeting. "This is Adara."

"Hello Adara." Tempest flashed me a smile, her silver eyes glinting as she studied me.

"You're the girl from the prophecy, are you?" Cascada asked. Her face remained unsmiling, and there was wary look in her eyes as she scrutinized me that put me on the defensive. "You don't look like much."

My back stiffened, and I took a seat at the table, trying not to scowl. "Does everyone know about this prophecy but me?" I demanded, too out of sorts to touch the food. "I only just learned about it last night."

"There isn't a single person in Lochanlee who doesn't know about it," Cascada said. "King Aolis sends his shadow guard to search the newborn babes every year for a female with fire magic." Her eyes narrowed. "Can you really do it, then? Use water and fire magic at the same time?"

"Not at the same time," I admitted. "But I can use both." I glanced at the manacles on my wrists and sighed. "I would show you if I wasn't wearing these things."

"Hmm." Cascada seemed skeptical. "Are you going to use your magic to undo the shadow corruption?"

"I would, if I had any idea how to do that," I said. "But so far, all I can do is set things on fire and put them out."

"I would think you could do more than that," Tempest said,

sitting back. "You're not some youngling still trying to master your magic."

My ears burned with embarrassment. "I didn't know I had any fire magic until three days ago. And I couldn't use my water magic at all. My mother made me wear a primal stone that was spelled to keep my powers hidden, and raised me in a tiny village in Domhain. Everything I know, I've learned only recently."

"The last three days?" Avani asked, in disbelief. "That's hard to imagine."

I didn't know what to say to that, so I changed the subject. "Why doesn't Aolis have you three in cuffs?" I asked. "Isn't he worried about you three trying something?"

Cascada huffed. "Hardly. We may be powerful, but we are no match for his shadow magic, and besides, it is not us who would suffer for our disobedience. He would punish us by attacking our families instead."

"But wouldn't that just perpetuate a vicious cycle of war?" I asked. "Your families would retaliate too, wouldn't they?"

"They would try," Avani said slowly, "but it would be a losing battle. Aolis's shadow magic is insidious—it infects everything it touches, and while everbright potion is effective against shadow creature bites, there is no cure when the attack comes straight from the source."

"One of my cousins tried to rebel against the king once," Cascada said, a deep bitterness in her voice. "Aolis was taking too many of his people. The king decimated his lands in a single night, using shadow magic. That was ten years ago, and still nothing grows or lives there save the nightmarish creatures he left in his wake."

My stomach turned at the idea of so much senseless destruction. "That's awful."

"Still," Tempest said slowly. "I don't think the king truly

wants the kingdom to be consumed by shadow magic. He likely sees you as a solution to the problem he created."

I raised an eyebrow. "I have a feeling it's not as simple as that."

Tempest shrugged. "Perhaps. But what does it matter if Aolis is the one who unlocks your magic, so long as you *can* get rid of the taint?"

I opened my mouth, but before I could answer I heard a heavy door unlatch, followed by boots clomping across the floor. A soldier in jet black armor with a wicked-looking sword strapped to his side entered the dining room, and a shiver ran down my spine as I took him in. His snow-white hair, which was slicked back from his head, was nearly the same color as his skin, and I caught the shadowy outlines of black veins creeping up the sides of his neck and down his hands. Unlike Avani's, his did not disappear no matter how much I blinked.

"You're part of the shadow guard, aren't you?" I blurted. He wore the exact same armor Slaugh and his soldiers had when they'd stormed Mrs. Aeolan's house and taken me captive.

He nodded, taking another step into the room. Tendrils of shadow wafted from the edges of his form, nearly invisible to the naked eye, the same ones that clung to General Slaugh. Part of me wondered if I was the only one who could see them—no one else at the tryouts seemed to have noticed, or if they had noticed, they'd kept their mouths shut about it.

"King Aolis requires your presence at dinner tonight," he said, looking me up and down. "I am here to escort you."

My heartbeat tripled, and I felt sweat break out along the edges of my brow. So, the moment had finally come. Despite my best efforts to heed my mother's warnings, I was going to come face-to-face with the king. The fae who had apparently been searching for me my entire life, and who was responsible for the shadow sickness sweeping through our lands.

I clenched my fists at my sides, hating that I felt so powerless in this moment. But there was nothing I could do to resist—my magic was useless, and I had no weapons on me, while this soldier was clad head to toe with armor and likely had multiple blades on his person aside from the nasty-looking sword strapped to his hip. He would cut me down if I even looked like I was *thinking* about escaping.

Taking a deep breath to calm myself, I turned to Avani, who was watching us with open curiosity. "Am I dressed appropriately to meet the king?" I asked, trying to stall.

She gave me a quick once-over, her mouth twisting slightly. "A more elaborate gown would have been better, but it's best not to keep the king waiting," she said. "Your outfit is serviceable enough."

I sighed, then turned back to the soldier. "All right. Lead the way."

The shadow guard nodded, then motioned for me to follow him. He led me back through the sitting room, then opened the door leading out of the tower and stepped aside to let me pass. A shiver crawled down my spine as I walked past him—the inky darkness clinging to his body warped the air around him, giving him a sinister aura that made me want to shrink away. I took several steps away from him, wanting distance, and gave a little sigh as the feeling lessened.

The shadow guard locked the heavy reinforced door behind him, then led the way through a twisting maze of hallways. I could tell the castle had once been a grand and welcoming place —sumptuous décor graced every open room I glanced into, and symbolism representing the four elements was subtly etched, carved, and painted into every mantle, rug, table, and wall. But the shadow taint seemed to cling to everything, making it all seem older, warped, faded. I could even sense it in the surrounding air, and it made my skin crawl. No wonder everyone who lived here had to take everbright potion.

Eventually, we came to a pair of double doors with rose vines carved into whorl patterns all across the surface. The shadow guard knocked at the door, then poked his head in when it opened and muttered something to whoever was inside.

After a moment, the guard pulled his head back and turned to face me. My breath caught as I met his eyes—dark green with gold-rimmed pupils. Hadn't I seen those eyes before? I opened my mouth as he took me by the arm, but before he could say anything, the door swung wide, and he ushered me inside.

"Miss Adara of Fenwood," the guard announced me. He released me, and I felt him slip something into my skirt pocket before he stepped away. It settled heavily into the fabric, and I slid a hand in to feel the object—long, metallic, with a loop on one end and teeth on the other.

A key.

Resisting the urge to whip it out of my pocket and get a better look at it, I looked around, trying to take in the space's enormity. My gaze was inexorably drawn to the fae sitting at the head of the long table, and I swallowed hard as our gazes collided. I'd seen drawings of King Aolis, of course, and knew that he cut a fine figure, but those images paled in comparison to the majestic figure sitting regally in the ornate dining chair. He was lean yet broad-shouldered, clad in magnificent, multi-layered robes of gold and sea foam green. A golden crown that had been forged to look like an unending line of waves sat elegantly atop his long, silver-blue hair, which hung in loose waves down to his elbows. His tanned skin was smooth, his nose strong and straight, and I thought I could even see the barest hint of laugh lines around the corners of his eyes and mouth.

How is there no trace of shadow taint on him?

"You are the spitting image of your mother," King Aolis said.

His voice was soft and warm, like golden honey dripping off the edge of a teaspoon. He stared at me, and there was something in his gaze, past the cerulean of his irises, that made me feel like I was being devoured. It was his pupils, I thought dimly as I stared back. There was a yawning abyss within, and I felt as though I was being pulled toward it. Just a few steps forward and I would be at the edge, ready to tumble into the waiting darkness.

Blinking, I gave myself a mental shake, trying to clear my head. "I look nothing like my mother," I said, taking a step back. I looked around the room again, trying to see if she was here somewhere, but the only faces aside from the king and his staff were from the portraits of former monarchs that hung on the walls. "Where is my mother?" I demanded.

"She'll be joining us shortly," the king said with a broad smile. "In the meantime, have a seat. I have been waiting for decades to meet you."

King Aolis didn't seem perturbed by my lack of deference. In fact, he seemed genuinely delighted to see me. Bewildered by this unexpectedly warm reception, I found myself acquiescing to his request, my feet moving of my own accord. A servant appeared behind my chair to pull it out, and I sat down. A small part of me wondered if perhaps I'd misinterpreted the king's intentions.

"Why are we having dinner together?" I blurted out, anxiety propelling the words from my mouth without giving me a chance to think them through. A sumptuous dinner was spread out before us—tureens of soup, roasted fowl and venison, and a number of breads, sauces, and other dishes. "Why am I even alive? Isn't my power a threat to you?"

The king threw back his head and laughed. So loud and long, in fact, that my cheeks began to sting with embarrassment. "You, a threat to me?" he chuckled, his eyes sparkling with mirth. "You might be the girl from the prophecy, but you're still a child, Adara. You are no threat to my rule."

I lifted my chin in defiance, my spine ramrod straight as I sat up tall. "If I defeat the shadows, as the prophecy says I must, then you won't be able to rule Ediria anymore. Your shadow magic is the only reason you have the throne in the first place, isn't it?"

King Aolis sighed, shaking his head. "You've clearly misunderstood my reason for bringing you here," he said, reaching for a soup tureen. "But before I explain, let us eat. You must be starving."

Before he could close his fingers around the handle, a servant was at his side, pouring the soup into a delicate bowl for him. A second servant came and did the same for me, and despite my nerves, my stomach growled at the delicious aroma wafting from the bowl. I could definitely stand to have a meal, but...

"How do I know this hasn't been doctored?" I asked suspiciously. "That you haven't laced this with some kind of potion that will compel me to do your bidding?"

The king smiled. "I don't need to do that," he said. "I have Gelsyne still, remember?"

I fisted my hands in my lap as a wave of fury raced through me like wildfire. "Yes, you do," I said through clenched teeth. "Your soldiers took her, and destroyed our home."

"A regrettable incident," the king said, "but it really was imperative to get you here by any means possible. Besides, now that you're here, you won't be going back to that hovel, anyway. You and Gelsyne will have every creature comfort you deserve, as befitting of a Greater Fae."

He brought a spoonful of soup to his mouth, and I reluctantly did the same. As I expected, it was delicious. Everything on the table was, and I quickly devoured a small army's worth of food. The lull in conversation gave me time to gather my thoughts and get a sense of my surroundings, and I let my gaze travel the room, studying the portraits on the walls. The one closest to our side of the room caught my attention—a fae dressed in turquoise robes with gilt-edged water lilies embroidered along the sleeves and hem. His lavender-blue hair was the exact same shade of mine, and he had the same slight up tilt to his nose that I did.

"King Cyrian," Aolis said with a solemn nod. "He was a wise and just ruler. I often wish he was still here, if only to offer me counsel. It was never easy, trying to fill his footsteps."

"I would trust you a lot more if you would drop the tragic king act and just tell me what you want," I said sharply.

The king arched a brow at me. "You think this is an act? That my words are not genuine?"

"I think that you told me that my mother would be arriving soon, and I've yet to see her." I leaned forward, splaying my hands on the table as I glared at the king. The manacles around my wrists bit into my skin, reminding me that despite our lavish surroundings and creature comforts, I was still a captive, still held here against my will. "How do I even know she's still alive?"

"Oh believe me, I wanted to execute Gelsyne for the treason she committed." The king spoke the words casually, but something ugly shifted behind his eyes that made my stomach twist. "She fled the court and kept you hidden all these years. Can you imagine how many lives could have been saved if I'd found you sooner? How much more wealth and freedom our kingdom would have?"

"Wealth and freedom?" I asked, confused. "I don't understand how my magic would help you accomplish any of that."

The king laughed again. "You must be joking," he said. "Surely you know of the treasures that lie in the Deadlands?"

I went still, my mind racing to catch up. I knew that the

Deadlands—formerly known as Hearthfyre, the fire fae realm—were full of veins of precious metals, and more importantly, primal stones, which fae used to store and harness fae magic. Access to those primal stones was one the main reasons we had fought so hard to reclaim the fire fae lands back from the dragons, but even though the dragons were no longer there, the mines were still inaccessible. Only those who had a death wish, or were exiled, traveled into the Deadlands. It was overrun with shadow creatures.

"You...you want me to use my magic to defeat the shadow creatures so that you can mine the Deadlands?" I asked, aghast.

"Well, not just that," King Aolis said with a wave of his hand. "I'd also like you to clear the taint from the rest of the kingdom as well. These shadow creature attacks have not been good for trade between the realms, and the house leaders have been making more noise about them. That's why I've been recruiting so heavily for the army. But," he said, his eyes gleaming as he leaned toward me and took one of my hands in his, "with you by my side, as my queen, there will be no need for that anymore."

"As... as your *what?*" the word came out in a shriek—I couldn't help it—and I snatched my hand back. "Why in the name of the Radiants do you think I would ever marry *you?*"

My heart thundered in my chest as I stared at King Aolis, and I gripped the arms of my chair until my fingers turned numb. I knew the king wanted me to use my magic, but marriage? This was just too much.

King Aolis raised his eyebrows. "I would think that obvious," he said. "I am the *king.* A marriage to me would be a great honor. And besides, as far as I'm concerned, your hand in marriage is owed to me, since your mother chose to marry someone else."

"Huh?" I stared dumbly. "My mother was supposed to marry you?"

King Aolis frowned, then chuckled again. "I keep forgetting

that you think Gelsyne is your mother," he said, shaking his head. "Allow me to correct that. Your mother was the late Princess Olette."

I stared at King Aolis, certain that I'd misheard him. "No," I said, my voice cracking a little. "That's not right. Chaya—*Gelsyne*—is my mother."

King Aolis scoffed. "You really think that Gelsyne, a powerful earth fae with a strong lineage, could have birthed a daughter without a drop of earth magic in her? No, my dear, you are not Gelsyne's child. Olette must have been pregnant when Gelsyne smuggled her out of the castle, no doubt to keep her away from me. King Cyrian had promised me her hand in marriage, before that blasted dragon prince stole her heart."

His lip curled at the mention of the dragon prince, and his cerulean eyes blazed with hatred. "I don't believe you," I said, my mind spinning. "I...I can't."

King Aolis smiled. "Well, if you can't take my word from it, let's get it straight from the horse's mouth." He clapped his hands, and a door on the far left side of the room opened. My heart dropped as two guards dragged my mother in, her too-thin form draped in a ragged, stained dress, her arms weighed down by chains.

"Gelsyne, why don't you take a minute to set Adara straight?" King Aolis asked, his smile widening. "After all, you *are* the one who's been lying to her all these years, haven't you?"

32

Einar

Gone.

The word echoed in my mind as I smashed into the china cabinet directly behind where Slaugh and Adara had been standing. Broken glass and china rained around me, but I barely noticed the shards slicing into my arm as I spun around, looking wildly for Adara as if she might reappear.

But in the back of my mind, I knew that was foolishness. Slaugh had taken her. And he wasn't coming back.

"Die, dragon!" one of the shadow guard soldiers yelled, charging at me with his sword drawn. I dodged the blow and blasted him with a torrent of fire, but unfortunately, the flames licked harmlessly against his inky black armor.

My fire wouldn't be of any use here. It was time for a good, old-fashioned brawl.

The soldier swung for me again, but this time I grabbed his wrist before he could bring the sword down, then kicked him in the stomach. He flew back against the wall, sword flying from his fingertips, and I was on him in an instant, tearing off his helmet. His eyes widened as I opened my mouth and spewed fire at his head. A scream ripped from his throat, but it died quickly as the flames quickly ate through his flesh. In seconds, his head was nothing more than a blackened skull, the stench of charred meat and black magic clinging to him.

Sensing movement behind me, I spun around and chucked the body at another soldier charging at me. The soldier stumbled back, stunned by the unexpected weight, and I wasted no time, snatching up the fallen sword of the soldier I'd just killed and hacking at the weak point right at his shoulder. Blood spewed from the wound, but instead of going down, the warrior sprang back, out of my reach. Dark magic coalesced around the wound, and I gritted my teeth as the blood flow ceased, the wound healing before my very eyes.

"You're going to have to try a little harder than that," the soldier said smugly.

He raised his hand, and I cursed as he blasted me with a gust of wind. Shadow magic crackled along my exposed skin, and I hissed as the taint bit into me, finding weaknesses in the myriad cuts along my arms. These soldiers might have been fae, but they were fae who had been gifted with shadow magic.

"Don't let them hit you with their magical attacks!" I shouted at the others, who were locked in their own battles. "You'll be infected!"

Gritting my teeth, I resisted the taint and squared off against the soldier again. This time, when he lashed out at me with his magic, I went high, flipping overhead and avoiding the attack. Landing behind him, I spun around and grabbed his head, then twisted sharply until a fatal crack echoed through the room.

Two down.

The taint began to burn in my veins as I turned to confront yet another soldier, but I kept my head down and allowed my rage to overtake me. My anguish at being separated from my mate fueled my blows, and I attacked the soldiers relentlessly, avoiding their magical attacks and using brute force and agility to crush and kill them.

They had shadow magic, but I was faster and stronger, and they had just taken away the most important thing in my life. There wasn't a force on this earth that could save them from me now.

As I tore through the soldiers, I was dimly aware of the others fighting as well. Mavlyn lashing out with her thorny vines, Leap dancing around the room and shooting bolts of lightning at his targets. Even Mrs. Aeolan fought, expertly sliced at her opponents using sharp wind currents. They kept the soldiers distracted, allowing me to tear through them, painting Mrs. Aeolan's once-pristine walls with their blood.

Before I knew it, I was standing in the middle of the room, panting, covered in shadow guard blood. The bodies of the soldiers were littered all around, nearly every piece of furniture reduced to kindling. Leap, Mavlyn, and I exchanged wary glances, and I strained my ears, searching for the sound of any other approaching enemies.

But there was nothing, save for the sound of our harsh breathing.

"Well, that was far too much excitement for this hour of the morning," Mrs. Aeolan said briskly, propping her hands on her hips. "I'm going to have to have this entire room redone."

"You're going to have this entire room burned," Leap corrected. He grimaced at the dark blood staining his left sleeve. "And we're going to need some everbright potion for Einar and the rest of us. He was hit, and all this blood can't be good for us.

"I have a few doses upstairs," Mavlyn said. "I brought some along just in case."

"We're going to need to get rid of these bodies, too," Leap

said. "There's no way the neighbors didn't hear that commotion. Someone's going to come looking."

We leaped into action, Mavlyn fetching the potions from upstairs while Leap and Mrs. Aeolan used their air magic to float the bodies out into the backyard. We didn't have an earth fae on hand who could bury the bodies, which would have been easier, so I was forced to use my fire to make quick work of the corpses, scorching them at the hottest temperatures possible so we could reduce them to ash.

By the time I finished, I was nearly dizzy with exhaustion.

"We can't stay here," Leap said as I sat down on the edge of the fountain. A sharp ache gripped my heart as I remembered Adara sitting here with me less than a day ago, trying to bring me comfort after I'd stormed out of the house in a fit. I'd foolishly pushed her away, had pushed her away many times, but now that she was gone I fiercely wished that I hadn't. I couldn't bear the distance between us, and the beast inside me roared and beat its wings, frantic to chase after her.

"Of course not," Mavlyn said, folding her arms across her chest. "We've got to go after Adara."

"You three should clean up and leave now," Mrs. Aeolan said. "Don't worry about the neighbors, or about this mess. I can take care of that."

"Are you certain?" I asked, lifting my head to look at her. Soot and blood streaked her gown, her silver hair a frizzy halo around her head, and yet somehow, she looked more regal than any of us. "This isn't going to be easy."

"Oh, hush." She waved a hand at me. "This will be far easier than taking on King Aolis in his stronghold. Though I really do wish you hadn't destroyed the dining room quite so thoroughly." She sighed.

"I'm sorry, Mrs. Aeolan," Mavlyn said, looking stricken. "I didn't mean to bring so much trouble upon you."

"Nonsense." Mrs. Aeolan gave Mavlyn a brief hug. "It's been a long time since these old bones have seen any kind of adventure, and it was lovely to see you. You three had better get going, and don't worry about me. I'll be just fine."

The three of us quickly cleaned up, washing the blood off our skin and changing into fresh clothes, then hurried out the back, hoods drawn over our faces. Walking as fast as we could without looking like we were rushing, we made our way back down to the lower city, where we could hopefully find a place to hole up until night fell and we could sneak out of Wynth entirely.

"So what's the plan now?" Mavlyn asked as we slowed our pace, blending into the crowd. The streets were still decorated with the remnants of last night's festival, but I noticed now that wanted posters of Adara's face were plastered on the outside of some of the buildings. "Do we head to Castle Kaipei? General Slaugh had to have taken her there."

"I don't see any other choice," I said. The ache of Adara's absence was growing worse, especially now that I was seeing her face everywhere. I knew it was the mating bond punishing me for allowing her any sort of distance, demanding that I rectify the mistake at once and return to her side before someone else could claim her.

But it wasn't just the mating bond that compelled me to rescue Adara. It was the fact that the pieces were falling into place, and I was beginning to suspect I knew who she really was. The knowledge of her true identity was eating away at me, but even worse, the fear that I might be too late to save her. I'd never experienced terror the way I had when that soulless bastard had opened that portal and dragged Adara through it.

What was Slaugh doing to her now? Torturing her? Or had he already handed her over to Aolis, to use and abuse as he saw fit? Just the thought of that rotten king putting his hands on

Adara threatened to send me into a rage, and I had to take slow, deep breaths to calm myself.

Losing control wouldn't help Adara. I needed to keep a clear head, and get out of the city.

"We're going to need a few supplies if we're planning on storming the castle," I said. "I've never led an attack on Kaipei myself, but we had detailed maps of the defenses. It won't be easy to get through."

Leap nodded. "We're going to need some explosives," he said.

"And some everbright potion, to ward against shadow sickness," Mavlyn said. "Is there an apothecary here in the lower city?"

We made a list of the things we thought we might need, then spent the final hours running around the city and purchasing supplies. It seemed to take forever, but finally, the sun began to creep below the horizon, painting Wynth in fiery shades of red and gold. My shoulder blades itched with the need to sprout wings and fly as fast as I could toward Kaipei, but even though I couldn't see it, I knew the energy dome arcing over Wynth was still active. Flying directly out meant certain death, even for a dragon.

The shadows grew longer as sundown finally approached, and we headed for the alleyway that led to the secret passage Leap, Adara and I had used to get into the city. All seemed quiet as we entered the alley, but we only made it three paces before I heard the barely perceptible sound of several bodies dropping from the rooftops above. Tensing, I turned to see Storm and six other air fae youths with him, all armed to the teeth, weapons pointing straight at us.

"Not so fast," Storm said, taking a step toward Leap. Hatred glimmered in his eyes as a cruel smirk twisted his lips. "You didn't bring me my fan."

Leap crossed his arms over his chest. "So? You told me you were going to tell my uncle about me, but I don't care. I'm leaving the city now—there's no way he'll catch up to me. And besides, you never expected me to get the fan. You were hoping Madame Gale and her cronies would have me killed after they caught me."

"I was," Storm agreed, his eyes narrowing, "but you're a slippery one. You escaped Madame Gale, and even managed to evade General Slaugh and his shadow guards. Oh yes," he said with a laugh, noting the murderous expression on my face. "The moment I saw those wanted posters going up, I went straight to him. He was already here in town sniffing around. I was rewarded handsomely for the tip, too."

"You slimy piece of gutter trash," I snarled, igniting a fireball in my palm. In an instant, all five of Storm's crew turned their crossbows on me, and I froze.

"Ah, ah, ah." Storm wagged his finger at me. "I suggest you snuff out that fireball now, unless you'd like to become a pincushion."

"You seem to be under the false impression that we're outmatched," Mavlyn said, drawing Storm's attention. "But have you taken a minute to look down?"

"Keep your eyes on them," Storm barked at his crew, and I cursed inwardly—that would have been a perfect distraction. Slowly, he looked down, and I did as well, noticing for the first time the thin vines wrapped around all their legs.

"I wouldn't move too much," Mavlyn said with a sly smile as Storm tugged experimentally on one of his legs. "Leap and I spotted you, and I scattered those seeds behind us when we walked in. Those vines have tiny thorns on them that secrete a very special poison. If you move too much, you'll be dead."

Storm bared his teeth in a snarl. "We can still kill you," he snapped, raising his crossbow and pointing it at Leap's chest. "You take one more step—"

"Storm," Leap interrupted in a quiet voice. "Enough of this. I know why you're angry, and it isn't just because of me. You screwed up that night, too."

"*I* screwed up?" Storm hissed, his face turning bright red with anger. I tensed, noticing how his finger trembled on the trigger. One slip, and Leap would be dead. "You're the one—"

"Yes, yes, I'm the one who didn't vet our insider," Leap said. "But you're the one who got distracted by that stupid jewel-encrusted saber hanging on the wall on our way out. You're the idiot who just *had* to stop and pry it off the wall—"

"—I was trying to make sure the night wasn't a total loss!" Storm protested.

"—and you're the reason Skye jumped in front of that crossbow bolt that was meant for you," Leap finished coldly. "Are you really going to dishonor her memory by killing me in the same way they killed her while sacrificing her life for you?"

A heavy silence descended in the alley then, and several of Storm's comrades lowered their crossbows. "He's right," the girl with the pigtails who'd caught us sneaking into the city said in a quiet voice. "Skye wouldn't want this, Storm."

"We don't know what Skye would have wanted," Storm said through gritted teeth. Tears gleamed in his eyes as the last of the sunlight disappeared from the sky, plunging the city into twilight. "She's *dead*."

"She is," the girl agreed, "and I think we've had enough death, Storm. Let Leap and his friends go. Even if we kill him, that earth fae girl will kill us in retaliation. And I don't know about you, but I think Skye would be real pissed if all of us showed up to meet her in the afterlife with each other's blood on our hands."

A long silence passed, and I was just beginning to wonder if we really would have to fight when Storm finally lowered his crossbow. "Fine," he said with a sigh. "But will you at least release us?"

"The vines will loosen on their own once we're far enough away," Mavlyn said coolly. Her easygoing nature had evaporated, reminding me how deadly earth fae could be, especially the ones who controlled plant life.

Leap and Mavlyn turned away to leave, but I stood my ground for one last moment, looking Storm in the eye. "If Adara is harmed in any way because of your interference," I said in a quiet voice, "I will personally come back here and flay every strip of hide off you, boy."

I allowed a tiny bit of the shift to come over me, and Storm's eyes widened. I knew he could see the outline of wings behind my back, and the reptilian slits of my pupils. He nearly took a step back before he remembered the vines, and I grinned at him, baring sharp fangs.

"You're not fae," he accused, pointing a trembling finger at me. "What are you?"

"Let's hope you never find out," I said, then turned and followed my friends into the darkness.

33

Adara

"Mother!" I cried, jumping to my feet. My chair skidded across the floor behind me, but I paid it no mind as I raced around the table and tried to get to her side.

But before I could manage more than a few paces, a powerful hand closed around my wrist, pulling me to a halt. "No closer," King Aolis said, and though his voice was mild, I could sense an undercurrent of something sinister beneath it. "You can speak to her from here."

"You *bastard*." I spun around to face him, yanking my arm from his grip. "Look at what you've done to her!" I jabbed a finger in my mother's direction as I glared up at him. Standing, he was a towering figure, and I had to lean my head all the way back to look him in the eye, but I refused to allow that to intimidate me. The key that guard had slipped into my pocket was burning a hole in my skirt, and I wanted so badly to use it to free myself so I could incinerate the king where he stood. "She's skin and bones, and riddled with shadow sickness!"

"A regrettable side-effect of spending too much time in the

castle," King Aolis said with a sigh. "I make the staff take ever-bright potion, but we've had severe shortages recently, and I can't waste such precious supplies on traitors. But," he added with a sly smile, "you'll be able to restore Gelsyne to the picture of health. You just need to master your powers first."

I clenched and unclenched my hands several times, trying for patience. Too furious to even address Aolis's comment, I slowly turned back to face my mother. The guards had deposited her onto the stone floor, where she knelt, her ragged dress pooled around her knees. Her normally lustrous hair was dull and stringy, her skin sallow, and her green eyes glittered with anguish as she looked upon me.

"Adara," she croaked in a voice like rusted nails. "I'd hoped you would stay away."

"What are you talking about?" I wanted so badly to close the distance between us, to take her too-frail body into my arms and hold her close, but Aolis's unspoken threat hung in the air behind me. He wouldn't kill Mother, not when he was using her as a bargaining chip, but he certainly had the power to inflict more pain on her, and she had suffered enough. "I couldn't stay away. How could you think I would leave you?"

She shook her head, sadness overtaking her features. "I've fought my whole life to keep you hidden and safe, so King Aolis wouldn't be able to use you as a pawn. To see you here in his clutches now, after all I've sacrificed..."

She trailed off, and though she looked absolutely wretched, some of the pity I felt for her faded as my anger and frustration found its way to the surface. I knew she'd only been doing what she felt was best for me, but she'd lied about so many things...

"How foolish," King Aolis scoffed, his tone full of derision. I glanced behind me to see him curling his lip at Mother, looking down at her as though she were a dog unworthy of licking his boots. "You obviously heard about the prophecy, so you must have known this was inevitable—"

"I've told you and your minions a thousand times," Gelsyne snapped, "I knew nothing of a prophecy! Olette begged me with her dying breath that I would keep Adara away from you when she was born. She feared you would kill her once you realized Adara was Daryan's daughter, and with such strong fire magic, there was no way for us to hide her heritage!"

The words echoed through the room like a slap, and I stared at my mother, rooted to the spot. "D-Daryan?" I stammered, unable to believe what I was hearing. "The dragon prince was my father?"

"Of course he was," My mother—no, *Gelsyne*—said wearily. She scraped a manacled hand over her face, trying to collect her thoughts. "Olette had eyes for no one else, and the two of them were mated. The bond between them was so strong that she nearly joined him in the afterlife when he died—a foolish decision on your part, Aolis," she snapped, her eyes sparking fire as she glared at the king. "The only thing that kept Olette alive was Adara growing inside her. Once she was born, Olette passed within minutes. She barely had a chance to meet her daughter before she died."

King Aolis flushed. "How was I to know dragon mate bonds were so potent?" he snapped, his tone riddled with anger and embarrassment. "It isn't as though they've ever taken the time to explain their primitive ways to us!"

"Oh please," Mother said in a scathing tone. "You were too blinded by jealousy and hatred to ask those kinds of questions, and even if you weren't, it wouldn't have mattered. Olette was only ever a possession to you. You never loved her, or cared about her happiness. If you had, you would have let her and Daryan live out the rest of their lives in happiness. Instead, you risked the entire future of Ediria by ordering his assassination, and look where we are now!"

I glanced back and forth between them, trying to grasp everything that was being said. My world was tilting on its axis, everything I thought I knew about myself crumbling to dust beneath the crushing truth of the words being hurled back and forth across the room.

My mother was the princess, Olette.

My father was the dragon prince, Daryan.

King Aolis had assassinated my father.

And Gelsyne—who was *not* my mother—had hidden me away not because of my strange powers...but because I was *half-dragon*.

My legs threatened to buckle, and I gripped the table behind me, trying to steady myself. "Adara?" a voice asked, but it sounded so very far away, as if from a lifetime ago.

No, not a lifetime. A life. Another life, that had belonged to another person.

Because the old me, she wasn't real. She was a lie.

"How could you keep something so important from me?" I asked Mother. Stabbing pain radiated through my chest—the knife of betrayal twisting deep. "Something so vital to my identity? You let me believe my entire life that I was magically incompetent...that I was broken. That my only option was to follow in your footsteps as a healer, and to live my life out in a tiny village where everyone hated me for being different!"

All the repressed anger that I'd shoved back down rose to the surface, burning my eyes and filling my throat until I felt like I was choking on it. My vision blurred, and I blinked tears away as I clenched my hands, impotent rage eating me alive. I wanted to lash out—at Mother, at Aolis, for putting me in such an impossible position. For forcing me into the box I'd lived in my whole life and allowing me to believe I was weak and unworthy.

"I'm sorry," Mother choked out. Tears streamed down her cheeks unchecked, and there was such a stricken look on her face that some of the anger bled out of me despite my best efforts to hold on to it. "I see now how wrong I was to handle things the way I had. I should have known Aolis would find you eventually, should have prepared you so that you would have been strong enough to hold your own. I was blinded by my fear, and my promise to Olette..." she trailed off, letting out a shuddering breath.

"Well, this is all very touching," King Aolis drawled, drawing my attention to him, "but as much as we all wish we could have done things differently, the past can't be changed. And as the situation stands now, the kingdom is only going to continue to be overwhelmed by shadow magic. You are the only one with the power to truly fight back."

He softened his tone as he looked down at me, but though he looked perfect and magnificent as only a royal fae at the height of his power could, there was no mistaking the inky darkness shifting behind his eyes. Shadow magic, rooted deeply inside of him.

"You are the source of this corruption," I said quietly. "Do you really think that cleansing the land isn't going to involve cleansing it of you, too?"

King Aolis gave me a smile. "You'll find it a little difficult to do that once we're bound by the marriage covenant," he said, "which is the only way I'll agree to perform the ritual on you and unlock your magic. No one else will do it for you, not so long as I rule," he said when I opened my mouth to protest.

"You evil bastard," I hissed. "If you had even a shred of decency, you wouldn't force me to do this."

"You'll find that decency is a luxury those in power can ill afford to indulge in." King Aolis's smile turned vicious as he spread his hands, as if weighing something on each of his palms.

"So, what will it be, Adara? Will you agree to marry me, so you can save your precious 'mother' and be a hero to the people? Or will you reject me out of spite, and let the entire kingdom rot for the sake of your pride?"

I stared at him, caught between two impossible choices. To marry him, and enslave my magic to his whims, or remain free at the expense of the kingdom. I knew which choice the hostages would want me to make...but could I really go through with it? And what assurances did I have that King Aolis would keep his word?

Before I could make a decision, the castle walls began to rumble. My breath caught at the sound of explosions outside, followed by distant screams.

"What is that?" King Aolis demanded, striding to one of the floor-length windows. I hurried over to them as well, pressing my nose to them, and my heart leaped in my throat as I caught sight of a cloud zipping around in the sky. There was no mistaking the white-haired youth, or the bolts of lightning arcing from his fingertips as he zapped guards straight off the walls.

"Leap," I breathed, hope leaping in my chest. If Leap was here, that meant Einar and Mavlyn were too. Quickly, I fumbled the key from my skirt pocket, then inserted it into the tiny hole in my right manacle. The piece of metal popped open, and let it drop to the floor before I went to work on the other.

"Friends of yours?" King Aolis sneered, his gaze fixed on the sky. "That's no matter. Even if they make it past the defenses, they're no match for my shadow magic."

I shot out a hand, and King Aolis jumped back with a shout as I unleashed a gout of flame at him. The hem of his robes caught fire, but he quickly summoned a gust of wind to snuff it out.

"How did you get your manacles off?" he demanded, eyes flashing.

"I have my ways." Smirking, I stalked toward him, my arms engulfed with flames, ready to unleash them on him. "What's wrong, Aolis? Are you afraid?"

"Of you?" he scoffed. "Hardly." He raised his arms, and tentacles of shadow streamed from his body. My skin crawled as dark magic permeated the air, and Gelsyne coughed from behind me. "I would snuff those flames out, Adara. Someone is liable to be hurt."

"Threatening my mother won't make me agree to marry you," I pointed out. "In fact, it's guaranteed to ensure I won't."

King Aolis scoffed. "You seem to think you have more power here than you do," he said, circling me. "I can kill Gelsyne any time I like—you'll still fold eventually. Someone like you would never risk the lives of the entire kingdom for the sake of your own freedom."

He shot a tendril of shadow toward Gelsyne, and I flung out my hand in response. A whip of flame snaked through the air, catching the shadow, and a wave of satisfaction filled me as my fire burned the shadow tendril into nothingness.

"That's an interesting development," Aolis said, surprise flickering across his handsome features. "I didn't realize your fire alone was enough to stop my shadows."

"Guess you learn something new every day." Giving him a mean smile, I stalked toward him, summoning more flames to my hands. I felt powerful, magic surging to my fingertips as I finally gave myself the freedom to let loose. The flames around me rose higher and higher, and I allowed them to swirl around me, licking at my skin the way a puppy dog might lavish attention on its master.

The fire was mine to command. And I was going to destroy him.

King Aolis sneered at me, and he made a slicing motion through the air. I jumped to the side, but not before something invisible sliced through my sleeve, and I hissed as a long gash appeared along my forearm.

"You forget I am a master of both water and air," he taunted. "Do you really think a fledgling fae like you can keep up with me?"

I squared my shoulders, cursing myself inwardly. How had I been so foolish as to forget he had other weapons at his disposal? "I guess we're going to find out," I said.

Aolis sliced his hand through the air, but I was ready and waiting this time. I dodged the air attack, then tried to summon an ice stake and fling it at him. But the flames that roared around me were too hot for me to pull any moisture from the air, and I didn't dare let go of my fire magic. The moment I did, Mother was dead.

Instead, I grabbed a steak knife off the table, and flung it at Aolis. He used his air magic to knock it away, but the distraction allowed me to get in close, and I swung a flaming fist at his face. He caught the punch, then howled as the flames seared his skin, and I grinned viciously as I brought my other hand around in a right hook.

"That's enough!" he roared, blasting me back with a wave of air magic. The blast upended the dining table, sending food, dishes, and cutlery flying, and I cried out as a knife sliced into my upper thigh.

But somehow, I still found the strength to move, to put myself between Aolis and Mother.

"You'll have to kill me if you want to get to her," I said between clenched teeth.

Aolis laughed, his eyes glittering with something bordering on madness. The abyss that lurked within his pupils had expanded, engulfing the whites of his eyes completely. "If I have to kill you, I will," he said. "But is that really what you want, Adara? To throw your life away so needlessly, when you have the power to deliver our kingdom from the darkness?"

I opened my mouth to shout at him that *he* was the darkness, but just then the doors opened with a bang. We turned toward the sound, and my heart leaped as two familiar faces raced into the room.

They'd come. For me.

34

Einar

"Can't this thing go any faster?" I demanded as we puttered along through the sky on Leap's cloud familiar. It had been a full day since we'd left Wynth, and Kaipei was only just now appearing on the horizon. "If I were flying, we would have been there already."

"This thing has a name," Leap warned as Cirra rumbled ominously beneath us. "And feelings."

"All right, all right." I reluctantly patted one of the cloud's fluffy swells. "Cirra. Can't Cirra go any faster?"

"She could if it was just me she was carrying," Leap said, "but you two are heavy, and Cirra is stretching herself thin to make herself wide enough to fit all three of us. This is the best she can do."

"I think Cirra is doing a fantastic job," Mavlyn said, stroking the cloud fondly. It immediately ceased its rumbling, and instead started up something that sounded remarkably like a purr. The first few hours of travel had been rough on Mavlyn—earth fae weren't exactly fond of their feet leaving the ground—

but she'd acclimated quickly, and looked as comfortable as any air fae. Her auburn hair streamed out behind her like a banner, and her cheeks and the tip of her nose were pink with cold. "And besides, even you agreed that you can't fly us to Kaipei. You're far too visible in your dragon form during the day, and we don't have time to wait for nightfall."

"Not to mention that riding Cirra gives us the element of surprise," Leap said. "They won't see us coming until it's too late."

I sighed. "At least this gives us the opportunity to conserve our strength," I said, my gaze firmly fixed on Kaipei. It wasn't hard to spot—the dark clouds looming overhead drew the eye straight to the capital city. Kaipei was built on a mountainous island in the center of a vast lake, with massive, fortified walls that rose at least five stories up, enclosing the town that made up the lower part of the city. The castle itself perched at the top, with bridges running between the larger main building and the smaller sections. Lightning rods identical to the ones in Wynth topped its many towers and turrets, and I noted similar ones along the walls.

"How close will you need to be to take those towers out?" I asked Leap.

"At least fifty yards," he said. "It's harder to accurately aim lightning at distances greater than that."

"And you're sure you'll be able to subdue the poison vines?" I asked Mavlyn. Because fae from all four houses had ruled the castle, it had built in defenses from all the elements. Water and air would be the strongest, since those were Aolis's elements, but that meant the earth and fire elements would be underpowered.

"With ease," Mavlyn said. There was a beat of silence, and then she added, "you never did explain to us exactly how you'll know where to find Adara. Kaipei Castle is bound to be huge—she could be anywhere, and the longer we spend running around trying to find her, the bigger the risk we'll be captured or killed. The everbright potion will only last us a couple of hours."

"I'll be able to track her by scent," I said, the lie rolling easily off my tongue. I wasn't about to tell them the truth—that the mating bond was like an anchor hooked into my chest, the chain tugging me inexorably toward her. There was no place in Eidira where Adara could hide from me, no matter how treacherous or remote.

"By scent?" Leap asked, looking incredibly skeptical. "What, like a dire wolf?"

"Exactly," I said. "Dragons have to hunt for our food, you know. We're excellent trackers."

"Uhuh," Leap said, not sounding even remotely convinced. I couldn't blame him—dragons spotted our prey from the sky, after all. We were almost never close enough to track them by scent.

"There's something that's been bothering me since the shadow guard attack," Mavlyn said. "I don't know if you two noticed, but Slaugh called Adara "princess". And I don't think he meant it as a term of endearment."

"Did he?" Leap frowned. "I don't remember that."

"I do," I said quietly. I hadn't examined that piece of information too closely while we were in Wynth, but I'd had plenty of time to think about it since we'd been stuck on this cloud for hours. "If Adara really is a princess, then that means she is Olette's daughter."

"Olette? The dead water fae princess?" Mavlyn demanded. "But Olette was killed during the wedding feast. Everyone knows that. King Aolis mourned her publicly for months afterward. All the stories say he was deeply in love with her."

"She should have died the moment Daryan was killed," I said, "since the two of them were mated. But I was there. I saw her being dragged away by her lady-in-waiting, an earth fae noble. If she was pregnant at the time, the babe would have kept her alive. Long enough to see it born, in any case."

"But...but wouldn't that mean Adara is half-dragon?" Leap asked, his face scrunched up in confusion.

"Giant's teeth, it *would*," Mavlyn gasped, her eyes popping wide. "That would explain why she has fire magic! And why her mother wanted to keep it a secret!"

I gritted my teeth as I looked at the castle again. We were getting closer now, maybe an hour away. I was itching to see Adara again, to take her in my arms and really *look* at her. She favored her fae heritage so strongly that I hadn't noticed, but there would be traces of Daryan in her features.

My best friend. Adara was my best friend's daughter.

And the Radiants had made her my mate.

"Blast it all," I growled, balling my hands into fists. This wasn't supposed to happen! How could I possibly return to my role as a sleeping guardian, knowing that Daryan had a daughter who was not only alive, but also carrying the fate of the world on her shoulders? He would never forgive me if I abandoned her, and truthfully, I didn't think I'd be able to bring myself to leave her side once we were reunited.

"Are you okay, Einar?" Mavlyn touched my elbow, pulling me from my thoughts. "You look like you're ready to launch yourself off Cirra's back."

"You're not far off," I muttered. The desire to fly straight to the castle so I could tear it apart, find Adara, and stake my claim on her, was incredibly strong.

But instead of doing that, I grabbed my satchel and checked the contents. The explosives I'd spent the last couple of hours preparing nestled safely inside, just waiting for me to ignite them. I pulled one out and rolled it between my palm, the smooth glass ball comforting against my skin.

It had been a long time since I'd practiced warfare, but it was second nature to me.

"All right," Leap said, and Cirra slowed her pace. We were less than half a mile out now. He raised both of his hands, and lightning began to crackle from his fingertips. "Get ready, you two."

He stood up on the cloud, and I tensed, noticing that the guards on the wall facing us were looking up at us. A few of them were air fae, which meant they would be able to engage us in the sky. Leap pointed one hand at the lightning rod closest to us, and another at a rod higher up, close to the top of the castle. I sucked in a breath as he drew more lightning to his fingertips, building the energy in his hands into massive, glowing blue-white balls that hissed and crackled. This close, I could feel it snapping at my skin, and I winced a little at the pain. If Leap lost control for even a single second, we were all dead.

But he didn't. Instead, he snapped his fingers, releasing the charges. The guards shouted as massive bolts of lightning streaked through the sky, hitting their targets unerringly. The entire energy field lit up with a shriek as the lightning zig zagged through it, then abruptly went dead, the two towers Leap had hit charred and smoking from the overload.

"It's down!" Leap shouted. "Hurry, before they get it back up again!"

I snatched Mavlyn by the waist and leaped from the cloud, my dragon wings already bursting from my back. A volley of arrows sang through the air, narrowly missing me, but I didn't stop to worry—Leap was covering us, using his wind magic to knock the arrows out of the sky and distracting the guards. I lit a couple of bombs and dropped them in strategic places, blowing up two bridges, one guard tower, the stables, and the courtyard outside the main entrance to the castle.

"This is insane!" Mavlyn shouted as explosions shook the air.

Her eyes were wide as she looked down at the screaming guards, and I caught the stricken expression on her face as she watched a griffin stumble out of the stables, one of its great wings engulfed in flames. It let out a shriek of agony, and even I felt a twinge of guilt as I watched it suffer.

But the last thing we needed was another griffin attack. They'd nearly gotten us when Adara and I had fled Lady Mossi's. And while Leap was formidable on his own, even he wouldn't be able to withstand an entire fleet of them.

Satisfied that I'd put a dent in the castle's defenses, I flew straight to one of the main towers, where purplish black vines writhed along the stone walls, just waiting to snatch us up in their clutches.

"There, there," Mavlyn crooned, stretching a hand out toward them. "It's all right. We're friends."

The vines reluctantly lowered themselves away from the window, but I could see it was a struggle. "Damn shadow magic," Mavlyn grumbled under her breath. "It's interfering with my ability to control them."

I tucked Mavlyn tight against my body, then folded my wings around us and aimed feet first for the window. We crashed through the glass, and I hissed as shards ripped at my wings, sending streaks of burning pain through them. Several guards who had been playing a game of dice shouted in alarm, and they jumped up from the table, already drawing their swords. I was on the first one in a second, using my clawed hand to rip out his throat, and blasting the other two with fire. Their screams, along with the scent of charred flesh, would draw attention, so I tossed the dead body aside and yanked the door open, then began running down the stairs.

"Where are we going?" Mavlyn panted as she ran behind me. I could hear the sounds of fighting outside, and I hoped Leap was doing all right. It was incredibly brave of him to take on the guards outside like that, but I'd left him half the bombs, and he was quick-witted and resourceful. I had to believe he would be okay.

"Following the scent," I answered, reaching the bottom of the tower. I flung open the door, and we ran down a wide hallway, past dozens of rooms. I expected to run into guards, but the halls were suspiciously empty aside from a few servants who scurried fearfully the moment they saw us coming.

"Where the hell is everyone?" Mavlyn voiced my thoughts aloud. "Why isn't anyone trying to stop us?"

"I don't know," I admitted as I turned a corner, passing an enormous set of double doors I suspected led to the great hall. I didn't sense Adara in there, though, so I kept running. "This smells like a trap. Is there any way they could have known we were coming?"

"Anything is possible," Mavlyn said darkly. "But there's no way we can turn back. Not as long as we're sure Adara is here."

"Do you hear that?" I asked, slowing my pace. I could hear the sounds of fighting down the hall—shouting, the roar of flames, someone laughing darkly.

"It sounds like a battle," Mavlyn said grimly. She reached into one of her pockets and withdrew a fistful of seeds as we followed the sound, stopping in front of a door. "Is Adara in there?"

"Yes." I could feel the bond tugging, demanding that I storm in there and take what was mine. "Are you ready?" I asked Mavlyn, grabbing the doorknob.

"Ready as I'll ever be."

I wrenched open the door, and Mavlyn and I charged through, only to skid to a halt at the sight before us. We were in a large, well-appointed dining room, except the massive table that had likely sat in the center had been thrown to the side, the room littered with broken furniture, dishes, candelabras, and food. Adara and Aolis were engaged in a fierce battle in the center of the room, a clash of fire against shadow.

"Ahh, we have company," Aolis said in a bored voice, glancing toward me. His arms were outstretched toward Adara, shadow magic pouring in snake-like rivers from his body. It looked like he was trying to plunge the entire room in darkness, and an icy shiver raced down my spine at how close to death we all were.

"I know." Sweat poured off Adara's brow as she countered with fire magic, and I watched in astonishment as her flames ate away at the shadows. It was one thing to use fire against shadow creatures, but I'd seen Aolis use his magic firsthand to cut down dragons as though they were nothing more than blades of grass. Even the strongest of us hadn't been able to use our fire to stop him, but Adara was keeping him at bay somehow. "Meet my friends, Aolis."

Adara didn't turn to look at me, and I didn't blame her. I could see that it was taking every ounce of effort to keep Aolis back, and I frowned, wondering why she even bothered when she was impervious to shadow magic. But then I spotted a huddled form in the corner a few yards behind Adara, and the two guards flanking her. Chills ran over my skin as I recognized one of them as General Slaugh, but it wasn't him who had my attention.

It was Gelsyne. Adara's guardian.

"Please," she whispered, turning to face us. Even bedraggled and ruined as she looked, I recognized her instantly as the lady-in-waiting who had dragged Olette away during the wedding feast. "Help her. She can't hold out much longer."

"There's nothing any of you can do to help," Aolis scoffed. "Adara may be strong, but she's no match for my shadow magic. Not while her light magic is still locked away. She'd have to complete the ritual first, and I won't allow it unless she marries me." He smirked at her.

A haze of red swam over my vision, and I nearly shifted into dragon form on the spot. "Marry you?" I thundered, taking a step toward Aolis. "It's not enough for you to steal one dragon bride, eh? You have to go for two?"

King Aolis froze, and his shadows faltered. "You two aren't mated," he said, his gaze cutting to Adara. "Are you?"

"Not that I'm aware of," Adara said through gritted teeth. She used the distraction to blast more fire at Aolis, and he hissed as a flame latched onto his arm, burning through his robes. Snarling, he waved his hand, and a current of water flew across the room from an upended pitcher, dousing the fire.

"Then you have no claim over her, dragon," Aolis sneered. He gestured to General Slaugh and his guard. "Kill them," he ordered. "They are of no use to me."

To my surprise, the soldiers didn't move. "I don't know about that," General Slaugh drawled, a lazy smile curling his ruined mouth. "I think it might be fun to keep a dragon chained up in the dungeons as a pet."

"I didn't ask for your opinion, Slaugh," Aolis snapped. "Kill them, now."

But Slaugh merely inspected his fingernails, looking completely disinclined to move. I stared at him, puzzled—I knew the bastard hated dragons with a passion. Why was he staying his hand?

"How dare you," King Aolis seethed when Slaugh continued to ignore him. "You refuse to do as your king commands?"

Slaugh narrowed his eyes at Aolis, and I watched the exchange, fascinated despite myself. "I've done everything you've asked, remained one of your most loyal supporters, given you my council repeatedly. Yet you do nothing but cower inside the castle, refusing to use your magic, letting the other houses run roughshod over the kingdom. You've become weak, King Aolis. Unworthy of the throne, unworthy of the powers the shadows have gifted you."

"Fine," Aolis snarled. His handsome face mottled with fury, and blackness swallowed his eyes, from the depths of his pupils all the way to the corners of his whites. "If you won't do it, then I'll kill all of you!"

He took a step toward me, shooting a tendril of shadow my way. I dodged, but before he could strike again, Adara jumped in front of him, putting her body between Aolis and me. Pride and anguish swelled inside me as I watched her—she was like an avenging goddess, her lavender-blue hair and the skirts of her gown floating all around her as she commanded the raging flames.

"I'm your opponent, Aolis," Adara said in a voice like hardened steel. "If you want to get to my friends, you'll have to go through me, first."

Aolis sighed. "If I must," he said, closing his eyes. Every light in the room winked out as he pulled the shadows to him, and a wave of terror rose inside me as the shadow tentacles coalesced into a monstrous, hulking form behind the king. It towered over both of them, larger than any flames Adara could hope to summon on her own. She would survive the assault, but she would be completely drained of magic, and Gelsyne would be left to Aolis's mercy.

I couldn't allow that to happen, but I knew that my magic was useless here. There was only one thing I could do...

"Adara." I stepped into the fire, allowing the flames to lick at my skin as I came to stand by her side. Adara whipped her head around to look at me, the flames flickering as her concentration wavered for a heartbeat. My heart ached as I looked into her face —behind the determination, I could see the terror, the exhaustion, the grief etched into her soul. This close, I could make out her wounds—a gash on her arm, a knife wound in her thigh, and numerous nicks and cuts.

Without breaking her gaze, I unclasped the cuff around my wrist and fastened it around her upper arm.

"What is this?" she asked, looking at it.

"It belonged to Daryan." I swallowed hard, then added, "To your father. The primal stone in it has vast fire magic reserves." I stepped back, but instead of withdrawing, I stood behind her, placing my hands on her shoulders. I couldn't offer her my magic, but I could offer her strength and support. "Use the primal stone, Adara, and defeat King Aolis. The throne he sits on belongs to you, and it's high time you take it back."

35

Adara

I sucked in a breath as Einar's hands curled around my shoulders. Strength flowed through my body, and I knew it wasn't just from the primal stone he'd given me. No, his very presence seemed to seep into my bones, warm and reassuring, bolstering my resolve. My heart swelled—for once, we were united, our differences fading away in the face of our common enemy. I felt as tall and strong as a giant, as mighty as a tsunami, as fierce as a firestorm. Like nothing could stand in my way, not even a wicked king overflowing with dark magic.

I didn't have to ask how to use the primal stone—I could already feel the energy humming along my wrist, just begging to be released. Silently, I opened myself up to it, and gasped as pure magic rushed through my veins, making me blaze from the inside out. I felt like I was bursting with power, and I gritted my teeth, my body shaking as I struggled to control the sudden surge of energy.

"Step away from her, dragon," Aolis sneered, raising his arms. The shadow monster moved through him, stepping in front of him like a champion ready to fight on his behalf. "She's mine."

"No, she isn't," Einar said. "Adara belongs to no one but herself."

I flung my hands out, releasing every ounce of power inside me. The flames roared as they barreled through the shadow monster, punching a hole straight through its chest. The firestorm engulfed Aolis, and the king let out a deafening shriek as the flames ate at him. He fell to the ground, flailing and thrashing as the shadow monster evaporated, trying to douse the flames with his magic, but my fire was stronger. I pushed relentlessly, powering through the gusts of wind until they became feeble wisps, and finally, the king succumbed, his screams fading as the flames ate through his vocal chords, his lungs, his heart. Fierce pleasure whipped through me as I watched his entire body crumble to ash, and a heady wave of relief nearly threatened to take my knees out from under me.

"It's all right," Einar murmured in my ear as I sagged against him. "I've got you."

I tilted my head to look up at him, and for a heartbeat, it was just the two of us. "Thank you," I murmured, my forehead brushing the underside of his chin. "I couldn't have done it without you."

He pressed a kiss to my brow, and we said absolutely nothing. There were many things unspoken between us—questions, thoughts, revelations we would have to discuss.

But for now, it was enough that we were here, and that we'd won.

The flames finally winked out as the last of my strength left me, and my vision swam. "Adara!" I heard Mavlyn cry, and the next thing I knew, she was at my side and I was sitting in a chair, trying to regain my bearings.

"Are you alright?" she asked, placing a hand on my forehead, but I was barely looking at her. My gaze fixed on Gelsyne, who had passed out on the floor, still between the guards. The heat must have gotten to her, I thought dimly. I needed to check on her.

"My mother..." I began, but then I noticed movement coming from the charred husk of Aolis's body. My blood turned frigid as I watched shadows curling upward from the ashes, far too thick to be smoke. A sinister laughter filled the air, and I watched in horror as the shadows traveled through the air, heading not toward me, or Einar, or even the guards, but straight toward Mother.

"No!" I shrieked as the shadows engulfed her. They poured into her through every orifice—eyes, nose, mouth, ears—and I ripped myself from Mavlyn and Einar's hands, rushing over to grab her shoulders. "No, please!"

Mother's eyes opened, and my heart sank—they were filled with pure blackness. A smile that could only be described as pure evil spread across her face, and she sat up, her movements far too fluid and graceful.

"What's the matter?" she asked in a sing-song voice that was both hers and not hers. There was an undercurrent of darkness beneath it that made me want to gouge out my eardrums, and I recoiled instinctively as I felt something sinister shifting beneath her skin. "Aren't you happy to see me, Adara?"

"You're not her." I stood up, backing away. Not-Mother rose to her feet, and before my eyes, she transformed. Her stringy hair turned dark and lustrous, her haggard skin smooth, her ragged dress into a flowing black gown. She looked regal, powerful, and if the magic humming in the air around her hadn't been so dark and ugly, I might have been relieved. "Who are you?"

"You can call me Nox," she said. "Mother of Shadows. I've been waiting a long time for you to come and kill Aolis, and you've brought me the perfect vessel to top it all off. I can't thank you enough."

"What are you saying?" Einar demanded. He stepped up by my side, Mavlyn joining me on the other, and I was grateful for their presence—I felt like the world was sliding out from beneath me once more, everything I thought I knew changing. "You *planned* for Adara to kill King Aolis?"

"Of course I did." Gelsyne—no, *Nox*—gave him a sly smile. "Why do you think you encountered such little resistance when you stormed the castle? Did you really think it would be *that* easy? And why do you think my handsome general here spared your lives?" She sauntered over to Slaugh and pressed a hand against his ruined cheek. "You've done so well, my brave soldier. Your loyalty will be rewarded."

"Anything for you, Mother of Shadows." Slaugh smiled, and the look of pure devotion in his eyes made me sick.

"So you meant what you said earlier, about the king," Mavlyn said. "You thought he was too weak to rule, so you replaced him. I'm guessing you're the one who gave Aolis his powers in the first place?" she asked Nox.

"I did, and it turned out to be a mistake." Nox sighed. "Apparently Aolis had a conscience—he felt bad that his shadow magic was poisoning everything, so instead of using his powers, he kept himself shut up in the castle to stop himself from doing any more damage. Cowered inside his chambers like a sniveling fool, whining about the prophecy. Unfortunately, he had a rather strong mind, and I was unable to get him to do my bidding," she added, curling her lip. "Thankfully, Gelsyne isn't nearly as powerful, and torture and shadow magic have weakened her. She's barely putting up any fight at all."

"So she's still in there?" I asked, hope and fear churning in my gut. "My mother is still alive?"

"Of course she is." Nox grinned at me. "She has to stay alive, or I won't be able to use her body as a vessel. Don't you worry, she'll remain safe and sound. I have far too many things planned to discard her now."

"And what things would those be?" Einar growled.

"Oh, this and that." Nox shrugged. "Slaugh, would you be a darling and take these prisoners to the dungeons? I'm weary of this conversation, and there is much I need to take care of."

"Certainly." Slaugh gave us a vicious smile. The door behind him opened, and ten more shadow guards filed in, bristling with weapons and armor. My stomach sank to my boots—I'd used every drop of magic to kill Aolis, and had no reserves left to fight these fae.

"We're not just going to let you take us," Mavlyn said, stepping forward. "We'll fight you with our last breath if we have to."

"That's fine by me," Nox said in an airy voice. "After all, it's not as if I need any of you alive."

The guards sprang into action, but Mavlyn was faster, tossing her seeds at them. They exploded as they hit the ground, growing quickly into thorny vines that snagged at the guards' feet and dragged them down. Einar blasted them with fireballs, setting several of them aflame, but more of the guards were breaking free already. I gripped the edge of the table behind me as Slaugh stalked toward me, a sick look in his hungry eyes. He was coming for me, and I had no power to fight him with.

"Stay away from her," Einar snarled, stepping in front of me. His wings flared out wide as he shielded me from Slaugh, making it impossible for me to see the other fae.

"So eager for death, are you?" Slaugh sneered. I peered over Einar's shoulder to see Slaugh draw the sword at his hip, and my heart dropped. Einar was strong, but he couldn't hope to win against Slaugh unless he shifted, and there was no room in here. If we could just get outside—

The doors to the dining room burst open again, cutting off

my train of thought, and my jaw dropped as Avani, Tempest, and Cascada sprinted toward us. "Go!" Avani yelled as she charged Slaugh, vines whipping from her outstretched hands to wrap around his sword arm. "Run, while you still have the chance!"

Slaugh turned to face the new threat, and Einar snarled. I thought he would attack the general and try to finish him off, but instead he grabbed me and threw me over his shoulder, then raced out of the room, Mavlyn covering us. I watched as the three hostages faced off against the shadow guard, Tempest using a pair of fans to slice at her opponents with wind, while Cascada slapped a hand on one of the guard's faces and drew every drop of moisture out of him, turning him into a husk. Then we were gone, sprinting down the hall as fast as Einar and Mavlyn's legs could go.

A door opened as we raced past it, and the same guard from before, the one who had given me the key, stepped out. "This way!" he shouted, and Einar and Mavlyn stopped abruptly.

"Who are you?" Einar demanded, swinging around to face the guard.

I twisted around on Einar's shoulder to look at the guard. "It's all right," I told them. "He helped me. We can trust him."

"Slaugh technically helped us too, and that didn't turn out so well for us," Mavlyn pointed out. "How do we know he won't lead us back to Nox?"

I stared at the guard, taking in his golden-green eyes. "I've seen you more than once," I said, my hazy mind slowly putting the pieces together. "In my mother's apothecary shop. Then in the woods, when you pointed me toward the tower where Einar was sleeping. And then again in the air temple."

The guard nodded. "I'll tell you who I am, but first, we have to get out of here." He opened the door wider, and I saw a set of descending steps beyond it. "You can stay here if you want, but

Nox's minions will find you, and she'll torture you until you beg for death. If you don't want that, I suggest you follow."

He disappeared down the stairs, and the three of us exchanged glances. "Certain torture and death versus possible death?" Mavlyn shrugged. "I think I'll take my chances."

She followed the guard down the stairs, and Einar sighed and did the same. A lump of dread settled in my stomach as he closed the door behind us, and pitch dark descended upon the stairwell. I didn't know what lay beyond, and didn't even have enough magic in my fingertip to light a flame to see the way.

For the first time in my life, I was truly powerless.

And I had no idea what came next.

The End...for now.

Adara and Einar's story will continue in Forged in Frost, Book Two in Of Dragons and Fae. Head over to www.jasminewalt.com for more information on where you can find it!

P.S. Did you enjoy this book? Please consider leaving a review. Reviews help authors sell books, which means they can continue writing sequels for you to read. Plus, they make the author feel warm and fuzzy inside, and who doesn't want that? ;)

ABOUT THE AUTHOR

NYT bestseller **JASMINE WALT** is obsessed with books, chocolate, and sharp objects. Somehow, those three things melded together in her head and transformed into a desire to write, usually fantastical stuff with a healthy dose of action and romance. She also writes reverse haram under Jada Storm.

Her characters are a little (okay, a lot) on the snarky side, and they swear, but they mean well. Even the villains sometimes. When Jasmine isn't chained to her keyboard, you can find her practicing her triangle choke on the mats, spending time with her family, or binge-watching superhero shows. Drop her a line anytime at jasmine@jasminewalt.com, or visit her at www. jasminewalt.com.

ALSO BY JASMINE WALT

Secret of the Dragon

Her Dark Protectors

Written under Jada Storm, with Emily Goodwin

Cursed by Night

Kissed by Night

Hidden by Night

Broken by Night

The Dragon's Gift Trilogy

Written under Jada Storm

Dragon's Gift

Dragon's Blood

Dragon's Curse

The Legend of Tariel:

Written as Jada Storm

Kingdom of Storms

Den of Thieves